Praise for *Favourite Daughter*

'This book is so stunningly fresh and darkly funny that every page surprised me. Morgan Dick doesn't just craft a clever plot – she writes brilliantly about grief and addiction and inheritance and, yes, redemption. What a massive talent! My perfect reading experience was marred only by envy'
Catherine Newman, author of *Sandwich*

'Brilliant. Darkly funny, gently devastating and so deftly written, with characters so finely drawn I keep expecting to recognize them on the street. I'm fairly sure *Favourite Daughter* will be massive'
Lauren Bravo, author of *Preloved*

'A vast and ambitious novel of sisterhood, generational trauma, redemption and forgiveness. Morgan Dick writes with a rawness and ferociousness that will take your breath away'
Kirsty Capes, author of *Girls*

'A gripping, deeply honest and tender story, with characters that wove their way into my heart and stayed there. Dick's writing is witty and packed with insight, making her a new favourite author of mine'
Natalie Sue, author of *I Hope This Finds You Well*

'I am in such awe – the characters, the plot (delicious!), the various voices, the deliberate tenderness. And what an amazing job Morgan has done of presenting addiction as the commonplace condition it is . . . She has profound compassion for all her characters, withholding judgement for any of them. This is a serious and important book but it's also charming, funny and sweet'
Marian Keyes, author of *My Favourite Mistake*

'Rich, complex and astute – *Favourite Daughter* is a precise rendering of experiencing the worst time of your life while the rest of the world keeps turning and how possible it is to possess the indomitable spirit needed to keep on going, even when everything kind of is your fault'
Rebecca K Reilly, author of *Greta & Valdin*

'Refreshingly dark and dryly funny, as well as perceptive and moving on the nature of addiction. Morgan is great at dialogue too, especially when she's showing people talking at cross-purposes. I loved how understated the humour was'
Rebecca Wait, author of *I'm Sorry You Feel That Way*

FAVOURITE DAUGHTER

Morgan Dick

PENGUIN
VIKING

VIKING

UK | USA | Canada | Ireland | Australia
India | New Zealand | South Africa

Viking is part of the Penguin Random House group of companies
whose addresses can be found at global.penguinrandomhouse.com

Penguin Random House UK,
One Embassy Gardens, 8 Viaduct Gardens, London SW11 7BW

penguin.co.uk

Penguin
Random House
UK

First published in Canada by Doubleday Canada,
a division of Penguin Random House Canada Limited 2024
First published in Great Britain by Viking 2024

001

Designed by Josie Staveley Taylor, adapted from an original design by Kate Sinclair.

Printed and bound in Great Britain by Clays Ltd, Elcograf S.p.A.

The authorized representative in the EEA is Penguin Random House Ireland,
Morrison Chambers, 32 Nassau Street, Dublin D02 YH68

A CIP catalogue record for this book is available from the British Library

HARDBACK ISBN: 978-0-241-74024-8
TRADE PAPERBACK ISBN: 978-0-241-74077-4

Penguin Random House is committed to a sustainable future
for our business, our readers and our planet. This book is made from
Forest Stewardship Council® certified paper.

For Cameron, Levi, and Beckett

MICKEY

Mickey learned of her father's death from the obituary. She wasn't listed among his loved ones, which didn't surprise her. It didn't offend her either. Wildly indifferent, she slapped the newspaper into a pile on her desk and shoved it aside and resolved to never think about the obituary, or her father, ever again.

She swiveled for a better view of the lone kindergartener squatting on the classroom carpet. "That's a cool airplane."

Ian did not look up from his Lego. "It's a starfighter."

"Oh. My mistake."

In the forty-five minutes since school ended, Mickey had scoured the floor for every scrap of tissue paper, stub of crayon, and crust of Play-Doh. She'd scrubbed the tables clean of white glue and applesauce. She'd tucked away the cars, the trains, the glassy-eyed babies, the pink stethoscopes. All that remained was the Lego. And Ian.

Mickey let her gaze drift toward the bathroom for half a second. It had been hours. "Does it go fast, your starfighter?"

Ian muttered under his breath and kicked off his shoes for no apparent reason, pouting in that despondent way of his, as if everything in the whole world insulted him.

Mickey suppressed a smile. This kid was quite possibly her favorite.

From the doorway came a clopping of boots and a jangling of keys. Mickey spun, searched the battle-worn face of Jean Donoghue, school principal, and found . . .

A frown. Damn.

"Hi, Ms. Morris," Jean said, her voice as full of artificial sweetness as the can of Diet Coke she toted everywhere. "Hi, Ian."

Ian shot her a glare and returned to his Lego. He was definitely Mickey's favorite.

After traversing the classroom and perching on the edge of Mickey's desk, Jean gave a tiny shrug that confirmed the worst: it was time to call the cops.

"No answer on her cell?" Mickey asked.

"I tried it four times."

Mickey felt the cold trickle of disappointment. "Let's give her ten more minutes? She deserves that much." According to Ian's file, his mom was twenty and his dad was nowhere.

Jean threw back the last of her pop and crunched the can in her fist. Foundation had caked in the crinkles around her hard gray eyes. "It's school policy."

Easy excuse. Yes, Ian's mom should've been here at 3:50 with all the other moms. She should've greeted Ian outside the classroom with a hug and a kiss and a specially prepared snack of apple slices and peanut butter. But this situation wasn't her fault. She was probably stuck working overtime at a waitressing job she hated but couldn't quit because her landlord had raised the rent by thirty-five percent. And now Jean wanted to involve the cops?

Mickey thought of her own mother and the one-bedroom apartment they'd shared all those years. Empty fridge, lights that only sometimes turned on. All because her father—

No. She wouldn't go there. She wouldn't think of him, of the newspaper now neatly tidied away as if it were completely unremarkable—nothing more than fodder for papier-mâché projects.

Mickey took a deep breath, which did nothing for the blood thumping in her ears or the sudden tightness in her throat. "His mom's having a tough time."

"*I'm* having a tough time. I've got date number three with the accountant tonight." Jean tossed her empty Diet Coke into the recycling bin beside Mickey's desk, where it clattered to the bottom and fell silent. "Date number three. I need to leave."

Mickey couldn't believe this. Except that she totally could. Jean was nearing retirement and spent much of the workday watching TikTok videos of people cutting into ultra-realistic cakes. "Go ahead. I'll stay."

"I can't let you do that."

"It's no trou—"

"Are you sure?" Jean whipped off her lanyard and dropped it beside Mickey's laptop. "Here are the keys. You're a saint. Seriously. You were put on this earth to teach kindergarten."

This was a fact. Mickey had the face of a kindergarten teacher, heart-shaped and plain, with a broad forehead and wide-set eyes that evoked a certain wholesomeness. She had a cheery singing voice. She had a toothy smile. She had the patience to stuff twenty-six pairs of hands into twenty-six pairs of mittens. Kindergarten was her calling, her destiny, the single reason she hadn't yet expired in a ditch somewhere.

"I'm giving you a raise." Jean let out a bark of laughter. "Except that I can't. If I could, I would. You know that."

The pay was insulting, and Mickey's expenses were high.

Speaking of which—"I might use the bathroom before you go."

"Of course, of course."

Mickey snatched her purse off the desk and tipped her head at Jean knowingly. "That time of the month." Which could easily have been true.

Jean raised a three-finger salute.

Mickey ran a few steps, walked a few steps. Ran, walked. Ran, walked. Snaked her way between rhomboid tables and little yellow chairs. Pushed her way through the bathroom door. Plopped down on the child-sized toilet and dug around in her purse. Wallet, sunglasses . . . packet of antiseptic wipes, extra Band-Aids . . . the Hillary Clinton biography she'd taken from a Little Free Library eight months ago and never opened . . .

Mickey scrunched the faux leather in her fists. Why did they make bags this big? Why? She'd filled it with crap out of obligation. Now the non-crap things—the things she wanted, the things she needed—were impossible to find.

Hillary Clinton hit the floor. Chargers and earbuds spilled out over Mickey's knees. Bile stung her throat. Where was it? Maybe in her desk? She couldn't have left it at home.

Then her fingertips brushed cool plastic, and the cosmos realigned, every scattered moon and star sliding back into place. Here, finally, was the cheap water bottle she'd filled before leaving her apartment that morning.

She yarded off the lid, raised the vodka to her lips, and glugged.

A bulb flickered in the ceiling, its light shrinking and swelling and shrinking again. Here came that blissful sense of focus. Mickey felt calm, attuned. Like she'd developed microscopic vision. Wasn't there a poem about that? Something about holding eternity in a grain of sand and infinity in an hour. Or was it the other way around? She made a mental note to Google it later.

After another gulp or two, Mickey put the bottle away and stood without even trying to pee. Kindergarten teachers never peed. They'd evolved past it.

Back outside, Jean was gazing at her phone with wonderment and delight. "Can you believe this is a cake and not a ski boot?" she asked, showing Mickey the screen.

"I can't." Mickey contained a burp.

Jean started shuffling away. "Don't wait more than half an hour."

Then it was just the two of them.

As Ian made another starfighter, Mickey sat calmly at her desk and thought rational thoughts. It was bad, minding a child under the influence of alcohol. Mickey knew it was bad. That was why she never did it, ever, except for this once. She'd had a rule since teachers' college: not a drop of liquor until the bus ride home. Which, the gnawing sensation in her gut reminded her, was supposed to be right now.

And wouldn't it be even worse to call the police? To launch Ian into the swirling vortex of the child welfare system? Most foster parents were kind and well-meaning, Mickey had no doubt. But even if Ian ended up with someone good—someone who appreciated his creativity and enjoyed hearing his many facts about space travel—that person still wouldn't love him like his mom. Today would live forever in his memory as the day he was taken. *Apprehended.* That was the term.

No. Better to sit and wait.

Mickey hugged herself. She wasn't thinking about the bottle in her bag or how much she wanted another sip. She definitely wasn't thinking about her father. Not his belly laugh, not his Tigger impression, not those summer Sundays when they'd ambled down to the river and sprinkled pieces of bread for the ducks. He liked being outside, Mickey remembered. He liked lying under tall trees and pruning those bushes in the yard, the ones with the puffy white flowers.

Mickey flinched. Her butt cheek was vibrating.

UNKNOWN CALLER

Third time that day. She put the phone back in her jeans, put her hands back in her armpits, and watched evening push in on the sky through the classroom's small window.

Ten minutes later, her butt vibrated again.

UNKNOWN CALLER

Mickey put the iPhone on her desk and stared at it. She could answer, see who it was. Whether a telemarketer or a pollster or a scammer demanding an immediate wire transfer of ten thousand dollars, this caller might just have some interesting things to say. Mickey could ask them about the weather in Toronto or Dallas or wherever. She could ask about their family, maybe hear about the in-laws who dropped by unannounced and refused to leave, or the teenagers who holed up in their bedrooms vaping and eating cereal. There would be laughs, maybe even some tears. She would lose herself in the conversation entirely.

She swiped to answer. "Hello?"

A half second of static.

"Michelle?"

Mickey's throat sealed over. Nobody called her by that name.

"Michelle Kowalski?" A weathered, masculine voice.

"Yes?" she said. "I mean, no. But yes."

"Okay." The second syllable dragged its feet: *Okaaaaaay.* "Sorry—so, are you? Michelle Kowalski?"

"I'm Michelle Morris."

"Oh. I'm looking for Michelle Kowalski, the daughter of Adam Kowalski."

"That's me. Also. Sort of." Mickey had used Morris, Mama's maiden name, since she was fourteen. Despite splitting from Mickey's dad almost thirty years ago, Mama still used her married name, Kowalski, which was so fucked up Mickey couldn't even talk about it. "Who is this?"

"My name is Tom Samson. I'm a lawyer at Samson, Baker and Chen, LLP."

Mickey remembered, all at once, the income taxes she hadn't filed and the overdue library books she hadn't returned and the first chocolate-chip muffin she'd shoplifted at age ten. She felt an urge to cover herself, to hide. "A lawyer?"

Ian's big blue eyes flashed up to meet hers for a moment before returning to the fleet of spacecraft he'd assembled on the carpet: in formation and ready to strike.

"I'm calling about your father."

There it was again: his laugh, Tigger, the bread, the ducks. Piggyback rides. His broad shoulders and woodsy smell. Ice cream cones. Rubber boots and muddy puddles. A little pink bicycle, no training wheels, and his voice in her ear saying, *Go on, Mickey girl. You can do it.*

"He hired us some years ago to handle his estate planning," the lawyer continued. "I'm not sure how often you speak with him."

Not once in twenty-six years. Now they would never speak again, which was both a relief and . . . not, for some reason.

"I saw the—" Mickey caught herself. *The obituary,* she'd meant to say. "I mean, I know about—about the—that he's dead."

"I'm sorry for your loss."

There was something deeply offensive about these words. "Thank you."

"I'm, uh—I'm sure you know where I'm going with this."

Mickey did not know in the slightest.

"He thought of you in his will."

Mickey held this phrase in her mind, turned it over and twisted it, examined it from different sides. *He thought of you in his will.* She knew what the words meant individually. Together, they meant nothing. A word salad, a non-sentence. "What?"

"Your father left you some"—a tiny but distinct pause—"assets."

Assets meant property, investments, shareholdings. Assets meant money. Assets were what loving parents left their children—a gift from one generation to the next.

"I don't think that's right," Mickey said.

The line went quiet. She could hear her heart beating and the clock ticking and Ian humming the theme from a certain space opera.

"This might be easier in person," said the lawyer. "Our office is downtown, or maybe I could meet you somewhere?"

Mickey found the newspaper in the pile on her desk, flipped back to the obituaries, and examined the picture of her dead dad. Twenty-six years, and he hadn't changed a bit. Well. A bit, yes. But beyond the bald scalp and the jowls, he had that same old shine to him—the same broad grin and twinkle in his eye.

Hang up the phone, she told herself.

"Michelle? Are you still there?"

Hang up this second. "Yes. I'm here."

"Any chance you're free this evening?"

Ian was staring at Mickey openly now, his expression inscrutable. Almost five o'clock. He must've been tired and hungry and more frightened than he'd ever let on.

And Mickey could really use a few more sips from her bottle about now.

"Could I get a ride?" she asked.

A yellow poplar leaf skimmed across the sidewalk and pasted itself to Ian's ankle. He glanced down and sighed, gazing blandly at the leaf for several seconds before shaking it away. The whole thing made such a depressing sight that Mickey wanted to cry.

She knelt down to his level, like always. "We'll have you home soon."

He fiddled with one of his starfighters, lifting the cockpit's tiny lid to reveal the Lego person inside—a sumo wrestler, if Mickey wasn't mistaken. "My mom gets really busy sometimes. But she loves me very much."

Mickey filled with a sudden desire to bring him home and run him a warm bath, to put a cup of cocoa in his hands, to read him a story and make him his favorite dinner, which she knew was mac and cheese. She couldn't, of course. Instead, she zipped his jacket and fixed the collar where it had rolled up underneath. "Of course she does."

For the next ten minutes, they stood at the curb with their backs to the school, long shadows dangling from their feet. September wasn't yet over, but the days were short, and the air had bite. In this part of the country, winter had a habit of arriving early and staying late.

Ian's pants slid an inch down his hips as he stuffed the Lego in a pocket. "Can I go on the slide?"

"No, sorry. Our ride is coming any second."

Mickey's stomach lurched with each passing car. She hadn't thought to ask what the lawyer drove.

"Why are you nervous?" Ian asked.

"I'm not nervous."

"Why are you tapping your foot?"

"I'm not tapping my foot."

Ian crooked a brow.

"My so-called father died," Mickey conceded. Kids made such good bullshit detectors.

"Your what father?"

"He doesn't deserve to be called a father, but that's what he technically is." Mickey shook her head. "Was."

"Oh," Ian said in a sagely sort of way.

Not that Mickey was messed up. She had a bachelor's degree. She ate leafy greens. She managed to keep the lights on and a small fern alive. She'd made her way in the world just fine, thank you very much, with almost no help from anyone. So what if she had a few vices here and there? It was only liquor. Cannabis sometimes. *Bridgerton* on occasion. What did any of it matter? She was a thirty-three-year-old woman. If she wanted to come home and drink a pint of vodka and watch eight episodes of smutty Regency romance, then that was her goddamn choice.

"Miss Morris?"

A man approached them in the slow, limping manner of fifty-somethings with old sports injuries. He wore a navy suit and a pair of narrow sunglasses that made Mickey think despairingly of the early 2000s.

"You must be Mr. Samson," she said.

The lawyer removed his sunglasses and blinked at Ian. "Is this your . . ."

"My student."

"Ah," he said but appeared no less flummoxed.

"His mom got tied up with something, so we're dropping him at home," Mickey said firmly. She would knock on the front door, and Ian's mom would answer, sweaty and flustered and still wearing her waitressing uniform—in Mickey's mind, a baby-blue dress with buttons down the front. *I'm so sorry*, she would say, pulling Ian into a tight hug. *Thank you.* And then the lawyer would ferry Mickey home to her small apartment, where she could resume her usual evening activities. Yes, this was the plan. "Ian, this is Mr. Samson."

"Tom." Samson stuck out his hand. Ian only stared at it. "I'm, uh . . ." The hand fell. "I'm parked around the corner."

The three of them clambered into a glossy black Mercedes. Mickey took shotgun and put Ian's address into Google Maps. Her phone began to spout directions, and off they went, gliding away from the shawarma places and half-built condo towers and fore-closure signs of the inner city. Samson's cologne crowded the air, a peaty fog.

Mickey retrieved the newspaper from her purse, unsure why she was doing so, unsure why she'd even brought it. She would throw it away the second she got home.

It is with profound sadness that we announce the passing of Adam Kowalski, aged 61, after a long illness.

He'd been sick. Cancer? Liver disease? Why, why did Mickey care?

He is lovingly remembered by his wife Leonora and daughter Charlotte.

Mickey folded the newspaper in half, then folded it in half again, and again and again until it would fold no further. She'd be twenty-five by now, this Charlotte, a grown woman with travel stories and coffee preferences. No longer the pigtailed little princess Mickey had always imagined. *Imagined* because Mickey had never seen a picture of her. She'd never wanted to.

Mama had kept close track of Dad and his new family through the years, never failing to make a cool, casual inquiry with a mutual acquaintance when she stumbled on one. She would inevitably par-rot this information back at Mickey, who could only plug her ears. ("They've got her enrolled in private school, do you believe that? Apparently, she golfs. A nine-year-old.")

Samson glanced over at Mickey, his gaze flitting from her chest to her face and back again. "You look a lot like your mom, don't you?"

Mickey felt a swell of nausea. This guy reminded her of the busi-ness types she used to meet in her early twenties, the ones who fed her shots of top-shelf tequila and rubbed their pelvises against hers on sticky dance floors. The men she couldn't bear to look at in the morning. "How would you know?" she asked.

"Your dad showed me a photo once."

Mickey's heart punched against her rib cage. "Please don't call him that."

"The service is tomorrow."

Mickey ignored this.

Samson eyed Ian in the rearview mirror as they rolled up to a red. "I like your airplane."

"It's a starfighter," Ian snapped.

They parked in front of a towering infill with front-facing windows that looked into a sleek white dining room. A pair of yellow Adirondack chairs sprouted from the tidy lawn. Even after double-checking the address, Mickey still wasn't sure they'd come to the right place.

She twisted to peer at Ian in the backseat. "Do you live here?"

But he had already unbuckled his seatbelt, opened the door, and gone bounding toward the house. Mickey caught up in time to ring the doorbell.

The man who answered had a cologne-ad appearance she found vaguely gross: stubble, brooding eyes, dress shirt unbuttoned halfway. He seemed to register Mickey first—"Hi?"—and Ian second. "*Hi.* What's going on?"

Ian pushed inside and wriggled free of his backpack, which fell to the hardwood with hardly a sound. He disappeared around a corner, and a door slammed.

Foreboding dripped through Mickey. Something about this didn't feel right.

"Are you Ian's dad?" she asked.

The man laughed. "Uncle."

Mickey peered around him for some sign of Ian's mom. She would be here. She had to be. "And you live here?"

"It's my house."

His house. So, they all lived together?

"Sorry—who are you?" he asked, as concern gathered in his face.

"I'm the teacher," Mickey said carefully. "I was hoping to chat with Evelyn for a sec."

The man scratched the nape of his neck, head tipping far enough forward to reveal a thinning patch at his crown. "I thought . . . I thought Ian went with her. She left this morning."

The words lodged in Mickey's soft tissue one by one, each its own twist of shrapnel. *She. Left. This. Morning.*

"Evelyn's your sister?" she asked, thinking quickly.

"Half-sister."

Mickey examined him more closely. His jaw was too square. His pecs were too bulging. His hair had been sculpted into a handsome swoop at the front. But however douchey-looking, this guy was still Ian's next of kin. He'd have to do.

"School starts at nine on Monday," she said. "You'll make sure he's there?"

He pointed to himself. "Me?"

"You."

"I can't look after him. I'm not a—a—I can't." A flush rose up his neck and into his cheeks. "I just can't."

"I didn't catch your name," Mickey said in the steadiest voice she could manage. She'd taken another swig from her bottle before leaving school, but the buzz—the calm, rather; the clarity—had long since worn off. The world had clouded over again. She needed to get home.

"Christopher. Chris."

Mickey reached up and planted her hands on his shoulders. "Look, Chris. Here's the deal. That little person back there? He needs someone to make him dinner. He needs someone to play with. He needs someone to run him a bath and read him a bedtime story. He needs a hug. These tasks, for better or worse, have fallen to you. Tonight, you're the guy. If you don't do it, no one will. Do you understand me?"

His eyes had grown to globes. "I—I do."

Mickey spun on her heel and started down the walkway. "Drop-off is at nine a.m. Don't forget to pack lunch and a snack."

"But . . . what if I suck?"

She glanced back to find his handsome features wilting somewhat. Without the cocky airs, he looked a lot more like his nephew. Something about the eyes and how they slanted downward at the outside corners.

She jogged back to the porch, then gave him her number and what she hoped was a reassuring smile. "This way you can get in touch if "—when, come on, it was a matter of when—"things go sideways."

Back in the car, a file folder lay open across Samson's knees. "I'll cut to the chase," he said.

Although the engine was off, Mickey buckled her seatbelt. Whatever this was about, she wanted it to be over. "Please, do."

"He left you some money."

Mickey felt her own mouth drop open. The first half of that sentence had rung clear and true. The second half had not. Her father was one to take, not give.

Samson handed her a small manila envelope. "The release of the funds is conditional upon your agreement to several terms and the completion thereof."

She tore the flap and shook out the contents, a single piece of cardstock paper. Heat crept up her arms and neck as she scanned the cursive text, the fancy trim. It did not make sense. "This is a voucher for seven therapy sessions."

"Yes, from"—Samson consulted the file—"Momentum Counseling."

Mickey flapped the paper in the air. "What is this supposed to mean?"

"These are the conditions you must complete."

Conditions, meaning . . . But no. That couldn't be right.

"I don't get the money until I go to counseling?"

"That's the long and short of it, yes."

Mickey flung the voucher on the dash. "What the fuck."

"It's somewhat unusual."

Mickey was fully overheating now, the waistband of her pants growing damp with sweat. She poked the button on the passenger door to lower the window, but it wouldn't budge. "What the actual fuck."

"There's a note here from him. Shall I read it?"

Mickey snorted. Thirty minutes from now, she'd be tucked up at home with a bottle of Russian Standard. She didn't need this stupid lawyer with his stupid sunglasses. She didn't need whatever pennies her father had chosen to fling at her. She didn't need any of—

"*To my daughter Michelle I leave a sum of five and a half million dollars.*"

Mickey drew a breath, or tried to.

"*Acknowledging the harm I caused her as a young father and understanding the need for professional services to redress it, I ask that these funds be held in trust until Michelle has completed seven fifty-minute psychotherapy sessions. Should Michelle not complete these sessions within three months, my wish is that the money instead be donated to the Sunrise Hospice Foundation.*" Samson closed the file. "That's it."

Mickey tried to swallow, but this function too evaded her. God, why was it so hot?

"I go to counseling, you know," Samson offered with a shrug.

"You do?"

"If it can help me, trust me—it can help anybody." As Samson turned in his seat to face her, he looked strangely desperate. "I'm a real asshole."

"I wondered," Mickey said weakly. The words *five* and *million* were still ricocheting off the walls of her skull, pinging from one side of her brain to the other.

"I had an affair with a junior associate at my firm. Cheated on the best girl I ever had. Lydia—sweet, funny, smart. She's a doctor. A doctor! And that's not the half of it. I'm quick to anger. I'm a workaholic. I'm a narcissist. I'm a misogynist."

Mickey pushed random buttons on the console trying to start the air con. "Why are you telling me this?"

"Because it works. Going to someone and talking about your problems? It works." He opened his mouth, shut it, opened it again. "And who knows? You might get along well with this therapist."

Mickey could only laugh.

ARLO

"What am I supposed to do with his shoes? There are mountains of them. Dress shoes and sandals and hunting boots. The hunting boots! There must be ten pairs. And loafers, you know, the ones with the little tassels on them? Never threw a thing away in his life, that man." Mother turned the funeral card over twice, as if she hadn't read the thing eighty times already. On the third flip, the card slid through her fingers and sailed down onto the marble floor. She kept her nails so long and heavily shellacked that her hands were basically nonfunctional. "Oh, fuck."

Arlo gazed at the tiny picture of her father now upside down on the ground. She couldn't shake the feeling that even now, forty thousand dollars in funeral costs later, she'd failed him. This reception was all wrong. It was too cold in here, too echoing. There was nowhere to sit. And the music—ugh, the music. "Is this ABBA playing right now?"

Mother wriggled down to the floor in her pencil skirt, retrieved the fallen funeral card, and took a swill of Riesling as she rose, leaving another cherry lip print on the rim of her glass. People were staring, but then they'd been staring all day. "Does Goodwill accept men's dress shoes from the eighties?"

"Maybe?" Arlo said, her ears stinging with smarmy, jangly, disco-inflected Eurojunk. Daddy would never have listened to this. He was one for jazz, roots, soul. Gritty vocals, stirring ballads. Feeling! He was a man of such feeling.

"What about the diabetes people?" Mother asked.

And tenderness. No one had a heart like his. He'd never missed a ballet recital, school play, or soccer game. He'd cried at Arlo's wedding. He'd refrained from saying *I told you so* when she got divorced ten months later. Daddy had been there for her, even at his sickest, even when earlier this year The Thing happened, and she lost her job.

Twenty feet away, Arlo's ex-boss stood at an otherwise-empty cocktail table with a glass of red, looking as calm and collected as ever. Arlo couldn't decide if Punam's presence here today was a touching gesture or a total dick move.

"Charlotte? Are you listening to me?"

"No. Yes. What?" Arlo opened Shazam on her phone.

"Who has that many shoes? *I* don't even have that many shoes. And I'm a shoe person." Mother adjusted the feathery black fascinator (six inches tall at least) she'd purchased for the occasion. "The whole thing is ridiculous."

Arlo seethed. "It *is* A B B A."

"I might just keep the shoes."

"Why would they play this right now?"

"Would that be weird?"

"What is this, someone's fiftieth birthday party? I have to do something about this." Arlo pressed off into the crowd.

She ran a few steps, walked a few steps. Ran, walked. Ran, walked. Wove around easel-mounted wreaths and servers with trays of caviar tartlets. Skipped over a fallen suit jacket. Planted her elbows on the bar. "Excuse me."

The bartender was polishing a champagne flute with a linen napkin. Arcs of white light spun off the glass and lodged like grit under Arlo's eyelids.

"Could we change the music, please? My dad hated ABBA. Hated them."

The bartender continued to stand there polishing his glass, not changing the music. Below the bar, a small dishwasher hummed and gurgled.

"Sorry," Arlo said. "It's just that he would really, really hate it."

Stoic, the bartender gave his champagne flute one last dab, set it down, and spun to face a silver MacBook open on the counter behind the bar.

"Thank you," Arlo said to his back. She clasped her hands, which had been so busy these past months stroking Daddy's brow and fluffing Daddy's pillows and wetting Daddy's lips with a small pink sponge. Now her hands were empty. She didn't know what to do with them. Nor did she know how to act, or stand, or set her face. She imagined how a person might look whose dad's ashes weren't sitting on a pedestal at the front of the room in a pearly white urn, and she tried to look like that person: casual, mature, composed.

Half of Daddy was there, a pile of dust in a stone pot, and the other half of him was in the ground a short drive away. There had been much discussion over the ratio—how much to bury and how much to keep. Even more discussion was had over the choice of grave marker. They'd settled on an upright headstone, marble with bronze accents and custom engraving, to be unveiled in a second ceremony in a few months' time. And no, it was not too grandiose.

The ABBA song cut. An Ed Sheeran ballad took its place. It was . . . worse? Somehow?

"Are you Charlotte?"

A man appeared at Arlo's side. Fiftyish, with a strong brow, a bolo tie, and some silver in his hair. One of Daddy's associates from the firm?

"Yes," she said. "But people call me Arlo."

"That's a cute nickname."

Arlo wanted to say something prickly but didn't. Because she was a casual, mature, composed person. "My dad gave it to me."

"Ah. Of course." The man looked embarrassed. Arlo was pleased. "I'm Tom Samson, your father's lawyer."

"Pleasure." Arlo turned her attention back to the bartender, who'd begun mixing a slushy green cocktail. She strained her voice over the grumble of the blender. "Excuse me. *Excuse me.*"

Samson's hand alighted on Arlo's elbow. "I know you and your mom don't want to get into the legal stuff right away—"

"No," Arlo said, staring at the gaudy, jewel-encrusted signet ring on Samson's pinkie finger, "we don't."

"—but the three of us should find a time to talk. Soon."

Arlo caught the bartender's eye again, finally. "Sorry. This isn't quite . . . It isn't quite right either. Jazz, maybe?"

The bartender gestured to the computer. "Do you want to come take a look?"

Arlo bit the inside of her cheek. She was being overbearing and weird, wasn't she? But it wasn't her fault. It was the fault of this day and her empty hands and the stupid, annoying lawyer, who was still touching her. "Oh, no. It's your—and you should decide . . . But maybe Ella Fitzgerald, if you have it?"

The bartender turned his back again.

"You see, there are some things to iron out," Samson said. "With the will. I mean, *iron out* probably isn't the right expression. It's a little complicated."

Arlo gave a noncommittal grunt. Why was this guy still talking? Did he struggle to pick up on social cues? Or was he just really self-important, his arrogance a mask for deep-seated feelings of inadequacy? On a normal day, such questions might've tempted her.

"I would hate for you to be surprised."

Arlo shushed him. "Bewitched, Bothered, and Bewildered" had come on the speaker overhead, and she was seven years old again, dancing on Daddy's feet in the living room while one of his forty-fives spun on the turntable. He was so tall, and Arlo was so small, and for a brief moment in time, everything was perf—

Her heart jolted before she'd fully registered the clamor, not one sound but three: wood splintering, porcelain shattering, and a good many gasps. Across the room, a cocktail table lay on its side, and an older woman in jean overalls shoved her way through a circle of Mother's spray-tanned tennis friends, waves of cornsilk hair rolling down her back.

Instantly, Arlo knew who she was.

"Piss off. All of you." The woman turned for the pedestal, her eyes set on the urn that contained half of Daddy, beautiful Daddy, Daddy with his broad shoulders and woodsy smell.

The ballroom darkened in Arlo's periphery. Everything fell away—everything but that pearly white urn. She had to get there first.

Arlo hurtled forward. Shoved her way to the pedestal. Caught the woman's wrist.

A pair of hooded eyes met hers.

So, this was Daddy's first wife. Deborah. Even now, with her pulse ticking under the pad of Arlo's finger, she hardly seemed real. She was a wisp, a flicker, an afterimage of the person from that Polaroid Daddy used to keep in the bottom drawer of his desk. *Who, her?* he'd said, that day he caught Arlo snooping. *She's no one. Somebody from a long time ago.*

Moving at warp speed but also in slow motion, Deborah reached out with her free arm and scooped the urn into the crook of her elbow.

21

Arlo let go. In her mind, she saw Deborah drop the urn, saw the ashes spill out over the floor, saw a biblical wind surge through the ballroom and carry half of Daddy away forever and ever.

"Put him down!"

Mother waddled into the scene in her pencil skirt.

All conversation had ceased, all eyes now fixed on Deborah. The servers stood frozen with their trays of food. The bartender, Arlo noticed with a pang of fury, was rapt.

"That's my husband." Mother pointed a sharp finger at the urn.

Deborah raised her chin, stretching the wattles of her neck. She was older than Mother, much older. "He was my husband, too. Ask his creditors."

"Let's all take a breath," Arlo said. She stammered something about empathy and perspective-taking—words she barely heard herself. She was too busy thinking through the situation, trying to imagine an outcome in which her beloved father wouldn't end up on the soles of people's shoes.

"You crazy fucking bitch." Mother stood nose to nose with Deborah and pursed her lips sphincter-tight for a moment. "You know what you are? You're a *parasite*."

Deborah raised her barely there eyebrows. "I'm not the one dressed head to toe in Gucci."

"Alexander McQueen," Mother spat. "This is all Alexander McQueen."

Arlo wedged herself between them. No one else would de-escalate this, she knew. No one else would be the adult. "Mother. Take a walk."

"I can't go for a walk. This crazy bitch is trying to steal my husband."

"She's not a crazy bitch," Arlo said. "She's a person, and she's sad."

Mother laughed. "This is just like you. Compassion, forgiveness, kumbaya. Well, tough shit, because I'm not about to let—"

"Stop," Arlo said, so firmly that shock rippled through Mother's dewy, Botox-infused facial tissue. She put her hands on Mother's shoulders and spun her. "I'll deal with this."

Just like she'd dealt with the funeral home, and the bank, and the credit card companies. She'd stood in line for ninety minutes at the registry to get a statement of death, a medical certificate of death, and a death certificate, because apparently those were all different things, and who knew which ones were actually required, and while she was waiting, she'd called to cancel Daddy's health plan, pension plan, senior's benefit, passport, driver's license, life insurance, car insurance, and membership to the local gun club.

She looked around at the crowd and said. "Don't you have anecdotes to swap or something? Salmon puffs to eat? Give us some air."

The people turned away, all murmurs and shamed expressions.

Arlo took a cleansing diaphragmatic inhale, trying to forget her mother and the caviar tartlets and just focus on the person in front of her. She could talk her way through this mess. The words were there, ripe for the picking.

"Deborah?" she said gently. "What is it that you want?"

Deborah adjusted her grip on the urn. "It's not fair."

Arlo gave the silence a few moments to sprawl—a trick of her trade. Wait long enough for someone to talk, and odds are, they will.

"How come he gets such an easy out?" Deborah said. "I mean it. I want to know."

"I wouldn't call it an easy out," Arlo said, shaking away the memory of Daddy's distended belly and how it had bulged under the hospital sheet.

"We have to live with everything he did. Everything he was. *He* doesn't. *He* doesn't have to live with any of that. Sometimes, I swear . . . I'm so angry still. At him. And now that he's dead, there's nowhere for it to go. The anger. And I deserve to be angry, you know. He was a mean, selfish drunk who ruined my and my daughter's lives. Michelle is so messed up she doesn't even know it."

Arlo flinched. *Michelle*. That name was—had always been—a fly in her ear.

"He made me feel small. Worthless. Helpless." Deborah's body caved around the urn as she crushed it to her chest, elbows tucked at her sides like brittle wings.

Arlo knew instantly what needed to be said. "People change a lot over the course of a life."

Anger flared behind Deborah's sunken eyes. "I don't want to hear what a—what a good dad he was to you, or whatever. What a good husband to your . . . to your . . ."

"I didn't mean him. I meant you."

Deborah's lips parted.

"You've held a lot of hurt. I can't imagine. But it's not thirty years ago anymore. You're not helpless now. You're the protagonist of this story. Please, Deborah. Put him down."

Five seconds passed, then ten, then fifteen. Deborah said nothing, did nothing. Arlo began to feel doubt creep in. Had she miscalculated? But she never miscalculated.

Finally, the sands began to shift behind Deborah's eyes, desperation hardening into resolve, and Arlo knew it was over.

Deborah returned to the pedestal in three long strides and set down the urn. She drew a breath and let it go as a laugh. "You know exactly what to say, don't you?"

As well Arlo should. She was a psychologist.

Later, Punam approached Arlo at the bar and squeezed her arm with a just-right amount of pressure, somehow managing to make Arlo feel valued and accepted with a simple touch. It was a skill Arlo both admired and resented. Punam had placed her on an indefinite suspension from their two-woman psychology practice, and still, Arlo couldn't bring herself to hate the woman. Not fully, anyway.

"How you holding up?" Punam asked.

Arlo summoned a sober expression. "Pretty much how you'd expect." In truth, she was fucking fantastic. The encounter with Deborah had left her vibrating. What a thrill, getting down to the heart of someone, mining their hopes and fears and hammering these feelings into something stronger—action. How she'd missed it.

Punam gestured to the area around the pedestal. "That over there did not look easy, whatever it was. You've got some skills, kiddo."

Arlo felt a rush of pride. Was that terrible? She'd defused a near catastrophe with poise and tact. And on five hours of sleep, no less.

Punam added, in so casual a voice Arlo wasn't sure she'd heard correctly, "I think you should come back."

"Back where?" Not work, surely.

"I spoke with the college—" Punam began.

Arlo held her breath. *The college*: regulatory gods who, balancing their scales with feathers and stones, decided which psychologists were allowed to practice and which weren't.

"—and now that the lawsuit is settled, they agree it's time."

Arlo didn't know what to say. Punam was hot shit in the therapy world. She won international awards, published books. A *New York Times* reviewer had dubbed her the next Brené Brown. She styled her bangs into a long side-parted curl that swooshed perfectly across her forehead and grazed the outside corner of her left eye. Getting one chance to work with her was miracle enough, but two?

Arlo would get her old office back, Punam said, and a pay raise after the first six months. Arlo didn't need it—the starting salary was over six figures, not to mention the inheritance was coming— but if her skills were worth that much . . .

"There would be a probationary period, of course. Regular supervision and case reviews. We'd test things out for a few weeks, see if it's a good fit. See how you're doing with clients. But, yeah—job's yours as soon as you're ready."

As soon as I'm ready, Arlo thought, staring into her fourth glass of wine. She was pretty much ready now. "I'll let you know."

"Rest up. Treat yourself to something nice." Punam chuckled darkly. "God knows you deserve it after this shit."

Arlo did deserve a little something. A bit of fun, perhaps.

Across the bar, Tom Samson was watching her again.

MICKEY

Daria's eyes, usually hard and stoic, softened with surprise. "Five million dollars?"

"And a half," Mickey said. "And a half!"

They sat together in Daria's kitchen with a box of breadsticks and a bottle of Absolut—their Saturday-evening tradition. Mickey had always admired her fifty-something neighbor across the hall, whose Slavic lilt, pixie cut, and perma-scowl spoke of a person who clearly didn't give a shit.

Daria tipped back some vodka like it was apple juice and plunked her shot glass upside down on the wobbly table. "So, what is problem?"

Mickey didn't know where to start. She'd always known her father was rich, but not five-and-a-half-million-dollars rich. And the fact that he would use that wealth to bait her into a therapist's office . . . "The problem is it's absurd."

"Absurd to go to therapy?" Daria asked.

"Absurd that he would absolve himself of the trauma *he* caused *me* by making *me* relive that same trauma." Mickey paused to appreciate her own eloquence. "It's the stupidest, most arrogant, most egotistical thing I've ever heard."

Something pounced across the tile in an orange blur and settled at their feet.

Mickey glanced under the table at Daria's new kitten, a scruff of spotted fur named Rybka. "She has the biggest ears."

"She is Ashera cat. Part leopard. Very expensive." Daria was a successful artist, or so she'd always claimed. Her sculptures, metal-work figures of varying nakedness, weren't quite to Mickey's taste. "When she is grown, she will be tall as Doberman."

"That's . . ." *Terrifying*, Mickey thought. "Cool."

Daria delivered a face-melting stare—another of her talents.

"What?" Mickey said, when she could take it no longer.

"Arrogant and egotistical—it means same thing, no?"

"That's not the point."

"I think it means same. Hang on—I check." Daria slipped into the adjoining den, a jungle of fringe lamps and antique maps. As she heaved a Polish-English dictionary off a bookcase by the window, sunlight strained through her pale kaftan dress, her legs a pair of slim shadows.

"Forget it," Mickey said. After everything she'd been through yesterday, the least Daria could do was exhibit some outrage on her behalf. There should be swears and sympathetic groans. Head-shaking. Some eye-rolling at minimum. God!

"Yes, is as I thought." Daria clapped the dictionary shut, replaced it on the shelf, and returned to her spot at the kitchen table. "But you know, is easy thing. You sit in chair, you talk to therapist person forty, fifty minutes, you go home. Me, I do much harder things for much less money."

"I don't think it would be easy, exactly." Mickey had done enough therapy in her teens and early twenties—prostrated before the altar of the Kleenex box and said all the things she was supposed to say.

"Because you are traumatized?" Daria asked.

Mickey winced. "I'm not traumatized."

"You say this. Just now."

"Nuh-uh." She had not! Had she?

"Not one minute ago. You don't want to 'relive the trauma.' This is what you say."

Mickey searched for him in her mind, this time reaching past the Tigger impression and the puffy flowers and into a darker corner of her memory. There she found her father's beer-stench, his half-naked body sprawled across a couch, the natty blue quilt Mickey would pull over him as he snored. And then, later, the endless phone calls from collection agencies, the knocks on the door, the moving crew in matching polo shirts who came to—

No. She couldn't think about it.

"It was a trauma, but I'm not actually trauma*tized*," Mickey said. "I was only saying . . . It's the principle of it."

Daria's eyes hinged open and shut a few times. "Which is what?"

"He left. Took off one day when I was seven. Went out to buy a loaf of bread and never came back. That's actually what happened. Do you know how cliché that is?"

Daria's mouth twisted, her tongue bulging inside one cheek. "You think about this still, this loaf of bread."

"How could I not?" Mickey asked. "Bread changed the course of my life."

"My father, you know, he was bad man also. He beat me and my mother every day for thirteen years." She rolled up the sleeves of her dress to reveal the pale marks along her elbows. Long lines bisected smaller ones like railroad tracks. "I have surgery to put bones back in. You know how often I think about this now?"

Mickey swallowed hard. "How often?"

"Never. Never is how often I think about this." The sleeves fell, and the scars were gone. "This therapist . . . maybe is good thing for you."

"I don't want the money." What would Mickey even do with it? Buy a boat? A yacht? "My teaching salary is more than enough."

"You live in five-hundred-square-foot apartment," Daria said with a laugh.

Mickey didn't get the joke. "So do you."

She gestured to Mickey's outfit, an old t-shirt under an admittedly ill-fitting pair of corduroy overalls. "Your clothes all are from Superstore."

"I'm thrifty."

"And you drink more than me, even."

A thorny feeling crawled up Mickey's spine. She used to get this shit all the time from people. From Mama. It was always *I'm worried about your health* or *I wish you wouldn't sleep all weekend* or *I just don't think it's normal to go through a whole liter of vodka in four days.*

Daria nodded to Mickey's glass. "This one is how many?"

"Two," Mickey said carefully.

"You've had five."

"I have not." She had, of course.

Daria's expression shifted. Mickey couldn't categorize it at first, this tiny smile, this slight pinching together of the eyebrows. Then she realized—affection. Daria was gazing at her with affection. Mama used to do that, too.

Mickey downed the last of her vodka. It had been a mistake, coming here. "Thanks for this. My treat next time."

There would be no next time.

"You come back tomorrow?" Daria asked, her voice tinkling with hope. "Sunday I walk usually. You come. We talk some more."

"I'll have to check my schedule. I might be busy."

Daria's eyes hardened up again. "I see."

Mickey strode into her classroom on Monday morning to find Jean waiting for her. The principal wore a dour face, the brackets around her mouth especially deep. At her side, a heavily made-up stranger in a beige pantsuit was glancing back and forth between her two iPhones. They sat together in tiny chairs at a tiny table, looking deadly serious.

"What's happened?" Mickey asked.

Jean and the stranger bolted to their feet, each glancing at the other.

A third woman, a stranger in a tea-length polka-dot dress, sat at another table scrubbing the rainbow keys of a xylophone with a wet wipe.

"Hi," Mickey said. "Who are you?"

The woman scrubbed the xylophone more furiously.

"Who is that?" Mickey asked Jean.

"She's the sub," Jean said.

A knot cinched in Mickey's gut. Whatever this was, it wasn't good. Very, very not good. "I didn't call for a sub."

"Let's talk in my office."

"After school, maybe?" Mickey said. "I need to get my stuff ready. Hey—that doesn't go there." The substitute teacher had risen and was stowing the xylophone on the shelf by the wall calendar instead of the shelf by the phonics chart, how dare she.

Jean reached under her glasses and pawed at her eyelids, smearing mauve eyeshadow onto her cheeks and the sides of her nose. "My office, Mickey."

Something told Mickey not to go—an urge of self-preservation. Terrible things awaited her in that office. "I don't want to."

"Fine." Jean lowered into her chair, as did Pantsuit. "We can talk here."

Pantsuit's manicure glimmered under the fluorescent lights. Each nail had been filed to a point and tipped with green.

"You can talk, but I need to get things ready. Mondays I always set out the sensory bins first." Mickey made her way into the corner and peeled the lid off a massive container of gelatinous round water beads. She was flooded with the impulse to busy her hands, to do normal things. "I thought I'd do beads instead of sand today. Ian makes too much of a mess."

Pantsuit flipped open a leather notebook, uncapped her probably-eighty-dollar fat ballpoint pen, and scrawled something on a blank page.

"Ian is why we're here," Jean said.

Mickey froze. A series of images sprang to mind, each more devastating than the last: Ian huddling alone in a bus shelter; Ian wandering the back alleys of downtown in his Spiderman shoes; Ian lying on a slab with a tag on his toe and a Y-shaped autopsy incision in his chest. She should never have left him with that skeezy, bro-ish uncle. "What happened? Is he okay?"

"Ian is fine," Jean said.

"Are you sure?"

"Yes, I'm sure."

Mickey's heart began to beat again. "Then what's the problem?"

Eyeshadow was all over Jean's face at this point. "Why would you think it was okay to take a child off the school grounds?"

Pantsuit threw Jean a sharp glance.

Mickey blinked. Had she taken a child off school property? Well, yeah. She had.

"I—I only meant to . . ." She'd begun this sentence with no idea how to finish it. What was happening right now? The sensory bins. She took the lid off another sensory bin. Children would be here soon, and they needed tactile stimulation. "It was the end of the day, and his mom clearly wasn't coming."

"I told you to call the police."

"Let's not get sidetracked here," said Pantsuit, speaking for the first time. Her voice had a certain sizzle. "The fact is . . ." She fixed Jean with a wide, encouraging stare.

"The fact is . . ." Jean said. "You're fired."

"Placed on unpaid leave," Pantsuit said.

"Placed on unpaid leave," Jean said.

There was more—a lot of legal jargon and something about the teachers' union? Mickey was handed a business card at one point. By whom, she couldn't say. The world had dissolved into specks of light and shadow. When the classroom drifted back into focus, Jean and Pantsuit were on their feet again, and the sub was arranging all the wrong toys—castles, train tracks, dinosaurs—on the carpet.

"Not that." Mickey pried a miniature bulldozer from the sub's soft warm hands. "I meant to get rid of this thing. Sidak and Ella won't stop fighting over it."

The sub took half a step backward, her eyebrows disappearing under her Bettie Page bangs. "Oh—I thought—"

"And I never set out the trains until after circle time." Mickey pushed past the sub and heaved the toy kitchen set out from the corner. This place was a mess, and she had no time to fix it. "Where are the little ketchup bottles? Did someone move them?"

Mickey turned to the sub, who had shrunk backward into the whiteboard. "Did *you* move them?"

The sub shook her head. "I swear, I—"

"Why would you mess with my kitchen set?" Mickey asked. "Why would you—"

A hand landed on Mickey's bicep.

Jean gazed at her sadly. "Buddy. You've got to stop."

Mickey scuttled out of Jean's reach. She would not be pitied or placated. This was her class. These were her kids. The school year was only a month old, and already she knew which ones needed extra help to get their shoes off, which ones would burst into tears when a crayon snapped in half, which ones were most likely to stick their hands down their own—

Her feet tangled. The room catapulted upward, her vision filling with rows of fluorescent lightbulbs, white-painted pipes, a mildewed ceiling panel. The ground rose up to meet her, and she landed flat on her back.

Pain radiated outward from her shoulder, where she'd landed on . . . what? She twisted an arm beneath her and pulled out a plastic snowman. His carrot nose and one of his tree-branch arms had snapped off in the collision.

Jean's voice rang from a distance: "Oh, Jesus."

Pantsuit towered over Mickey. Her features appeared longer and narrower from this angle, as if her whole face had been squeezed in a vise grip.

"It's 7:50, Ms. Morris. Children will be here soon. This is their classroom, the place they come to make friends, to have fun, to explore the world. The place they come to for routine." Pantsuit smiled. "Stability. That's the key word here. Children need their adults to be stable. And that is not you right now."

Mickey propped up on her elbows and scrutinized herself. She was on the floor. Her back hurt. Her lip, which she must've bitten during the fall, tasted of tin and salt. And something was rearing up inside her—a feeling she couldn't name, dark, clawing, threatening to burst out. All she knew was that if she stayed here, she might cry. The children would stare, or try to hug her, or cower in their seats, deeply afraid.

Maybe Pantsuit had a point.

Gritting her teeth, Mickey flopped onto her side and gathered the pieces of broken snowman off the floor. After lumbering upright, she offered the pieces to the sub, who folded her arms and looked away.

Mickey placed the debris on a shelf instead. "Some superglue should fix it."

Her gaze went to the row of little hooks on the wall, the cubbies where children would soon hang their jackets, their hats, their *Paw Patrol* backpacks. "You said *un*paid leave?"

Pantsuit had returned to her tiny chair at the tiny table. "Pending an investigation."

"Into what exactly?" Mickey asked. What had she done? Kept a vulnerable child at home where he belonged. That's what she'd done.

Jean examined herself in the floor-length mirror by the reading nook and wiped her cheeks with a tissue. Mickey had glued laminated circles around the frame, each proclaiming a different self-affirmation (*I work hard, I am smart, I can do anything*). "You can't take off with a kid in your own car, Mickey."

"It wasn't—" Mickey shut her mouth. Bringing up the lawyer would only make this worse.

"You'll get your next paycheck as usual," Pantsuit said, scrolling her two phones again. "Then nothing after that."

ARLO

Arlo woke with peaty fumes at the back of her throat. The scent seemed to come from everywhere—her hair, her pillow, the designer bedsheets she'd once spent half a paycheck on. Cologne, she realized, shaking away dim visions of a man between her thighs and a damp face in her neck. Because surely not. It hadn't actually happened.

She reached under the covers and patted herself down. Bare breasts weren't the best sign, no, but Arlo clung to hope. There was still the tiniest possibility it had all been a dream. She cranked one eyelid open, then the other, and peered through the sludge of her day-old mascara.

There he was, lying naked atop the covers: the caretaker of Daddy's large and complicated estate, from which Arlo was set to inherit over five million dollars. The lawyer.

Samson lay on his side facing Arlo with his hands gathered under one cheek. Black hair spurted from his chest—much darker than the salt-and-pepper stuff atop of his head. Arlo pitied herself. Knowledge of Samson's body hair was knowledge she didn't want.

"Mr. Samson," she said, wriggling a hand up from under the covers to poke him in the sternum. "Mr. Samson."

As his lashes fluttered apart, his eyes lit with recognition, memory, and lastly shame. He twisted his upper body to face the ceiling a bit more and her a bit less. "Hi."

Arlo had a flash of her ex, Hayden, half-asleep on the pullout couch in his parents' basement after they'd both lost their virginities. Hayden half-asleep on the cruddy futon in their first apartment. Hayden half-asleep on the Swiss-made mattress Daddy bought them as a wedding present. Hayden sulking as the delivery guys wrangled it through the door. His face had said, *Who needs six thousand pocket coils? What does* pocket coil *even mean?*

"Why would you do this?" Arlo asked the lawyer because a) it certainly wasn't her fault, and b) she was curious. What a fascinating choice for a person to make.

"You mean, why would I want to . . ." Samson gestured back and forth between them.

"I'm half your age."

"Well, yeah. You're young and"—his cheeks reddened—"completely gorgeous, obviously." He flopped around until he was able to pull the bedsheet over his waist.

At the funeral, Arlo had found him overbearing and arrogant and generally oafish. But there was always more to uncover. Blind spots, misbeliefs. A person was a ripe, ripe orange. She couldn't help but dig in her thumbnails and squeeze until the juice streaked down her wrists. "And what does that matter for you?"

Samson frowned. "I don't get what you're asking."

"Why me? Why now? What was important about this?" Arlo bit the tip of her tongue. She had a bad habit of overtalking, of asking too many questions in a row. It overloaded clients. Totally counterproductive.

"I guess, um, getting old is hard?"

Arlo cheered inwardly. Now they were getting somewhere. "Go on."

"I mean, I've done well. I live alone in a two-million-dollar pent-house full of Red Sox memorabilia. I've got it good. I know that." He said how secure he was, how grateful. Yes, he'd always wanted a family. No, it hadn't happened. He wasn't married. He didn't have kids. He didn't have any of the things he thought he'd have at this age. He was fifty, and there was no pretending anymore. "God. What's wrong with me? You don't want to hear this."

Arlo desperately wanted to hear this. She loved this shit. Watching people take their oldest, ugliest feelings and shake them out in the light of day . . . Hearing people voice thoughts they may never have acknowledged . . . It was a magic Arlo hadn't touched since working with her last client, Laura Hedman, a nineteen-year-old with crushing anxiety and a thing for the cottage-core aesthetic. Arlo's heart still lifted at the memory of what they'd achieved together—all the emotional boundaries they'd worked on setting, all the distorted thought patterns they'd wrangled into submission.

"It's good to talk about these things." As Arlo touched the lawyer's shoulder, his hands slid away to reveal a pair of wide puffy eyes. Pure vulnerability. Made Arlo shiver every time. "It's too much to carry on your own."

Laura's burdens had been heavy, too. In the end, she couldn't withstand the weight. Her parents blamed Arlo, and there followed the baseless accusations, the unceremonious suspension, then the hearing in that courtroom with the blinding white walls, where Laura's father had sobbed into the heels of his hands, and Laura's mother had glared at Arlo with disdain, with hatred, as if Arlo weren't also grieving the loss. As if Arlo hadn't watched the court-room doors like a hawk, hoping against hope that it was all a mis-take, and that Laura might stride inside at any moment, revived and smiling and wearing one of her usual elaborate side-braids.

But reason had prevailed. As the judge had put it when he dis-missed the lawsuit, it was *mere chance* that Laura had killed herself after a therapy session. *A calculation of fate.* She might've gone to class that day, or to the store.

Arlo offered Samson a smile and swung out of bed. She found a satin robe in the dresser and wove herself into it, then fumbled around in her desk drawers for a few handouts.

"It's important to know what resources are out there," she said, handing him a small stack of papers. "There are some great groups and meet-ups in the community for people looking to expand socially—if that's of interest to you. And of course, therapy is helpful." Better for Samson to call a helpline and find a different practitioner. He couldn't continue these conversations with her; that would be inappropriate.

Samson's mouth puckered as he flipped through the handouts. "Oh. Thanks, but I've got somebody already."

"You do?" Arlo asked. *He doesn't*, she thought.

"I see a private gal. Two hundred bucks a pop."

"A private gal." Arlo sank onto the mattress, feeling oddly deflated.

"It's worth it, though. She helps me with my cognitive distortions. Fortune-telling, mind-reading, all-or-nothing thinking." Samson counted these on his fingers. "And I've got a bit of an anger problem. Men, you know—we're not taught how to regulate our emotions."

"Right," Arlo said.

A phone chimed on the far bedside table. Samson reached out to silence it. "Sorry. That's my reminder to meditate."

"To what?" Arlo asked. There was no way.

"I have an app. Guided visualizations, mostly. Some belly breathing."

Arlo pictured this man sitting cross-legged on a yoga mat, palms turned upward on his knees, and her head exploded. It did not compute. She'd pegged him for the kind of cringey but ultimately harmless fifty-something who made people uncomfortable at parties, always jingling an expensive watch and mansplaining mutual funds.

"You people do good work," he said. "Things really turned around for me when I started therapy."

Arlo crossed the room with no particular destination in mind. She pushed aside the Moleskine notebooks and rose-gold writing implements that cluttered her desk and sat on the edge with her legs dangling. Sunlight slanted through the window at her back, gently roasting her nape. "This"—she gestured between them, as he'd done earlier—"won't affect our working relationship, I hope?"

"Our working relationship?" Samson said, his voice scaling into the next octave.

It felt like she'd lost the upper hand somehow and needed to regain it. "You're still the lawyer. We still have to sit down and figure out the estate stuff. The house, the inheritance."

Samson inspected his thumbnail. "I've been meaning to set up a meeting with you and your mom. There were some changes made in the last few months. To the will, I mean."

Changes, Arlo thought darkly. Daddy had always planned to divide the estate more or less down the middle. Mother would keep the house but share the liquid assets fifty-fifty with Arlo. Unless Daddy had reconsidered that split? Maybe he'd grown weary of Mother's crystal-embellished Manolos and boozy brunches and four-hundred-dollar facials. Arlo certainly had.

"Let's talk about it this week?" Samson smoothed the comforter flat over his lap. Was he trembling? "You could come to the office."

"Why can't you tell me now?" Arlo asked.

"We're downtown. Central location. Easy to get to."

The heat on Arlo's neck was growing painful now. She wanted to move again but thought it would look odd, even weak. And a dark sense of foreboding had snuck up on her, pinning her to the spot. "Mr. Samson."

He scrunched his eyes closed.

"*Mr. Samson.*"

The lawyer opened his mouth, and for a terrible moment, Arlo wondered if he might vomit. Then he drew an audible breath and said, very quickly, "The will no longer mentions you."

Arlo held this phrase in her mind, turned it over and twisted it, examined it from different sides. *The will no longer mentions you.* She knew what the words meant individually. Together, they meant nothing. A word salad, a non-sentence. "What?"

He'd gone pale. "You're not in it."

"In what sense?"

"In the sense that he didn't leave you anything."

Arlo laughed. What a weird joke. What a weird lawyer.

"I'm sorry," he said. "This must be so hard."

Arlo detected care and caution in his voice.

"You're serious," she said. Her vision blurred, the bed and the lawyer melting into one another. "You're actually serious right now."

Samson said something vaguely kind and reassuring. Arlo didn't register it. She couldn't register anything, not even her own body. Where were her arms, her legs?

She'd spent the last eight months taking care of Daddy. Except no. People *took care* of goldfish. What Arlo had done for her father—spoon-fed him pudding, soaped his sallow belly, lifted him on and off a commode every morning—wasn't care. It was devotion. Not to mention everything she'd done before his liver failed.

"Arlo? Arlo."

She blinked her surroundings back into focus. The lawyer had scooted to the foot of the bed and was gazing up at her with the most crushing look of concern, his eyebrows fusing into one long furry ridge.

"Sorry, what did you say?" she asked.

"I said, do you have somebody to talk to?"

"About the will?" Surely, that's what he'd meant.

"Feelings like this are too much for one person to shoulder," he added.

"Oh," Arlo said. "Somebody, as in . . ." A counselor. A therapist. A professional, because that's what he thought she needed—professional help. "Right. Yeah. Yeah, I'm good."

There was a long silence, then he asked to use the shower. Though she said yes, he seemed hesitant to stand.

"Would you mind? I'd rather you don't look."

"Of course," Arlo said and shut her eyes.

MICKEY

Mickey vaulted over Question 19 (*Is there a concern about alcohol, drug abuse, or overuse of prescription or nonprescription drugs?*) and went straight to the next section on the intake form, which asked her to rate a series of statements on a scale from *very untrue* to *very true*. She circled *somewhat true* for the first item—*I feel sad, depressed, or hopeless*—and promptly crossed it out. She didn't want to sound overly confident, but she also didn't want to sound wishy-washy. This form was a piece of art, a self-portrait her new therapist would inspect with a magnifying glass. This form was everything.

"You okay over there, hun?"

The receptionist flashed Mickey a gummy smile.

"You were muttering to yourself," she added, which might've been true.

After returning the form, Mickey settled into the same chair in the empty waiting area, where a small fire twitched and whimpered in the stone hearth. The décor was more ski lodge than psychologist's office, which made sense, actually, given that Adam Kowalski had chosen this place. Only the best to fix his fucked-up firstborn.

She opened the email app on her phone. Nothing from the teachers' union. She closed the app and opened it again. Still nothing.

Someone had called yesterday saying an investigation would be launched, but they hadn't given any dates. Would she be back in time to make holiday crafts with the kids? Felt snowmen with googly eyes? Penguins fashioned from toilet paper tubes? God, she hoped so.

Across town, a substitute teacher would be calling Mickey's kids back to their desks now for midmorning snack. In Mickey's mind, it was that same woman with the polka-dot dress, only her eyes were glowing a demonic shade of red, and her teeth had sharpened into fangs. She wouldn't remind the children to wash their hands, nor would she help them open their juice boxes and yogurt tubes. She'd be too busy scrolling through something stupid on her phone, TMZ probably, and so the children would languish, thirsty, hungry, yogurt-less. Later, when the class came together for end-of-the-day circle time, the sub wouldn't play any of their usual clapping games. Would she even know to sing the Goodbye Train song? It was their favorite.

When Mickey shut her eyes, she could still see them gathered on the front carpet in the classroom, backpacks on, legs crisscross. Their chubby cheeks and messy hair.

"Mickey Morris?"

The person waiting at reception was not what she'd expected. To be a psychologist, Mickey knew, this girl must've been at least twenty-four or twenty-five. She wore a blazer and round wire glasses and carried a clipboard under one arm. But her hair—so lank, so gingery. And her skin—so bare, so freckled. She might've been twelve.

"I'm Arlo." Her whole face flexed into a smile.

Mickey felt a strange swell of affection. "Hi."

"Come on back."

Arlo led Mickey to a door at the end of the hall, her chunky heels clopping with every step. Like the wearer, the shoes were small, maybe an adult size five or six. "Here we are."

Shuffling inside, Mickey jolted to find a familiar face staring back from the far wall, someone with impeccable eye makeup, ramrod posture, and shiny teacher-hair.

"Don't mind the mirror," Arlo said. "There's an observation room on the other side, but no one is watching our session."

Mickey turned from her reflection and took in the rest of the space: pastel-blue wall paint, box of tissues, mass-produced art print of lighthouse on pebbled shore. It was, she thought grimly, familiar territory.

Arlo tugged the door shut and folded herself into a leather armchair at a small table. "Any troubles getting here today?"

This struck Mickey as a loaded question to be asking right off the bat, but she would roll with it anyway. She'd been in half a dozen rooms like this one during her university years, mostly at Mama's urging. She'd talked to psychologists, psychiatrists, psychotherapists, certified counselors, licensed clinical social workers. If nothing else, this meant she spoke their language. She would do the right things, use the right words, and get out—with her money—as fast as possible. Yes, she could do this. She could play the game.

"No, getting here was pretty easy for me." Mickey sank into the other chair and its overly squishy seat cushion, which had clearly been designed to ensnare. "I'm doing pretty well. I thought I'd come in for more of a—a check-up, you know?"

A small silence sprouted between them.

"But no traffic or anything like that?" Arlo asked.

"Oh." Mickey produced a laugh, light and good-natured, the laugh of a well-adjusted, stable person who led a balanced lifestyle and didn't misinterpret simple small talk for existential questioning. "No, it was fine."

"Glad to hear it," Arlo said, clasping her hands. "Let's get started, then."

First came the classic speech about confidentiality. Basically, Arlo was legally bound to keep Mickey's deepest, darkest, most incriminating secrets unless Mickey was deemed at risk of harming others or herself. Mickey wanted to ask what counted as harming oneself but thought better of it. A well-adjusted, stable person would probably not ask that question.

"I see you're already paid up for seven sessions total, which is great. Most people only come once or twice. Good for you, making that investment."

"About that—" Mickey said. "I wanted to ask if I could book sessions back-to-back?"

Arlo narrowed her eyes slightly. "Back-to-back."

"Like, um . . ." Mickey thought quickly, ". . . immersion. You know, do a bunch of days in a row." That was a thing, wasn't it? Wellness retreats, ashrams, etc.?

"I generally suggest two weeks between sessions. One week minimum. It gives time for growth to happen." The psychologist's head canted to the side at the end of her long neck. "Was there a reason you wanted to book the sessions so close together?"

Mickey recalculated. "Self-care. Figured I'd do a deep dive."

"Why now?" Arlo asked.

"Hmmm?"

"Why do the self-care now?"

Balls, Mickey thought. She should've crafted a narrative, made up a backstory. Her true self, though completely acceptable and in no need of alteration whatsoever, would probably not do. Not here. "Um . . ."

Arlo's gaze whirled down through Mickey's skin, her skull, her brain matter.

"I don't know," Mickey said to make it end.

"That's okay. We can come back to that." Arlo moved the clipboard into her lap, which Mickey did not take as a particularly good sign. "Let's hear a bit about yourself."

Easy: "I'm a kindergarten teacher. Have been for twelve years."

No harm in offering a few facts. Spies were taught to stick as closely to the truth as possible when being interrogated. Mickey had read that somewhere once.

That smile again, the one that gripped every muscle in the therapist's face. "Sounds fun. And busy. Your students must be important to you."

Mickey let herself relax a little. "The most important."

"Who else is important to you?"

"I read a lot of Murakami. Weird, dreamy shit, you know? Italo Calvino. Kafka. I like Wes Anderson movies. Especially the ones with Bill Mu—"

"Right. And who are the important people in *your* life? People you know personally."

Heat pooled in Mickey's cheeks. "I . . . don't see how that's relevant."

"Humans are social creatures. That social impulse is what separates us from other mammals." Arlo went on to talk about the vagus nerve, the parasympathetic nervous system, something about mirror neurons.

Mickey wasn't sure how to respond. How could she say she hated people and wanted nothing to do with them without sounding vaguely psychopathic? "I guess my independence is important to me."

"I see." Arlo jotted a note on her clipboard, probably something about Mickey's *affect* or *thought content*. Instantly, Mickey felt nineteen years old again. Were these people incapable of having a normal conversation? Must they always be studying and assessing and writing things down? "For your emergency contact, you've put someone called Daria. Who is that?"

Mickey rubbed her suddenly clammy palms on her jeans. "My neighbor."

"You're close?" Arlo asked.

"Right across the hall."

Arlo made another note. "Family?"

"Nope."

"None?"

"Don't talk to my mom much." Mickey peeled off her sweater and balled it in her lap. She glanced at the wall clock and found she still had, God, thirty-seven minutes left.

"And your dad? Is he in the picture?"

He might've been. In an alternate universe, he might've arrived on Mickey's doorstep one day with an apology and a gift of some kind, a token of goodwill. Flowers, maybe. A pie. Yes, it would've been a pecan pie. They would've sat together in Mickey's kitchen with a slice each.

"Gone since I was little," Mickey said.

Arlo perched forward in her seat, like a spectator at a high-stakes sporting event. How entertaining this must be for her. "Sounds hard."

Mickey clenched her jaw, managed a shrug.

"Talking about your dad is tough for you, huh?" Arlo said, scribbling and scribbling and scribbling some more.

"Not really." If the topic was tough for Mickey, then it was only because this girl had stirred it up with a stick. Mickey had decided long ago what to think about her father—when she thought about him at all, which was basically never.

"I only mean that our feelings toward family can be complicated," Arlo said. "People are complicated."

A laugh erupted through Mickey's nose, carrying with it some of the heat that had built behind her ribs. She couldn't help it. "People are simple."

Arlo's pen fell still. "How so?"

ARLO

"And your dad?" Arlo glanced at the wall clock and found she still had, God, thirty-seven minutes left. Thirty-seven minutes until she could return to her office and scroll through Daddy's Facebook page, and all the texts he'd sent her, and all the photos of him she'd kept on her phone, which was what she'd been doing all day every day since the lawyer had uttered those six terrible words: *The will no longer mentions you.* "Is he in the picture?"

"Gone since I was little," Mickey said a little too evenly. They'd touched on something here, unearthed an old trauma, and now she was trying to bury it.

Parental abandonment wasn't something Arlo had experienced until last week. Except no, that wasn't right. She wasn't a child, and Daddy hadn't dumped her on the street. He'd merely made a change to his will, that was all, a small change, completely within his rights. But why? Why, instead of giving her five and a half million dollars like he'd always planned, had he opted to strike her name and give her . . . nothing?

Refocusing her attention on the new client, Arlo perched forward in her seat. She needed to get out of her own head and into someone else's—and body language was key to establishing any therapeutic alliance. "Sounds hard."

A muscle quivered in Mickey's jaw as she managed a shrug.

"Talking about your dad is tough for you, huh?" Arlo said, making a few quick notes on her clipboard. *Neat appearance. Organized thought content. Constricted affect.*

Annoyance flashed in Mickey's eyes. "Not really."

"I only mean that our feelings toward family can be complicated," Arlo said, backtracking. She'd pushed too far too soon. "People are complicated."

Mickey laughed through her nose. "People are simple."

"How so?" Arlo asked.

"Adults act in their own self-interest. We might huddle together for warmth sometimes, but when hunger strikes, we'll fight to the death over a—a deer carcass or whatever."

"A deer carcass?" Arlo glanced down at where she'd written *organized thought content* and scratched it out.

Mickey squirmed in her seat, growing taller for a moment before hunching again. "All I'm saying is, at the end of the day, people do what's best for them. If that means stabbing you in the back, that's what they'll do."

But that wasn't true at all! People were inherently worthy and whole. Inherently good! This was one of Arlo's core beliefs—her guiding value as a therapist. She felt warm and tingly just thinking about it.

"That's why I don't do people," Mickey added. "That's why I don't talk to them."

"You don't talk to people?" Arlo asked as gently as she could, because wow—this poor, paranoid, angry woman.

Mickey pawed at the stray hairs that had fallen into her eyes. "I—what I meant was—I talk to people. Obviously, I talk to people. I'm talking to you right now. I just don't get too close.

To people. People are bound to disappoint you. Even the good ones. Especially the good ones. Your closest friends, family. These are the people who screw you over the worst."

This tweaked something in Arlo's brain, and the lawyer's words rang out all over again. *The will no longer mentions you.* And again. *The will no longer mentions you.* And again. *The will no longer mentions you.* At some point, the emphasis started shifting around. *The* WILL *no longer mentions you. The will no* LONGER *mentions you. The will no longer mentions* YOU. But the phrase never softened, each variation as brutal as the last.

"People do strange things sometimes," she said, suddenly light-headed. "But if a loved one screws us over, as you've put it, then surely they will have had a reason."

"Egocentrism," Mickey said pointedly. "Self-preservation. Looking out for numero uno. That's the reason. That's all there is to understand."

No. Not in Daddy's case. Arlo would prove it if she had to.

She looked Mickey in the eye and said, "I respectfully disagree."

Tom Samson's personal secretary was stabbing some spinach with a fork when Arlo strode up and flattened her hands on his desk. She'd thought carefully about her expression, adopting a steely gaze and a certain don't-fuck-with-me positioning of the mouth. It seemed to be working. Wide-eyed, the secretary wheeled backward in his chair and crushed his plastic salad container against his chest.

"I need to talk to him," Arlo said, nodding to the wall of frosted glass behind the secretary's desk. Samson was back there, a grayish man-shape hunching in front of a computer. "It's urgent."

The secretary shook his head and, through a full mouth, produced a sound Arlo took to mean *Absolutely not.* A few grains of quinoa rained onto his shirt.

"I'll let myself in. Thanks." Arlo dove for the door handle and took one step inside before halting, confronted by a wall of floral smell.

Samson glanced up from his desk, eyebrows soaring. An oil diffuser puffed away at his side while instrumental music drifted from his laptop—harps, flutes, and fiddles, all vaguely Celtic-sounding. Something about the wispy melody, together with the lavender scent, made Arlo want to slither down onto the carpet and coil there forever.

The secretary barged in. "I'm so sorry, Mr. Samson. I couldn't stop her."

When Samson stood, Arlo's first thought was of how wrinkly he looked—not only his face but his entire being. One corner of his half-tucked dress shirt stuck out the fly of his pants. She noticed then the pillow and blanket lumped on the sofa against the wall.

"It's okay, Dean," Samson said to the secretary.

The secretary—Dean—threw Arlo a snide glance and retreated, reaching for his back molars with one finger as he stepped out and closed the door behind him.

Samson gathered the pillow and blanket into his arms and chucked them on the floor. From the coffee table, he cleared an empty takeout box, a cloudy Scotch tumbler, and a bulk-sized bottle of soy sauce. He gave no explanation for the presence of these things, saying only, "Pardon my mess."

He dragged a chair over and sat in it, offering Arlo the whole sofa with a sweeping sort of gesture. "What can I do for you?"

Arlo tried to reconjure the don't-fuck-with-me face. "Why did he do it?"

Samson smudged his lips together. He was calculating, clearly, which was not what Arlo wanted. She hadn't come here to be handled. She'd come here for answers.

People are simple. The new client had said that yesterday. But it wasn't true. People weren't simple. Daddy, for example, would've had good reasons—good, profound, decidedly not simple reasons—for cutting Arlo out of his will. He wouldn't have done it selfishly, nor would he have done it out of spite. Maybe he'd meant it as a compliment. Yes, that was it. Arlo was such a strong, independent woman that she didn't need an inheritance.

"You're talking about your—"

"You must know," she said.

"I can't discuss client matters." He touched his fingertips together, acting suddenly professional in his crinkled clothes and bare feet.

But Arlo wouldn't accept this. "He came to you and told you do it, right? To change the will. He must've said why."

"It would violate confidentiality."

"So he *did* tell you."

"You're a therapist. You understand."

Arlo found this mildly offensive. Why should she understand anything? The situation was not understandable. "Don't do that."

"Do what?"

"Presume to know what's happening inside my head."

"I'm not presuming anything."

"You don't know me, okay?"

Samson laced his fingers together and squeezed hard enough to make his knuckles blanche. She'd irritated him. Good. "I didn't say I—"

"And you certainly didn't know my father. He was—he was—"

Arlo couldn't pick an adjective. Memories had started to bubble up, and half of her was five years old again, bouncing on Daddy's knee outside an ice cream parlor. Riding on his shoulders at Disneyland. Standing in line for a roller coaster, and later, falling asleep against his soft cotton shoulder while they waited to see a parade. The pictures from that trip had turned out blurry, she recalled, but they'd kept them anyway, slotted them into plastic sleeves in an album with a tartan-print cover.

"Was he mad at me?" What a violent thought. It sliced and pummeled her from the inside out. "Because if he was mad at me, I really don't get why."

Samson placed his hands on his belly. They rose and fell as he breathed. "Life can take some shit turns," he said softly.

The fire she'd stoked inside her chest shuddered out. How could she despise this man? Beneath the pompous exterior, there was a wholesomeness to him she couldn't deny. He reminded her of someone. Not Hayden, obviously. Hayden was Arlo's age, for starters. He wore a beard and a man-bun and did pull-up exercises using a special device that hooked on the doorframe.

"But you?" Samson said. "You'll be okay. You're still young enough."

"For what?" Arlo asked.

Samson's knees made a popping sound as he stood. Only after crossing the room and stowing the soy sauce in a mini-fridge behind the desk did he give an answer. "Self-reinvention."

Then it came to her: Tom Hanks. He reminded her of a mid-2000s Tom Hanks, the handsome but slightly doughy one who'd bunked up in an airport terminal and fallen for Catherine Zeta-Jones. The Tom Hanks of her childhood. Yes, this man was sweet and soft underneath it all. He would help her if she played her cards right.

"How did Daddy seem to you when he made these changes? Tell me that at least."

Samson walked out in front of the desk and thrust his hands in his pockets. "He was dying."

Eye-roll, thought Arlo. "Yes, I know that."

"Tired. He seemed tired."

Arlo pressed up off the couch and joined Samson where he stood, stepping close enough to count the blackheads on his nose. "I went to the hospital every day."

Samson shrank backward into the edge of the desk. "I'm sure he appreciated it."

"Have you ever done that for someone? Cared for them as they died?"

"I was in a strange place when my mother passed," Samson said, mostly to the floor. His eyes flashed up to meet Arlo's in brief spurts. She could feel him warming up, turning to clay in her hands.

"You pour yourself into them," she said.

"My sisters were better equipped to look after her anyway. Caregiving is . . . well, I'm not good at that sort of thing."

"*I* was," Arlo said, trying not to think too hard about patriarchal gender norms. Finally, she was gaining some ground. Samson would spill the truth any second now. "I was great at it. I read to him, clipped his toenails, moisturized his feet."

"That's honorable," Samson said with a wince.

"I changed his clothes, brushed his teeth."

Samson swallowed, his Adam's apple bobbing once, twice in his throat. "Wow."

"I bathed him. All of him. Even made sure to get his scrot—"

"Please—stop." Samson threw his hands up. Victory. "I do have something that might help. Hang tight for a minute here."

Arlo waited until he'd left the room before she doubled at the waist and let out a huge sigh.

There would be an explanation for all this. Of course there would be an explanation! Daddy was a good man. No, he never got sober. Alcohol had saturated his blood, his brain matter, and every one of his relationships right to the bitter end, when the last healthy cells in his liver turned to scar tissue. But it wasn't his fault. Few people swapped fists with addiction and came out the winner. Besides—he made Arlo laugh. He sang her funny songs. He sent her a rose and a teddy bear every Valentine's Day. These things outweighed the broken promises, the lies, the empties clinking around the floor of his Beamer.

"Why are you hanging upside down like that?"

Arlo swung upright so quickly she saw stars.

Samson had returned with a steaming ceramic mug, a small carafe of milk, and a few paper packets of sugar. He positioned everything on the table just so.

Arlo's heart sank. "I thought you were bringing me secret files or something."

"This is better. Bengal Spice. You know, the one with the tiger." He brought his fingertips to his mouth and made a chef's kiss. "Oh, it's good shit."

"Good shit," Arlo repeated slowly. She wasn't sure what else to say.

Samson must've seen something dire in her face because his own grin sloughed away. "You don't need me to tell you who got the money."

Arlo moved toward the door. What a tremendous waste of time. "Look, if you're not going to help me—"

"You don't need me to tell you *because you already know*."

Arlo shook her head. Riddles. First he'd given her tea, and now he was giving her riddles.

"I assure you," she said. "I don't know. I don't know a thing about this."

"Besides you and your mom, who else would your dad want to take care of? Come on. It's obvious." Samson plopped down on the couch and sipped Arlo's rejected tea. "That's why it's so hard to accept."

○

Apparently, Deborah Kowalski liked to garden. Squash, kale, onions, peas, heirloom tomatoes—the photos littered her Facebook page in bursts of red and green and yellow. As Arlo scrolled, she saw that Deborah had a friend group of similarly barefaced, weather-beaten sixty- and seventy-somethings. They went on hikes in the nearby mountains and met for evenings of crochet in each other's living rooms. Deborah was always pictured in one of three outfits: cream slacks with a flowery top, a frumpy brown wrap dress, or the jean overalls she'd worn to Daddy's funeral. And always, *always* the same bucket hat.

In short, there had never been a woman less like Arlo's mother.

Arlo scrolled back up and inspected the profile picture, a grainy close-up taken in front of a nondescript body of water. Deborah looked tan and happy. By any indication, her life had turned out fairly okay. Sure, her marriage to Daddy—and its subsequent combustion—would've left a nasty mark. But that was decades ago. It was honorable but unnecessary, this effort of his to balance the books.

She opened a new tab and typed Deborah's name into Google. Top hits included a LinkedIn profile with no picture and no text, the results of a half-marathon from 2013, and the link for a boutique hair salon in a suburb just south of the city. Arlo clicked.

So, Deborah was a hairdresser. She specialized in dye jobs and offered a ten-percent discount to first-time customers. A button under her bio read *Book now*.

Arlo jumped out of her chair and went to the fridge, where she caught a glimpse of herself in the small mirror affixed to the door. Her hair had grown long and lank. A good cut would probably take an hour: ample time for them to get to know each other and talk things through.

But no. Show up at Deborah's place of work? Arlo wouldn't. She couldn't. Even if she wanted to. Even if she deserved the money, and Deborah didn't. If Arlo was certain of anything, it was that Deborah did not deserve Daddy's money. Where had Deborah been when the doctors started calling Daddy's liver failure *end-stage*?

Where had Deborah been when Daddy broke both legs trying to jump into the pool from that balcony in Vegas? Where had Deborah been when Daddy fell asleep in the snowbank outside Limerick's and lost three of his toes?

Arlo was Daddy's greatest protector. She was the one who chopped vegetables for his salad lunches and brought them to the house in a giant Tupperware container. She was the one who called the pharmacist to make sure they put his pills in special blister packs. She was the one who, since age ten, had remembered to buy toilet paper and pay the electric bill and pick up a rotisserie chicken for dinner. Not Deborah. Deborah hadn't done anything.

"Not a thing," Arlo muttered an hour and a half later as she shouldered open the door to Diva Hair Designs Ltd. A chime of three ascending notes strained against the song playing from the ceiling speakers. Arlo's blood ran cold: ABBA.

Bent over a broom, Deborah swept a few wisps of hair out from under the lone stylist's chair behind the reception desk.

Arlo coughed.

Deborah gave no sign of having heard, baying along to "Chiquitita" as she swirled across the hardwood. It was a small space made even smaller by its clutter: candles, dream catchers, shelves stacked three rows deep with shampoo bottles and salt lamps.

Arlo tapped the desk bell, which made a tinny, futile call. What pitiful customer service. "Deborah. *Deborah.*"

Glancing up, Deborah made an exaggerated surprise face before propping her broom against the wall and swooping in behind the counter. "I'm so sorry! I didn't see—oh." She smiled with such genuine warmth it made Arlo's toes curl inside her boots. "It's you. Hi, honey."

Arlo bristled from head to toe. *Honey* was a term of endearment. *Honey* signified a closeness and affection she did not want. She hadn't come here to be coddled. She'd come here to understand how Deborah could accept so much money from a man she hadn't spoken to in almost three decades. How she could justify it to herself, this gross wrongdoing, this theft.

But instead of the dignified speech Arlo had mentally prepared and rehearsed during the drive over, what came out was "He chose us."

Deborah flinched ever so slightly, as if struck by a tiny whip.

Arlo's stomach lurched. Had she actually just said that? *He chose us*? It was the kind of thing an angry teenager might shout before stomping into her bedroom.

But compassion rather than insult reared up behind Deborah's eyes. "I think you could use a trim." She took a smock from a drawer and swung it through the air. "*Olé, olé.*"

Arlo hesitated. The prospect of spending time alone with this very bubbly, very blonde woman suddenly held no appeal. Ten seconds into the interaction, and she'd already humiliated herself. What was she doing here? "Oh—I—"

Deborah jerked her head toward the stylist's chair. "On the house."

"No, thanks."

"Come on, honey."

"I really can't."

Deborah glanced at the ceiling. "You know what, give me a sec. I need to change this music before it rots my brain. There's a type of old biddy who comes in here who just friggin' loves A B B A . I mean, I liked some of their stuff. I really liked their outfits. Is that embarrassing? You know, the boots, the bell-bottoms, the minidresses with the cats on them. Do you know which ones I'm talking about? You're probably too young."

She fiddled with an ancient green iPod, still talking, talking, talking. Arlo felt simultaneously dizzy and immobile, like a fly being spun in a spider's silk.

"My generation really did have it all. What do you kids have? TikTok? Taylor Swift? Actually, I don't mind her. I like that she writes her own stuff. And she's got great hair, great natural curl. She straightens it, of course, because all women want the opposite of the hair they have. Which reminds me of something my mother used to say . . ." Deborah went on, somehow.

"Chiquitita" cut out.

"It's a shit time, isn't it? When a parent passes." Deborah's voice was at Arlo's back suddenly, her cold fingertips on Arlo's neck. She fastened the smock a little too tight. "I was a total wreck both times. Hey—you want some tea? I've got Bengal Spice, the one with the tiger."

"Everyone keeps offering me tea." Arlo was half-aware of a hand on the small of her back, pushing her toward the salon chair. Her and Deborah's reflections filled a mirror framed by twinkly lights.

"People probably want to make it better for you. Which is stupid. I'm sorry."

No sooner had Arlo's butt hit the seat than Deborah spun the chair 180 degrees. Arlo stared up into the caverns of Deborah's nostrils, transfixed.

"Both my parents died from cancer. Mom had it in the lungs— big smoker. Dad had it in the bladder. Dad went quick, but Mom? She was in the hospice for ages, which meant *I* was in the hospice for ages. It's a full-time job. Reading to them, feeding them, sponge baths and all that. Then it's over. Boom."

"Boom," Arlo said weakly.

Deborah took a pair of scissors from the pocket of her apron, smoothed Arlo's bangs, and started snipping. Arlo suppressed a sneeze as the cuttings dusted her nose.

"Your dad's hair was this color when I met him."

Once again Arlo tried to recall her dignified speech, but the best she came up with was "What will you do with the money?"

Her vision smeared as Deborah whipped the chair back around. She had a flash of a carnival she'd attended as a seven-year-old: neon lights, bright colors, rides that made her dizzy. A lot of screaming.

Deborah mussed Arlo's bangs, expressionless. "What money?"

Arlo clutched the armrests of the chair to steady herself. "From Daddy's estate."

"He didn't leave me anything," Deborah said, bitterness entering her voice for the first time, "although that would've been nice of him."

Arlo scrutinized her in the mirror. She wasn't fidgeting or blinking too much. She wasn't turning red or avoiding Arlo's gaze or showing any other signs of lying. All Deborah did, actually, was yawn into one shoulder. As new wrinkles sprang up around the hairdresser's eyes, Arlo realized no one who'd just scored five million bucks could possibly look so . . . used up.

"You're serious," Arlo said.

Deborah opened and shut her scissors a few times. "Honey, I'm too old to bullshit."

Arlo eyed the collection of bottles and sprays on the counter, the various curling irons, the stack of fashion magazines—anything but her own reflection. Feeling herself blush was enough; she didn't need to see it, too. "There's something funny happening with the will. He set aside a bunch of money for someone. I—we don't know who."

Deborah laughed darkly. "Well, all I'll say is let's hope he didn't give it to Michelle."

"Michelle." It occurred to Arlo that she'd never spoken this name aloud. There had never been a reason to. Daddy's other child had never factored into his life, or Arlo's, or anyone's.

"She's your—"

"I know who she is."

Deborah took a random chunk of Arlo's hair and sliced off a good inch. "I'll take care of the split ends here."

"Thanks, but that's not nec—"

"Never overestimate the power of clean ends." Deborah wrinkled her nose. "Under? Never *under*estimate."

Arlo watched helplessly as hair collected on her shoulders. "Where is she? Michelle."

The resulting silence was a dark void, an endless tunnel, a wormhole to another dimension. At least ten different emotions swept across Deborah's face.

"You don't know?" Arlo asked.

Deborah's expression finally settled into something like dread.

"You don't *want* to know."

Deborah shrugged.

"You *do* want to know?"

She tucked her chin into her shoulder for a moment.

"Deborah? Deborah."

There was an air of futility about her as she pocketed the scissors again. "It's hard to set boundaries with people you love."

MICKEY

The cabinet by the till at the vegan café displayed tray upon tray of unappetizing hippie food, the broccoli quinoa bites and no-bake power balls stacked into three-feet-high pyramids. Mickey buttoned her cardigan up to her neck and ordered a coffee. "Dark roast, please," she said, sliding a pair of sunglasses down over her eyes as late-afternoon light bulldozed through the windows. "With room."

"Do you want that bulletproof?" asked the barista, a university-age kid whose trendy square glasses had no lenses in them.

"What?" Mickey said.

"With butter."

"In coffee?"

"Don't worry—it's plant-based."

"I'm very confused," Mickey said.

She'd entered another universe, one of potted lemongrass, hanging succulents, and Dalai Lama quotes on heart-shaped chalkboards. After paying her seven dollars, she found a seat in the corner near a trio of post-yoga twenty-somethings with glowing skin and Apple Watches. *Perfect*, she thought, flipping open her notebook. She clicked her pen and listened.

"You're not giving yourself enough credit." One of the yogis, a sliver of a person wearing a sports bra and no shirt, sipped from a cup of something yellow and frothy.

"Absolutely," said another, clad neck to toe in orange athletic wear. "It's like you're having all this uncertainty, right? And you're not trying to change it. You're just, like, chilling."

The one in the sports bra nodded. "Sitting with it."

"Exactly," said Traffic Cone. "Sitting with the feelings."

Mickey jotted these phrases, doing her best to keep up with the conversation. There would be no repeating Wednesday's debacle at the therapist's office. Next week, she would start the session with enough psychobabble up her sleeve to fool anyone.

"Thanks, guys," said the third yogi, who sat facing away from Mickey: high bun, long neck. "It's hard to make space for it, you know? But I think you're right. You can hold the pain in one hand and with the other reach for calm, peace, even . . ." a pregnant pause, ". . . joy."

"That's beautiful," said Sports Bra.

Mickey's hand was cramping. Fucking jackpot.

"It's about expanding your awareness," said Long Neck. "At any moment, you might be feeling ten different—"

An espresso machine sputtered to life, and the rest was inaudible.

"Excuse me," Mickey said, when the noise had stopped, "but could you repeat that?"

Long Neck peered back over her shoulder. Perfect eyebrows. Figured. "I'm sorry?"

"The last thing you said." Mickey consulted her notes. "After 'expanding your awareness.' You said, 'At any moment, you might be feeling ten different . . .' and I couldn't hear the rest."

Long Neck gaped.

"Are you transcribing our private conversation?" said Sports Bra.

"Oh my God," said Traffic Cone.

"It's okay—it's research." Mickey had it in mind to pretend she was getting a call when she took out her phone and saw she actually was getting a call. No ID. The teachers' union? "Sorry. I have to take this."

She hurried outside with her coffee, grabbed one of the patio seats, and swiped to answer. "Hello?"

A shaky voice: "Ms. Morris? Mickey?"

Cradling the phone in her neck, Mickey peeled the plastic lid off her coffee cup and began to top it up with vodka from her bottle, which had found its way out of her purse and into her hands. Four-thirty was a little early for a first drink, but at least it was closer to evening than morning, and really, what else was she going to do? "Yeah?"

"It's Chris, Ian's uncle."

Mickey righted the bottle. "Oh. Hey."

Then came the unmistakable mewl of an upset child.

"I'm sorry, but I didn't know who else to call."

○

Sickness hung over the house and settled on the browning yard, the leaf-strewn walkway, the stoop full of lawn-care flyers and still-bundled newspapers. There was panic, too—a stench that seeped out under the front door and billowed up into Mickey's face. Yes, a child here was ill.

There was no answer when she rang the bell, so she let herself in. "Hello?"

The door butted against a mound of shoes—men's, mostly—tumbling from the open front hall closet. Dress shoes, some mesh-top trainers. Ian's Spiderman runners.

"Chris?" Mickey called with an odd pang in her chest.

It was near sundown, but all the lamps were off, the room's only source of light a flat-screen TV turned to *SportsCenter*. The sound had been muted, the broadcasters' lips wriggling noiselessly. Mickey slung her jacket on the leather sofa and stacked her mittens on top.

Footsteps thumped back and forth across the ceiling. Someone up there was pacing—panicking over what was probably nothing. In all likelihood, Ian just had a stomach virus. Mickey would give him a quick hug, and the uncle a few pointers, then retreat back to the safety of her own life. Easy.

Up she went, dodging the stray socks and Lego pieces on the stairs. A light shone in the hallway above, where Ian's backpack lay open and empty on the floor, a gutted fish. Mickey could hear rushing water, a man muttering.

She found Chris bent over the bathroom sink, shirtless and splashing himself. "Oh, God," he said. "Oh, Jesus."

Mickey lingered outside the door, where the air was less pukey.

He wedged his entire head under the tap. "Oh, Jesus. Oh, Jesus."

She reached inside the bathroom and poked him between the shoulder blades.

With a yelp, Chris launched himself backward into the towel rack. A framed photograph of Peyton Manning rattled on the wall.

"It's okay," Mickey said. "It's me."

Recognition, then gratitude flooded his face. "Oh, thank God. I'm so glad you're here. You've gotta help me."

"It's cool, man," Mickey said. "Relax."

"He keeps throwing up. Every time I think he's finished, and I manage to get him back asleep, it only lasts like eight minutes. He wakes up, again, and he sits up, *again*, and he pukes absolutely fucking everywhere." Chris gestured to the bathtub and the bedding balled there. "I'm out of sheets. I've got him wrapped up in a sleeping bag right now. I put a pot beside the bed, but he never makes it that far. It's like he doesn't know how."

It took a great deal of effort not to laugh. This poor guy was so out of his depth.

Still dripping, Chris plunked his hands on Mickey's shoulders. Their weight was . . . pleasant, Mickey decided. Weirdly pleasant. "You've gotta help me," he said again.

She couldn't not stare. The gray-blue irises, the long lashes, the cheekbones. The cheekbones, God. At their first meeting, she'd found his whole vibe much too slick for her liking. Now, like this, bloodshot and crazed and more than a little ridiculous, he was absurdly, inhumanly handsome.

"You should turn that off," she said. "The tap."

Ian occupied about five percent of the king-sized bed in Chris's room. Pink-faced and shiny, he tossed back and forth inside a slippery green sleeping bag that had been zipped to his armpits. He moaned: a noise worse than a dentist's drill, a train wreck, a building collapse.

"You know what I keep thinking?" Chris said. "What if he's patient zero. What if he's the first case of a killer flu virus that will inevitably go airborne and wipe out ninety-nine percent of the world's population?"

"You need to shut that shit down," Mickey said, laying the back of her hand on Ian's forehead. Warm—way too warm.

"What if he's already infected me?"

"He's dehydrated. Do you have some sports drink or something?"

Chris went away and returned thirty seconds later with an entire flat of orange Gatorade.

Mickey helped Ian sit up and propped some pillows behind his back. "Hey, buddy. Have a drink of this."

He took a dutiful gulp and promptly coughed it back up. Gatorade rained onto the sleeping bag, the mattress, Mickey's bare arms.

Ian looked moonily at Chris. "Can we still play basketball tomorrow?"

Chris retreated in half steps, as if backing away from a large predator. Coward. "We'll see, sport."

Mickey unzipped the sleeping bag to Ian's knees. "That's better." She turned to Chris and tried to keep the edge out of her voice. "Were you trying to roast him?"

"Is he too hot?" Chris asked from the doorway.

"He's sweating."

"Well, I don't know." He stuck out his bottom lip. "I don't know anything."

After trickling some more Gatorade into Ian's mouth, Mickey cracked the window and found a dingy stuffed bunny on the ground beside the bed. She rubbed its nose against Ian's until he smiled, then rested the bunny in the crook of his neck. His eyelids fluttered down, down.

"How do you know what to do?" Chris asked a few moments later, as Mickey guided the door shut behind them. "Is it a girl thing? It must be a girl thing."

Mickey swallowed a comment about patriarchal gender norms. Never mind this pretty man. Her work here was finished. Now she could go home and—

"Drink?" Chris offered, raking his hair back over his crown. "I certainly feel like one."

The liquor cart was beautiful, to be sure, with all its gleaming shelves and shimmering bottles, but Mickey most appreciated the music it made. The soft clatter of wheels as Chris pulled the cart out from the wall. The tinkle of glasses rubbing shoulders. Understated. Harmonious.

"I don't have company often, so this thing is pretty well stocked." He retrieved a pair of tumblers from the bottom shelf. "Ice?"

"Never," Mickey said.

She sat on the big leather sofa with her legs curled beneath her. Chris had turned off the television and turned on a single lamp in the corner, everything awash in drowsy amber light. Outside, it had begun to rain.

Chris passed her two fingers of Scotch and sat at the opposite end of the couch. "I've had a hell of a week." He worked in finance—something about securities. Mickey didn't understand the details and didn't seek clarification. More interesting than what he did was the way he talked about it: in pressurized bursts, the words welling up.

"This week has sealed it for me—I'm not meant to be a dad."

"There's time for you yet." Mickey pegged him at thirty-six or thirty-seven, that age when a man had both status and youth. A liquor cart and liver function. "You could do it. You've got some dad energy."

He sniffed his Scotch. He had a habit of holding the glass right in front of his face, as if he were trying to hide. "No, I don't."

"You called him 'sport.'"

"What?"

"You called Ian 'sport.'"

"No, I didn't."

"You totally did."

"No way," he said. Was he blushing?

"I heard it. I was like, What is this guy, fifty?"

A muscle tightened in his jaw, and Mickey realized she'd offended him. "Sorry," she said.

Chris waved this away. "It's hard to picture myself as a dad. I never really had one myself." He lowered his glass, revealing a deep frown. "Mine bailed pretty early."

"Same here." Mickey took a measured sip of Scotch. She was trying not to finish the glass before Chris finished his, but he was desperately slow.

"You get it, then. It isn't that I think I'd be good or bad. The whole idea of me as a parent is just . . . impossible."

When Chris was in junior high, he told Mickey, his mom had gotten pregnant by a guy named Steve who sold weight-loss vitamins door-to-door. "He also sucked. He was shitty to my mom and shitty to Evie. Which is maybe why she's had such a hard time." Growing up, Evelyn was always getting busted for something—selling her Adderall to other kids at school, shoplifting eyeshadow from the mall. She had Ian at fifteen. "They showed up here in June with all their stuff. She said it would be a month, two tops."

"That's a big thing, taking them in," Mickey said.

"I didn't think twice about it at the time, which was stupid." He peered over the back of the couch at his dimly lit home. "The place had felt pretty empty since my ex moved out."

A pulling sensation gripped Mickey's stomach. She'd taken Chris for a serial dater, but maybe she'd been wrong. Maybe he'd loved this ex of his. Maybe he'd worshipped her athletic, five-foot-ten body and effortlessly clear skin and genuinely funny jokes. They'd probably gone on ten-mile runs together, cooked elaborate meals together. Had sex no fewer than four times per week.

Mickey allowed herself a gulp. "What will you do?"

Chris stared down into his glass. "Evie will come back. And my mom might fly in next week to help. So, you know, it'll be okay." He repeated this softly, as if to himself. "It'll be okay." His eyes caught a gleam of lamplight as he glanced up, his irises briefly golden. "I meant to ask. Did you get in trouble for bringing him home the other night?"

Some Scotch went down the wrong way, and Mickey coughed up fire. "Why?"

"Somebody called me from the school," Chris added.

Pantsuit, Mickey thought bitterly. "They put me on leave. For now." She coughed again. Things were loosening inside her chest, channels unclogging. "But it'll work itself out. I have no doubt. And financially, you know, I'll be okay." Fuck everything. "I came into a lot of money recently. Or I *will* be coming into a lot of money, as soon as I finish the therapy."

A stitch appeared between Chris's pleasantly bushy eyebrows. "As soon as you what?"

Mickey recounted what had happened with the lawyer and everything he'd told her about the will. The whole miserable tale spilled out with surprising ease—maybe because Chris seemed so genuinely interested to hear. The more she said, the wider his eyes grew.

"Wow," he said, when she'd finished. "Five and a half million?"

"Yep," Mickey said.

"But you have to do the . . . the stuff first."

"Yep."

He sat back and was silent for a moment. "That's fucked up."

"It *is* fucked up," Mickey said, deeply validated. Finally, someone who understood! "Thank you!"

"Have you started it yet?"

Mickey remembered the first session and groaned.

"That good, huh?" Chris said.

"She kept going on and on about what my goals were," Mickey said, thrumming with the same righteous anger she'd felt in that stupid little room. "What my values were, what I wanted to achieve. Which is so presumptuous. Why should I want to achieve anything? I'm fine the way I am. I pay taxes. I stop at stop signs. I stay out of everyone's way."

Chris raised his glass to toast her. "Absolutely."

"And if I don't want anything to do with people, that's my decision." Better to save herself the disappointment and avoid personal attachments altogether. Her father had not, after all, shown up at the doorstep with that pecan pie. There had been no chance to tell him about her life or her students or any of the things she'd managed to achieve in his absence. His eyes had not gone rheumy as he stood back and marveled at the woman she'd become. None of this had happened because, ultimately, her father was just another asshole in a great wide sea of them. This was what the psychologist had refused to understand. "Right?"

Chris looked lost in thoughts of his own. "My sister," he said, shaking his head ruefully. "*My sister*. I mean, do you believe this? She abandoned me with her five-year-old."

"Technically, she abandoned the five-year-old with you, not the other way around."

"I don't have any clue what I'm doing."

"That part I agree with."

"He's like another species."

Chris wasn't far off the truth there. Children were categorically different than adults—another life-form: gooey, screamy, frantic. Good. Mickey's draw to them was based more on survival instincts than maternal ones. Being with kids, she explained, was like huddling in front of a flame.

He tilted his head to one side. "You're deep, you know that?"

Mickey laughed. He sounded like a surfer bro sometimes.

"I mean it. You're wise. The wisdom, like, radiates off you."

"Well," Mickey said.

She glanced outside, where night had settled. The streetlamps beamed down, huge nets of light that engulfed car windshields, plains of asphalt, trim plots of grass.

"Is it really so bad?" Chris asked. "Seven appointments total? Think of it as . . . three hundred grand per session."

"Did you do that math in your head just now? Impressive."

He shifted in his seat, drawing close enough that his knee touched hers. "What are you so afraid of?"

Mickey thought of the bottle in her purse and wondered, inexplicably, what this man would say about it. What would he have said, for example, if he'd seen her sloshing vodka into a cup of coffee today at four in the afternoon? If he'd seen her stealing sips on the bus ride over? Would he make a joke and laugh it off only to throw concerned glances her direction later? More importantly, why did she care?

"Nothing," she said. "Yeah, no. Nothing."

ARLO

There were seventy Michelle Kowalskis on Facebook, thirty-one on Instagram, and nineteen on TikTok. The youngest was seven, the eldest seventy-four. They worked as nannies, doctors, bartenders, manicurists, dairy farmers, plumbers, dry cleaners, and accountants. They lived in Portland, Dublin, Gdansk, New Jersey, Chennai, Winnipeg, Iowa City, and Cape Town. Michelle Kowalski, Michelle Kowalski, Michelle Kowalski. The world was awash with them.

"Tell me about this next gentleman," Punam said, running her pen down a list of Arlo's clients. They sat across from each other in a small boardroom at the office with a now-empty pot of tea.

"He's, um . . ." Arlo minimized Facebook, opened the desktop folder where she saved her documentation, and scrolled through her case history. "He's a former gymnast. National level. PTSD diagnosis last year. History of emotional and verbal abuse."

"Coaches?"

"But of course."

"I used to do a lot of work with swimmers," Punam said. "Different sport, same shit. I find ACT is helpful. A-C-T. Acceptance and commitment therapy."

Arlo knew what ACT was. She didn't need Punam to explain. But off Punam went, jumping into a lecture about functional behaviorism before Arlo could protest. This mentorship arrangement was nice but often felt wholly unnecessary and actually sort of demeaning.

"The key, really, is that idea of self-as-context," Punam said.

"Self-as-context," Arlo said reverently as she opened Facebook again. According to the search results, only one Michelle Kowalski lived within a hundred miles—someone with an illustrated pink handprint for a profile picture. No other images were visible on the page, only a few comments from 2009, when eight people had wished her a happy birthday.

Across the desk, Punam continued on: "The Observer Self. That's another way of thinking about it. It's about asking, 'As I notice something, who is it that's doing the noticing?'"

Arlo nodded along, making occasional eye contact to feign interest.

The About section of Pink Handprint Michelle's Facebook profile listed her favorite movies (*The Royal Tenenbaums, Doctor Zhivago, Snatch*) and her favorite musical artists (Modest Mouse, The Shins, Joni Mitchell). She sounded like someone who collected vinyl records and rolled her own cigarettes—back in 2009, anyway.

Punam's voice began to drift in and out, as if through radio static: ". . . facilitate contact with the present moment . . . attending to internal and external experiences . . . access a transcendent sense of self . . ."

Arlo's mind swirled with hypothetical Michelles. Was she homeless? Incarcerated? Addicted to substances? Though Deborah hadn't specified what sort of problems haunted her daughter, Arlo wouldn't be surprised if Michelle was coping with some seriously dark shit. Holed-up-in-a-boarding-house-somewhere, huffing-spray-paint-out-of-a-paper-bag kind of dark. Dark enough that

Daddy had felt compelled to strip Arlo of her rightful inheritance and shunt it toward Michelle instead.

But all of it? Had he really needed to give her all of it?

"Does that give you a few ideas to get started?" Punam folded her hands and leaned back in her seat.

Arlo blinked her parched eyes for what might've been the first time in several minutes. The psych lecture had, apparently, concluded. "Definitely."

Cheek dimples flanked Punam's smile: two depressions about big enough to jam a pinkie finger in. Arlo sometimes imagined herself doing that—poking Punam in the face.

"Last but not least is . . ." Punam looked to the bottom of her list. "Mickey Morris?"

Arlo recalled the woman's blonde hair, pink lipstick, and obvious attachment problems. "We've only done one session, and what I see so far is a big fear of getting close to people. One of those reject-the-world-before-it-rejects-you types."

"What's your plan then?" Punam asked.

Arlo licked her lips, which felt crackly all of a sudden. "My plan?"

Those dimples again.

"Your intervention approach," Punam said.

"I, um . . . I haven't decided yet." Arlo felt a twitch of panic. She'd been too busy with Samson and Deborah and the hypothetical Michelles to do much planning. Not that much planning would be needed. Mickey Morris had arrived on Arlo's desk a neatly wrapped parcel. All she had to do was pick at the tape a little, peel back the paper, lift the flaps. Easy.

Punam dropped the smile. "You seem distracted."

Arlo felt herself shrink as Punam's heavily made-up eyes bored into her. "I'm not distracted." She clapped the laptop shut. "I'm present."

"I've been meaning to ask you how you feel."

Arlo's chest tightened up. Hopefully this wasn't going where she thought it was going.

"About the lawsuit," Punam added, and yes, there it was. There *she* was: Laura. Kind, sweet, chronically depressive Laura. Laura who recorded friends' birthdays in a special notebook and sent thank-you cards with looping calligraphy. Arlo still had a few in her desk. She even pulled them out from time to time and ran her fingertips over the bumpy homemade paper. *Thanks for everything,* one said. *You're a real lifesaver.*

Arlo bolted upright and went to the window, her heart fluttering in her throat. She'd had enough of this table, this room. "What do you mean?"

"It isn't exactly a linear journey, processing something like this."

But Arlo had finished processing it. She'd done the reflection, the reframing, the replaying every conversation, and her part in Laura's story could be summed up in four short words that she now said aloud: "It wasn't my fault."

Punam's voice had softened by the time it arrived at Arlo's back. "It's never anyone's fault. You know that."

Arlo watched the rush-hour traffic parade by, all these normal people driving home from their normal jobs. What constituted a bad day for a shopkeeper? Poor sales? What about an accountant or a PR person? For them, bad days meant numbers that didn't balance, emails sent out with typos. None of these people, Arlo was pretty sure, ever got blamed for someone's death at their places of work.

She turned away from the window. "You're a great therapist, Punam, but you're not my therapist."

"Are you getting therapy?" Punam asked.

Arlo held in a laugh. God forbid anyone take her side. "I was cleared, wasn't I? The lawsuit was dismissed. The end."

"See? That, there." Punam speared the air with her pen. "That's what worries me. It's not over. It won't be over so long as you live because that's not how it works. This thing is inside of you, and if you don't at least acknowledge it, the feelings will fester. Believe me—I know. I've fucked up with more than a few clients over the years."

"But I didn't fuck up."

"Do you really think that? I'm asking."

Arlo searched Punam's face for judgment and found only kindness, which was somehow worse. "I have some planning to do for this new client." She returned to the table and began packing her things, taking care to slide her laptop into its case slowly and gently rather than shoving it inside and running away, like she wanted to. "As you've pointed out."

"But it's raining," Mickey said the next morning, planting an elbow on the reception counter as the cords tensed in her neck. Arlo could almost smell the stress hormones.

"No problem." Arlo produced the pair of umbrellas she'd brought from home: one black, the other pink with purple polka-dots. "Which would you like?"

Mickey glanced between the umbrellas, frowning. "I can't decide."

Arlo handed over the pink one. "It suits you."

"Does it?" Mickey took the umbrella by the handle. "Yes, I suppose it does."

The city hung on a knife's edge between fall and winter, the mid-October sky overcast and sharp with cold. Wind funneled through the streets at odd angles, tossing the rain sidelong and kicking up leaves from the sidewalks. Fitting weather, Arlo thought, for a moment of personal challenge and change. This excursion was one of her better ideas.

"Why a walk, exactly?" Mickey asked as they set off.

"There's this thing called a Chatty Café happening at a café down the street," Arlo explained. They would move from table to table making conversation with strangers in what was essentially speed-dating for the socially isolated. Mickey would hate it, but that was the whole point. While unpleasant at first, the chat—the people and her burgeoning sense of connection with them—would leave her feeling buoyant. Arlo, too. She needed this today.

"You'll rate your mood before and after to see what happens." Arlo massaged a cramp in her side. Their pace had sped to a near jog, glass storefronts and scrawny poplar trees gliding past in her periphery. She wasn't sure who was setting the pace. "It's an experiment, that's all."

"This café isn't a vegan place, is it?" Mickey asked darkly.

"No?"

"Oh, good."

Mickey agreed to the field trip with a shrug and rated her mood at four out of ten, about what Arlo would've guessed. Less expected was the varied crowd at the coffeehouse: teenagers in baggy light-wash jeans; punks with neck tattoos and studded leather jackets; moms with babies; beefy gym rats; and an old guy in a skin-tight Playa del Carmen t-shirt. Despite their many differences, they'd gathered here to cultivate a shared sense of community. Was there anything more profound, Arlo wondered, as the old guy threw her a gap-toothed grin. Her heart brimmed over with love for her fellow man.

Shortly after, she and Mickey found an open table, and one of the baristas chimed a bell at the front of the room, signaling the start of the event.

Mickey flopped around in her armchair. The plush cushions appeared to have swallowed her. "Wait—so, what am I supposed to do here?"

"Talk to the person," Arlo said, trying not to smile. This new client was cynical and combative, but Arlo would break through her defenses soon enough.

"Talk about what?" Mickey asked.

"Food, music, the weather. Anything."

"What will that help?"

Arlo explained the power of superficial conversation and the growing body of evidence that suggested small talk fostered connection and well-being.

"That's interesting," Mickey said flatly. What she clearly meant was *That's a load of horseshit, and you're a silly little girl who doesn't know what she's talking about.*

But Arlo was unfazed. It wasn't horseshit. She wasn't little or silly, and she did know what she was talking about. She'd read seven peer-reviewed research articles in preparation for this excursion, including two randomized controlled trials! "What do you have to lose?"

"For starters, what if I don't want to connect with these people?" Mickey asked, with a glance over her shoulder. "What if they're terrible?"

Someone must've done a real number on this woman. *Or,* Arlo thought, maybe it was the other way around. Maybe Mickey's distrust of people stemmed from her own self-loathing. At some point—or multiple points—in the past, she'd acted badly toward others, and now she saw herself as a malevolent force in the world.

"Look," Arlo said, swelling with empathy. "I work with people who've done some seriously bad things. Like, *bad.* Highly illegal, highly amoral things. But I've yet to meet a bad person."

Mickey opened and shut her eyes, very slowly, which Arlo did not find super encouraging.

"All people are deserving of compassion," she added quickly. Someone was coming their way. "There's innate goodness to everyone.

Happiness is a universal experience, but so is suffering. We're all in this together."

"Holding the pain in one hand," Mickey said drily, "and reaching for joy with the other?"

Arlo wasn't sure what to make of this. "Exactly."

A guy in a suit set down his coffee and plunked into the third armchair at the table. Clean-shaven, bolo tie. He was—

He was Tom Samson, Arlo realized with a sickening jolt. The lawyer.

Samson crossed his legs, uncrossed them, crossed them the other way. He'd gone even paler than usual, clearly horrified, and was it any wonder? The last time Arlo had seen this man, she'd also seen his penis, and now, like it or not, that penis would live in her memory forever.

"Hi," she said with a rush of nausea. Normal, she thought, trying to steady herself. She would act normal. They would make pleasant chit-chat for a few minutes, then the barista would chime her little bell, and they would all move on with their lives. She could do this. "I'm—"

"It's you," Mickey said, her eyes on Samson.

Samson's gaze slowly drifted up from where it had landed on his hands, and they shared a look of . . . mutual recognition?

"Have—have you two met?" Arlo asked.

Samson looked at his hands again.

"Briefly," Mickey said.

"Professionally," Samson added.

A small knot of dread tightened in Arlo's stomach. *Professionally*, meaning what? He'd provided legal services for Mickey? There were, Arlo supposed, only so many estate lawyers in the city. Still, she didn't like this. She never liked it when her work and personal lives overlapped. She'd spotted the gymnast with PTSD at a supermarket the other day and had taken great pains to avoid being seen, hiding behind a cupcake display for four whole minutes while her client stared numbly at the wall of bread loaves. Decisions were always tricky for him.

After a moment of awkward silence, Samson rose. "Maybe I'll just go find another table or something."

"No," Mickey said, so sharply the lawyer seemed to flinch. "Stay."

Arlo couldn't categorize the expression forming on Mickey's face, but it reminded her of that meme with the lady and the floating math equations.

Samson sat back down. Then they all stared at each other for a while.

Arlo reached for one of the index cards stacked in the middle of the table and bolstered herself with some positive inner self-talk. She was a skilled practitioner. She could manage a messy situation like this. It was going to be fine. Totally, totally, super fine. "Shall we start with a prompt?"

Mickey propped one elbow on her knee, rested her chin on her fist, and smiled sweetly. "We were just saying how great this event is. Isn't it great?"

"Yes." Samson sipped his coffee. Milk foam clung to his upper lip. "Great."

"We came to discover the innate goodness in others," Mickey said. "You?"

Arlo wasn't sure where this was going but didn't like it. "*Would you rather go into the past and meet your ancestors*," she read aloud from the card, "*or go into the future and meet your great-great-grandchildren?*"

"Guess I was looking to branch out a bit," Samson said.

"You're lonely," Mickey said.

Samson undid the top button on his shirt. As a tuft of black chest hair sprang free, Arlo remembered that morning in her bedroom and the handout she'd given him with event listings for isolated people. It seemed he'd not only read the handout—something few people did—but actually found the courage to turn up. What Arlo didn't get was why Mickey seemed so keen to bug him about it.

"Have you ever thought about the reasons why you're lonely?" Mickey asked, and if the alarms hadn't already sounded in Arlo's brain, they would've gone off then. *Why* was a dangerous question best pondered in the safety of a psychologist's office. *Why* led to doubt, guilt, and shame. *Why* was a powder keg.

"I'm sorry?" The foam on Samson's upper lip was starting to deflate.

"There has to be a reason, right?" Mickey said. "Nobody starts off alone in the world. We end up this way because of our choices."

"I guess," Samson said. "Yes. Yes, that's right."

Arlo detected a tremor in his voice and decided to act. "I would for sure rather meet my ancestors," she said, remembering the index card in her hand. "What do you guys think? Mickey?"

But Mickey's gaze was set firmly on Samson. "Let's explore that a little, shall we? Tell me—who was the last person you dated?"

"You don't have to answer that," Arlo told Samson. This was a sore subject. She could tell by the way he was curling into himself, shrimp-like, his chin tucking into his chest, his shoulders drawing up around his ears.

"Their name," Mickey pressed.

"Her name was Lydia," Samson said quietly. "Is. Lydia."

Mickey nodded. "Go on. Tell us about her."

"She's a gastroenterologist," Samson said. "She's smart, obviously. Pretty. Funny."

Arlo lay a hand on Mickey's elbow, hoping the gesture wasn't too patronizing. She wanted to imply kindness and warmth and unconditional positive regard, but also she needed her client to fucking quit it with this shit. "Medicine—such a demanding career, isn't it?"

Mickey yanked her elbow away. "So, what went wrong?"

"We grew apart," Samson said, which was obviously a lie. He was turning pink.

Mickey made a confused face. "*Is* that what happened?"

"Yes," Samson said.

Mickey made a *hmmm* sound.

"What?" Samson said, sweating now, the poor man. "That's what happened."

Mickey sat back. "Okay."

Silence unfolded, and for a blissful five seconds, Arlo thought it was all over. She'd drawn another prompt card and was about to read from it when Samson blurted, "Fine. I cheated on her. I did. I cheated."

"You what?" Arlo said, couldn't help but say. Cheating was common. Half her client roster were cheaters. But Samson? With his lavender oil and his Tom Hanks face?

"How many women in total?" Mickey asked. "*Girls* might be the better word. Waitresses, interns."

Arlo saw them in her mind's eye: a long line of perky young women with smooth foreheads and bright smiles and minimal cellulite. Women like herself. And suddenly it was obvious: Samson was a total douchebag. The douchebaggery shrouded him as thickly as his peaty cologne. She hadn't noticed before. She'd slept with him, but she hadn't noticed, taking him for a pompous but ultimately tenderhearted oaf when actually he was a player, a snake!

"She was a junior associate, not an intern." Samson shut his eyes for a moment. "Okay—there was also one intern."

"Because you're a womanizer," Mickey said.

Samson's lip trembled. "I'm not. At least—I don't want to be."

"A misogynist," Mickey said. "A narcissist."

"Stop." Samson began to rock forward and back in his seat.

"Yes—*stop*," Arlo said, a little frightened by how angry Mickey looked right now, how vindictive. What was she trying to gain here?

"And you know what?" Mickey said. "It's boring. You're another one of *those men*. Men who fuck women over their whole lives and wake up in middle age all alone."

People were starting to stare.

"Men who can't accept the reality—"

Samson licked the fronts of his teeth while Mickey spoke; at the same time, a breath left his nose as an audible shudder. He was teetering on the brink of something—rage, maybe even violence. Arlo glanced at the polka-dot umbrella Mickey had hooked over the armrest of her chair and imagined Samson snatching it up. Imagined him wielding it overhead like a weapon and smashing the shit out of everything.

"—that you reap. What. You. Sow."

Samson curled his hands into fists. Arlo was about to throw herself between him and Mickey—to shield Mickey from the imminent blows—when Samson brought one fist to his mouth, screwed up his face, and began to cry. He cried as Arlo had never seen a man cry in her whole life as a therapist, shedding big fat tears that ran down his cheeks and darkened the lapels of his suit jacket. He cried so loudly, with such lurching gasps, that the rest of the café fell quiet, and people began to gather round: a few of the gym rats, one of the moms, the barista with her little bell. The old guy in the Playa del Carmen t-shirt looked particularly concerned.

Whatever Mickey had hoped to achieve from this encounter, it was clear from her wide eyes and dangling jaw that it wasn't this.

"We'll go now," Arlo said, reaching for their coats.

They sat together on a park bench across the street and watched a Canada goose waddle past. The rain had stopped, and some sun was starting to break through, the bird's slick feathers glinting with wet. Pausing, it craned its long neck at them and threw a menacing stare. Arlo held her breath, too tired to contemplate another confrontation—even with a goose.

"Well," she said, once the bird had carried on and she could exhale, "this is the part where I ask you to rate your mood a second time."

Mickey kicked her heels into the ground, seeming neither to care nor to notice that muck was splatting her legs. Maybe it was the light, or maybe it was the fact that she'd just bullied a grown man to tears, but she was looking a little gray, her mouth sloping into a lazy, almost catatonic frown. "Two? Maybe a three."

"So, worse than before." Made sense. Victimizing others, Arlo knew, rarely gave people the satisfaction they craved.

"I knew the café thing wouldn't help," Mickey said softly, staring off at nothing.

Arlo felt a surge of empathy and goodwill toward her client. She wasn't sure where it came from, this habit of liking people best when they behaved their worst, but it had always served her well as a therapist. It would serve her well now.

"How did you know that guy?" she asked.

Mickey seemed to choose her next words with care. "He handled my father's estate."

"I see," Arlo said calmly, as a firecracker exploded in her nervous system.

She wanted to ask a million questions. When had Mickey's dad passed? If it was recent, had she cried yet? What kind of relationship had they shared? Had Mickey played the caregiver, like Arlo? Had she also shuttled her father between dialysis and physio, the endocrinologist and the hepatologist, the dietitian, the orthotist, the outpatient wound clinic? Did Mickey also know the smell of a Stage Three pressure ulcer?

But all this would have to wait.

"Did he . . . take advantage of you?" Arlo asked, afraid to hear the answer. Fingers crossed they hadn't both slept with the lawyer.

Mickey snorted. "No."

Thank Christ, Arlo thought.

"He told me some things about his problems," Mickey said, rubbing her face in her hands. "How he goes to therapy."

"So, he confided in you," Arlo said, deciding to take a risk and deliver some truth, "and you used that information to skewer him in public."

Mickey exhaled long and slow through pursed lips. "Yep."

"And did it help?"

"Not really, no."

Mickey met Arlo's gaze for half a second, which Arlo took as a small win. Here was a sliver of space—a crack in a window on Mickey's inner world. Arlo would nudge it open bit by bit, session by session, until she could climb inside.

Another goose waddled past.

"Those things have always scared the shit out of me," Mickey said, grimacing.

MICKEY

When Mickey strode into Chris's apartment Friday evening—she hadn't knocked; they were beyond that now—Ian was sitting cross-legged on the floor three feet away from the TV, craning his neck to watch a show about anthropomorphic pigs with English accents. Some color had returned to his face, and he wasn't vomiting every-where, which were good signs.

Mickey sank beside him on the carpet. "Hey."

Ian lifted a hand in greeting without looking away from the screen. "Hey."

The pig children were flying a kite. If memory served, the kite would soon catch in a tree, and the pig father would have to scale the branches and shake it loose with some skillful maneuvering of his hooves. It was without question the most boring children's pro-gram ever produced, and Mickey's hatred for it burned in the deep-est parts of her being.

"This is a good one," she said.

Ian shrugged. "I guess."

"How much screen time you getting these days?"

"Too much."

Mickey had accepted Chris's dinner invitation out of 1) ongoing concern for Ian, and 2) practicality. She'd depleted her stores of microwavable pasta dinners and resorted to toast and/or cereal for meals. The nearest Superstore was a short bus ride from home, but the thought of getting up and going there—of finding a coin for the cart and traversing those mile-long fluorescent aisles in search of frozen peas—was simply too much. Then there was the fact that her checking account had $181.91 in it.

"How was it being back with the new teacher today?" Mickey hadn't planned on asking. In fact, she'd decided against it. Someone else was still running her classroom, screwing with her carefully planned desk arrangements while she sat around at home doing nothing. Hearing about it might make her crazy, and she'd already gone over the edge once this week. But with the child here in front of her . . . with news of her students so close at hand . . .

Ian's expression was grave. "She doesn't sing."

"Oh," Mickey said, deeply troubled. How could someone teach kindergarten without singing? It would be like riding a bike without wheels, like launching into space without rocket fuel.

"She doesn't dance."

"Oh, no." Kindergarten teachers had to dance. They had to hop, shake, wiggle, twirl.

"She won't help me put on my mittens."

"Oh, no, no, no." Mickey pressed up off the floor.

They'd taken away her classroom—her life's work. That was bad enough. But to have replaced her with a teacher who didn't sing or dance? It was beyond insult. And who would suffer most for this oversight? The kids. They would never learn the days of the week if their teacher refused to sing.

Ian was on his feet now, too. "Where are you going?"

Mickey halted. She hadn't realized she was in motion. "Nowhere."

He placed himself between her and the front door. "Why are you marching around?"

"I wasn't marching. Was I marching?" Pacing. She'd been pacing. "I'm sorry." She knelt in front of him, got back on his level. "That was confusing, what I did. But I'm not leaving yet. I'm staying for dinner."

Ian bowed his head. A pink gob of Silly String or possibly yogurt had crusted in the hair behind his ear. "No Goodbye Train?"

Mickey died a little inside. "No Goodbye Train."

Ian plopped down on the carpet again. The pigs were on a Ferris wheel now, and the ride was picking up speed, the world around them a smear of color and noise.

Chris appeared in the doorway from the kitchen wearing oven mitts and a novelty apron emblazoned with a giant arrow and a crude slogan about sausage. "Wow. You look . . . wow."

She'd put on some extra eyeliner, some lip stain, her favorite sweater-dress. It wasn't much.

"Can I get you anything?" He yanked off the oven mitts and did the thing where he flopped his hair back. "Water? Or I've got root beer."

"No whiskey?"

"Had some bad wine the other night and had to pitch everything." Chris nodded at the wooden contraption in the alcove under the stairs—the liquor cart, Mickey realized, squinting. Only without any liquor. "Sorry."

She went to the cart and inspected the holes in the dust where bottles had been. "You threw it all away?"

"Some of that stuff was super old."

"You don't have anything?" Mickey asked—croaked, really. It was hard to speak all of a sudden.

"Is that okay?" he asked.

She'd seen a liquor store down the block. It would still be open. She could try to sound casual about it. *Shame not to have wine with such a beautiful meal*, she could say. *Why don't I pop out to get some? A Malbec, maybe? No, no—really, I don't mind. It'll take ten minutes.*

Then she noticed Ian watching out the corner of his eye.

"Root beer sounds great."

Mickey lounged at the kitchen table and watched him work. How better to evaluate Chris's child-minding abilities than to sit around doing nothing while he toiled? It wasn't fun. She didn't like the steamy warmth of the kitchen. She didn't like the scents of cream and lemon or the way they fused at the back of her throat. She *definitely* didn't like Chris's handsome smile, or his funny jokes, or his charming anecdote about the first time he'd made this dish back when he was studying business abroad in Burgundy. No, she didn't like any of this in the slightest.

Chris poked around in a pan with a wooden spoon. "I hate that pig show."

Mickey laughed. They'd left Ian in the other room.

"We've all got one we hate," she said.

"I dream about them sometimes, the pigs." Chris brandished his wooden spoon through the air, flinging cream sauce onto his apron, the countertops, the backsplash. "They come to me in my dreams. My dreams, Mickey."

It startled her, this combination of his voice and her name.

"He's got this storybook, right? *Five-Minute Stories*, it's called. The thing must be two inches thick. But the problem is he never wants just one."

She picked one thing in her line of sight—a bottle of white wine vinegar, as it turned out—and stared at it to steady her pulse. But then she caught herself wondering if vinegar was drinkable, whether it still contained any trace amounts of alcohol, how it might warm her throat on the way down, and her heart beat faster.

"'One more,' he says. 'One more.' If I say no, he starts throwing shit. I'm a hostage in my own home."

Did cooking sprays contain alcohol? What about very old apple juice? Surely, apple juice turned to alcohol eventually. Something happened with the sugars.

"How many do you end up reading?" she asked, digging her fingernails in her palms. Wow, she needed to get a grip.

"All of them. I read all of them. It takes an hour." He laughed at himself—a quality Mickey hadn't encountered often in people of any ilk, let alone successful, single thirty-somethings with pleasantly muscled forearms.

"I'm sure you'll get used to it," she said, feeling wobbly now on top of everything else.

"Well. I won't have to, luckily." Chris was no longer laughing. He lifted the lids off various pots and peered down inside as if he'd misplaced something. "My mom is flying in soon. To take over."

Mickey didn't love this idea, though she couldn't say why. "When?"

"She has to figure out the time off, but as soon as she does, you know, she'll be here." He put his hands on his hips and pouted at the pots. "What was I doing?"

"Are you sure you can count on her?" Mickey asked. "Your mom, I mean."

"Well, historically, she hasn't been the most dependable," Chris admitted.

If his mom was anything like Mickey's, then she definitely wasn't coming, and this story was about uncle and nephew now. Would the uncle set aside his self-doubt and take up the banner of parenthood? Would the nephew learn to risk his wounded heart again? It was the stuff of maudlin sitcoms. Mickey could almost hear the laugh track.

"*Dishes.* That's what I was doing." He turned and went to the sink. "I sort of went zero for two in the reliable parents department."

Maybe it was the heat of the kitchen, or maybe it was the rushing sound of the tap, but for one reason or another, Mickey's tongue loosened up. "Ha! Me too."

Chris glanced at her over his shoulder. "Really?"

Mickey flashed back to a cold dark February in her last semester of teachers' college. The mauve carpet in the hallway outside Mama's apartment. Mama's voice seeping under the door as Mickey jiggled the knob, and jiggled it some more, her shoulders aching under a backpack full of textbooks, her toes frozen inside her boots. "Did your mom change the locks on you, too?"

Chris turned off the tap and faced her again, silent.

His handsome features had crumpled into an expression of sympathy—sympathy for *her*, Mickey realized, as her stomach lurched. Because she'd gone and confided in him.

She leapt upright. "Let me help with something."

Chris looked startled. "Oh—you don't have to—" His face changed as some kind of understanding settled in. "Maybe you could put the potatoes in a dish? And the green beans?"

Mickey did as he said and ferried everything to the table, grateful to be away from him for a few moments. Ian, she reminded herself. She was here for Ian.

"I don't want this," said the five-year-old, grimacing at the food from atop a booster cushion a few minutes later.

Mickey pinched her lips together. These next moments would be crucial.

"Sure you do," Chris said. "It's delicious."

"It looks weird and gross," Ian said.

"I saw you eat your own boogers earlier."

Ian shifted sideways in his chair, turning his body away from the French food and toward the wall. "No, I didn't."

"If you eat the food, I'll give you ice cream after."

"I don't want ice cream."

Chris scooped out a chicken breast and began shearing it into cubes. "Cookies. I've got cookies."

"I don't want cookies."

"What do you want then?"

"I want the five-minute stories."

In the TV version of their lives, the shot cut to a close-up of Chris and his bulging forehead vein. He'd frozen with his fork hanging midair en route to his mouth.

"Mom says reading stories makes flowers grow in your brain," Ian added.

"Your mom's not here," Chris said and buried a hunk of meat in his cheek.

"So?" Ian said.

"So, it's off the table."

"What's that mean?"

Chris chewed his chicken as if to inflict pain upon it. Shreds flew around the inside of his mouth as he talked. "It means it's not going to happen."

"Why?" Ian asked.

"I don't like those stories."

"Why?"

"There's too many of them."

"Why?"

Quiet fell over the kitchen. Mickey held her breath.

"Why?" Ian asked again.

Chris dropped his fork and drove the heels of his hands into his eye sockets. This was it: the climax, the big moment, the point at which time would slow, and string music would swell, and viewers would perch on the edges of their seats. Soon the reluctant hero would embrace his sense of duty, open his mouth, and say—

"We can read the five-minute stories."

In that second—there at that table, surrounded by gourmet cuisine—the carefree bachelor died, and from his ashes rose a parent. Mickey would know one anywhere. Parents had a scooped-out appearance that couldn't be replicated.

She took an exultant slug of root beer. That was that. Her professional obligation was fulfilled. Ian and Chris would take care of each other, somehow, and she would no longer have to worry about them. She wouldn't have to think of them at all.

"I want Miss Mickey to read some, too."

"What?" she said.

Her name had bounced off Ian's pale little tongue and traveled through the air via his squeaky little voice, and now he was staring at her with the kind of nuclear intensity only a child could manage. Three, four, five seconds later, he hadn't looked away.

"Is that okay?" Chris asked, and Jesus, now they were both staring.

Mickey tightened her grip on the glass of root beer. It was dewy and cold, about as cold as a pint of vodka straight from the freezer, and if she shut her eyes, she could imagine it as such. The scent so stiff and cleansing. The taste a pleasant knife in her mouth.

"We can clean up, have some ice cream, get the gremlin ready for bed. I think he might need a bath. And then . . ." Chris shrugged.

"And then?" She couldn't decide if he was propositioning sex. She had a hunch he wasn't, which frightened and perplexed her more than anything.

"I don't know," Chris said. "Hang out? Watch some TV?"

"Like, what?" Mickey said. "Make a bunch of popcorn? Play a board game? Fall asleep on the couch under a pile of blankets watching old episodes of *The Office*?"

"Why not?" he asked.

"Like a fam—" The word wouldn't come. And no wonder it wouldn't. That wasn't Mickey. She didn't do this. She didn't bond with people over chicken dinner and root beer. She moved through the world on her own. Life was a solo effort, and people who claimed otherwise were anesthetizing themselves.

Mickey jumped out of her chair.

"Where are you going?" Chris asked.

"Bathroom." Mickey did her best not to run.

After locking the door, she hunched over the counter and tried to breathe. The sink was predictably scummy. Two of the three lights above the mirror had burnt out.

I love you, but I need to set this boundary. Those were Mama's words, the actual words that had come out of her actual mouth, as if she were so mature, so psychologically evolved, as if she weren't just another asshole who'd shoved her daughter's stuff into garbage bags and dumped them in the third-floor hallway. It had been over a decade, but Mickey still thought about it all the time. Because she was foolish. Because she was weak. Because no matter how many times the human race shit-kicked her, she couldn't give up the fight.

Tonight, for instance. She'd walked straight into this.

"You're pathetic," Mickey whispered to the girl in the mirror, the silly girl with her matte lip stain and frumpy sweater-dress. Still trying to make herself fit.

An impulse arrived.

She checked under the sink but found only toilet paper and boxes of soap. "Come on," she said, throwing the cupboard doors shut.

Then she saw it. There—in the mirror above her right shoulder. A medicine cabinet.

◎

Mickey walked the streets with a dull ache in her stomach and a bottle of blue mouthwash in her armpit. It was a slow process, the walking, like wading through dense forest or floodwater or no-man's-land on a World War I battlefield, one of those great plains where dead horses ballooned in the bomb craters, and stars burst overhead, and all that gravity sucked your feet so far down, down, down into the muck that no one would find you for a hundred years.

"Strange," she said and brought the bottle to her lips again.

She'd run straight for the front door without saying goodbye. It was a dick move, which was maybe why her thoughts had turned so suddenly to Tom Samson. Him with his salt-and-pepper hair and his little bolo tie and his crocodile tears.

Mickey drew the deepest breath of her life, threw her arms wide, and sang into the night: "*Oh, the Goodbye Train is coming, see you soon! Choo! Choo! Oh, the Goodbye train is—*"

Along came the automaton drawl of Google Maps: "You have arrived."

"Have I?" Mickey glanced at her phone. "Shit, I have!"

The office tower went on forever, its little lights climbing to infinity. It was nine o'clock on a Friday night, but she figured he might still be there, working late or maybe screwing around with a secretary. Unless he'd taken the week off to recover from the café incident. Mickey covered her eyes, which didn't at all help, the scene playing out in her mind again and again and again and again and again.

"You alright, miss?"

Mickey parted two of her fingers and peeked through. A security guard stood in front of the revolving glass door with his hands in the pockets of a jacket so puffy it made his head look somewhat miniature. His face was kind, but his stance was wide, and Mickey had the impression he wouldn't hesitate to bulldoze her if the situation called for it.

Mickey pulled her jacket further across her chest and squeezed the bottle of mouthwash against her ribs. "It's my b-b-boyfriend."

She'd always had an easy time getting past security guards, and tonight was no different. Some tears, some sniffles, some lies about how she'd meant to leave a birthday present on his desk as a surprise but forgotten until now, how bad she felt, how much she loved him, blah, blah, blah, and bingo—she was in, striding across the marble floor of the lobby.

After scanning the directory on the wall—*Samson, Baker and Chen*, LLP; eleventh floor—she hit the up button and climbed aboard a golden elevator. All four walls were mounted with mirrors, none of which made a very pretty sight, so Mickey shut her eyes and clung to the railing until the car swooped to a halt and the doors sighed open.

Though the main reception area was empty, all the lights were still on, and half the offices were full, their occupants hunched over laptops with cups of coffee or cans of beer or both. No one paid Mickey any attention whatsoever. Like day and night, she was extraneous here.

She found the nameplate that read THOMAS SAMSON III and strode inside only to be met by a sweet floral scent and the mumble of ocean waves. Mickey steadied herself against the wall; the tranquility was clobbering.

Samson lay curled on the sofa in his underwear with his big limbs tucked into his chest and a blanket strewn over his shoulders. Files splayed out all around him on the floor. He brought to mind a sort of big graying baby. Mickey did him a kindness and kept the lights off.

Crouching, she drew closer and closer until they touched noses. "Hey."

His eyes hinged open.

"Christ!" He threw off the blanket, flopped onto his feet, and staggered backward into a probably-silk fern in the corner.

"How were you already asleep?" Mickey asked. "It's like nine-thirty."

"Fuck." He scrubbed his face in his palms. "Actually. What the fuck."

"And why does it smell like an old white lady in here?"

"It's lavender. From the diffuser." He gestured to a contraption puffing away on the side table next to what Mickey assumed was an infant's sound machine. "It's nice."

Mickey sat on the edge of his desk. "It's something."

His plaid boxers had hiked up; he tugged them lower and shifted his junk around, then returned to the sofa and pulled the blanket over his lap. As he looked up at Mickey, concern and revulsion mingled in his face. "Wow. You look . . . wow."

"I'm a terrible person," she said.

"What?"

"I humiliated you." She'd been trying to make a point, certain that if she poked and prodded him in all the right spots he would inevitably explode in a fit of misogynistic rage, thus proving the therapist wrong about humanity's inherent goodness. But instead of yelling at Mickey, or calling her a bitch, or grabbing one of the umbrellas and threatening her with it, as she'd envisioned, he'd done something so much worse. "You cried. You *wept*."

"I remember," he said.

"I've never seen someone cry that hard. And I teach kindergarten."

Samson winced. "Okay, enough."

"I was terrible. Am. Terrible."

Ian probably hadn't cried; no, that wasn't his style. He would've heard Mickey scamper away—heard the front door creak open and shut—and shrugged the whole thing off. He would've taken the evening and stuffed it down in that place where he stored all his disappointments. And Chris . . . he probably gave Mickey the benefit of the doubt, made an excuse on her behalf. It wouldn't have crossed his mind that she might drink his mouthwash.

Mickey suppressed a minty burp. "Don't you think?"

His gaze settled on the bottle under her arm, which she'd given up trying to conceal. This man already knew her for what she was.

"I don't know," he said.

She swallowed hard. Her tongue was growing heavier, the words harder and harder to form. "You're a total creep, but that's not a . . . not a 'scuse."

Samson brought his fist to his mouth for a moment. Finally, he was starting to look annoyed. Good. She deserved it. She deserved whatever vitriolic speech he was about to hurl her way. "I'm fucked up. I get it. But at least I'm trying. You know? At least I'm not hiding."

She took another swig. The mouthwash seared all the way down. "Do I look like a person who's hiding?"

"You look like a person who's sick," Samson said.

Mickey hung her head. Really? Was this the best he could do?

"You need help," he added, or maybe he didn't. Maybe he hadn't said anything at all, and Mickey was only remembering all those other times over the years when a concerned friend or teacher had pulled her aside to deliver the same awkward speech: addiction was a disease, a terrible disease, but nothing to be ashamed of, not in this day and age, and did she want a leaflet with some resources? What about a business card with the numbers for some crisis hotlines? She could keep the card in her wallet for quick reference.

Mickey groped for an intelligent argument—something about society and the urge to pathologize things. The ideas were there, but the sentence refused to assemble itself.

"What do you want?" Samson asked, and this time, Mickey knew for sure it was him talking because she'd seen his lips moving.

"I want to teach kindergarten," she said. "Then I want to come home and sit by myself in a quiet room. That's all I want." That's all she'd ever wanted. Was it really so much to ask? Yes, she drank, but only at the end of the day, or sometimes in the middle of the day, only sometimes, and really, she couldn't not. It was just a thing that she did.

Samson shook his head. "That's not what you want."

The heat from her stomach migrated down into her toes and up into her cheeks. She tugged at her jacket, but it wouldn't come off. "It is."

"It's not." His body closed in on hers.

"Why are you standing so close?"

"I'm afraid you'll fall over."

"Who are you to give me shit? You don't know me. You're not a—a mind reader." This came out whinier than Mickey had intended. The venom she'd summoned at the café evaded her now. It was all she could do to stay awake.

"How much of that shit did you drink?"

The world was melting. An ocean tide rolled in and out.

"Mickey? Mickey."

The floor gave way.

ARLO

Punam went a long time without speaking. "Explain it to me again."

Arlo recounted the events of the session exactly as they had unfolded: the Chatty Café, Tom Samson, his crocodile tears. She could've lied but there was no reason to. A clever therapy intervention had gone sideways through no fault of her own. Yes, Mickey had made a scene, and yes, she'd inflicted emotional trauma on an unsuspecting bystander—but all of this only pointed to how deeply she herself was suffering. And she'd come away from the encounter with vastly improved insight into some of those feelings. Really, it had been quite a productive session.

"I wouldn't say it was your best idea," Punam said.

Arlo bit the inside of her cheek. "Why—why is that?"

They sat on opposite sides of Punam's desk for today's supervision. Her office was bright but small, the walls cluttered with master's degrees and certificates of appreciation from volunteer organizations and photos of the lakefront cottage she talked about constantly but seemed to barely ever visit.

"You brought a client into a triggering environment. An environment that happened to be full of other vulnerable people."

Arlo remembered the warm atmosphere, the pleasant hum of small talk, the old guy with the Playa del Carmen t-shirt. Hardly *triggering*. "It was basic behavior activation," she said.

"But was it safe?"

Of course, it had been safe. Arlo hadn't taken Mickey cliff-jumping. All they'd done was sit down for a chat in the company of other humans, and surely there was nothing so inherently danger-ous about that. "She gave consent beforehand."

"But was it informed consent?" Punam leaned forward and planted her elbows on the desk, stacking one forearm atop the other. "Did she know the risks? Did you? This work is hard enough when it's just two people in the controlled space of a therapy room."

"We encountered a challenge point," Arlo said, trying not to sound too terse. Punam and all these buts. "Challenge points are good. They mean we're getting somewhere."

"I've been doing this a long time, Arlo. I know what challenge points are."

Indeed: Punam's sixty-five years weighed on the folds of her neck and the papery skin under her eyes. Here was an older woman clinging to what little influence she had left, Arlo reminded herself. Punam's power was waning, and no amount of vacation property could change that.

"Of course," Arlo said. "Sorry."

Punam's features softened in a troubling way. "Let me just ask you this." Sympathy. Her face was twisting up with terrible, abject sympathy. "Do you trust yourself right now?"

Laura Hedman wandered out from a dark corner of Arlo's mind exactly as she'd appeared at their final session: wingtip glasses and nail polish the yellow of baby chicks. They'd talked about her uni classes, her friends, her plans for the weekend. She'd seemed so light, so bright, so totally fine.

Nothing like that awful letter she'd written.

Arlo shooed the memory aside. But Yellow-Nail-Polish Laura was just one of many, and another soon came forward to take her place. There was Exam-Season Laura, with her beige knit cardigans, caffeine jitters, and tendency to catastrophize; Put-Together Laura, who wore lipstick and oversized blazers and tried so very, very hard; Nineties-Inspired Laura, who favored space buns and metallic shades of eyeshadow. There was Tired Laura, Restless Laura, Mascara-Down-Her-Face Laura. On and on they went, these Lauras, always breaking free from their pens. Trampling the ground. Barging into places they had no business being.

"The café thing was an error." Did Arlo really believe this? No. But the truth didn't matter now. What mattered was turning Punam's frown upside down and getting out of this room. "Come on. You know the work I've been doing with my other clients."

The gymnast with PTSD, the medic with the eating disorder, the insomniac homemaker—they'd all turned corners. Why? Because Arlo was an excellent therapist.

Punam tilted her head to one side. "Have you thought any more about Laura?"

"No," Arlo said.

Punam tilted her head to the other side.

"You're doing the thing where we wait for the client to talk," Arlo said, as heat built in the pit of her stomach. But it wouldn't work. She wouldn't be baited into saying anything because there wasn't anything to say. Arlo had provided Laura with some very effective therapy. Laura had said so many times. *Thanks for squeezing me in. I honestly don't know what I'd do without you.* Plus, sometimes memories were just memories. Not everything had to mean something.

Punam hoisted her head slowly back to center. God, she was good.

"A little bit," Arlo conceded. "I've been thinking about her a little bit."

"Only a little bit?"

"It's not productive to dwell."

"Mhmmm," Punam said, though her tone was not quite one of agreement. Her gaze drifted to a framed photo on her desk: the stone façade of her cottage at dusk. Then she looked up with such laser intensity that Arlo recoiled into the backrest of her chair. "Well, now you've made one mistake. You've still got a full case-load of people to see. How can we recharge your batteries and make sure you're ready for next week?"

There was a right answer. Arlo needed only supply it.

"Maybe," she said, wincing inwardly at the prospect of what was to come, "a bit of time off with family?"

○

She lay starfished on the floor inside the walk-in closet with her cream pantsuit bunching in all the worst places and Daddy's favor-ite silk pajama shirt folded over her face.

"Mother?" Arlo prodded her with one foot. "Mother."

She hinged upright like Dracula rising from his coffin. The pajama shirt tumbled into her lap, exposing silver roots, sloppy lip-stick, and a string of false lashes that dangled from the corner of one eye.

Arlo couldn't help but flinch. "Dear God."

Mother glanced left and right. She found one of Daddy's neck-ties on the floor beside her foot and gazed at it inquisitively, as if she'd never seen a necktie before and could only imagine what pur-pose it might serve. Then she bowed her head and wept.

Arlo had seen Mother cry only twice before. The first time, Arlo was eleven, watching from the living room couch with her favorite stuffed mermaid while her parents stood in front of the TV argu-ing over a recent dinner party and whether Mother had shown too much cleavage, whether she'd appeared too sullen, whether she'd had one too many gin martinis. The other time, Arlo was seventeen, and Mother had spent forty-five minutes on hold with a Clinique representative to learn they'd discontinued her favorite brand of night cream.

Steeling herself, Arlo knelt at Mother's side and rubbed the firm nubs of her vertebrae. "It's hard. I know it's hard."

"I'd forgotten," Mother said. The false lashes had come fully unglued and now clung to the cliff's edge of her cheekbone. "For a split second, I forgot he was gone. Does that happen to you? You wake up in the morning, and for a moment it's like everything is normal. It's like before. Then you remember."

"Yes, Mother. I know what you mean."

Cloudless sky filled the small window above the dresser. Luckier people were out there carving into brunch tostadas or wandering the streets with oat lattes in hand. Not Arlo. Arlo would spend the whole day here, patting Mother's back and sorting Daddy's things. All so she could look Punam in the eye on Monday morning and say, *The time really helped me refill my fuel tank. You were right—self-care. So important.*

"Where are they?" Arlo asked.

Mother showed her to the living room in the basement, where men's shoes covered the sectional couch, the coffee table, half the floor. Runners, rain boots, loafers, oxfords, soccer cleats, sandals, golf shoes, and at least five pairs of hockey skates. Some shoes were worn and muddied, others brand-new and still in their boxes.

"Holy shit," Arlo said.

Mother sighed. "I know. He hid them everywhere."

Arlo had always attributed Daddy's hoarding to his having once been poor. The first few years of her parents' marriage had been famously impoverished. To Arlo, who had known only brand-name cereal and luxury sedans, that time felt like a fable.

She dug a plastic bin out of the storage room and began to fill it.

"Woah—hey." Mother snatched away a pair of pilled gray slippers. "Not those ones. He wore those every day."

"Fine." Arlo picked up some random dress shoes.

Mother stole those as well. "This pair is Italian leather. He only bought them maybe six months ago. You can't—I mean, it seems silly to give them away. They're new."

This day, Arlo thought. "What, you're saying you want to wear them?"

"Well, maybe."

"They're men's dress shoes."

"So?"

"You wear a women's size seven."

Mother set down the Italian loafers and stepped into them with her chin held high. "Well?"

Arlo considered her. "You look like a bourgeois clown."

"I didn't ask for your help, you know."

"You literally did."

"Why don't you start over here." Mother steered Arlo toward the bar, where some of Daddy's personal items had been laid out like artifacts in a museum display. Watches, pens. His passport. "Decide if you want any of this."

Arlo brought Daddy's wallet to her nose for a sniff, but the paled brown leather had lost its smell. Inside were his credit cards, a crisp hundred-dollar bill, an expired boating license, faded receipts, and a folded photograph. At first, Arlo wasn't sure what she was looking at. The light-wash quality of the early nineties. An impossibly young, mustachioed version of Daddy sitting on a picnic bench in jeans and a t-shirt. A pigtailed little girl on his knee. She looked up at him so adoringly, her smile as bright as her white-blonde hair. How devastated she must've felt when, no more than a year or two after the picture was taken, he went away and began a new life without her.

Arlo refolded the photograph, then folded it again and again until it would fold no further. Then she tucked it in the pocket of her sweater. "Can I ask you something?"

Mother was waddling around in a pair of Daddy's cowboy boots, transferring shoes from one pile to another for no discernable purpose. "What's that?"

"Do you think all people are terrible?"

Mother froze, flip-flops in hand, her expression inscrutable.

"Like, inherently," Arlo said, thinking briefly of Samson. How many other grieving daughters had he slept with over the years? Was this a thing he did, trawling for hookups at clients' funerals? And how could Arlo get him so wrong? She never got anyone wrong. "Are people just . . . bad?"

"I'm not sure what you're asking," Mother said.

"I used to think—I *do* think—that people are complex. Well— simple. The complexity of it is simple. People are layers of experience." This wasn't coming out right. "I always thought that if you really drilled down, at the core of it, people were . . . not bad. Do you know what I'm trying to say?"

Mother was quiet for a long time. She set aside the flip-flops and turned to Arlo with her chest puffed out. "I'm not weak, you know."

"I—I didn't say you were."

"Your father had the biggest heart. He was a good man. If he wasn't, I wouldn't have stayed. You're acting very insensitive for a psycho—psychothera—whatever you are."

"I didn't mean . . ." Arlo was no longer sure what she had meant.

"He was sick, that was all."

"I haven't forgotten," Arlo said. How could she? She'd been managing Daddy's addiction since she was very young. That period felt distant but distinctly real, as if her child-self might still be out there somewhere, sponging Daddy's vomit out of a carpet in a country across the sea.

"And if things went a step further—if he raised a hand to me, say—then I was prepared to leave. Really. I was. And all this?" Mother gestured to herself. "The turtlenecks and the suits and the pearls? I wore them for me. Because I wanted to make him happy. It was my choice." Her voice wobbled. "He had the biggest heart of anyone. But I would've done it."

A question rose in Arlo's throat. She couldn't hold it down. "Did you know?"

"Know what?" Mother said, picking at the knotted sleeves of Daddy's pajama shirt, which she'd tied around her waist.

"That he cut me out of the will." Arlo hadn't thought to ask before now.

Mother gathered the pajama shirt in her arms and squashed it against her chest. "The lawyer came to see me a few days after the funeral."

"And?" Arlo wasn't expecting Mother to split her share. She didn't want pity. What she wanted was for someone to please, for the love of God, just explain it to her, here, now, in simple terms, because she'd tried working it out on her own, she really had, and none of it made any sense. This wasn't in Daddy's character. He wouldn't use someone up and throw them away—especially not Arlo.

Mother shrugged. "I'm sure he had his reasons."

Arlo reached into her pocket and closed the photograph in her fist. "That's it? 'I'm sure he had his reasons'? That's all you have to say?"

"He took care of us." Mother stepped close and used a corner of Daddy's pajama shirt to wipe Arlo's cheeks. "We took care of him, and he took care of us. So, yes. He will have had his reasons."

A terrifying possibility bubbled up.

"Do you think he loved her more than me?" Arlo asked.

Mother smiled sadly. "I ask myself that question all the time."

MICKEY

The bed was not hers. Mickey was certain of this before she had even opened her eyes. The mattress was too firm. The sheets were too tight. The pillow was starchy and coarse and smelled of chemicals. The air was full of distant pager alarms, rickety wheels, footsteps of varying squeakiness, and snores.

She pressed up, wincing at a painful pinch in the crease of her left elbow where a rubber tube poked through the skin. Over Mickey's shoulder, a half-empty bag of saline hung from an IV pole. Yes, it was as she'd feared.

Her purse. Where was her purse? They'd taken her sweater-dress and replaced it with this cheap polka-dot number, which meant they'd probably done something with the rest of her stuff. Hung it up, stashed it somewhere safe. Hopefully. Was there anything so awful as losing an iPhone?

She scanned the room. Nothing on the side table, nothing on the counter by the sink. And on the chair—yes! There it was: her stupid, beautiful, enormous purse, bundled up with her coat and her heel boots. In Tom Samson's lap.

He snored, mouth gaping, head flung all the way back.

Mickey squeezed a single word from her mangled throat: "Hey."

He wheezed a little but gave no sign of waking. Light dripped in from the hall, casting him in a jaundiced hue.

"Hey," she said again, as loudly as she could manage. The sound of her own voice chafed.

Samson's head snapped up. He sniffled, coughed. "Hi."

Mickey's nose began to prickle. She was here, and her purse was all the way over there, the distance between them insurmountable. "I want my purse."

"What?"

"My purse."

Samson followed her gaze into his lap. "Oh." His eyebrows drew down and together. "You're not leaving, are you? I don't think you should—"

"It's my purse," Mickey said, as something surged inside her—a tide she couldn't contain. It was the memory of Ian's tiny voice, but it was also the memory of Chris's stupid apron, and the pig show, and a golden elevator. Sirens. A bumpy ride in the back of a truck. An astringent taste in her mouth. Yes, the tide was all these things at once. "I want it."

"Are you . . ." He stiffened. "You're crying."

"Yes, I'm crying. I don't have any of my stuff. They took my clothes, my purse, my ph—my ph . . ." She couldn't say it.

"Okay, okay." He lumbered upright and approached her slowly.

Mickey snatched the purse out of Samson's arms and scraped its contents onto her lap. "I'm thirty-three years old. Almost thirty-four. I need to keep track of my purse. If I can't keep track of my own purse, then what am I? I'm nothing." The phone slid out, sleek and shining: a marvel of human innovation she would never take for granted again. "Even my kindergarteners can keep track of their backpacks."

"Why do you carry around a Hillary Clinton biography?"

Mickey held the iPhone to her heart. "Because I'm going to read it someday, okay? Leave me alone."

And he did. Well. He didn't *leave* leave, but he did give her some space, striding over to the window despite the fact there wasn't much to see as far as Mickey could tell. The brick face of another building, an eavestrough, a strip of starless night sky.

"You went down pretty hard," he said after a while. "One second you were fine, the next you were on the ground."

Yes, there had been a floor. Carpeted, Mickey was pretty sure. The scratchy stuff designed for high-traffic areas.

"When was that?" she asked. "Like, how many hours ago?"

"I don't know, eight? Nine?" As he turned from the window, he fell into silhouette. What he said next made Mickey grateful she couldn't see him clearly. "Someone's coming to talk to you. The social worker."

"About the . . . the . . ." Mickey willed herself to stop crying. She wasn't ashamed. Why would she be ashamed? It was her body, her mouthwash. Well, technically not her mouthwash. But whatever.

"Yeah. About that."

He stepped into the light, and Mickey could see him properly again. She searched his face for judgment but found none. Her relief was swift and unexpected.

"And they told you all this?" she asked.

He sank into the chair again, still holding Mickey's coat and shoes. The boots were scuffed to shit, probably from all the curbs she'd slipped over. The gutters she'd trod through.

"I said I was your father."

Mickey felt another, gentler tide beginning to rise. What a creep this lawyer was. What a wonderful, wonderful creep.

"What?" he said. "Why are you looking at me that way? I thought someone should be here for you, make sure your purse didn't go missing. Places like this, you know, stuff gets lost all the—shit.

What did I say? I'm sorry. Don't cry again. Or do. Sorry. I'm a jack-ass. Cry if you want to cry."

"This is the nicest thing anyone's ever done for me," she said.

"Really?" His tone was one of sad disbelief.

Samson's kindness was almost too much—especially given that only a few days had passed since Mickey verbally assaulted him for no reason.

"I'm really, um . . ." Sorry. She was sorry. How hard was it to say? "I shouldn't have—you didn't deserve what—" Jesus. "Do you know what I mean?"

Samson leaned forward, elbows on his knees, nose pointed at the floor. "I deserved everything you said. All of it. Truth is, you didn't make me cry. I made myself cry by being such a sorry-ass piece of shit."

A light knock came at the door.

"Good morning."

She had a silty voice, a triangle of mousy gray hair, and a scowl reminiscent of border guards and junior high lunch ladies.

"Are you the social worker?" Mickey asked doubtfully. This woman was at least seventy and smelled like cigarettes.

She introduced herself as Vera. "Mind if I turn on the light?"

"I'd rather we didn't," Mickey said.

Vera's hand fell away from the switch. "All the same to me." She nodded at Tom. "Hi."

"I want him to stay," Mickey said, surprising herself.

"Okie dokie." Vera hoisted herself onto the empty bed across the room, chuffing as she rearranged the waistband of her pants.

There were some demographic questions to begin with—how old was Mickey, where did she live, etc. Vera made a few scribbles on a clipboard, which she tilted at different angles in the dim light and occasionally lifted near her face, squinting. "Hang on." She pulled a circa-2010 BlackBerry out of her pocket and shone its light on the paper. "There we go. Okay, let's see. Do you use substances? If yes, which ones, and how often?"

Mickey laced her fingers in her lap and squeezed. "What does that even mean? 'Substances.' Isn't everything a substance?"

"Alcohol and drugs."

"I don't want to talk about that," Mickey said.

Vera set her clipboard aside, expressionless. "Okay."

"Seriously?" Mickey asked, because nobody had ever left it alone that easy.

"Why not? Makes my life simpler. But look, let's forget all that stuff"—she gestured to the clipboard, wrinkling her nose—"and have a chat."

Mickey looked to Tom, who gave a tiny encouraging nod.

"Fine," she said.

"Who are your people?" Vera asked.

Mickey snorted. "Why does everyone ask me that?"

"It's important for most of us," Vera said. "Not all of us, I'll grant you. But most of us."

"Well, I don't do people. People are the worst."

"Fair enough. It's your life."

What a terrible social worker, Mickey thought.

"Tell me about last night," Vera said.

Mickey relayed what she could remember, from the French exit she'd made at Chris's house to collapsing on the floor in Tom's office. She spoke with as little emotion as possible and stuck closely to the facts. If ever there was a time for the spy strategy, it was now.

"Huh." Vera put a finger to her lips in a contemplative way, doing the thing where they wait for the client to talk. But it wouldn't work. Mickey wouldn't be baited into saying anything because there wasn't anything to say. She'd done something deeply self-destructive, but this was a free country, and people were allowed to make poor decisions.

"Huh," Vera said again.

Mickey hugged her purse. She definitely didn't like herself very much. If this whole episode had proven one thing, that was it.

"Huh," Vera said, actually said, an actual third time.

"Oh my God, what?" Mickey snapped.

Tom spoke before Vera had the chance. "If you really don't care about people, then why go out of your way to avoid them?"

This question lodged painfully deep in Mickey's brain.

"I don't avoid them, per se," she said.

"Then why isolate yourself?" Tom's eyes had grown wild and bright. *Pick me*, they said. *I know the answer.* "If you truly don't give a shit what anybody else does or says or thinks?"

"I don't isolate myself." That word conjured images of frail seniors and depressed people.

"You don't 'do' people," Tom said, making air quotes. "That was how you put it."

"Well, it wasn't what I meant. And I thought *she*"—Mickey jerked her head at Vera, who was smiling for the first time since she'd walked in, baring a set of dingy teeth and bright red gums— "was supposed to ask the questions."

"This Chris guy, for example," Tom said. "If you really didn't care about him and his kid, I don't see why you would run out like that. We run when we're scared."

Mickey considered this. Yes, panic had made her run last night— but also confusion. Her relationship with Ian used to begin each morning when he tottered into class, and it used to end each afternoon when he tottered out of it. Now she was a person who showed up at his house to watch TV and read bedtime stories and eat dinner with his attractive, bumbling uncle, a man who was sweet and surprising and somehow single. It just didn't make any sense.

"We get scared about things that matter," Tom said. "People who matter."

Mickey wasn't stupid. She saw his point. She also knew it was moot.

"*If* there were people out there I didn't hate," she said, with another glance at the IV pole, "and *if* I wanted to spend time with them . . ." Mickey couldn't finish the sentence, though the words gonged in her head: *Why would anyone want to spend time with me?*

"Yeah." Tom sighed. "That's the hard part."

◎

That afternoon, Mickey dusted the baseboards, emptied the recycling, vacuumed the carpets, clipped her toenails, flossed her teeth, crushed five episodes of *Bridgerton*, and dusted the baseboards again. Eleven and a half hours after Tom had dropped her off at home and with nothing else to clean, fix, or watch, she took a swig of Russian Standard straight from the bottle and knelt on the bedroom floor beside the wall outlet. Holding her breath, she plugged her phone into the charger and the charger into the wall. The Apple logo appeared white against a purgatorial black background and hovered there for three impossibly long seconds. She punched in her passcode, and the home screen materialized.

A red bubble in the top right corner of the phone icon told her she'd missed four calls. Four. That was bad. Or good. She couldn't decide. Four missed calls meant she'd made him worry. It meant she'd burdened him. But maybe it also meant he cared? At least a little?

Mickey opened her text messages.

Where did you go?

Are you coming back?

I hope you're ok

She stared at the last text for a long time. Mickey wasn't used to taking up space in other people's heads. But she wasn't used to taking up space in a hospital either, which had definitely happened. She still had the ID band on her wrist to prove it.

The phone erupted in her hands with a flash of light and the violent, trilling ringtone she hated desperately but was too lazy to change. It hit the floor screen-down.

She turned it over with one flick of her finger and yanked her arm back. Chris was calling. Again. For the fifth time. Probably to yell at her, to say how badly her departure had rattled poor Ian, and what had she been thinking, running out like that? Bad thoughts piled up in Mickey's head, as relentless as this Godforsaken fucking phone, which was still ringing. How was it still ringing? She had to make it stop.

She swiped to answer. "Hello?"

"Are you dead? Did you die?" There was heat in his voice—not anger exactly, but something close. "What happened to you?"

"Yeah. Sorry. I got this weird stomachache all of a sudden, and, um . . ." She held the phone in the crook of her neck and wrenched at the hospital band. It did not break.

"A stomachache."

"It's been happening a lot lately—this, like, sharp pain." She put the phone on speaker, pressed off the ground, and went to her craft table in the corner to look for a pair of scissors. She was making her students glittery new name tags despite not being their teacher anymore, and no, that wasn't weird. "I think I must have an ulcer or IBS or . . ."

One snip, and the hospital bracelet fell from Mickey's wrist.

"I got freaked out," she said. "I got freaked out, and I ran. Bathtime and movie night and—do you know what I'm saying? I'm not used to being part of that stuff. And there are some things I shouldn't be a part of. I want to be your friend, not a stand-in for Ian's mom. I won't drop everything and run over every time he's sick or needs a bedtime story." However much she might want to. Because that wasn't the point. "You can't treat me like that."

Mickey dropped the hospital bracelet in a waste bin under the table and waited for the blast of the hang-up tone.

"You're right," he said. "I'm sorry. Honestly? I like it when you're around. And not just for the kid stuff. I mean, you know what you're doing way better than me, clearly, but that's not—it isn't why . . . I just—I like you."

Mickey pulled out the chair and fell into it. He liked her. He *liked* her. But how, exactly? Did he like her in a buddy-buddy, let's-go-out-for-trivia-night-and-get-hot-wings kind of way? Or did he like her in another way? And how could she find out? Besides asking him, which she obviously couldn't. That much vulnerability might kill her.

"Hello? Mickey?"

An idea sprang up out of nowhere and raced laps around her brain. "My birthday is on November tenth," she found herself saying.

"Happy early birthday."

"I might have people over for food. And, you know, drinks."

"Nice," he said, with a smile Mickey could somehow hear. "That sounds great."

She grabbed a squeeze bottle of turquoise glitter paint and added an extra swirl to the name tag she'd made Ian. It needed a little more sparkle—a little more pizzazz. Plus, this next bit would be easier to say if her hands were busy. "I think you and the kiddo should come."

The line went quiet for an excruciating quarter of a second.

"The third, you said?"

"The third," Mickey croaked.

"Ian might be gone by then, is the only thing."

She rose from the craft table and went back to where she'd left the phone plugged in on the floor. "What do you mean 'gone'?" That word didn't go with Ian's name.

"Back with my sister."

Mickey found the bottle of Russian Standard and peered into the bottom. Whether in five minutes or in five hours, she would get up and go get another bottle from the fridge, and she would drink that one, too. Not because she particularly wanted or needed it. She just knew it was going to happen. "Did you hear from her finally?"

"I give it another week. Ten days, tops."

She also knew, logically, it would be best for everyone if Ian's mom came back. Logically, she knew this. And yet.

The last time Mickey had celebrated a birthday—properly celebrated—was on a trip to Holland over a decade ago. It was the same year Taylor Swift released a song about being twenty-two, and there had seemed to her a touch of divinity about this. Dodging bicycles and trams, she wandered along in the rain in search of accommodation and eventually checked in to a hostel where she met some exchange students from Serbia or Slovenia or somewhere. Mickey was pretty sure they took a boat ride at some point.

She was proud of herself for collecting these memories of swan-cluttered canals and wet cobbles. Even if Mama had cried when Mickey arrived home four days later, jet-lagged and wearing all sorts of entry stamps on her arms from bars she couldn't quite remember visiting.

Mickey rarely thought about these events now. She definitely wasn't thinking about them that week at therapy, her third appointment of the requisite seven.

". . . which makes it four people coming including me," Mickey said. Daria had also accepted her birthday invitation and dutifully offered to make a dessert Mickey had never heard of. "I guess that's not a lot. Is it still a party if there are only four people?"

Five. She would invite Tom, too. "Do you know what a Napoleon cake is?"

"Let's Google it," Arlo said, pulling out her phone.

There was so much to do. Mickey had to decide on decorations, pick an outfit, figure out what food to order. "Am I supposed to make gift bags? My last birthday party was in grade six. I remember there were gift bags."

"Holy shit, it looks so good." Arlo showed Mickey her phone and swiped through a few images: layered puff pastries topped with various configurations of berries. It did look good. "Is someone making this for you?"

"My neighbor across the hall."

"Wow." Arlo put her phone away. "Well, *my* neighbor leaves me passive-aggressive notes about the noise volume, which is basically the same as an elaborate pastry."

Mickey let herself laugh.

Today's therapy session felt different. She hadn't dreaded it, for one. Part of Mickey was actually pleased to be here, wedged into this tiny room with a woman who looked like the Little Mermaid. She'd had more annoying counselors. At least this one wasn't afraid to swear.

"I always forget how much work it is to host people," Arlo said.

"Totally," Mickey said.

Arlo flipped through the papers on her clipboard for what must've been the third or fourth time since Mickey sat down. She kept glancing at a page near the back. Chart notes from last time? Maybe she couldn't remember what they'd talked about. "Why have a party this year?"

"Just thought it would be nice," Mickey said. "You know—get people together for food, some drinks."

"Some drinks," Arlo said, her eyes flashing up.

The muscles of Mickey's abdomen seized. Had she remembered to cover her breath with a swig of milk before leaving the house? No, she hadn't. She hadn't even brushed her teeth. Or maybe she had, and she just couldn't remember? Maybe it didn't matter. They weren't sitting that close together, and vodka barely had a scent, anyway. Maybe Arlo hadn't smelled it.

"I was taking a second look at your intake form just now," Arlo said, "and I noticed you left the question about substances blank."

Fuck. She'd definitely smelled it.

"Did I?" Mickey said. "I must've missed it."

"That tells me it's worth exploring a bit. Do you mind?"

Yes, Mickey minded. This wasn't Arlo's ground to dig up. And wasn't Mickey doing enough already? She was hosting a party. Mickey! A party! "I guess that would be fine."

"Some coping strategies are helpful in the short term but not the long term. These questions will help me—us—understand whether the drinking is getting you where you want to go." Arlo's tone was so devoid of judgment it was actually offensive.

"I already agreed," Mickey said. "Go ahead."

Arlo read aloud from another of her papers: "*Have you ever wondered if you should reduce your drinking?*"

This was such bullshit. "No," Mickey said.

"*Does it frustrate you when people criticize your drinking?*"

"No."

Arlo set down the clipboard and held her pen horizontally between her hands in a scholarly way. So studious, so interested. As if Mickey were a case study to be pored over.

But she was not a case study. She was a person, and people couldn't be reduced to a set of probing questions some addictions researcher had devised back in the eighties. That's what this was—a standardized questionnaire. Mickey knew because she'd been asked these exact questions at least seven times in her life. "What?"

"I wasn't sure if you had more to say."

"Oh," Mickey said. "Nope. Next?"

"*Have you ever felt guilty for something you did while drinking?*"

Mickey remembered stepping off the airplane from Amsterdam, as hungover as she'd ever been. Falling into Mama's arms at baggage claim. Entering their shared apartment to find streamers and helium balloons still crowding the ceiling and an untouched cake forgotten on the kitchen table. Candles lying sideways in the melted icing. "No."

"*Do you ever have an eye-opener after waking up in the morning to calm your jitters or get rid of a hangover?*"

"I—" Mickey hesitated, weighing how much truth to tell. She'd taken her first sip at 7:56 that morning, which wasn't exactly first thing. She'd combed her hair and put on underwear first. And she'd paired the alcohol with dry toast. Plus, lots of people drank at breakfast. It was a brunch thing. "An eye-opener? I'm not familiar with that."

Arlo shrugged. "A drink in the morning. Hair of the dog."

"I used to only do that on weekends," Mickey said, because this point should count for something. She never drank on workdays—not until the bus ride home. Except for that once, with Ian. "It's been different since I got laid off."

Arlo pursed her lips—a look of deep concentration, as if she truly were trying to understand. "How does it help?"

This question caught Mickey by surprise. No one had ever asked it before.

"I don't know. Fills the time, I guess." Or softened it. Sanded the edges of this unbearable reality she'd built. Something along those lines. "It's a nice thing to have."

Arlo's mouth bent into a thoughtful frown. "A nice thing to have."

"Yeah. Like a treat."

"A treat."

"Why are you repeating everything I say?"

"Sometimes it helps to hear our words said back to us."

"Us?" Mickey was really starting to hate this woman.

Arlo removed her glasses and folded them on the table. Her eyes glimmered, small and diamond-hard and strangely familiar. "Any big drinkers in your family?" she asked.

Mickey scratched her forearms, her wrists, everywhere those stupid entry stamps had been. Everything itched. "My dad. Why?"

ARLO

"Any big drinkers in your family?"

Mickey began scratching her arms so suddenly and compulsively Arlo wondered if she might be having some kind of tactile hallucination. "My dad. Why?"

Arlo felt a zing of good adrenaline. She'd hoped to broach the subject of Mickey's father during today's session. But then Mickey had shown up smelling like a distillery, and the conversation had gone another way. Unless it was all the same thing—the liquor, Mickey's dad, her deep-rooted (and as yet unacknowledged) need to be loved and accepted. God, human beings were compelling creatures.

"Nobody drinks, like, automatically," Arlo said, trying not to sound preachy. Mickey hadn't been the most receptive to the screening questionnaire, and she needed to tread carefully. "It's a learned behavior."

A soggy laugh scrabbled up Mickey's throat, almost a cough but not. Her neck had all but disappeared, her shoulders surging up beside her ears. A gargoyle in a pink cardigan. "I didn't learn a thing from my dad. I promise you that."

"When did he pass?" Arlo asked.

"Like a month ago."

The adrenaline doubled. *Same*, Arlo wanted to say, as her heart began to spasm. *Same!* But she did not say this. She did not say this because she was a good therapist with good boundaries. Self-disclosures of this nature—*Guess what? My dad also died super recently! It was and continues to be extremely traumatic, and now I'm questioning everything I thought I knew about him!*—only deflected focus away from the client and were thus unhelpful. Better to home in on Mickey and foster some internal awareness.

"It's tough for you to talk about him, huh?" Arlo gestured to Mickey with her pen. "You're all hunched up."

Mickey frowned at her reflection in the observation mirror but made no apparent effort to fix her posture. If anything, her hunch deepened, which Arlo admired in a strange way. Irreverence was a quality she'd always enjoyed in people, not least of all Daddy.

"What was he like?" Arlo asked, wondering if Mickey's father had also hoarded Italian leather loafers.

Mickey took a tissue from the box on the table and began shredding it into tiny pieces in her lap. She eyed the clock; Arlo was losing her.

"Tell me one thing." *Please*, Arlo thought. Just one thing.

"I remember . . ." Mickey gave a half smile. "I remember his mustache. Big and kind of, I don't know, sandy-colored."

"Go on," Arlo said.

"I remember running around the park with him. He used to play with me a lot when I was little. He would pick me up and spin me. Constantly. He was either playing with me, or he was passed out on the couch. One or the other."

Sounded a lot like the two iterations of Arlo's father. Fun Daddy and Tired Daddy, as she used to call them.

"I remember how he used to yell at us. The names he would call my mom."

Mad Daddy—his most frightening persona. The one who slammed doors and broke plates.

"I remember sitting on his knee sometimes, and not knowing what scared me more—having him so close or knowing that sooner or later he'd disappear. How messed up is that? Having a parent who's that awful and still . . . loving them." There was something slightly crazed about the way Mickey's lip curled as she said this. "Needing them."

A wave of heat rolled up Arlo's spine. "You make it sound pathetic."

"It is. Pathetic." Mickey brushed herself off with the sides of her palms, and all the bits of Kleenex snowed onto the floor.

"Children can't choose who they form attachments to," Arlo said, which was true, but also no parent was only good or bad. It wasn't fair to parse out the failures from the successes. Yes, Daddy was a drunk. Yes, he made a lot of messes and left most of them to Arlo. But there had been good stuff, too—all those imaginary tea parties, the games of tag and tic-tac-toe, the bike rides, the piggyback rides, the water balloon fights, the limited-edition Bratz dolls he'd bought her, the books he'd read her, and later, the skiing lessons, the driving lessons, the Beach Boys singalongs, the third-degree interrogation of any male who came within ten feet, the way he'd cried at her high school grad and again at her wedding, when she'd surprised him with "God Only Knows" for the father-daughter dance. "I do wonder, though. These tough feelings you've held on to—the shame, the resentment . . ."

Anger flashed in Mickey's eyes. "I don't resent anything, and I'm certainly not asha—"

"Is it really about your dad?" Arlo was pressing hard. She had to. They were on the brink of something here. "Sometimes we direct our emotional energy toward the people in our lives because we're afraid of directing it toward ourselves. We scrutinize others—or the memory of others—when we would do better to look inward."

"You didn't have to scrutinize my father. The faults had a way of jumping out."

Mickey turned her attention back to the wisps of Kleenex at her feet. She bent over and started picking them up one by one, collecting each scrap in her cupped palm.

"He left when I was seven. Just up and left. Randomly. Went off and made a new life with a new family."

Arlo was speechless for a moment. Was she overthinking this? Spotting connections where there were none?

"Kids only see their parents from a certain angle," she said, recovering her composure. "Remembering things from childhood is a whole other question. Most of our memories are constructed from vague feelings and other people's stories."

Mickey straightened. "I haven't 'constructed' anything. I knew him, okay? I knew the—the stupid shuffle of his steps. I knew his favorite TV channels. I knew the sound his Coors made when he cracked it. He crushed a can of beer first thing every—"

Her mouth shut and opened and shut and opened, as if a fuse had short-circuited in her brain, and now all the signals were misfiring.

"Every morning?" Arlo said. "An eye-opener?"

The conversation had come full circle: from Mickey's drinking to her abandonment issues and back again. Arlo couldn't have planned it better. Yet her stomach was rolling, and sometime in the last five minutes, the good adrenaline had turned bad.

Arlo veered her Prius to the curb, slammed the shifter into park, and tumbled out into the cold. She knew what she had to do. And while some people might call it wrong, breaking into legal offices in search of confidential documents, she saw no reason to feel guilty. She deserved to know for certain who'd walked away with Daddy's money. She deserved a name, an address, a phone number. Yes, it was the middle of the night. Yes, she was wearing pink flannel pajamas. What did it matter? She was out for justice.

The security guard sitting on a stool inside the vestibule regarded her with mixed apprehension and pity. He didn't bother to stand. Didn't bother to even fold his newspaper, a tabloid with a car wreck on the cover. "Can I help you, ma'am?"

"My boyfriend works at the law firm upstairs." She launched into a story about how she'd meant to hide a gift in his desk for their anniversary tomorrow but had forgotten until now. Desperation came to her voice quite readily.

The security guy set the newspaper in his lap with a sigh. "Who's your boyfriend?"

"Tom Samson. He's a lawyer."

He scratched a scab on his bald head and squinted at her for a long moment before erupting in laughter. Not that Arlo cared. Justice! This was about justice!

The security guard rose from his stool and swiped his badge against a sensor on the wall. "He good to you, this Tom Samson?"

Tom Samson was a greasy player who preyed upon grieving women. Worse than that, he was a brick in the bureaucratic wall separating Arlo from the knowledge that was rightly hers. She hated him and all he stood for.

"He's the best," Arlo said.

The security guy smiled, not unkindly. "I bet he is."

The elevator was full of mirrors. Dodging her own gaze, Arlo watched the floor number tick upward: seven, eight, nine . . . She dug in her coat pocket for the photograph from Daddy's wallet— the photograph of Michelle.

This lapse in judgment was so unlike him. Daddy made sound decisions, gave good advice. He'd foreseen every mistake Arlo ever made. *Isn't that tree a little too tall to climb? Isn't your course load a little too heavy this semester? Isn't this boy, this Hayden, a little too . . . average for you? I mean, a plumber. Really?*

A horn sounded. The floor shifted. The elevator doors and the button panel tipped sideways, and Arlo collided with the wall, ramming shoulders with her reflection.

She found the brass railing and steadied herself. The horn— music; it was music—pounded through her ear canals and the gray matter of her thalamus.

Her phone. Jesus. It was just her phone.

PRIVATE CALLER

She hit the red button to decline. Her ringtone, the main theme from Tchaikovsky's *Swan Lake*, fell silent.

The elevator car halted with a swoop of gravity, and the doors parted.

Draped in shadow, the reception area was full of odd shapes: the jagged angles of armrests, the long spine of a floor lamp, a plant with leaves like outstretched claws. A lone vacuum cleaner shored up in the middle of the carpet. Gone were the secretaries and the assistants; all but a few of the rooms dark.

The door to Samson's office had been left open by a crack.

Arlo took a finger and ran it downward along the gap between door and frame. This was so easy, so right. All day yesterday she'd been toeing an edge in her mind, circling something she couldn't yet see. Now she wanted to face it—to face *her*.

No floral smells tonight, only a faint muskiness as Arlo pressed open the door and stepped inside. She scanned the room: desk, mini-fridge, filing cabinets, couch, sleeping person, side table—

Her gaze swung back to the person, to Samson, who lay on his back with his bare feet sticking over the end of the sofa and a blanket drawn up to his nose. File folders, loose papers, and empty chip bags encircled him like a sad shrine.

Arlo glanced back and forth between the lawyer and the door, unable to move. *Fuck*, she thought. *Fuck, fuck, mother fucking fucker of all fuckers.*

God knows how long she stood there. Long enough for sweat to soak the waistband of her pajama pants. Long enough to consider every possible course of action.

Option 1: Slink away and forget she'd ever come here. Accept what she'd been given—nothing, in a word. No money, no answers. Carry this nothingness on her back for the rest of her life while the elusive Michelle frittered away Daddy's hard-earned cash. Arlo imagined her lying on a beach somewhere, sipping a cocktail out of a coconut while waves lapped and palm trees swayed in the distance. Big sunglasses obscured her face.

Then there was Option 2.

Arlo tiptoed behind the desk, lowered into the chair millimeter by millimeter to avoid any squeaks or creaks, and spun to face the row of filing cabinets behind the desk. A–C. D–F. G–I. J–L. Bingo. Trapping a breath of air in her chest, she reached out and tugged the handle.

Locked.

Okay, so this wasn't going to be as straightforward as she'd initially thought. But everything was still fine. Totally, totally, super fine. Every lock had a key.

Pawing through the desk drawers, she found pens, bottles of essential oils, Visa gift cards, a Tibetan singing bowl, business cards for massage therapists and real estate agents, incense sticks, and an assortment of male enhancement pills. But no key.

Then she noticed a groove in the top piece of the desk. She nudged the loose papers and sticky notes aside, revealing a square section that appeared to flip open.

Arlo buzzed from the tips of her toes to the crown of her head. So, this was crime. *Resistance*, she corrected herself. It was resistance.

She gripped the top piece, peeled it open, and found—

Nothing but dust and a single dime.

"Come on," she said, letting the lid fall.

A snore rumbled through the air.

Arlo went crashing backward in the chair, which butted against the filing cabinets with a scuff and an excruciating clang. When at last the noise settled, she stood.

He'd rolled onto his back, but his eyes were—mercifully—still shut.

Arlo's guts twisted as saliva filled her mouth. She might get fined for this. Do jail time. Lose her license—her career. The thing she was best at, the thing she wasn't whole without. And for what? It was the middle of the night. She was wearing pink flannel pajamas, rifling through a lawyer's desk in search of . . . what? What was she doing here?

Her vision narrowed, and for a moment, all she could see was the strip of gray light squeezing through the office door. But as she passed the couch, inching closer to escape, her gaze fell on one of the files surrounding Samson, and she paused. KOWALSKI, M. M for Michelle.

Her knees found their way to the floor. The file found its way into her hands.

"Fucking jackpot," Arlo said.

A phlegmy sound erupted from Samson's throat. His eyelashes fluttered.

Shit.

He was waking up.

Shit!

The door. Could she make it there? No, she couldn't.

Arlo tugged open her coat, squashed Michelle's file against her abdomen, and cinched the coat tight again.

Doom set in as Samson's eyes fluttered open. She'd been caught. She'd been caught, and now her life was over. The small-headed security guard would drag her away in handcuffs and turn her over to the cops. She would spend the night in one of those holding cells with fifty people and one toilet. Mother would have to come and post bail. When Punam heard the news, she would shake her head and say, *I knew it. I knew that girl would throw away her vast potential in a misguided act of hubris.*

But rather than swear and jump to his feet, as Arlo might've expected, Samson rubbed his face and groaned, sounding more aggrieved than surprised. "Seriously? Tell me this isn't about the café thing."

A tiny ray of hope shone through the doom.

The café thing. The café thing! Maybe Arlo hadn't come here in a misguided act of hubris after all. Maybe, *maybe* she'd come here to talk about the café thing!

"I—I wanted to apologize," she said.

Samson swung his legs down off the couch and sat upright, peering around at the office through squinted eyes. "And you couldn't do it in the light of day? What time is it?"

"Three, maybe? I was having trouble sleeping." True enough. She'd been awake all night, plagued by visions of faceless Michelle. "That was my client who bullied you. I shouldn't have brought her there."

Samson produced a phlegmy cough and rubbed his jaw again. There was nothing incredulous about his expression—no narrowing of the eyes or arching of the brows. He looked weary and . . . contemplative. But was that good or bad?

Arlo sucked in her bottom lip to keep it from quivering.

"I have a phone," he said finally. "You could have called."

The doom began to dissipate. He was buying it. She was saved!

"You're right." Arlo eyed the door again. Her future was out there waiting, bright and warm and fully intact. "I'll just go."

His voice arrived at her back as she was lunging for her escape. "Wait."

Arlo froze with the door handle in her fist. A hard lump formed in her throat.

"You came here to say something nice—to take responsibility for something, which is hard. I would know. So, uh . . . We should go somewhere. Let me buy you breakfast."

"I'm not hungry," Arlo said to the door.

"Coffee, then. There's a place down the street that's open all hours."

Arlo glanced over her shoulder to find Samson had cast off his blankets, a tiny bit of his penis visible through a hole in his boxer shorts.

She tightened her grip on the door handle and blurted, "I can't. I have things to do."

"Such as?"

"I have to get ready for work."

"At four in the morning?"

"It takes a long time to do my hair."

"Unless," he said, doubt creeping into his voice, "there was some other reason you came here?"

So close. She'd been so close.

She let go of the handle. "Of course not."

Ten minutes later, they slid into a red vinyl booth in what might've been the warmest diner of all time. Heat pressed on Arlo from all directions: the vent at her ankles; the faint shroud of steam and smoke overhead; the coal fire under her own ribs, which was slowly turning her organs to jerky.

"It's toasty in here," Samson said. "Aren't you toasty?"

"I'm fine." Arlo pushed her glasses up her nose. They slid back down. "I feel fine."

"Why don't you take off your coat?"

"Nah."

This was like hot yoga. Arlo would drip, and she would wobble, and she would hate every second. But after—oh, after! The relief! She would step outside, feel the brittle November cold on her face, and rip into Michelle Kowalski's file. Every second—every sweat droplet—brought Arlo closer to that moment.

"Maybe I'll have eggs." Samson flipped his menu. "But their French toast is really good here, too."

Soon Arlo would have a phone number. She could call Michelle later this morning.

"Oh, but the tostadas . . ."

Or—*or*—Arlo could show up at her house unannounced as a fun surprise. Why not? They were sisters. Arlo would stride right up to her door and knock loudly, confidently, with purpose.

"No, don't think that's the ticket. If I eat too much too early, it does weird things to my gut. I get really bloated and gassy, do you know what I mean? Have you ever had that?"

And finally, Michelle would have a face.

Samson clicked his tongue. "Did you decide?"

"Yes." Arlo hadn't meant to shout but definitely did.

A waitress in an ill-fitting blouse appeared with a notepad in hand. "Ready?"

Samson planted his elbows on the table and squished his fists in his cheeks, studying the menu with renewed fervor. "You go first."

Arlo ordered coffee and slid her menu across the table.

"What's the soup today?" Samson asked.

"No soup until ten," the waitress said.

He gave a grunt of disapproval. "Your eggs—are they free range?"

The waitress pouted. "What does that mean?"

Samson returned the frown. "I think I need another minute."

"Oh my God, pick something," Arlo said, for she could take this no longer.

"I don't know what I—"

Arlo stole his menu and passed it to the waitress. "He'll have eggs and toast. Sunny side up. Whole-wheat bread."

The waitress scribbled on her notepad. "You two are cute."

As she wandered away, Samson looked at Arlo with a kind of awe and said, "I didn't know it, but what you ordered just now was exactly what I wanted."

"I'm good at reading people," Arlo said. Sometimes, at least.

A flush crept up Samson's neck. "Look, you made all this effort to come and apologize for your, um, your client. I should also take responsibility for some things."

Arlo filled with foreboding. Surely, he wasn't about to—

"Your dad's funeral."

"We don't have to do this," she said.

"I took advantage of you. You were grieving, and I took full advantage. I'm sorry."

Arlo felt herself soften toward him. This poor man. He was trying so hard to change, to be better. The least Arlo could do, especially after breaking into his office late at night and stealing his stuff, was respond with a bit of honesty. "Thank you, but that's not necessary."

Arlo was an adult. Not one with a particularly high sex drive, but still. When the impulse struck, she deserved to bang whoever was present and willing. And the impulse *had* struck. The unsettling truth was this: Samson had capitalized on her grief, rubbing her back at Daddy's funeral and feeding her glass after glass of wine, but she hadn't particularly minded.

"I'm not saying it's okay to search out hookups at funerals, but for what it's worth, I"—oh God, she was about to say it—"really did want to sleep with you."

"But why? You're, I mean . . . Look at you. I'm sure you've got ten guys' numbers in your phone who you could've called. I don't see why you would pick me. I'm just some old guy."

Arlo had no good answer for this question.

You two are cute, the waitress had said. Cute how, exactly? Surely not as a couple. Samson was easy enough to talk to, especially for a lawyer, and he was handsome in a way. But as a partner? For Arlo? He was at least twenty years her senior. It was almost like having sex with—

Arlo sundered that thought.

"You don't give yourself enough credit," she said.

Samson crooked a brow. "You're saying I'm not an old guy?"

"I'm saying you're an *attractive* old guy."

"Oh," he said with a wry smile. "Well, thanks."

They shared a not-unpleasant silence.

"And on that note," Samson said, "excuse me for a sec while I use the bathroom. My bladder's not what it used to be."

Arlo watched the back of his head bob away over the tops of the other booths. Then she ripped open her coat.

Cool air lapped her clavicle, the notch of her throat, her armpits. It was swift. It was merciful. It was the air of the future.

She cracked open the file. The first page was blank but for one word: CONFIDENTIAL. A line near the top of the second page was marked BENEFICIARY. A trio of names followed, and time seemed to slow to a crawl:

Michelle Kowalski AKA *Michelle Morris* AKA *Mickey Morris*

Arlo clapped the file shut and sat on it.

"You look sick."

Samson slid back into the booth. A chipped brown mug full of coffee had appeared in front of Arlo, which meant the waitress must've returned at some point, too. Arlo wasn't sure how much time had passed, what with all the firecrackers bursting at the base of her skull. Each explosion obliterated another region of her hindbrain. Goodbye, pons. Farewell, medulla. Never again would these neurons direct Arlo's vital functions. Never again would she breathe, or sneeze, or swallow. Because Mickey. Because Mickey!

"Do you feel okay? Are you gonna throw up?" Samson reached across the table and draped a hand on her forehead.

Arlo batted him away.

A tiny part of her must have suspected. Their stories matched too cleanly: the dead dads, the mutual connection to Samson. And the way Mickey talked about Daddy, as if he were solely to blame for every ounce of pain and sorrow that had ever befallen her. Yet Mickey, rather than Arlo, would get his money. Mickey who had never really known him. Mickey who had so much growing of her own left to do. Arlo still didn't understand it. And she had to understand.

The firecrackers fizzled and fell quiet.

"What's she like?" Arlo asked, following an instinct. Samson must've known the truth. But he didn't know that Arlo knew, which presented some interesting possibilities. "Michelle."

"I'm sorry?" Samson gulped from a streaky glass of water.

"You met her, I'm assuming, or at least talked to her. Tell me. What's she like?"

"I can't confirm or deny—"

"Tom. It's okay."

He set his glass on the table and rotated it quarter turns at a time. "She's, you know, a person. She's got stuff like the rest of us. Issues. But she's caring, I think. Kind."

This was true; Arlo just hadn't expected to hear it from him. All the names Mickey had called Samson at the café—all the vitriol she'd hurled at him—and now he was calling her *kind*?

"What are her plans for the money? Do you know?"

Samson stared off into the distance for a moment, then laughed. "Part of me thinks she'll give it all away to charity or something. Someone who deserves it."

Yes, Arlo thought, as the pyrotechnics in her brain stem started up again. Mickey would do that.

MICKEY

"I think I might be having a seizure."

Chris rubbed his eyes and shrank into the collar of his peacoat. And fair enough. Industrial lights beat down on the converted warehouse, the floor an endless turf of trampoline pads that flexed and sprang and catapulted dozens—nay, hundreds—of tiny children into the air. They bonked noses, banged elbows. Burst open with screams and occasionally blood.

"Yeah, this place is kind of a nightmare," Mickey said, swirling the inch of backwash and foam at the bottom of her plastic beer cup. "That's why they serve booze."

They sat together on a bench at the sidelines, his left thigh almost brushing her right. Mickey could practically feel it, this not-quite-touch, his molecules fizzing up against hers.

Ian was out there in the middle, bounding up and down in a Darth Vader t-shirt and the lime-green knee-highs the trampoline park forced everyone to buy at admission. His hair had grown long, falling flat over his face every time he jumped and flouncing upward as he came plummeting back to earth.

"I still don't understand how a pair of socks could cost eighteen dollars," Chris said. "Also, you really didn't have to pay."

Between the socks, the price of admission, and the beer, today's excursion had cost Mickey almost a hundred bucks—more than half the funds left in her checking account.

"It's the least I can do after last time," she said. "And look how happy he is. This was a good suggestion."

"You mean it?" There was doubt in Chris's voice, but also hope.

"You're doing a great job." Mickey touched his knee in a way she thought would be sweet but turned out to be weird. Instead of laying her hand on him in a brief, delicate motion like a normal person, she'd sort of poked him by accident, tapping on his knee with two fingers like a morse code operator relaying news of a maritime disaster.

She retracted her hand and sat on it. This wasn't a date.

"Up till now I've had a hard enough time doing my own laundry and packing my own lunches."

"I know what you mean," Mickey said.

It was kind of a date. He'd asked her to hang out on a Friday night—to meet at an agreed-upon location at a specified time for no real reason except to enjoy each other's company. He was wearing a dressy-casual checked shirt and smelled of aftershave. She was wearing mascara and a real bra. So, yeah, maybe it was a date.

He shifted slightly, and boom, there it was—their legs were touching, fully touching now, just like that first night at his place. The rain, the Scotch. "I have a confession to make, on that note. I might've misled you about something."

Mickey swilled the last of her beer, steeling herself. He didn't mean what he'd said on the phone the other day. He didn't like her. He didn't feel anything toward her at all. She was nothing to him. A passing thought, a bit of fluff on the wind.

"I can't really cook." Chris inspected the creases of his palms. "That French dish I made you? It's one of three things I know how to make. Literally three. I'm thirty-six years old, and I still cycle between three meals."

All Mickey could think to ask was "What are the other two?"

"I can't tell you. It's too embarrassing."

"Come on," Mickey said. "Now you have to."

"Well, one is spaghetti."

"Obviously."

He hitched his knee on the bench and turned so that his whole shin pressed against the side of Mickey's thigh. "And for the other one, what I do is I make a grilled cheese sandwich—a really big one, right—then I heat up a jar of tikka masala sauce and use it as a dip. Sometimes I eat the leftover sauce with a spoon."

"Honestly, I think that sounds really good," Mickey said, trying hard to focus. *Thigh-shin contact!*

"It is really good! Thank you. I feel validated now."

They watched Ian in silence for a few moments.

"Why is he clucking like a chicken?" Mickey asked.

"He's weird," Chris said fondly. "Really fucking weird."

A whole future seemed to solidify as they laughed together. They would sit side by side like this on the couch in their apartment every morning as they drank French-pressed coffee. They would get a dog and call her Ruby. They would squabble over who stole the blankets at night and which color to paint the accent wall in the living room.

Mickey felt a dry itch at the back of her throat, remembered the empty cup in her hand.

Chris's expression sobered. "You're the first person who's made me feel like I could actually do this. You know—take care of someone. A kid."

Mickey glanced over her shoulder at the weary parents waiting in line at the concession stand, all of them puffy-eyed and stooped and ready, dear God, for a beverage. *Drinking is a learned behavior*, Arlo had said. But wasn't everything? Walking, talking, coughing into one's elbow. Learned behavior, learned behavior, learned behavior. Who cared? The holidays were coming, a season of early sunsets and maxed-out credit cards, and these people deserved a drink. *She* deserved a drink. So what if it was her fourth—fifth?—of the day.

"I still think Evie's coming back. I do. But in the meantime, I'm starting to think we'll be okay, me and him. And that's because of you." He shook his head. "Not that—I mean, I heard what you said on the phone about not being a stand-in for his mom. I get that. You're not her. You're you. Obviously, you're you. That sounded stupid."

Mickey stared at the shining residue at the bottom of her cup. Would it look desperate to shake those last few drops into her mouth? Probably, she figured. There was barely enough left to wet her lips.

"*Thank you* is what I'm trying to say."

Thoughts like these had come to occupy her mind day in and day out. How many minutes until the next drink. Where it would come from. What it would cost.

"You're welcome." She patted his knee again, this time in a matronly way, the way an elderly woman pats the knee of a great-nephew who's just brought her a slice of cake, before bolting to her feet. "I'm gonna get another. You want anything?"

He blinked a few times, the emotion clearing from his face. "I'm okay."

Mickey jogged over to the concession stand and joined the long queue. Despair set in. There was only one person working the till, which meant she'd be waiting forever.

The day of her thirty-fourth birthday, Mickey woke gasping for oxygen. She'd buried her face in the pillow sometime over the course of a nightmare she already couldn't remember—something to do with the waitressing job she'd quit over a decade ago. The past had a way of lingering in the body, tucking into brain folds and between molars and under ribs. Unfairly so.

She got out of bed and did not drink. She went to the bathroom and did not drink. She splashed her cheeks with water and patted them dry and slathered them with noncomedogenic SPF 30 face cream and did not drink. She put on a bathrobe and did not drink. In the kitchen, she tugged open the window blinds and stared at the foot of clean snow covering the alley and did not drink. She dropped the last slice of bread in the toaster and did not drink, and when it popped out brittle and blackened, she also did not drink.

Her mind devoted itself to non-drinking thoughts: what music she might play tonight, what food she might order, how all her clothes were such trash. She took every item from the dresser drawers—jeans, cardigans, midi skirts, maxi skirts—and found each of them wanting. Clothing piled on the floor.

Mickey laid back in the middle of all these wrong-looking, wrong-feeling clothes. She examined the ceiling stucco, and when it started to swim, she closed her eyes. When the darkness, too, became unbearable, she opened her eyes and examined the ceiling again. And so it went, open and shut, open and shut, until she sat up, shaking with sudden cold, and groped around for her phone. Twenty minutes had passed.

She staggered into the living room and wrapped herself in a blanket from the couch. The roots of her hair were damp with sweat, her skull brimming with heat while a chill spasmed through her limbs, as if her body could no longer make sense of the air around it.

But why? Today was no different than yesterday or the day before. Nothing had changed between this week and the last. This confusion, this pervasive sense of icky-ness—it was the therapist's doing. She'd prodded around in Mickey's psyche for sport, planting all kinds of ideas. Just because Mickey drank in the morning and on the bus and at the trampoline park, that did *not* mean she was like her father.

Mickey sank to the floor and stared up at a different ceiling, a different configuration of stucco. "I'm a completely dissimilar person!" she proclaimed.

If her father were there—if he'd ever shown up with that pecan pie—he would've gazed at Mickey proudly then and said, *You're right. Of course you're right. I am a villainous scumbag, a thief, a ruiner-of-everything, whereas you, my daughter, are a ray of sunshine, a brave and graceful heroine, a truly well-formed adult.*

She'd long forgotten the sound of his voice, but when he spoke in her imagination, it was with the deep sonorous timbre of James Earl Jones.

I mean—look at you! You have a bachelor's degree.

"That's true," Mickey said to the stucco.

You have a fern!

"Also true."

Then what are you so worried about?

Mickey sat up. Her subconscious was right: she could have a drink. It was her birthday, and she was thirsty, and the bottle of vodka was right there on the counter. There was no deeper meaning in it. She would have a small glass, jump in the shower, and begin the day again.

No clean glassware to be found, so Mickey splashed the vodka into a mug and held the mug for a long moment to prove she could wait. Then she tipped the mug against her lips and took a sip. Not a big sip, mind you—big enough to taste the stuff properly, but nothing crazy.

She swallowed it down, and the scattered pieces of the universe clicked back together. A little more light fell through the windows. Mama Cass's "Dream a Little Dream of Me" spiraled up from Mickey's turntable, a rope of a song so thick and real she could almost grab the thing and coil it around her wrists. Her body crooked and contracted to the rhythm.

Mickey put her empty mug in the sink, then took it out again. She felt good, so good she thought she'd pour herself another, and maybe another after that. She twirled around some more. If there was ever an occasion to dance, it was one's thirty-fourth birthday. Never mind that she was alone. Why was it socially acceptable to dance with others in the morning but not by yourself? Other thirty-four-year-olds happened to live with roommates or partners. Just because she didn't live that life . . . just because she didn't have anyone . . .

But Mickey did have people. A handful, at least. Three adults and one child would be attending her birthday dinner.

She halted mid-spin. Her birthday dinner. She still hadn't decided about the food, or her outfit, or anything. And she would have to clean, a prospect so crushing she fell to the floor again.

Mickey forgot about the mug and brought the bottle to her lips and took a gulp, because . . . because . . . because fuck it.

Daria arrived ten minutes early with a plastic cake container, a bottle of wine, and her cat. "You take," she said, thrusting the wine at Mickey's chest. "I will put cake in fridge."

She pushed inside and set Rybka on the ground. Both had a choppy way of moving, teleporting from one spot to another like characters in a bad stop-motion film. There one second, gone the next.

This was how Mickey knew she was very, very drunk.

To be fair, she'd been drinking all day, which she never did, like, practically ever. She never ever did this because she wasn't an alcoholic and thus didn't need to. Logic!

"Where is your decanter?" Daria called from somewhere.

Mickey shut the door, surprised to find herself still standing in front of it. As she did this, the door made a gushing sound so enchanting she couldn't help but open and close it several more times. *Prrssshhhhhhhhhhhh.*

"Mickey?"

She spun. "Mhmmm?"

Daria was standing there with her arms folded. "You have no decanter."

Mickey grunted apologetically. Was she supposed to own a decanter? Was it something all good adults owned, like a slow cooker? Because Mickey did own a slow cooker.

"I bring," Daria said, striding out into the hall again.

Mickey went into the kitchen to compose herself. Unless her self didn't need composing because her self actually wasn't that drunk? The reflection in the microwave door was hardly that of a shit-faced person. She was wearing eyeliner and lipstick and a gold velvet evening gown she hadn't even known she owned. The table had been set with plates and takeout containers. Indian, by the looks of it. There must've been a delivery guy at some point.

Daria took a piece of naan from the basket and promptly dropped it back inside. "Soggy."

Mickey jumped. She hadn't seen Daria return.

"What?" Daria held a glass decanter up to the light. It was a misshapen thing, with a wide base and a neck that stuck up at a weird angle. Wine pooled and shimmered at the bottom.

"Dintseeoothere."

Daria set down the decanter, her eyes at half-mast.

146

Mickey gave her head a shake. She hadn't meant to say it like that. Her tongue had grown too big for her mouth. Or her mouth had shrunk. One or the other. "Didn't . . . see . . ." She could form intelligible words. She could do it if she focused really, really hard. ". . . you . . . there."

Daria said something in Polish and walked away.

Mickey poured some wine. Rather, the wine poured itself, speeding through the spout and into the glass quite readily.

So, she was drunk. It wasn't her fault. Definitely, for sure, super-duper not her fault. As long as she kept her mouth shut, nobody else would know.

The apartment buzzer sounded, unleashing a blast of static.

With expert coordination of her limbs, Mickey strode slowly and purposefully toward the button on the wall that would admit her guest. She managed to press the button on only her second try and proceeded to stare at the door. When a knock finally arrived, Tom was standing in the hall with a bowl of what appeared to be salad.

"Happy birthday." He leaned forward and put one arm around her without touching his chest to hers, patting her back stiffly while cradling the salad bowl in his other elbow. Tears glittered in his eyes as he pulled back. "Shit. I wasn't going to do this. This time of year, you know. The holidays are coming. For me, right now, getting invited to something like this? I don't have a lot of, uh, community."

Mickey bent her mouth into a sympathetic frown and shrugged.

"Do you know what I'm trying to say?"

She put one hand on his shoulder and pressed the other to her own heart.

"Exactly." Tom nodded at the bowl. "Oh—I hope you like chia seeds."

He joined Daria in the living room, where the two exchanged introductions and eventually settled into a conversation about their favorite Wes Anderson movies while Mickey lingered back in the kitchen with her wine. So far so good. She could make it through this party. One great advantage to people being narcissists was that they could be counted on to talk about themselves. She wouldn't have to open her mouth once except to eat something. She should probably eat something.

Mickey grabbed the basket of naan and went to town.

". . . nothing like *The Royal Tenenbaums*," Daria said. "All his new movies, I swear, they are garbage."

"Do you actually think that? Tell me you don't actually think that." Tom threw Mickey a glance over the back of the couch. "What are you doing there by yourself?"

Addiction had nothing to do with Mickey. How could it? How could she, an educated, reasonably successful woman with a slow cooker, also be an addict? Addicts led far more exciting lives than hers. Addicts snorted coke off glass tables in smoky backrooms or popped little pills on dance floors while laser beams and strobe lights flew overhead. Mickey wasn't that. She was a kindergarten teacher.

"Bill Murray should retire," Daria said.

"That is the cruelest thing I've heard in my entire life," Tom said.

Daria laughed. Mickey had never heard Daria laugh before.

"I mean it," Tom said. "You're vicious."

Mickey ripped off another piece of naan with her teeth. She was plowing through the basket pretty fast, but whatever. She'd paid for it, presumably. And she could stop whenever she wanted.

The buzzer went again. Mickey took up her position by the door.

"Sorry we're late," Chris said. "Someone here took forever to get ready."

Smiling up at Mickey in a miniature bomber jacket, Ian held out a bouquet of lilies and baby's breath. "We got these for you. They smell really good." His recently cut hair had been gelled into a tiny mohawk. "Happy birthday."

Mickey's arms strained under the bouquet's surprising weight.

Ian began to sing: "Haaaappyyyyy biiiiirthdaaaaaaay tooooo youuuuuuuu. Haaaaappyyyy biiiiiiiiiirthdaaaaaay toooooo youuuuuuuuuuuuuuuu. Haaaaaaa—"

"Not yet, buddy," Chris said, patting Ian's shoulder. "Not yet."

Tom came around the corner. "Who's got the great pipes over here?"

Rybka strode in figure eights between everyone's legs.

"Why are her ears so big?" Ian asked.

"She is part leopard," Daria said.

Ian stroked between the cat's eyes. "Cool."

While her guests introduced themselves, Mickey slipped back into the kitchen and rummaged through the cupboards for a vase. The best she came up with was a dusty cylinder of purple plastic, something she'd bought at the dollar store a million years ago. She filled it at the sink and wrangled the flower stems inside. Poor things. A pity that such prize lilies had ended up like this. Mickey bowed her head for them.

Chris piled more biryani on his plate. "So, how's it feel? Another year older. Stupid question, isn't it? I don't know why people ask that. It's not like you're any different today than you were yesterday."

Mickey didn't mind his habit of overtalking. Any excuse to stare. The room had listed one degree for every minute that had passed since they sat down to eat, Chris the one focal point keeping her steady.

Tom was predictably optimistic: "People change every minute."

Daria was predictably incredulous: "You think this? Really?"

"To be human is to evolve," Tom said. "We struggle, and we grow. Simple."

"Not sure that's true in every case," Chris said lowly. He turned to the head of the table, where Ian sat on a stack of dictionaries

Daria had graciously supplied. "What do you think, buddy? Do people change?"

Ian moved some chicken tikka masala around his plate with a spoon. "I'm bigger than I used to be."

"That is so profound," Tom said.

Daria laughed for the second time that evening. So weird.

"You've hardly spoken a word all night," Chris said suddenly, his almond-shaped eyes boring into Mickey with the heat of a thousand suns.

She shrugged, trying to look casual while her heart withered in her chest cavity.

"Seriously," Chris said. "What's wrong?"

Daria interjected: "Leave her alone. Birthdays for women— you know, it's complicated."

Tom held up his hands. "Enough said."

For a brief, blissful moment, Mickey thought she was saved.

"Why are you sad?" Ian asked, a slight pout on his lips. Of course he'd be the one to put it like that. His keen child's eye had seen right through her bullshit.

Silence fell across Mickey's shoulders and pushed her down into the floor. Her guests were watching, utensils idle in their hands, the food on their plates forgotten. She had to give an answer—a coherent answer, ideally.

Mickey willed her liver to work faster. And behold! The alcohol left her blood milligram by milligram, the molecules dividing into finer and finer pieces until eventually they ceased to exist. She felt logic and reason and motor coordination returning to her body. When the next breath left her lungs, she would be stone-cold sober.

She sat tall, adopted a dignified facial expression, and said, "Sssssmyyybirday."

"Oh," Ian said, in a tone of such clear understanding Mickey wanted to put her head down on the table and never lift it again.

"Are you wasted right now?" Chris asked.

Mickey tried to voice a denial, but what emerged was a hiccup.

Daria's head was in her hands. Ironwrought, unperturbable Daria.

"You are." Chris was grinning. He thought this was funny. "You're completely wasted."

"Not," Mickey said.

Chris bumped shoulders with her in a soul-crushingly buddy-buddy way. "Don't be embarrassed."

Mickey found herself standing. She was not embarrassed. There was nothing to be embarrassed about. She said as much, or tried to. What came out was a jumble of verbs and pronouns and prepositions. She snatched the decanter off the table.

"Sit down, Mickey," Daria said.

But why should she? It was her apartment. It was her party. It was her fucking birthday!

"Don't swear in front of the kid," Tom said.

Had she said that aloud?

"Yes," Tom said.

The room slanted another ten degrees. Where was Mickey's glass?

Someone gripped her elbow.

"Hey," Chris said. "It's going to be—"

The air buckled into a million pieces.

Her hand was open, empty. Where had the decanter gone? She was holding it a moment ago.

Ian was clutching his face. His mouth hung ajar, and from it came the most unholy noise Mickey had ever heard. How such an enormous scream could pour from such a small person, she had no idea. All these sounds—Mickey had no room for them.

"It's his eye," someone said. "There's glass in his eye."

"Go," said someone else. "Go now. Where's his coat?"

"Don't be stupid. Call 911."

Mickey could no longer tell one voice from another. Panic had blended them. Her surroundings, too, had lost definition. Wood, glass, wine, human—it was all one: a great and terrible murk.

"Ian, buddy, it's okay. It's gonna be okay."

"Does it count as an emergency?"

"Of course, it's an emergency. He could lose his fucking eyeball."

"I promise, it'll be okay."

A child was hurt. A child was hurt, and it was Mickey's fault. She could still hear him wailing and gasping somewhere across the room, across the murk. She tried to swim through it, to reach him, but something caught her and pulled her back. Big arms bound her. She fought, kicked, yelled, anything, anything to get free, but nothing, nothing worked.

Her feet left the ground. Someone had scooped her up and was carrying her through the kitchen, down the hall, and into her room. Laying her on the bed.

"You're no help to him," Tom said. Yes, it was Tom. He materialized in front of her, a look of abject pity on his face. "You're no help to anyone like this."

ARLO

Arlo slotted the stolen file beside her non-stolen files, locked the cabinet, and closed the key in her fist, the jagged metal biting her palm. It was ten in the morning on a Monday, and she had plenty to do—sessions to prep, referrals to review. For some reason, though, she couldn't bring herself to do anything.

It was unethical, providing mental health counseling to one's half-sister. Especially unethical given that the half-sister in question probably had no idea. Unless she did know? Unless she'd known all along? But why seek therapy from the half-sister you've never met? It wasn't like Arlo could ask. She had to cease all communication with Mickey. Arlo would offer a vague excuse for why she could no longer be Mickey's therapist—something about caseload numbers—and that would be that.

Unless that was dishonest. Say Mickey hadn't known. Say this whole mess of a situation hadn't been her doing at all. In that case, she deserved to know the facts, and providing them would be the most ethical course of action.

Ethics. It had been her favorite course in grad school. How little she'd known then.

She opened her emails and scrolled to find the message she'd received that morning about Daddy's headstone, which was ready for installation. The picture showed a tall slab of pearly marble with carved colonnades on either side and an ornate, scroll-like top. It was perfect.

ADAM KOWALSKI
LOVING HUSBAND AND FATHER

Father of two, Arlo thought.

It occurred to her, not for the first time, how much easier it all might've been had she grown up with someone else in the house— someone older and wiser. Someone to tuck her in those evenings when Mother was busy performing a fad skincare routine with expensive serums and toners, and Daddy was busy sleeping on the sofa (or on the floor, or in a field somewhere). Someone to hold her close when two burly police officers brought Daddy home from said field. Arlo was only six or seven the first time it happened, but she remembered the moment with flashbulb acuity: Daddy at the front door, dress shirt hanging open, shoes gone, an arm around each officer because he couldn't stand on his own. The guns on the officers' hips. The cold hardwood floor under Arlo's bare feet as she stood there in her pajamas. And the look of shame on Daddy's face as he saw her seeing him. She would remember that look all her life.

Her ringtone filled the office, *Swan Lake* pushing into every corner. She recognized the number, had practically memorized it.

"Hello?" she said, a tingling sensation spreading through her chest.

Over the line came a heavy draught of breath. "Hi. It's Mickey— Mickey Morris."

Arlo squeezed the phone so tightly it hurt her hand.

"I was wondering if you might have any time today? I know we have an appointment booked for next week, but I—something— something happened, and I . . ." Mickey was crying. Weeping, by the sounds of it. Snotty, throaty, grief-inflected weeping.

Arlo spurred into action. "Let's take some breaths. Ready? In for one—two—three—four. Out for one—two—three—four—five—six."

Truthfully, Arlo could barely breathe herself. Mickey had reached out during a moment of crisis. This could be her catalyst, the turning point at which she finally acknowledged her need for serious help. And she did need serious help. That much was clear.

"Now, let's try again," Arlo said, not gleeful per se.

"I got hammered at my birthday party and dropped a wine decanter and the glass flew up into a little boy's eyeball."

"I see." Excited. Arlo was excited about this. How could she not be?

"They had to sedate him in the ER."

"Were you there for this?"

"No. Tom wouldn't let me go."

Tom. Tom?

"They saved the eye, thank God," Mickey continued. "He has to wear a patch for a while, but eventually it'll be like it never happened."

"Oh, good. I'm so glad."

This birthday party had razed Mickey's old self and all the lies it fed on. From the charred detritus would rise a new woman, a new life, and Arlo would be there to sow the seeds, to sprinkle the water, to—to—

No, Arlo wouldn't be there. She couldn't be.

Mickey sniffled. "Yeah. But it's just—it's just—"

"It's too much. That's fair." Arlo clicked through her Google calendar. "I've got an opening at three this afternoon. Why don't you come by, and we'll talk it through. Together."

She stared at the computer screen for a long time after they'd hung up.

During case review that afternoon, Punam's flowy white top and braided side-bang, along with the way she lorded over the conversation, gave her the air of a warrior queen in an HBO fantasy series, and not in a good way. Near the end of the meeting, she said, "I got an email from one of your clients."

Arlo gripped the edge of the table. Mickey knew they were sisters. Somehow, Mickey knew, and worse yet, she knew that Arlo knew and that Arlo had kept the information to herself. Maybe their call this morning had been a test. Maybe Mickey had hung up the phone and gone straight to Punam to complain.

"The gymnast with PTSD. What's his name?"

Arlo let go of the table, the tension softening in her shoulders and arms. "Oh. George?"

"Yes—George," Punam said. "It was a glowing review."

"Good. That's good." Arlo was pretty sure she said this aloud.

"I've supervised a lot of therapists in my life. I've never had one of their clients email me with praise." Punam did not sound particularly impressed.

"Might have more to do with him than me."

"It might." Punam wrote something on a notepad in microscopic printing. She hadn't taken many notes today. She hadn't needed to. They'd skated through Arlo's caseload in record time. "Alright—out with it."

Arlo searched Punam for signs of displeasure, disappointment, ambivalence, anything. Her cheeks had a sullen way of sagging, and her brows stitched together somewhat angrily—but then she always looked like that. "Out with what?"

"Something's got you stumped."

Hardly! Arlo didn't get stumped. She worked through problems with empathy and patience. "It isn't a conflict of interest. More of an ethical . . . sticking point. A gray area."

"And you can't tell me anything else?"

She could tell Punam everything. Now would be the time.

"I don't think so, no," Arlo said.

"Well, these things come with the job. One time, I—" Punam laughed. "One time—oh my God, I forgot about this—I had a client who was facing spousal abuse. Physical, verbal, financial. Nasty stuff. And you know where the husband happened to work? My office. Different department, but I saw him every day. Sat beside him in meetings. And you know what?"

"What?" Arlo asked, indulging her.

"It's like this," Punam said, and thank God. Thank God Punam was here to tell Arlo *how it was*. "You have two selves. One version belongs to you, the other to your client."

Once again, Arlo felt Laura Hedman's presence as keenly as if the nineteen-year-old had wandered through the door and joined them at the table. It wasn't fair. There wasn't enough space.

"The moment a client leaves after a therapy session, I forget they exist. Everything they said, every disclosure they made—it's all gone. Because a different me holds that information. By the same token, of course, I have to forget my personal self while I'm working with the client. I have to leave my own feelings and problems and baggage behind when we enter that room together."

Arlo wasn't, like, a killer. It wasn't like she'd given Laura the pills and said, *Have at 'er.* She'd said some unhelpful things, yes, but what difference did it make? In all likelihood, Laura would've killed herself no matter what Arlo said or did. Even if Arlo had been at her best that day, it probably wouldn't have made any difference.

"The question becomes Can you do it? Within this ethical sticking point of yours, can you maintain that separation?"

Punam covered her mouth with two fingers, waiting, Arlo realized, for an answer.

Mickey wasn't Laura. Mickey was on the brink of meaningful change, and it was within Arlo's power to nudge her over the finish line. Mickey could get sober and stay sober. She could succeed where Daddy had . . . not quite. And if that meant Arlo needed to divide herself—to split her own mind down the middle, one half to give away and one to keep—then so be it.

◎

"Thanks for fitting me in."

Mickey stripped off a dingy gray scarf and balled it in her lap. She looked wan without any makeup, her lashes stubby and faint.

Arlo saw the resemblance now, and it struck her as terribly ironic. That Mickey would look so much like Daddy . . . Mickey who rejected him, who hated him, who hadn't really known him at all. Were Arlo not so skilled at compartmentalizing her own feelings, she might've called it an injustice. How unfair that Mickey should have Daddy's money *and* his cheekbones. His slender nose. His wide-set eyes. She had his whole face—which was maybe why, despite everything, Arlo wanted so badly to reach across the table and hug her.

"No problem." Arlo shifted in her seat. She couldn't quite get comfortable, her bones crushing together at strange angles. "It sounds like you could really use someone to talk to."

Mickey shrugged, and together they spiraled down into the silence.

The wall clock moved faster than usual, its hands swatting away the time as Arlo blinked and breathed and waited. One minute . . . two minutes . . . three minutes . . .

Mickey looped the scarf around her neck and yanked it off again. She clutched opposite elbows and rocked forward and back in her seat—suffering, clearly, and no wonder.

When Mickey did finally speak, it was in so low a voice she sounded like someone else. "Nothing good comes from it."

"From what?" Arlo asked, fizzing inside.

"Vodka."

And there it was: a change point. A breakthrough.

Mickey shook her head. "Not just vodka. Wine. Other things."

"What does the drinking give you?" Arlo asked. The first time she'd posed this question, Mickey hadn't been ready to answer it. But that was then. This was now. They'd entered a new, post-decanter-smashing world. "What does it add?"

Mickey's gaze settled somewhere above Arlo's left shoulder. The mirror. She was looking in the observation mirror. Having a deep moment of introspection? Reckoning with her self-destructive impulses and resistance to meaningful interpersonal connection?

"You know when you're outside—driving or walking around or whatever—and the sun is so bright it hurts?" Mickey said. "And you put on some sunglasses, and all of a sudden, wow, everything is so much better? So much easier? It's like that."

"You get a sense of escape," Arlo said.

"Sometimes. Other times, I drink because I know I'm going to, if that makes sense. Almost like it's already happened. All I'm doing is following along, reading the script."

I don't know what to tell you, Daddy would often say, when Arlo caught him drinking (or snorting, or both). *This is me. This is just what I do.*

"Your idea with the sunglasses," Arlo said in a perfectly steady voice, because she was a professional, an expert professional, and she was talking to her client right now, not her sister. "It's like this: they shield your eyes from that painful sun, yes, but they also keep you from seeing the world as it really is. Maybe you stumble around because you can't see the ground too well. Any coping strategy is great so long as it's working. For you, the drinking . . . maybe it's not doing the trick anymore."

Mickey said nothing. She hadn't glanced away from her reflection.

"What thoughts are showing up for you right now?" Arlo asked.

"My dad. Memories of him."

Arlo swallowed hard. "Go on."

Mickey's gaze snapped away from the mirror and landed on the Kleenex box on the table between them. "He used to drag my mom off to these parties and tell her what to wear, what to say. Then they'd get home and he'd call her a slut for something stupid. Even though he was the one who slept around. Everyone knew. I was a little kid, and I knew."

Yes, that did sound familiar.

"She couldn't call him on it or else he'd say, 'You're being dramatic. It didn't happen like that.' Then he'd sit down on the couch and tell her to get him a beer."

Also familiar—the lying, the cheating. The flagrant if not cliché pattern of emotional abuse. But that was the disease, not Daddy. Daddy was kind. Daddy was generous. Flawed? Sure. But he went to AA sometimes. He tried his best. He was a good person, fundamentally.

"He was a fundamentally terrible person."

Heat flushed through Arlo's chest. "And you don't want to be like him."

Mickey nodded.

"So, then, uh—what, um . . ." Arlo realized, with a sudden ache in the back of her throat, that she had absolutely no idea what to say next. She coughed to buy some time. Coughed again. Grabbed a tissue and wiped some imaginary snot from her nose. Crumpled the tissue and threw it in the bin. "Sorry—give me a sec here."

Therapy was a dance. Most days, she knew exactly where to step and when. Now, the rhythm escaped her. The words wouldn't come. But then she remembered Daddy's belly laugh, and the cheeky way he revved the Harley, and his Tigger impression, and suddenly the way forward was clear. "What else was he?"

Mickey twitched. "What?"

"Nobody is only one thing," Arlo said, and there it was, there was the beat. She'd found it again. "What else was he?"

"You're saying it doesn't matter that he used to gaslight my mother?"

"Of course it matters. But if you had no warm feelings toward your dad at all, then you wouldn't feel his absence like this. The way I see it, loss is the other side of love."

Arlo couldn't quite hear Mickey's response, but it sounded like "Oh, Christ."

"There must've been other parts of him—other facets to his personhood—that you appreciated. Parts of him you miss."

Daddy couldn't be reduced to the debris he'd left in his wake. Yeah, okay—he was a little bad. He was also good. He was kind and cruel and thoughtful and ignorant. He was all kinds of things! That was the complex reality of human beings—a reality that Mickey's all-or-nothing thinking style couldn't accommodate. Yet.

"Facets to his personhood." Mickey clicked her tongue. "Let's see . . . facets. Hmmmm. Facets, facets, facets."

Arlo waited her out.

"He was, um, a singer." Softly, almost a whisper—"He used to sing all the time."

Yes, always. Springsteen hits, especially.

"What else?" Arlo asked.

"He was a gardener. He liked to grow things. Herbs, I remember. There was a big long planter in the kitchen on the windowsill. A massive thing of basil. Massive. Every time he went to the sink, he would stick his nose in there for a sniff."

Arlo's hands buckled into fists beneath the table. "What else?"

"He was silly. He used to do funny voices for me." A haze descended over Mickey's eyes. "Tigger. He could do a mean Tigger."

Arlo would not, could not, cry.

"He left me some money when he died," Mickey added. "A lot of money."

Any satisfaction Arlo had garnered from this conversation instantly withered away.

"But to receive it—to access it, I guess—the will said I had to do therapy."

Arlo blinked. That—what Mickey had just said—didn't make any . . . any . . .

"He left me vouchers for seven sessions with you. Three more after today."

Mickey sounded far away. The room and all its contents had receded somehow, as if Arlo were staring into a long tunnel.

"Do you believe that? He left us. Abandoned us. And now, all these years later, he gets to be the hero who finally fixes me? I mean, look at you. Your reaction. You're shocked. Because it's shocking. The self-righteousness, the cowardice. Isn't it so wrong?"

It was so, so wrong.

"You know what I'm gonna do? I'm gonna stop drinking." Mickey dusted her hands, as if that did anything, as if that could really be the end of it. "I'm just gonna stop."

Arlo struggled to assemble the facts. Daddy had snatched away her inheritance and given it to someone else, a practical stranger, and on top of that, he'd had the balls to charge Arlo with said stranger's psychological well-being. Yes, that was the gist of it. And it actually made sense in a perverse way. Arlo had been such a good girl, a good daughter, always jumping in to clean up Daddy's messes. Why not this one, too? He probably hadn't thought twice about it. *This is me. This is just what I do.*

"I'll drink juice instead. Juice is great." Mickey was blubbering now, mopping her cheeks with the scarf. "Oh my God, what's wrong with me?"

A lot was wrong with Mickey Morris. Challenges. She had a lot of challenges. But then, Arlo was a good therapist. She could steer clients in all sorts of directions.

"I need to nip this in the bud," Mickey said. "Before it becomes a real problem."

Three sessions from now, this woman would walk away with all Daddy's money. Or maybe she wouldn't. Who knew what might happen between now and then, what decisions Mickey might make, if only Arlo could foster a little more self-awareness from her. Three sessions gave them one hundred and fifty minutes of therapy.

They could achieve a lot in one hundred and fifty minutes.

MICKEY

Mickey skirted a trio of construction workers waiting to cross at the stoplight and plowed straight across the road. Her pants didn't quite cover her ankles, which was bad news on a blowing-snow, biting-wind day like today. Stupid pants. Stupid winter. Everything in the whole world was stupid, and of all this stupid, stupid stuff, Mickey was by far the stupidest thing of all.

A city bus plodded past. Mickey could've been on it—but then she wouldn't have suffered, and suffering was the whole point of this trudge. Mickey deserved all the pain she could drum up. The shaking and the sweating and the low-grade fever weren't enough.

The houses grew taller, slimmer, sleeker. Spasms overtook her body every few blocks, and she had to pause, groping the nearest For Sale sign or utility pole for stability. Her vision blurred with pickup trucks and BMWs, bushy Christmas wreaths and giant inflatable reindeer. It was only mid-November, but Rudolph's simpering face was everywhere.

Nineteen hours since her last drink. And it *would* be her last. No need for helplines or AA meetings or thousand-dollar-per-day treatment centers. A lot of people quit cold turkey. She wasn't even quitting, per se, because to quit something implied a kind of dependence. Drinking was an unhelpful habit, like when Mickey left her clean laundry in a heap on an armchair because she was too lazy to fold it. The drinking simply had to stop; and stop, it would.

After dragging herself up the porch steps, Mickey crunched her fingers into a fist and knocked.

Ian's pallid face glowed between the plush green jaws of what appeared to be a fleece dinosaur costume. A black patch covered his left eye. "Hi, Miss Mickey."

She remembered the sound of the decanter smashing, and Ian screaming, and her guests squabbling over what to do, and Ian screaming some more, and it took all her concentration to stay upright. "Hi, Ian."

He glanced back over his shoulder. "I was just watching my show."

"I'm not staying. I came to say . . ." No point in lying. He understood everything, this child. All she could do was turn up and look him in the eye (singular) and ask forgiveness. "I drank too much wine the other night. It made me silly. I'm very sorry."

He gave a gracious little shrug Mickey did not deserve. "It's okay."

Another voice carried from inside. "Ian? Who is it?"

A young woman appeared in the doorway wearing a white bandeau top and baggy jeans, a glass of purple smoothie in hand.

Mickey felt a peculiar desire to cover herself. Before now, she'd glimpsed Ian's mom only in passing at pick-up and drop-off in the schoolyard. Up close, Evelyn was unnervingly pretty, even without makeup, and her dark shiny hair, gathered into a perfect topknot, brought to mind the kind of horror-movie ballerina who descends into madness and eventually murders everyone.

"Mom, you remember Miss Mickey." Ian gestured from one to the other and back again, as if this was an interdepartmental office mixer. "Miss Mickey, Mom."

Mickey offered a smile. Ian's mom returned it, her teeth so beaming and white they left an afterimage on Mickey's retinas.

"I—I'm sorry. I didn't mean to drop the—the thing." Mickey couldn't remember the name for it all of a sudden. Woozy, she planted a hand on the brick exterior of the townhouse. "It slipped right out of my grip."

"Kiddo, go play." Ian's mom shooed him inside and closed the door halfway. Her smile shrank and shrank and finally disappeared. "The glass in his eye is one thing. I mean, I'm not sure why my kid was at his teacher's birthday dinner in the first place. But it was an accident. I get that. Then I find out that you also, like, abducted him."

Were it not for the knee-buckling force of that phrase—*abducted*—Mickey might've laughed. "That day after school? I drove him home, that was all. Jean wanted to call child protective services. They might've taken him into care."

"That's kind of beside the point."

As Evelyn swirled her smoothie, Mickey imagined her chucking ripe blackberries into a blender and sealing the lid tight. Standing back while the blades chopped everything up.

Mickey's stomach churned. "Where's Chris?"

He would vouch for her. He would explain. Unless he wouldn't? Unless Mickey had sufficiently repelled him. Neither of the two dinners they'd shared had gone particularly well.

"Dunno," Evelyn said.

A terrible thought took root. "You wouldn't—I mean—you're not going to complain, are you?" she asked. "To the school?"

"I haven't decided yet."

Here came another wave of nausea. Legit or not, a complaint like this really would be the end of Mickey's teaching career. No more songs, no more dances. No more penguin crafts.

"Please don't. Maybe we could—I mean, there has to be a way to settle this between the two of us. Some way I can make it right. I—I'll do extra tutoring for free."

Evelyn sipped her smoothie, then sipped it again, taking her sweet time, wiping the corners of her mouth with a pinkie finger. And Mickey knew exactly what this was going to take.

"I'll help with your expenses for a while." Why not? With a bit of extra cash, Evelyn could buy Ian a new winter coat, enroll him in skating lessons. Maybe even find their own place. And it was no skin off Mickey's teeth. She would be a rich woman soon. "I could give you a grand or two, just to keep you in the green?"

Evelyn was silent.

"Five grand?"

Nothing.

"Ten?"

"I was thinking more like fiftyish," Evelyn said with another blinding smile.

Mickey's heart didn't sink so much as plummet through her abdomen. Of course, Evelyn had been *thinking* about it. She'd heard the story of Ian's eye and seen an opportunity for fast cash. Here was another trap Mickey had walked straight into.

"Fiftyish?" Mickey said. "Ish?"

"Fifty. Yeah. Let's say fifty."

There would be no skating lessons or winter coats, Mickey realized. Evelyn would blow the money on designer sneakers or wine subscriptions or some kind of all-inclusive breathwork retreat in the Caribbean—a lavish and lengthy trip to get her away from Ian. Again.

Evelyn stepped backward into the house. "Are you okay? You look, like, really sick."

Mickey had never felt so gut-twistingly ill in her entire life. "I'm fine."

"Well, that's good. Phew, it's chilly." The door was closing, framing Evelyn's lovely, dainty, perfectly punchable face. "I'll take ten grand in two weeks and the rest by Christmas."

A dart of panic flew through Mickey's chest. Not a dart—a poison-tipped arrow. A javelin. She wouldn't be done in therapy for at least another month, the inheritance a distant glimmer on the scorched, post-nuclear horizon of her life. "I—I can't get it to you that soon. I don't have it yet."

"Three weeks, then," Evelyn said brightly.

The door pounded shut.

Mickey stomped away, heart racing, arms pumping, brow dripping with sweat.

That was Ian's mom? That silly, self-interested, would-be H&M model sipping from a fucking smoothie? Ian deserved better. Mickey deserved better. After everything she'd done to keep social services away from this family. After everything she'd done to keep Ian at home.

Home. What a concept!

How different Mickey's life might've been had she known a proper home. Had she grown up here, for example, in one of these narrow townhouses with *Let It Snow* doormats, there might not be so much pain spiking through her gut right now. She might've made real friends. She might've formed different habits.

Mickey stopped in front of a brick duplex with one of those stupid inflatable reindeer in the yard. Swaying in the breeze, the ungulate seemed to mock her. Rudolph, the smug asshole.

She drilled the toe of her shoe straight at the reindeer's belly. Affixed to the lawn by a series of bungee cords, the reindeer toppled onto its side before swinging upright.

Mickey kicked it again. And again. Each time, the reindeer righted itself.

Other people didn't have these problems. Other people were born into families where love poured freely, and there was no turning the tap on and off at will. Other people's dads didn't walk out on their families at eight o'clock on a Tuesday night. Or if they did walk out, then they at least had the decency to turn up twenty years later with an apology and some fucking pie!

"Hey!"

Mickey glanced up to find a very large man looming at the front door.

"What the hell are you doing?" He seized a shovel (also very large) from a nearby garden bed.

She ran. Across the street, down an alley, and up another alley. Through blurring scents of garbage dumpsters, laundry room vents, and backyard firepits. Around golden retrievers, baby strollers, and games of street hockey. Across patch after patch of ice.

Two or three blocks later, she dropped onto all fours and came to sit crisscross-applesauce on the sidewalk. Because yes, this was her life right now. She was rocking back and forth on the cold ground, facing immense debt and cramping in places she'd never cramped before. Worst of all, she was alone.

But maybe she didn't have to be.

There was only one option. Well, there were a few. But one option—one person—stood out as the least humiliating.

"He's not here," said the receptionist forty-five minutes later, when Mickey lurched through the elevator doors and asked to see Tom.

"What do you mean 'he's not here'?"

"He's not in."

"He's always in."

"You could try calling him?"

Mickey paced the waiting area and dialed Tom's cell.

"Hello?"

"You're not at work," she said, so loudly that the DoorDash guy waiting for the elevator flinched and gave a small cry.

"I'm not always there," Tom said, "despite what you may think."

"Can we talk? In person. It's kind of urgent."

The resulting silence was long enough that Mickey checked to see if he'd hung up.

"I'll be there in twenty," he said.

Those twenty minutes were to be the longest and slowest of Mickey's life. She flicked through a copy of the *Wall Street Journal* and tried to read an article about cryptocurrency, but the topic was too boring, and the room was spinning too violently. She ducked into the bathroom and puked, which helped with the nausea but worsened the ache in her core muscles. It hurt to sit, to stand, to move, to stay still, to close her eyes, to keep them open.

But she had been right to come here. Even if Mickey sold her TV, her laptop, and her slow cooker, she would still be at least eight grand short of the first payment.

Shortly after Mickey limped back into the waiting area and slumped into another chair, Tom appeared in emerald-green track pants and a matching jacket.

"What are you wearing?" she asked.

"It's Saturday." With an unsubtle glance at the receptionists, he pulled Mickey upright, clopped a hand between her shoulder blades, and steered her into the elevator. As the doors shut, he turned to her gravely, a shining mass of athletic wear, and asked, "Are you on something?"

For all the places Mickey had turned up drunk in her life—lecture halls and potlucks and baptisms—no one had ever asked her this question.

"I haven't had a drink all day." Twenty-one hours and twenty-seven minutes.

"Are you in . . . you know . . ." He made an ambiguous gesture, swirling the air with one hand. "It can be very dangerous."

Withdrawal, he meant. But that wasn't possible. Mickey wasn't in withdrawal because Mickey wasn't an alcoholic.

"This is going to sound weird," she said, holding fast to the elevator railing, "but I would please like to borrow eight thousand dollars if that's okay."

Tom winced. "Mickey, I . . . I can't."

"Why not? You're made of money."

"It's enabling."

It took her a moment to understand his meaning. "No—it's not like that. I'm being blackmailed." This was at least fifty percent true. "Ian's mom is blackmailing me."

The elevator whooshed to a halt and spat them out into an echoing foyer. Tom's hand was on Mickey's back again, pushing her through a thin haze of people.

"Stop that." Mickey shrugged him off.

"Sorry, sorry." He stepped off to the side, sat on a leather bench by a big window, and waved for her to join—which she did, like an obedient dog.

She had the will at least to remain standing. She needed to make herself tall.

"I'll help you find a treatment program. I've got a buddy who went through a residential thing a couple years back. I'll call him right now." Tom patted the place next to him on the bench. "Here—come sit."

Mickey shaded her brow. The lights hurt. "This is a completely unrelated issue."

"Come on." His tone was doubtful, almost mocking.

"A thousand dollars?" Fuck this guy. "Can you lend me that much?"

"Mickey . . ."

"Couple hundred bucks. Anything would help."

"You must see that this—you, how you are—isn't right. You're sick. And me handing over a bunch of cash? It wouldn't help in the long run."

Rage crackled through her. How many times in Mickey's life had someone presumed to know what was best for her? What she was. What she needed.

She pulled her shoulder blades onto her back. "I thought we were friends, but you know what? Maybe not. Friends actually listen to each other. Friends believe each other. Friends certainly don't shit on each other like this."

She dragged herself outside and collapsed against a wall, resting her head on a NO LOITERING placard.

The sign for a business across the street flickered neon green in the falling snow.

○

There were no stools, so Mickey planted her forearms on the bar top and clasped her hands and hoped to God she would stay upright.

"I'll be with you in one sec, babe." Flexing an ultra-cut bicep, the bartender pulled one of the twenty taps and caught a stream of something dark and frothy in a pint glass. Like everyone else in this hipster microbrewery, she was all smiles, saturated with dopamine from the active lifestyle she probably lived, the weights she probably lifted on her days off, the omega-3s she probably consumed. Everywhere Mickey turned, people were aglow, chatting, laughing, petting the resplendent Bernese mountain dogs that lay curled on the cement floor between mismatched couches and lawn chairs. Under the twinkly lights, everyone seemed to sparkle.

Mickey watched beer flow from the tap. Nothing was stopping her from vaulting over the bar, shoving the girl aside, and sticking her whole head right there, right under that stream. The beer would flood her mouth hard and fast enough to make her choke.

The bartender threw Mickey a glance as she passed the pint to a waiting customer. "Are you okay? You look super—"

"I know how I look." Mickey scanned the chalkboard menu behind the bar. There were too many choices—sours, stouts, porters, IPAS. "What would you recommend?"

"Do you like hops?"

"I don't know." Mickey had never fully understood what hops were; past a certain age, it seemed impudent to ask.

"Do you like citrus?"

Mickey hadn't eaten a fruit or vegetable in at least seven days. "I don't know."

The bartender stepped forward into the light, and her wrinkles sharpened—crow's-feet, forehead lines, brackets around the mouth, what were those called, smile lines. She was older than Mickey had first thought. "What do you like better—light or dark beer?"

"I don't know." Mickey didn't know anything. She was a useless, ignorant blob who couldn't be counted on for even the simplest task. She couldn't even order a beer.

The bartender grimaced. "Are you sure you're alright? You're sweaty and sort of gray."

Unsurprising. Mickey's heart was pounding at a rate of at least 130 beats per minute. Her fingertips had grown numb. She was starting to see spots. "Give me anything. Truly. I don't care so long as it comes in a glass and contains alcohol."

The bartender fiddled with a buckle on her denim overalls.

"You remind me of my mom," Mickey said, only realizing it as the words left her mouth.

You have a problem, Mama had said, *a problem only you can fix*. That was the day she absolved herself of their relationship in the name of boundaries and her own wellness. Because Mickey was a disease that entered people's bloodstreams and made them unwell.

A glass of blonde ale appeared on the bar top. Notes of honey and peach floated up. Beads of condensation trickled down. Mickey brought her palms to the glass and felt the cold seep in. This beer was perfect, so perfect she couldn't inflict the damage of drinking it. She, small and broken and on the verge of vomiting again, was undeserving of this beautiful thing.

"It's okay if you don't want it."

The bartender was at Mickey's side all of a sudden: a soothing presence. Her messy bangs and crow's-feet conveyed a certain warmth, and she smelled like weed.

"Really?" Mickey asked.

"You've been staring at it for like seven minutes."

"How strange," Mickey said.

"Should I take it back?"

Mickey pulled her hands off the glass and wiped them on her pants. "Please."

The woman took the beer and retreated behind the bar. She placed the glass on a counter back there, where it glowed like a distant lantern. The room had darkened, the people and the dogs and the mismatched furniture all fuzzing together.

Mickey opened her wallet and pawed around for the cash she knew wasn't there.

"It's cool," said the bartender, with merciful nonchalance. "Seriously."

"Thank you," Mickey managed to say. She took out her phone; it was dead. "Hey—any chance you could call someone for me?"

—

She puked twice in the ambulance. The paramedics were kind. The nurses, too. They gave her a dose of valium, a juice box, and a pack of miniature chocolate chip cookies and put her on a gurney in the corner of the ER, where she would stay for the next several hours. The nausea got better, but the shame got worse, her slouch deepening with every compassionate glance from another health professional. The social worker from last time—Vera—was hanging around the nurses' station.

"I'll take this one," she said without any apparent attempt to lower her voice. "I know her."

The smell of cigarettes, dirty and sweet, filled Mickey's nose as Vera approached.

"Hey, honey. You want some more juice?" Vera flashed her yellow teeth.

"I think I'm good." Needing to do something with her hands, Mickey popped another cookie, which disintegrated into a candied paste on her tongue and took quite some time to swallow.

"Glad you came in," Vera said. "Detox is some nasty shit."

The doctors were monitoring Mickey for seizures, heart problems, and hallucinations, among other things.

"What's your plan?" Vera asked. "For after."

After. How was Mickey supposed to know what to do after? She owed Evelyn ten grand in a week. She had no job, no assets. She'd lost Ian. She'd lost Tom. There could be no more chicken dinners with Chris now that she was a person who drunkenly injured small children and was *known* to social workers. And the worst part—Mickey's deepest shame—was that these losses barely even registered. They were scrapes and scratches compared to the deep wound that had opened up inside her and now refused to close. Because all Mickey really wanted at that moment, on the most primal level, was a drink.

"This is the worst part, right? It must be the worst part."

Vera flipped through the papers on her clipboard. "You've got a shrink, right?"

Mickey's attention drifted to the translucent yellow box on the wall and the spiky shadows inside. To the left hung a poster about proper handwashing technique. This was a sad place, where she'd ended up. "Yeah, I've got a shrink."

"That's a good start." Vera's tongue made a slurping sound as it suctioned to her top front teeth. "I've got an in with the people at SkyView, you know. Big place on the West Coast. You like horses? They've got horses. Expensive as all hell, though. Would your dad chip in?"

"My dad?"

"Guy in the suit. Going gray. Kind of sad-looking."

She meant Tom.

"No," Mickey said. "My dad would not chip in."

"We can look at some other funding. There are cheaper programs out there, too, but SkyView's really the best. Better to invest up front and get the right treatment."

Mickey squeezed her juice box a little tighter. When had she agreed to treatment?

Vera clicked and unclicked her pen. "I'll do some digging and—"

"I'm good, actually," Mickey said.

She expected a pause, a hefty silence, a worried look. But Vera didn't miss a beat. "Gotcha. Works for me."

Mickey hit the bottom of her juice box with a final sputter of sweetness through the straw.

Vera held out a taxi chit. "See you next time."

ARLO

"Baby, It's Cold Outside" was playing as she walked in, the humid salon air suffused with cheer and a faint scent of peppermint. On a normal day, Arlo would've found Christmas music charming, even in mid-November. Today, somehow, it was an insult.

"Good timing," Deborah said, glancing over at Arlo as she helped an elderly customer rise from the hairdresser's chair. "I'm just finishing up with Mrs. Tremblay."

While waiting, Arlo took a miniature candy cane from a jar on the reception counter and shattered it between her teeth. Her phone rang.

PRIVATE CALLER

Probably a client. Arlo speared the decline button.

She'd woken that morning, a gray Monday, with the day's appointments weighing on her chest. The gymnast with PTSD at nine, the depressed homemaker at ten, the hypochondriac pharmacist at eleven, the rancher with BPD at twelve, half an hour for lunch, then an extra-long block of therapy with the army couple. They were all highly courageous, highly resilient people, and Arlo cared about them deeply. She really did. They were just such big talkers, all of them, and big criers, too. And today, well, she simply didn't have the space to hold their sorrows. Rather than risk burning herself out, she'd done the wise thing and cleared her schedule. Clients were gracious, in her experience, and she doubted anyone would complain. Besides she was allowed three personal days per year, no questions asked. Why not get her bangs trimmed?

Her phone again:

PRIVATE CALLER

Arlo turned it off and stowed it away.

"You've got some great natural highlights," Deborah said a few minutes later as Arlo settled into the salon chair. She mussed Arlo's bangs, flattened them, and mussed them again, as if there were nothing weird about Arlo showing up here for the second time in a month. As if Arlo were just another paying customer and not Deborah's daughter's sister. Arlo felt gratitude, then guilt, and could explain neither. "You want a shampoo?"

At the sink, Arlo sat with her legs outstretched and her head tipped back. Fake garlands drooped from the ceiling panels.

"Day off today?" Deborah asked.

"Playing hooky." Water rushed against Arlo's scalp and filled her ears, washing the clients off her brain for a few blissful seconds before they grew back again. How the gymnast hitched his knee up and down all session long. How the army husband blubbered.

"Good for you," Deborah said. "Life is short."

A cap clicked open. Shampoo squirted. Deborah's fingertips drew circles into Arlo's scalp, shooting sparks down her spine while a fruity smell stormed her nose.

"What do you do again?" Deborah asked.

"I'm a receptacle for other people's pain."

"What?"

"I'm a psychologist."

"Right. I forgot." Here came the water again. "You seen any good movies lately?"

Arlo tried not to frown. This was the hairdresser talk—the mindless chitchat Deborah must've dispensed on every customer who walked through the door. It wasn't what Arlo wanted. "I haven't, no." But was it fair, entrapping Deborah in a juicy conversation about her wayward daughter? *Entrap* wasn't the right word. Coax. Invite.

"I got Disney Plus recently," Deborah said. "Totally worth it." While smoothing conditioner into Arlo's hair, she gave a brief but spirited review of a recently watched Avengers movie ("That Hemsworth is a gift from God"), then went on to rank all nine *Star Wars* installments from "least bad" to "most bad."

Arlo half listened. It was perfectly reasonable for her to have questions about Mickey. She'd come here to learn about her sister, not her client. Mental health problems sometimes had a genetic link; it was important to learn the family history. She wasn't spying. Whatever information she chanced upon she would treat gently.

"I saw the third one in the theater in '83 when I was a teenager. I fell asleep. Actually. Is that awful? I remember my date was—"

"Have you heard from Mickey lately?" Arlo asked casually, because it was a casual question.

"Ha! No." Two syllables, heaps of bitterness. "Why?"

"Holidays and all that."

"I'm not sure what Michelle does for the holidays." Deborah turned the water back on and began rinsing the conditioner. "This is a really nice product."

"I wish I could get to know her," Arlo said.

"Redken. We've got it on sale."

"I always wished I had a sister." A half lie. Arlo had never wanted a sister. She could, however, see the appeal. Sisters were émigrés of the same distant—now disbanded—nation. "Even though— I mean, I always knew I had one."

"You can't trust that grocery store stuff, you know," Deborah said. "It coats your hair with all kinds of gunk."

"But that sister relationship. Telling each other secrets, braiding each other's hair . . ." Never needing to explain yourself too much because the other person already understood.

"Sulfates, silicones, weird acids and shit . . ."

"Do sisters actually do that sort of thing? See? I don't know."

Deborah scooped up Arlo's hair and tugged it into a pony so that all the water trickled out. "Done." She wound a towel around Arlo's head and walked out in front of the sink.

"Please." Arlo wiggled upright in the reclined seat, aiming a hopeful smile at the shadow looming above. Backlit by the ceiling fixture, Deborah had fallen into silhouette. "Tell me what she's like."

Deborah jammed her hands in her apron. "Michelle always had a big, big heart. Loved being around people."

"Really?" The towel came loose, cold wet hair collapsing down Arlo's nape. She barely noticed. Mickey? A people person?

Deborah turned away without a word.

Arlo followed her back to the salon chair and settled in. She was pushing into some of Deborah's worst memories, which might've felt cruel if it wasn't so necessary. "When did the drinking become a problem?"

Deborah plucked a comb from a jar of blue fluid labeled BARBICIDE and raked it down the back of Arlo's head. The teeth prickled. "Oh, I don't know. I'll never know." She froze. "How'd you know she was a drinker?"

"Lucky guess," Arlo said, keeping her voice light.

"Your dad." As Deborah resumed combing, her touch seemed to soften. "I'm sorry. I should've asked how you've been doing. The flowers stop coming after a couple weeks, but the grief doesn't."

That was true.

"I'm fine," Arlo said. "Thank you."

"And your mom?"

"Better now that she has Daddy's things organized."

"I bet. I've got boxes and boxes of my parents' stuff stored away. It's been a decade, and there are some I still can't open."

Arlo found herself nodding. A person left a lot behind.

"I still have a message from Daddy on my voicemail." Ninety-six seconds of breathy, opioid-inflected rambling recorded from his hospital bed. "It's over two hundred days old."

"Two hundred days? That's nothing. You should see all the home videos I've kept. Remember those little cassette tapes that used to fit into the bigger tapes? What am I saying—of course you don't remember that."

"I can't bring myself to—" The words tangled in Arlo's mouth as a realization struck. She saw what was happening here; Deborah was being kind, yes, but she was also deflecting. Dragging the conversation away from Mickey.

"I can't bring myself to listen to it," Arlo finished.

"That would be hard," Deborah said.

But maybe Arlo could spin this. Sometimes, she knew, you had to give a little to get a little. "They finished the headstone. It turned out really well."

"That's good, honey. I'm glad."

"I had to bribe the cemetery people to let us install it even though the ground is frozen. It cost like five times what it should've."

"Ah," Deborah said.

"We're having another little ceremony to unveil it, sort of like a second funeral." Arlo rattled off the date and time, directions to the cemetery. "You should think about coming. We would welcome you."

"Even your mom?"

Mother would lose her shit if Deborah came. But that was a problem for Future Arlo.

"We both felt really terrible about not inviting you to the funeral."

Something bit the cartilage of Arlo's ear.

"Oops," Deborah said. "Gotcha with the comb there. Sorry."

"*I'm* sorry," Arlo said, swallowing the pain, and her pride. "You didn't get a proper chance to say goodbye. That was thoughtless of us."

Deborah spun the chair to face her in one swift motion and began combing Arlo's bangs down over her eyes. "Thanks, kiddo. I'll think about it."

Arlo's vision filled with the soft shapes of Deborah's hands, the hard angle of the scissors.

"Michelle lived with me while she did her teachers' college. It started innocently enough, I think. Keggers, party buses. Kid things."

"Kid things," Arlo said, relishing the phrase. Oh, yes. This was the stuff.

"She was drinking every night. 'It's fine, Mom. I'm an adult, Mom.'"

Snips of hair skimmed Arlo's nose and chin.

"It was hard to argue with her because her grades were still so good," Deborah said, "but I knew something was wrong.

"Her twenty-second birthday, I had this whole big party planned. I bought steaks. I baked a cake. What does she do? She decides that morning to get on a plane to Amsterdam—fucking Amsterdam—and not tell anyone. I called the cops. I thought she was dead. I honestly thought that."

Arlo flicked the hair out of her eyes to find Deborah making wild gestures. The scissors, still in her hand, caught and threw the light with a kind of desperation.

"Three days later, I get a call, and it's her, and she's hammered, and she doesn't have enough money to come home. So, the sucker that I am, I burn all my savings on a last-minute, twenty-five-hundred-dollar plane ticket to get her home."

Codependency, Arlo thought grimly. *Classic.*

"'I'm sorry,' she says. 'I'm so sorry. I'm done now, I'm done doing stupid shit.'" Deborah dropped the scissors back in her apron. "But it only got worse. By the time she started her practicum placements, what, a couple months later, it was too much to watch."

"Too much how?" Arlo asked.

Deborah spun the chair to face the mirror again and ransacked a nearby cabinet. "I lost a lot of sleep when she started working in those schools."

A tingling sensation spread through Arlo's shoulders and down her back. Mickey had been laid off recently, she remembered. Unless that wasn't what had happened at all. "She was teaching drunk?"

"I don't know." Deborah resurfaced with a piece of plastic and screwed it onto the end of a blow-dryer. At least, she tried to. The attachment didn't seem to fit, though she kept trying to jam it on, pinching her lips together with effort.

"Do you think she still teaches drunk?"

"I don't know, and I don't want to know." Deborah gave up on the attachment and chucked it back on the counter. "That's why I set the boundary between us. I love my daughter—I do. You think I wanted to pack all her stuff in garbage bags and dump everything in the hallway? You think it made me happy, doing that?"

"Of course not."

"But the idea of her with those kids . . . No, I can't think about it."

Arlo could think about it. Arlo could see it perfectly.

MICKEY

Something glinted in the gray slush between her feet. She reached down, plucked a coin off the floor of the bus, and stowed it in her pocket for the return journey. The last of her savings had disappeared into rent, her phone bill, and a month's worth of couscous.

The bus lurched along under a low ceiling of cloud, passing nail salons and pho restaurants, snowy lots and liquor stores, a hookah lounge, a Salvation Army outlet, more liquor stores. Mickey had to be getting close.

She took out her phone and searched her destination on Google. The results page displayed an address here in the city's outer reaches, and the following:

People also ask:
Are loan sharks bad?
What happens when you don't pay a loan shark?
Do loan sharks murder people?

Mickey was no fool. This company offered the lowest interest rate she could find. Their online reviews weren't uniformly terrible.

Treated me with dignity wrote one person. *Quick and easy* wrote another. Mickey could get Evelyn her ten grand and repay the moneylender when the inheritance came in. It was all very prudent, very low risk. Plenty of people, and not just Mickey's father, used these sorts of services. Her situation now was completely different than his had been back then.

Seventy-two hours since her last drink. Most of the symptoms—the fever, the sweating, the darting thoughts—had passed. The chill lingered, and the clattering heartbeat, and that dull ache in her middle, where it felt like something had yawned open.

Mickey reached up and pulled the rope. This was her stop.

The sign over the door read DAISY'S MONEYLENDING, the words bookended with smiley faces. When Mickey caught sight of her reflection in the glass door, it displayed a somewhat different expression.

"Welcome!"

A saleswoman peered around the customer standing opposite her at the gleaming wooden counter. "Have yourself a seat, love, while I finish up with this gentleman." She sported leathery skin, a massive chest, and a wobbly English accent that might've been fake.

Mickey wandered into a small waiting area cluttered with macrame wall hangings, crinkled copies of *People*, and those brightly colored toys with the beads you push along the wire. A fireplace crackled on the mounted TV. It wasn't so bad.

She sat back and listened to the jazzy old Christmas songs that were playing—Bing Crosby, Elvis, Nat King Cole, etc. The recordings her father used to—

No. She would not go there. She would not think about him. Not about sitting between his outstretched legs on a toboggan and sailing down a snowy hill together. Not about the smoky, slightly spicy scent of his cologne. They were always broke, and always, he had to buy that cologne.

185

The saleswoman—Daisy, according to her name tag—appeared ten minutes later with a floral-patterned teacup on a saucer.

"I've put in some milk and sugar. Hope that's alright."

Mickey accepted the tea and took a sip: syrupy-sweet and scalding. "It's perfect."

At the counter, Daisy showed Mickey the laminated list of sums and interest rates she called a "moneylending menu."

"If you could tell me a bit about your situation—about what's brought you here—I can point us in the right direction," she said.

"I need fifty thousand dollars," Mickey said carefully.

Daisy examined her sidelong. "Because . . ."

I need to pay my blackmailer or else I'll never teach again, and nobody in my life will lend me any money because they think I'm an addict. "It's not relevant."

"I see." Daisy pointed to one of the bottom rows of the menu with her pen. "APR of forty-eight percent."

"What does that mean?" Mickey had a terrible suspicion.

"It's the annual cost of the loan, including fees and the interest expense."

"So, to get fifty thousand dollars now, I'll end up paying back seventy-five, when you add it all up."

"Or so. That's the idea."

Mickey was so tired of feeling nauseous.

A sympathetic expression formed on Daisy's face. Mickey was weary of this, too.

"Whatever's brought you here, it can't have been easy. But you'll get through it. My customers are survivors, every one of them. Doesn't matter what life throws at you. You'll rise the next morning all the same."

Mickey was more than a survivor. She was basically a cockroach. That part had never been the issue. And up until recently, it had felt like enough.

Chris had called three times so far that week and left three messages. Mickey hadn't listened to any of them. She hated checking her voicemail even at the best of times, when she wasn't grossly ashamed of herself, and so she obviously wasn't going to check it now.

"Shall I ring it through then?" Daisy asked lightly, as if Mickey were purchasing a pair of jeans or a bag of dinner rolls.

"Yes. Yes, do it."

"Excellent. I'm so pleased for you. Yes, so pleased." Daisy opened a laptop and clacked away merrily at the keyboard. "I'll let you know we also provide resources and referrals. Feel free to take these, or not." She pushed a stack of brochures across the counter. "Might be worth tucking them away somewhere."

One was entitled *Tips for Dealing with Collection Agencies.* The other, *How to Find a Licensed Insolvency Trustee.* The last brochure was glossy and thick and had a picture of a budding leaf on the cover. *What to expect if you file for bankruptcy.*

Time collapsed, and Mickey was eight years old again, standing by the open front door as a cold breeze blew against her bare calves, and men in matching blue polo shirts lugged away Mama's TV, the couches, the coffee table, Great-grandma's antique cabinet. They taped the drawers shut so the silverware wouldn't fall out.

"Love?"

Mickey blinked a few times. "What?"

"I said, let's start with your name and any aliases." Daisy had perched on a tall stool and donned a pair of glasses that magnified her dusty-green eyes threefold. It was like looking up at an owl in a tree. "Previous names. If you've been married, for example."

"Michelle Ko—" Mickey folded her lips under her teeth.

There would be no unsaying it once it was said. No undoing what it would make her: another Kowalski steaming toward ruin. Like father, like daughter.

"I can't do this." She pushed the brochures back across the counter. "I'm sorry for wasting your time, but I can't."

Daisy clawed her fingers around Mickey's wrist. "There's no shame in it."

Mickey wriggled free, staggered backward. The teacup and saucer went flying. Then came the sound of porcelain cleaving, and in Mickey's mind, the decanter was smashing all over again. Tom bound her arms. Ian screamed.

"Where are you going?" Daisy said sharply, eyeing the mess. "That was expensive."

"I'm sorry. I'm so . . . I'm so, so . . ." Mickey threw herself out into the cold.

Back at the bus stop, she sat on a bench in the glass shelter and took out her phone.

"I'm calling as a client. As a—a—" The term escaped her.

"A beneficiary?" Tom's voice brimmed with foreboding.

"I've only got three more therapy sessions left. I thought I'd give you some notice so you can start moving the money."

"Mickey—"

"I know the will says I'm supposed to get the money when I'm all done the therapy, but I thought maybe you might consider sending it a little early? Next week, maybe?"

"It doesn't work like that."

Mickey hung her head between her knees. "Why not?"

"We can't process a transfer until the conditions of the will are satisfied. The firm has a responsibility to the deceased."

The world dissolved into shimmering specks as Mickey lurched to her feet. "The deceased was an ass."

"Even so."

She plunked back down. The grimy walls and graffitied perfume ads of the bus shelter rematerialized. As did the crushing sense of dread.

"Why don't I look into it and call you back," Tom said.

The line disconnected just as a bus came grumbling up to the stop, splatting the walls of the shelter with slush from under its tires.

Mickey patted her pockets. Where had she put that coin?

◎

"You once told me all people are terrible," Arlo said during therapy that week. She'd pulled her hair back into the type of elegant bun Mama would've called a chignon. Her bangs fell in two freshly cut curtains around her eyes. "Do you still think that?"

"The *why* matters." Mickey coughed, clearing four days of sleep and silence from her voice. She hadn't spoken aloud since the phone call with Tom. She hadn't had a reason to. "People who do bad things have usually known a lot of bad things. Abuse. Neglect. These are the people who get the sickest, too."

Arlo raised her chin slightly and licked the fronts of her straight white teeth. She'd probably worn braces as a child. Eaten lots of vegetables. Always had shoes that fit. "Social determinants of health, is what you're saying."

"That's a nice scholarly term," Mickey said. She knew the idea well. The poorest and most marginalized of a society were the most vulnerable to disease and poverty. And crime.

But the episode at the moneylender had left her with few options. Fraud? Embezzlement? She didn't know what those things even meant, really, let alone how to achieve them. She could sell ova, hair, sex, or some combination thereof. Surrogacy was lucrative, she'd heard, but there wasn't enough time. Another solution had occurred to her—something she could steal and resell for more than enough cash—but there really would be no going back after.

"What about the kind of person who endangers others?" The hard edge in Arlo's voice caught Mickey off guard. The therapist was all pissy today for some reason. "Is there an excuse for that behavior?"

"Not an excuse. An explanation."

"But you agree that a person should be held accountable for the harm they cause."

This line of inquiry, Mickey was fairly certain, would not lead anywhere she wanted to go. Instead, she lost herself in the picture of the lighthouse on the wall to her left and wondered how the sand might sink underfoot. How the air might smell. Whether it would feel warm or cold on her skin. Warm, she decided. In the world of the lighthouse, temperatures never fell below shorts-weather. The seas were always calm, and skies was always clear—so clear that the lighthouse served a mostly decorative function. The shoreline was visible enough without it.

"Part of therapy is about facing up to ourselves," Arlo said. Yes, she was still talking, rudely intruding upon Mickey's pleasant maritime fantasies. "I'm not here to make things easy for you."

"That's obvious."

"I'm here to gently push your buttons."

Mickey laughed. What Arlo had meant was *I'm here to play with you. Because I get off on it.* "What if I don't want that?"

"You can leave whenever you want to. You're the boss here, Mickey."

If only that were true. No—Mickey was stuck. With this room, with this life, with a therapist who collected people's sorrows like seashells.

Sighing, Mickey looked away from the lighthouse. "So, you're saying I . . . harm people?"

"I don't know," Arlo said. "That's the question."

"Doesn't everybody hurt someone at some point? That's being human. We make mistakes. It's okay so long as we learn from it and apologize."

Arlo looked perplexed. "It's okay to hurt others so long as you apologize?"

"No. That's not what I said." Had Mickey said that? Maybe she had. "That's not what I meant."

"Think about one of your relationships, past or present. Let's say, for example, your mom."

A vise clamped around Mickey's heart. "My mom?"

"What sorts of things have you apologized to your mom for?"

"Why my mom?"

"Just think about it, Mickey."

Mickey was already thinking about it—Amsterdam. A pay phone receiver against her twenty-two-year-old ear.

"What's going through your mind right now?" Arlo asked.

"Nothing," Mickey said. Mama running to her at arrivals in the airport. Mama's swollen, stress-worn eyes. "My mind is blank."

"You're crying."

"No, I'm not."

No one spoke. Arlo was doing the thing—the waiting thing, each second of silence another pound of weight on Mickey's shoulders.

"There were times when I made her worry," Mickey offered, to make it end.

"Times such as . . ."

Besides Amsterdam? All the nights Mickey didn't come home because she'd fallen asleep in a field or on a bus or on some dude's futon. The nights the cops brought her back to the apartment—cops, plural, because it took more than one person to hold her upright. Then there were all the places she'd puked: vases and purses and carpets and sinks.

"I can't think of any examples," Mickey said.

"It takes a lot of courage to recognize what we do and do not deserve."

Mickey had absolutely no idea what Arlo meant by this but was not going to ask. A shadow was lengthening in her mind, darkness encroaching fast.

Arlo drew a long audible inhale through her mouth. "In the AA program, one of the twelve steps an addict takes—"

"I told you—I don't need that."

"—is to make amends with the people she has wronged."

"I stopped already. It's done."

"I'm not suggesting you do that now, but a first baby step—"

"No," Mickey said, as the last light drained away.

"—might be to build some simple self-awareness. When have you acted selfishly? Was there a time when someone trusted you with something very precious, and you let them down? Preyed on their trust, their vulnerability? You're a teacher. That's a big responsibility."

"I said stop." But it was too late. The shadow had arrived, and with it, the worst memory of all. Mickey flashed back to eight weeks ago, when she'd chugged vodka in an elementary school bathroom and taken innocent Ian into her care even though she was too sad, too damaged, and, most of all, too drunk to care for anyone. Only a deeply selfish person would do such a thing—the same kind of person who vanished overseas without a word of warning to her mother.

The same kind of person who stole.

ARLO

Arlo hunched over her keyboard and stared into the blinding white void of a Word document. The cursor blinked and blinked: a malevolent eye.

Thirty minutes until her next appointment. She'd hoped to make a dent in her speech for Daddy's headstone unveiling, but the office milieu had proven less than inspiring. All she had so far was

Daddy was a great man.

It wasn't wrong. It just wasn't right. She hit the backspace button and tried again.

Daddy was a tremendous man.

Arlo clapped the laptop shut. She needed to be at home or at a coffee shop or, well, anywhere but here. As soon as she got away from her files and Post-it notes and CBT textbooks, the words would fall right into place.

After bustling past Punam's office—Punam sat alone at her desk, thumbing dreamily through a passport—Arlo murmured something about a family emergency to Sam at reception and tried to look stressed. "Apologize to my two o'clock, will you? Thanks."

Stepping outside felt like waking up. Stillness hung over the street. Birds fluted in the snow-lined trees. It all seemed so perfectly right, the future so perfectly assured. Sometime soon—this week or next—Mickey would turn to Arlo with sad certitude in her eyes and say, *I'm a self-defeating alcoholic with a history of complex trauma and deep-rooted intimacy problems I have yet to fully recognize. My actions have had enduring and detrimental effects on those closest to me, and I therefore do not deserve five and a half million dollars.*

"That's true," Arlo muttered as she wandered toward her car. "At least for now."

If Mickey did the right thing and returned Daddy's fortune to the estate, Arlo could ensure a portion was set aside for the future if/when she finally got her shit together. Enough cash to give Mickey a comfortable quality of life, but not so much that it threatened her newfound sobriety? Arlo would have to think about it.

"Excuse me."

Arlo turned.

A woman of fifty or so was standing on the sidewalk in high-waisted jeans and an impressively stylish woolen shacket. There was something familiar about her full cheeks and broad mouth. And the way she carried herself, with her chin pointing slightly upward, as if Arlo owed her something.

"I'm Jennifer Hedman, Laura's mom."

A sinkhole opened in Arlo's abdomen and sucked her organs one by one into its depths. She willed herself to run, but her feet wouldn't lift.

"Don't worry," Jennifer added quickly. "I come in peace."

Yes, she certainly wore a friendlier face today on the street than she had last spring in court. No flaring nostrils or trembling upper lip. No hateful death glare. But her posture was almost too relaxed, her smile too easy. Arlo didn't trust it.

"Ha—have you been standing out here waiting for me?" Why? To yell? To fight? To break Arlo's legs with a steel pipe like that figure skater in the nineties, what was her name, Tina-something? Why couldn't Arlo remember? She'd seen like four movies about it.

"I know how it looks but hear me out." Jennifer tented her fingers. "Coffee? My treat."

"Absolutely not." Yet Arlo remained frozen.

A wrinkle appeared between Jennifer's manicured eyebrows. "Were you talking to someone just now?"

Arlo gestured to the space around her, the empty sidewalk. "There's no one else here."

"I thought maybe you had an earpiece in or something. Like maybe you were on the phone. I heard you saying . . . I'm not sure what I heard you saying."

Arlo offered no explanation because no explanation was necessary. Plenty of people muttered to themselves—and frankly, what she said to the air wasn't anyone's business.

"I called," Jennifer said. "Lots of times. You never picked up."

So this was PRIVATE CALLER.

"You never left a message," Arlo said.

Jennifer smudged her lips together. There was something judgy about it.

"I'm allowed to screen my calls. Boundaries are really important in what I do, and so is self-care, so you know what, no, I'm not going to pick up my phone every time it rings, and no, I'm not going to feel bad about it." There was no reason for this speech. Whatever Jennifer's angled chin might suggest, Arlo didn't owe her anything.

Yet the words kept coming. Arlo couldn't stop. "Because it isn't my job to solve every problem, and I need to have a life outside of my job, and plus, also, my voicemail says to call the distress center if you're in crisis, so that covers that."

She caught her breath and waited for the fiery rebuke.

"You're right. I'm sorry." Jennifer's voice dripped with humility. And indeed, remorse. Her gaze had grown weak, her smile uncertain. It was not the face of a person who was about to bludgeon someone's kneecaps with a pipe. Quite the opposite, in fact. "I'm starting to see things in a new light. I have a lot better clarity now."

Arlo felt a twinge of guilt. Was it possible Laura's mom hadn't come here to enact revenge, but to apologize, and Arlo was getting all defensive for nothing? Maybe she meant to acknowledge how wrong she'd been about the lawsuit and the hurtful accusations.

"One cup of coffee," Jennifer said.

This meeting might finally set her on a path toward healing and acceptance. And who was Arlo to deny her that?

"Please."

Ahead, the bumper of Arlo's Prius glinted in the winter sun. So close and yet so far.

Arlo sighed. "One cup of coffee."

They settled into a pair of hard wooden chairs inside the nearest Starbucks. Arlo couldn't figure out what to do with her legs. Cross one ankle behind the other like a duchess? Splay her knees wide like a cowboy? Nothing felt comfortable. In the end, she hooked each foot around a chair leg and held on tight.

"I'm a sucker for the Christmas drinks," Jennifer said after a healthy swallow of some peppermint creation Arlo could smell from across the table.

Arlo cradled an extra-hot oat latte between her palms. "I like the red cups."

"Yes. The red cups."

An electro cover of "Do They Know It's Christmas?" swirled overhead.

"This song is terrible," Jennifer said.

"Yes," Arlo said. "Terrible."

They drank their drinks.

Jennifer addressed her next words to the ceiling. "I've been going to therapy."

Ah, Arlo thought. It was all starting to make sense. Jennifer's therapist had probably encouraged this apology—maybe even helped her rehearse it.

"That's great." Arlo unhooked her ankles from the chair legs and relaxed a bit. "I hope it's been useful."

"Thank you," Jennifer told the ceiling.

"Do They Know It's Christmas?" came to the line about there being no snow in Africa.

Light skated across the whites of Jennifer's eyes as she slowly shook her head. "I didn't believe her. She came to me that morning and told me she was going to do it, and I didn't believe her."

Arlo allowed herself, for the first time, to imagine the weight of Jennifer's grief—and all the days she must've spent pinned under it, unable to move.

"She said it in a weird way. 'I made it to the end, Mom. This is it.' Something like that, like it was the last day of school or something. She seemed completely fine. She seemed happy. I nodded along and sort of brushed it off. I was—the truth is, I was very tired. It's hard work, loving someone who's that sick."

Things that came to Arlo's mind, in no particular order: the blue dispenser of hand sanitizer on the wall outside Daddy's hospital room; the snap of latex gloves; the squeak of a whiteboard marker; the nurses' billowing yellow gowns and big plastic face shields, constantly fogging up with breath; the sickly sweet smell of Daddy's toes, always crusting and flaking no matter how often Arlo lotioned them.

"We could never make plans—Bill and I—because we never knew if she could get out of bed that day. Christmases, birthdays, family reunions. Everything. We missed everything. We missed our whole lives. Because any commitment—anything in the world—came second to our child."

"Mhmmm," Arlo said. This, too, rang a few bells.

"Something I think about a lot—something I'm working through—is this idea that I'm here, and she isn't. Outliving your child is the worst kind of failure for a parent. The only failure if we're being honest. And I know what you're thinking. That I have survivor's guilt, that my daughter's suicide isn't my fault. Blah, blah, blah. Yes, I know all that, rationally. But it's hard to be rational. I'm sick of being rational. Mostly, I'm sick of being angry. And that's just it—that's what I've come here to say."

Here came the apology. Arlo couldn't decide if they should hug after. She took a hasty sip of her oat latte to buy time.

"I forgive you," Jennifer said.

The latte flooded Arlo's windpipe, and she choked.

"I was very angry at you. Now I need to let that anger go."

Arlo hacked and hacked, groping for air, for words. "Angry at—at me? Still?"

"Of course."

"Why me?"

Jennifer grew a second chin. "You know what was in the note."

The note, the note, the note. It was always about the note.

"You hurried her out the door," Jennifer said. "That's what she wrote."

"I would never," Arlo said.

"She told you she was going to attempt suicide, and you hurried her out the—" Jennifer braced her mouth with her fist.

"Do They Know It's Christmas?" reached its final verse.

"How is this still playing?" Arlo blurted. And how were they still having this same conversation, nine months on? Nine months and eleven days since Laura's memorial service. They'd draped the all-white casket with one of her high school field hockey jerseys and played Bob Dylan's "A Hard Rain's a-Gonna Fall" during the opening procession. Arlo had watched the live stream on her laptop because she knew she wouldn't be allowed inside the funeral home.

Jennifer prised the plastic lid off her cup and lowered her nose for a sniff. She stayed hunched like that, breathing deeply, for what felt like a long time. The peppermint stench wafted in Arlo's face.

"I shouldn't have raised my voice," Jennifer said. "That was unhelpful."

"She did not tell me," Arlo said. "Whatever she wrote, whatever she said happened, she did not tell me she was going to kill herself."

"Alright." A serene smile formed on Jennifer's lips, as if they'd been arguing over a dented back bumper or who had been first in line for the grocery checkout.

"You don't believe me," Arlo said.

"Thank you for listening. I really do appreciate it." Jennifer rose.

"Why don't you believe me?"

But Jennifer was already gone, the only sign of her the trash she'd left on the table.

○

The address on file was exactly what Arlo had imagined: a dingy apartment block with stucco exteriors and tiny balconies full of bikes and barbecues and Christmas lights. Reclining in the driver's seat of her car across the street, she watched the lights flicker on unit by unit, string by string. Two and a half hours, she sat there. Her bladder swelled. Her back seized. Still, she waited. She waited because it was within her rights to wait. Because there were no laws against sitting in a parked car and staring at the front doors of an apartment building until one's half-sister/client emerged from within. Because if Laura's mom could get away with a bit of light stalking, then Arlo could, too. She wasn't sure what she was looking for but knew there would be something—some evidence of wrong-doing on Mickey's part—eventually.

Memories of that morning bobbed to the surface of Arlo's mind like airplane wreckage. Woolen shacket. Oat latte. *I forgive you.* Arlo steered around these thoughts the best she could. Jennifer was grieving, and grief had a way of blinding people to the truth. That's all there was to it.

Arlo was reaching for another fistful of sour-cream-and-onion potato chips when there came a knock—a bang, more like—on the passenger window. The shiny, swoony face of a teenage boy filled in the glass. Though the temperature had dropped, he wore no hat, the tops of his ears a ripe shade of pink. A police emblem glittered on his breast.

Arlo rolled down the window, utterly calm and collected. She might've felt more threatened if the cop didn't look so silly, or if this episode of light stalking weren't so justified, or if she didn't happen to be a white woman. As it stood, she had no reason to feel afraid.

"Sorry, ma'am," he said. "Didn't mean to scare you."

"Scare me?"

"You screamed."

"Did I?" Yes, maybe she had screamed. Maybe she'd flailed. It would explain how the chips had ended up everywhere.

"This is two-hour parking."

"Okay." Arlo glanced back and forth between the young cop and Mickey's apartment building. Something flickered in the entrance vestibule. A flutter of movement?

"Ma'am? You have to move your car."

200

Arlo forced her attention back to the cop. "Right. Sorry." She put the car in drive and rolled forward about a foot, her eyes still on the building across the street. More commotion in the vestibule—more movement.

The boy knocked on the glass again. "You have to move it more than that. Like, further."

"How much further?"

"To the next zone."

"What's a zone?" Arlo asked, squinting. A shadowy figure had appeared in the building entranceway.

"Different parts of the street have different rates for parking," said the cop.

"But it's free after six," she said.

"Yes, for up to two hours."

The figure pushed through the glass door and stepped onto the sidewalk, a massive purse over one shoulder, her blonde hair almost greenish under the streetlamps.

Arlo's heart shifted in her chest cavity. Mickey.

"Alrighty then. License and registration?"

Arlo glanced up to find the cop readying a pad of paper. "What? No. I have to go."

"Oh, *now* you have to go, huh?" He clicked his pen with relish. "License and registration."

Arlo tracked Mickey in the rearview mirror as she fumbled around in her glove compartment. Mickey moved strangely, halting every few steps to readjust the strap of her bag. She approached a bus bench at the end of the block.

"Will this be quick?" Arlo handed over the documents. "Because I have to—"

The cop shot her a seething look of offense.

At the bus stop, Mickey rocked on the balls of her feet, reached into her purse, and took a drink from, what was it, a water bottle?

Vodka, in all likelihood. Maybe gin. Daddy had always liked his Tanqueray. Hendrick's on occasion.

"You know," the cop said, "bylaws are what hold a community together. It's an important responsibility to enforce them."

Arlo made a throaty noise to indicate polite interest. Another vehicle turned onto the street, beaming its headlights straight into the back of her brain. A city bus.

"Some might say the most important responsibility."

Arlo watched helplessly as the bus arrived at its stop with a hiss of exhaust out its tailpipe. A curtain of steam obscured her view of the bus bench. And Mickey.

The cop passed Arlo a pink slip of carbon paper. "You have sixty days to—"

"Thanks," she said, the ticket in her fist, her foot on the gas.

She pulled a U-turn in the middle of the next intersection and sped off in pursuit of the bus, past the apartment building and the boy-cop, who shook his fist at her like the self-righteous old man he would undoubtedly become.

For the next twenty minutes, Arlo trailed the bus by one or two cars, pulling to the curb whenever it stopped, squinting each time to see who had disembarked. As she and the bus tracked into the city's outer reaches, the coffee shops and clothing boutiques thinned away. Moneylenders and liquor stores sprouted up.

A few blocks later, Mickey stepped off the bus in front of a pawnshop.

MICKEY

Despite answering the door in a nightie that barely covered her mons, Daria's expression betrayed no shame whatsoever. Shame probably wasn't in her vocabulary. She strolled about the world exactly as she pleased: no regrets, no apologies, no evil deeds hanging over her head.

Mickey waved in greeting. "Hi."

Daria straightened, her nipples tenting the rose-colored satin.

Task number one was to get inside. Mickey had thought of feigning illness or inventing an emotional crisis but decided she was too shitty an actress to fool Daria. Instead, she kept her mouth shut, pasted a pained look on her face, and prayed it would allow her entry.

"Alright," Daria said mildly, opening the door wide.

This—what Mickey was about to do—was not the right choice. It was bad and wrong, but it was happening. Mickey was inside, and her shoes were coming off, and that was that. She followed Daria into the dewy warmth of the apartment, her almost-empty purse light on one shoulder.

Mickey sniffed the air. Lemongrass? Citrus?

"I borrow from friend." Daria gestured to the essential oil diffuser on the side table.

A meditation cushion, another new addition, lay on the living room floor. Mickey wouldn't have noticed had she not been scanning the room for expensive metallurgic artwork. The sculpture of the squatting man had been moved to one of the bookcases, where it now sat atop a few stacked volumes of Proust and Chekhov. Other sculptures shone out from different nooks: a body without a head, a head without a body, half a hand. They were small, each no bigger than a cereal box.

For all Daria's frankness about her successful sculpting career, Mickey hadn't truly believed it until this afternoon when she'd typed her neighbor's name into Google. Turns out Daria had won a MacArthur genius grant at age twenty-four. She'd taught at Emily Carr, Rutgers, UCLA. Her work was on display at French and Spanish and Danish museums Mickey had never heard of but which all sounded highly posh.

Daria lived too simply to be rich and famous, or so Mickey had always thought. There was no beach house, no swimming pool. She hung washing to dry on a wire rack and went around town on a bicycle. Not even a good one—a shitty three-speed. She did keep her apartment hot, a rare extravagance. And there was the leopard cat, Mickey remembered, as Rybka slinked toward the tree in the corner and hopped onto the highest carpeted step. The cat couldn't have been cheap.

Mickey held her arms aloft to air out her pits.

"Come," Daria said, poking her head out from the kitchen. "Sit."

Mickey waited at the table while Daria bustled around the kitchen. It was eight o'clock, and an evening news program burbled softly on the radio. The markets were trending high, or was it low, and someone was about to bail out someone else, which a lot of people were angry about. Or maybe they were happy about it.

Mickey couldn't grasp the words, too nervous to focus. She'd been drinking on and off all day, and it wasn't nearly enough.

The tinkling sound of glassware sent pleasant shivers down Mickey's arms. What would it be tonight—Absolut? Stolichnaya? Maybe Daria would break out a liqueur. Pálinka. Krupnik. Mickey would even go for some limoncello at this point.

Then Daria returned to the table with a glass of milk and a plate of wafer cookies. The nightgown rode up over her hips as she sat; again, she didn't seem to care.

"Oh," Mickey said.

"Tonight, we drink milk," Daria said. Yet there was only one glass.

Mickey forced a smile. She wanted to say thank you but found that on top of being unable to listen, she was also unable to speak. She picked up the glass and raised it Daria's direction, accompanying this gesture with a small tuck of her chin.

Growing up, Mickey used to steal little cartons of chocolate milk from the 7-Eleven near her elementary school. In junior high, she used to swipe socks and lipsticks from other girls' lockers when their backs were turned. On sleepovers at friends' houses, she would sneak away and raid the kitchen drawers for lighters, pens, spare change, anything, even stuff she didn't need, because why should her friends have stuff and not her? She took decks of cards, birthday candles, charging cables for appliances she didn't own.

These incidents, of course, didn't count. Children were excused from stealing. But when did this grace period end? Had she been blameless back in high school when she attended house parties to steal people's coats and sell them on Kijiji the next the day? In teachers' college when she would hook up with randoms just to steal the wallets from their jeans as she tiptoed out the door in the early morning?

Certainly, she wasn't blameless now. The gloss of childhood had long eroded, and if she was about to steal something, it was her own fault.

"Can I borrow a book?" Mickey asked.

Daria adjusted a spaghetti strap so it lay flat over the toned meat of her shoulder. She'd probably beaten people up before. "Which one?"

"I don't know yet. I just want something to read."

Daria nodded slowly at first, then faster. "I have something."

Mickey took her purse off the back of the chair and followed Daria into the living room, where Daria plucked a thin volume off the shelf: a worn copy of *The Little Prince*. "This one is good book for broken person."

Mickey accepted the book, too distracted to take offense. The squatting man would fit in her purse but probably weighed more than a bowling ball. One of the smaller, lighter sculptures might be a safer bet. Less obvious. The disembodied head, maybe, or the headless body.

"Do you have any Napoleon cake?" Mickey asked.

"You want cake." Daria looked more concerned than suspicious.

"It really is the best cake. If you happen to have some."

A rare smile broke across Daria's face. "Wait here," she said and padded away.

Mickey took a lunging step toward the shelf, tried to swallow, tried to breathe. It was decision time. Head or body? Body or head? Her hand hovered between them. *Choose*, she told herself. Only she couldn't. She wasn't this person. She didn't steal from Peter to pay Evelyn. Mickey was a teacher, a molder of minds, a guiding light. She was bound by certain moral obligations. Thou Shalt Not Pawn Thy Neighbor's Freaky Artwork.

But then the voice of her therapist came clawing back—*Was there a time when someone trusted you with something very precious, and you let them down?*—and Mickey remembered that, yes, she was indeed this kind of person.

She held open her purse and grabbed the headless body by the waist.

"Is this piece big enou—"

Daria. As she stood in the doorway from the kitchen with a plate of puff pastry in hand, her mouth contorted into an unfamiliar shape. Not disappointment—nothing so mild as that. Her expression pulsed and radiated.

Disgust. It was disgust.

The sculpture escaped Mickey's grasp and hit the floor with a sickening crack.

"I'll let myself out," she said, hot in the cheeks, already halfway across the room. Looking back over her shoulder, she glimpsed the curve of Daria's bare calf disappearing into the kitchen.

As Mickey jammed her feet in her shoes at the front door, a cat's meow rang gently through the air, lilting upward at the end as if to ask a question.

Rybka—rare, exotic, expensive Rybka—sat on her haunches and watched, head cocked to one side.

"No," said the guy at the till. He was only a kid—sixteen, maybe, with a math textbook open in front of him and a pair of enormous headphones around his neck. "No way, lady."

"Hear me out," Mickey said with the desperation of a person who'd crossed town in a bus with a leopard cat in her purse. Rybka scrabbled up out of the bag, launched herself at the counter, and landed lightly on the glass.

The kid regarded Rybka dubiously as she dipped her nose toward the counter and the watches gleaming beneath. "You seriously want to pawn a cat?"

"She cost thousands," Mickey said.

"You seriously want to pawn a cat."

"This is an Ashera. It's part leopard."

"Yeah, and I'm part Targaryen." Laughter fell from his chapped lips until Rybka flashed her slitted pupils at him, and his tone sobered. "Do you have any documentation for this Ash—Asher . . ."

"Ashera. And no."

"I see." He puffed his cheeks full of air and inspected Rybka from different angles, as if she were a chunk of zirconia. Just another piece of crap some loser had brought in for spare change. "There is something weird about her, isn't there?"

"She's very gentle," Mickey said, tamping memories of the birthday party and how Rybka had nuzzled Ian so sweetly. If Ian ever asked, Mickey would say Rybka had . . . what? Died? What could she possibly say?

The kid rubbed his brow, obviously conflicted. "Let me call my guy."

Mickey sat in a La-Z-Boy chair ($429) with Rybka in her lap and half watched the hockey game playing on a 55-inch TV ($699), feeling her own worth deplete with each passing moment. People weren't bad by default; she saw that now. Goodness of character was a luxury, like bath salts and speedboats, and in the great lottery of birth and biology, Mickey had gotten skunked. All those picture books she'd read her kindergarteners about friendship and loyalty and courage, as if she had ever in her life possessed such things. What horseshit!

Her phone rang while she was sitting there: Chris. Again.

She declined the call. A text arrived a moment later:

Hey, just thought you should know your voicemail inbox is full. It's probably full because I keep leaving you messages because you keep NOT PICKING UP THE FUCKING PHONE.

And another:

Please just let me know you're okay.

Mickey added his number to her blocked contacts list. She wasn't sure how to empty her voicemail inbox without listening to the messages and so left this problem for another day.

Forty minutes later, a mousy little man with a handlebar mustache popped in from the night. The kid introduced him as Henry. "He does our animal appraisals."

Mickey almost asked what sorts of animals this man appraised, then decided she did not want to know.

Henry pinched Rybka's scruff and examined the pads of her paws and even lifted her tail for a peek at her bum hole, all the while jotting in a tiny notebook he'd taken from the breast pocket of his Hawaiian t-shirt. After a few minutes, he estimated her value at twenty-five thousand dollars. "She's a beautiful specimen," he said.

The kid turned to Mickey with hunger in his eyes. "I'll give you ten thousand."

"Twenty," Mickey said.

The kid scoffed. "The cat has no papers."

"So? Eighteen."

"Twelve."

"Seventeen."

Cooing softly, Henry scooped Rybka in his arms and cradled her like a furry baby.

"I'll do fifteen," said the kid.

Mickey's conscience kicked and flailed and gave a final gasp. "Fifteen thousand five hundred, and you've got a deal."

"Fifteen five." The kid extended his hand for a shake, delight shining from his big greasy pores. "My dad's gonna be really impressed with this one."

Henry deposited Rybka on the counter. She took a few steps forward and a few steps back, seemingly unsure where to go. It was too much.

"Can you hold onto her for a few weeks?" Mickey asked. "I'll buy her back for twice as much."

The kid's top lip disappeared under the bottom one.

"I'm coming into some money soon," she added.

"Right," he said flatly, the asshole.

"I am."

"That's what everybody says," Henry chimed in.

"But for me it's actually true."

"Still . . . maybe you should say your goodbyes now," said the kid. "In case."

He turned away. Henry, too. Then it was just Mickey and the cat.

She gave Rybka one last scratch behind the ears. She wasn't sure how she'd gotten here and didn't want to reflect on it too hard. "Well, I guess this is it. I'm sorry. Truly."

The cat gazed up at Mickey curiously. The cat did not understand.

After they'd settled up, the kid went to the store entrance and flipped the sign on the door. Outside, the streetlights spat yellow light upon the snow.

"Do you even have a litter box?" Mickey felt her eyelids drooping. She wanted to go home, but she also couldn't imagine ever leaving this place, utterly unsure who she would be once she stepped outside.

The kid shrugged. "We'll figure it out."

"Will I figure it out?" Mickey asked.

No one answered. Maybe no one had heard.

ARLO

The gymnast with PTSD was halfway through a tearful account of his uncle's birthday dinner when Arlo realized she was doodling. She'd been doodling all session, cluttering the paper on her clipboard with squiggles, flowers, and stars.

". . . and when we sat down to eat, my mom put me at the head of the table with my back to the door even though I called her beforehand and asked her specifically not to do that. Which is a prime example of why I don't tell her things. It's like, what's the point?"

"Mhmmm, mhmmm." Arlo glanced at the clock.

Mickey had spent about a hundred years inside that pawnshop last night. But was she buying or selling? Selling seemed more likely. A diamond necklace or a catalytic converter—something that had fallen off a truck, as the saying went.

The gymnast rubbed his temples. "It got so loud. The kids. The dog."

Arlo would've gone inside to investigate, but the pawnshop had shuttered by the time Mickey emerged. Luckily, they were open until seven today. She would leave as soon as work ended, which was in . . . eight more minutes.

"The dog! He barks and barks and barks, and the whole house has hardwood floors, so the barking, like, reverberates. And my sister just expects me to . . ."

She would pick up a snack on the way—a glory bowl or some such thing. An expensive salad with enough quinoa and edamame to fulfill the day's nutritional requirements.

". . . calls me three times a day asking for . . ."

What with all the sleuthing last night, she'd forgotten to pack a lunch. Now it was almost five, and her stomach had resorted to eating its own lining. She felt a pang every few minutes.

"What do you think? Did I go too far?"

The gymnast's eyes had widened, seeking absolution. But for what?

"Can we pause for a second and appreciate that you're even asking that question?" Arlo said, improvising in her calmest therapy voice, a voice completely unlike her inner voice, which was going, *STUPID STUPID STUPID STUPID FUCK FUCK FUCK FUCK*. Her client could've just achieved a breakthrough, and she would have no way of knowing. The last thirty seconds, she'd heard almost nothing. "I'm so impressed with your impulse to reflect— you know, that self-appraisal piece."

The gymnast chewed on this for a moment. "Yeah. Yeah, I guess."

"That brings us to the end of today," Arlo said, vowing to herself that she would never doodle again so long as she lived. "Same time next week?"

After ushering the gymnast out the door, she jumped in her car and hauled ass to the nearest drive-through Mexican restaurant. She drove with her knees, a burrito in one hand and her phone in the other. Twenty-seven new text messages, all from the same person.

Do you want this

Or this

Do you want any of this

Tell me if you want this

Mother had sent no fewer than fifteen pictures: a hunting jacket, a hardback book about the Rolling Stones, a miniature Harley replica, a harmonica, a power drill, a Chicago Bears sweatshirt, a fountain pen, an ergonomic keyboard, a foot massager, a cooler bag, *The Godfather* trilogy DVD boxed set, a baseball mitt, and one of Daddy's beige hearing aids.

Arlo thumbed a reply as she pulled up to a red light:

Why would I want his hearing aid?

Mother pinged back within seconds:

I don't know that's why I'm asking

She refused to use punctuation. It was her greatest flaw, and the woman had a lot of flaws.

Can't talk now, Mother. I'm busy.

Arlo chomped into her burrito and chewed another mouthful of tender carne asada. She felt so alive.

The pawnshop looked even sadder in the dying light, if such a thing were possible. The golden arches of the McDonald's across the street reflected in the barred windows. A grubby sandwich board on the sidewalk shouted TOP PAY FOR GOLD! DIAMONDS! WATCHES! AND MORE! GET THEM ALL BACK AT EASTSIDE PAWN! The interior was so full of shadows Arlo's eyes needed a moment to adjust after she crossed the threshold.

A man with a thin comb-over and a teenager with thick acne sat side by side on stools behind the glass counter. The boy was doing homework and held a cat in his lap, while the father—Arlo assumed they were father and son; they had the same widow's peak and arching eyebrows—pecked away at a keyboard with his index fingers, concentration blanketing his face.

The teenager rested his pen between the pages of his textbook and smiled a smile of pointy teeth. "Welcome to Eastside Pawn. Let us know if we can help."

The dad muttered something at his computer screen.

"A blonde woman came in here last night." Arlo suppressed a burp. She'd eaten that burrito very fast. "Right before you closed."

Father and son shared a fleeting but distinctly worried look.

"We get a lot of customers." The dad shifted off his stool, stepped to the left of his computer, and leaned forward over the counter, hands rooting on the glass. He wasn't a big man, but his posturing made Arlo shrink away slightly. "Hard to keep them all straight."

"She sold you something," Arlo said.

"You'll have to be more specific than that."

"She's my"—Arlo flexed her neck sideways until it cracked—"sister."

"I meant the item."

"I can't say what it was exactly."

"Then it'll be hard for us to help you."

Arlo read their tense shoulders and clenched mouths. "I'm not a cop."

The teenager was skeptical. "That's exactly what a cop would say."

"Matthew—shush," said the dad.

The cat arched its spine luxuriantly. Its long face was . . . off, somehow. Freakish.

Arlo's phone rang. She saw the name on the screen and felt sorry for herself. "One second," she said, wandering away from the counter and toward a rack of power tools.

"I found more shoes," Mother said.

"How?" was all Arlo could think to say.

"The shed."

"He kept shoes in the shed?"

"Shoes, clothes, car batteries, old skis, stuffed animals—all kinds of shit. Shit I didn't even know he owned. It took me hours. I can't get the smell out of my nose."

"This isn't a good time, Mother." Arlo watched out the corner of her eye as the cashier poked at his keyboard some more. The son had set his textbook aside and was now affixing price stickers on porcelain teacups with a special gun. Poor kid. The hours he must spend in this sad crypt of a store, stocking the shelves with home audio equipment and greeting the weirdo customers and otherwise slaving away for his father, who probably didn't appreciate him, who probably never said thank you, who *probably* would end up leaving the store to someone else.

"There's never a good time with you," Mother said. "I need your help. I don't know what to keep. The donation people won't take anything with stains. What do I do? Throw it all away?"

"I said I don't care." Truly, she didn't. Not the teeniest, tiniest, most microscopic bit. "Get rid of everything." Arlo swiped to end the call.

When she turned back toward the counter, something furry was blocking her path. Sitting evenly on its haunches, the cat stretched its neck long and reached for the ceiling with a pair of enormous ears. The creature was intriguing, though hideous.

Arlo bent and held out the back of her hand. "Hi, kitty."

The cat hissed, revealing a maw of gleaming white barbs.

Arlo recoiled. The backs of her calves collided with something soft but solid, and she lost balance, toppling into what turned out to be a recliner chair. The green velvet-upholstered cushions released a puff of dust into the air.

The teenager reappeared a moment later, towering above Arlo with the now-docile cat folded in the crook of his elbow. "You're definitely not a cop."

"No," Arlo said, suppressing a sneeze. Humiliation settled with the dust. "I'm not."

He frowned. "You'll have to come back in three weeks when the pawn ticket expires."

"The pawn ticket?"

"For the cat. The seller has three weeks to buy her back." He shook his head as if to say, *Who are you? Don't you know how a pawn-shop works? Don't you know anything at all?*

"You mentioned you're about to inherit some money."

A week later, and Arlo was back in the therapy room with Mickey, who'd done nothing but stare at the lighthouse for the last twelve minutes. Was she dissociating? Was she drunk? Arlo couldn't smell it on her for once, but that didn't mean anything. So strong was Mickey's addiction that she'd stolen and pawned someone's beloved cat to buy booze. Any amount of Daddy's money—even an extra couple grand—would do her no good right now.

"Quite the loving gesture, for your dad to take care of you like that," Arlo said, raising her voice a notch. She would pry. She would dig. She would crank Mickey open with a crowbar if she had to. After all, it was for Mickey's benefit. "And it shows he trusted you. When you think of the time and effort it must've taken him to earn that money? It's an honor, don't you think?"

Mickey showed not a flicker of remorse. Or indeed a flicker of anything.

Her gaze, unfocused and vacant, brought to mind the dementia ward where Arlo had done her first student internship. Flat affect. Poverty of speech. Hair that hadn't been washed in at least two weeks, possibly three.

"Do you think you deserve it?" Arlo asked. "The money."

Mickey scrunched her nose and blinked rapidly, at last returning to consciousness. "Did you know I've never had a credit card? Or a line of credit, or a loan."

"Why's that?" Arlo asked, rejoicing. Finally! Something to probe.

"I don't want to make payments on things. Couches and cars and stuff like that. I don't want to"—Mickey's mouth puckered, as if she'd taken a sip of something sour—"owe people."

Not surprising behavior for a recluse who thought all human beings selfish vultures.

Mickey continued: "When my dad up and left, he disappeared. Like, totally. I think he went to Mexico for a year."

Costa Rica. He'd gone to Costa Rica. Arlo used to flip through the photo albums as a little girl, enchanted by the rainbow parrots, the green walls of jungle, Daddy lying in the sand with a hat pulled down over his eyes.

"His creditors took everything from us. I remember when the collections people came to take all the furniture away. They even took my bed. Left the bedding on it and everything. Sheets, pillows, a quilt I'd had since I was a baby. They looked so guilty, so sorry for me. But they still took it."

Had Arlo known about this? Yes, she supposed she had. But the facts of Daddy's departure from his first life had never really troubled her. The man who'd abandoned Mickey and Deborah wasn't Daddy. He was the man who'd preceded Daddy— a separate person. Psychologically, spiritually, even physically. Every cell in the human body died and was replaced many thousands of times over the course of a life. Arlo had read that somewhere once.

"Where did you sleep?" she asked.

"What?"

"After the collections people took your bed."

Mickey shrank to a child right there in her seat. No wrinkles, no scars. Skin the world hadn't left a mark on. "Mom and I shared. We shared until I was fifteen."

When Arlo was a child, she used to sleep in a queen-sized four-poster draped in a gauzy pink canopy that hung from the ceiling. Her fairy bed, she used to call it.

"I've spent most of my life trying not to be like my father," Mickey said. "I mean, it makes sense. When your whole childhood

217

is defined by this awful, awful person, goal number one becomes not turning out like that."

Arlo heard a tapping noise and glanced down to find her fingernail striking the metal bit of the clipboard. She set it aside.

"He's always been there in the back of my head," Mickey went on. "Guiding my decisions, if that makes sense. Like, in an opposite way. He's always been there telling me what not to do."

"And now . . . ?"

Mickey scooted to the edge of her seat and beckoned Arlo closer with a crook of one finger, as if about to share a terrible secret.

Arlo obliged, pulse quickening.

"He's dead," Mickey whispered.

"Yes, I—I know," Arlo said.

"Like, actually dead. Dead, dead, dead, dead, dead."

"And you're just realizing this?"

"Yes, I am just realizing this." Mickey smacked the table—"*Just.*" She smacked it again—"*Realizing.*" Smacked it once more—"*This.*" She sat back. "Logically, I knew that he was dead. But it didn't really register until now that he was gone."

Arlo felt a tweak deep in her forebrain, perhaps a neuron glitching somewhere near the amygdala. She briefly forgot who and where and what she was. "What's the difference?"

"He doesn't do anything or say anything. He doesn't think any thoughts. He can't see me. He can't hear me. He is a non-presence in the world. You know? He's not real."

Arlo reached for Daddy in her mind but couldn't quite grasp him. Disneyland, Ella Fitzgerald, the Harley—all of it was slipping through her fingers. "And what this means for you is that . . ."

Mickey threw up her hands. "I don't know. That's the problem. Before, I was living my life to prove him wrong. Now I'm living my life for nothing."

"You're saying that you don't know how to . . ." What was the right verb? ". . . how to *be*. Without him."

"That's the infuriating part. Even when he was gone from my life, he wasn't actually gone, and now that he *is* really gone, it feels like such a waste." Color fanned across Mickey's cheeks. "It's so stupid. All this time, I could've had a credit card. Who knew?"

"On the topic of money—" Arlo had lost control of the conversation, and now it was spinning uselessly, making her dizzy and somewhat nauseated. "This inheritance. I want to talk some more about that. What are your plans for the—"

"Can we stop there?" Mickey was rising from her chair. No! Why was she rising from her chair? "I'm sorry. I really need to get this afternoon over with."

"Get what over with?"

Mickey slung her coat on.

"Mickey?"

Turned away.

"Mickey."

Reached for the door.

"*Mickey.*"

And was gone.

MICKEY

After therapy, Mickey put herself on a bus and collapsed against the window.

She felt lopsided, her coat pocket heavy with ten thousand ill-gotten dollars. The extra five grand sat idle in her checking account, proof of her moral bankruptcy. How easy it would be to make that cash disappear. According to the rough calculations she'd done (and redone and redone) on her phone, five thousand dollars would buy two hundred and twenty bottles of vodka—one hundred and fifty if she splurged on Absolut. A paltry sum, especially when she remembered Rybka's soft weight in her arms.

She clutched the piece of paper she'd found taped under her peephole that morning. The picture, though grainy, was unmistakable.

LOST CAT
LEOPARD-LIKE SPOTS, ANSWERS TO NAME "RYBKA"
GENEROUS REWARD
CALL DARIA IF FOUND

It was a message: Daria knew. Of course Daria knew. She wasn't stupid. Her expensive-ass cat had gone missing mere seconds after she'd caught Mickey trying to steal one of her expensive-ass sculptures. It wasn't exactly a tough one.

You are the worst person, Rybka told Mickey with her angular face and big gray eyes. *You are the very, very worst.*

The truth shouldn't have hit so hard. Mickey had been on this track since her first sip of Coors at age seven, that day she found her father passed out on the couch with the can cupped loosely in his knubby fingers and his mouth hanging wide. She still remembered the Creamsicle-yellow fuzz on his tongue.

By that age, she knew the smell of beer (like a fruit bowl swirling with flies) and its color (golden as the star on a Christmas tree) and the way it frothed when poured (like bath bubbles). She knew the chink of the pop tab puncturing the can, and she knew the ding of an empty can hitting the floor. But she didn't know the taste.

Mickey's head rammed the window as the bus yawed over a speed bump, or maybe a pothole. Her stop. Shit! This was her stop.

Since her last visit, the neighborhood had accumulated several more inflatable reindeer, a hatted penguin, and a Grinch. Paper snowflakes gummed in the windows; garlands entwined the porch railings; pots of silk poinsettias stood sentry outside every other door.

"Fucking Christmas," she said, kicking through the inch of fresh snow on the sidewalk. It was still falling, landing in white clumps on her eyelashes and her lips.

Mercifully, Chris's house was the least festive on the block. No wreath and no electronic angels—only a snowman listing in the yard. Ian must've rolled the snow, found twigs for the arms, and jabbed in the carrot nose, all with his little hands.

Mickey raised a trembling finger to the doorbell.

Evelyn appeared behind the door. "Oh, hey," she said brightly.

Mickey held out the money. "I'll get you the rest by New Year's."

Evelyn stared at the envelope for half a second before accepting it with surprising reverence. As she lifted the flap and peered inside, her shoulders seemed to relax, and her smile caved, as if she'd been working very hard to buttress it but could manage the effort no longer.

"Oh, good," she said. "Good."

"Miss Mickey!"

Ian appeared at Evelyn's side covered to his elbows in some kind of shining grease. "At first, the eggbeaters made a really big noise, and I didn't like it, but then I covered my ears, and it was okay."

"That's right, baby," Evelyn said. "You did such a good job." She turned to Mickey and added, "We made cookies. Shaped like starfighters, obviously."

"Can Miss Mickey have some?" Ian asked.

Evelyn teased her fingers through Ian's hair, flopping it back over his forehead with . . . pride? And genuine delight? Like the normal, loving mother she couldn't possibly be, not in a million years, because did loving mothers behave as she had?

Something twinged behind Mickey's breastbone. She needed to get off this porch step. "Sorry, kiddo, but I have to—"

"Yes," Evelyn said, cranking the door wide. "Of course, Miss Mickey can have some."

Scents of ginger and molasses wafted from the glowing oven while a second tray of unbaked cookies lay waiting on the counter. Mickey stood there in the middle of the kitchen, unsure what to do with herself.

Ian climbed the stool in front of the sink and held out his hands, which Evelyn squirted with golden dish soap. She turned the left tap, tested the water, turned the right tap, tested the water again. Then she helped him lather, rubbing his hands delicately in her own and singing—*singing?*—in his ear: "*This is the way we wash our hands, wash our hands, wash our hands. This is the way we wash our hands, so we're nice and clean.*"

After toweling off, Ian hopped down from the stool and lifted his pant leg to reveal a single lime-green sock, one half of the pair Mickey had bought him at the trampoline park. "Look," Ian said.

"That was a fun day," Mickey managed to say.

Ian showed his sock to Evelyn. "I got this with Uncle Chris and Miss Mickey while you were away, Mama. Only I don't know where the other one went."

Evelyn flushed fast and pink with shame—the pure, unfiltered, entirely justified shame of having abandoned her child and misused everyone who cared for him. "Go check the couch."

As Ian's footsteps receded deeper into the house, Evelyn folded a tea towel against her chest, taking care to line up the corners. Twice, she shook it out and started over. There was something so quietly desperate about it that Mickey couldn't help but soften toward her.

"His face is different compared to before I left," Evelyn said quietly.

True. Ian's jaw had lengthened in the last month or two.

"And he's way taller," Evelyn said.

True again. They changed fast at this age.

Evelyn gave up on the tea towel and threw it aside. Her topknot was unraveling, sloping off the side of her head. "It got to be too much. It got to be too much, so I bailed."

Bailed, as if she'd canceled last minute on sushi plans or ditched her friends at some sticky college bar to hook up with a lacrosse player. Nineteen-year-olds did that sort of thing—most nineteen-year-olds. The ones whose lives hadn't imploded in ninth grade. It couldn't have been easy for Evelyn to walk the packed halls of her junior high school with a baby belly sticking out.

Mickey sighed. She'd found it so much harder to pass judgment since stealing that cat.

"And yeah, okay, I've done it before," Evelyn said. "But I'm back now, and I'm in this. For real. This time is different. That's what the money is for—so we can have a fresh start."

"Fresh start?" Mickey found this term worrisome.

"Hey."

Chris appeared in the doorway with a red plastic baseball bat in hand. Unshaven and barefoot, he wore jeans and a Harvard hoodie that would've looked obnoxious on anyone else.

"What are you doing here?" he asked. "I mean—I don't mind that you're here. I'm just surprised."

Evelyn snatched up the envelope, which she'd tucked in the fruit bowl beside a bunch of bananas. "She stopped by to see how my little man was doing."

Mickey remembered the nine unanswered messages still languishing in her voicemail inbox. Her turn to flush with shame. "Why are you home? It's Wednesday."

"To hang out with Ian." Chris took a mock swing with the bat. "Did you see our snowman?"

"I told her Ian is great," Evelyn said. "Ready for the move."

The ozone layer ripped, and the world deflated, its atmosphere siphoning out into space.

"The move?" Mickey asked.

Evelyn was refolding the tea towel again.

"The move?" Mickey repeated, to Chris this time.

"Uh, yeah—yeah, they're all packed." The baseball bat fell to his side. "Listen—it's been a while. You feel like a walk?"

He was already propping the bat against the wall, folding his body into a coat.

"They're leaving?" Mickey asked, once the door had swung shut behind them.

Chris sped his way up the sidewalk.

She ran to catch him. "Leaving to go where?"

"She's got a new boyfriend in Trail."

"That's hours away."

"And a job in a dentist's office."

"Who cares?"

"She's his mom. He loves her."

Name one force, Mickey thought, *that could lead a person further astray than love.* "She's a disaster."

"*She's* a disaster?" Chris said with a humorless laugh.

Her feet stalled. Chris had walked half a block before he seemed to realize she was no longer following him. He turned and jogged back, breath billowing up into his long eyelashes.

"A kid should be with his family," Chris said. "Don't you think?"

"Yes," she said. "That's exactly what I think."

He had such a delicate face. He was a delicate person, his fragility more obvious here, now, on a slippery street in December with the cold pressing on his pinkish complexion. Mickey wanted to shake him.

A man tinkered with an electric air pump in the next yard. The machine groaned to life, and a puddle of red plastic on the lawn sprouted into an enormous candy cane.

"Can we . . ." Chris cocked his head, gesturing for them to keep moving.

Mickey wouldn't budge. "She's in way over her head."

"I know."

"She abandoned him." Mickey was almost shouting, straining to hear herself over the whirr of that fucking air pump.

"I know."

"What happened to 'I could take care of him' and 'I could actually do this'?"

"Just because I *could* take care of him doesn't mean I *should*. It wasn't the plan."

"Kids never are. They just happen."

"What makes you the expert? Seriously. I want to know."

Because Mickey had once been abandoned. Because she, too, had been caught in a storm of reckless adults. Been bruised. Been damaged.

"I'm a kindergarten teacher."

Chris scoffed. "*Ex* kindergarten teacher."

This gave her pause.

The air pump went quiet, and Mickey could hear herself again: the breath whirling down into her teacher's lungs, the pulse of her teacher's heart.

"It's who I am," she said. "It's who I'll always be."

Chris rubbed his face in his palms, flustering those massive eyebrows of his. "This is ridiculous. Ian's home is with his mother. I thought you agreed. That's why you didn't call the police in the first place."

"That was before," Mickey said.

He stepped closer. "Before what?"

Mickey noticed, for the first time, the gray hairs scattered in his eyebrows and the tiny scar between his nose and upper lip. Before she knew it, she'd glimpsed that future again—the one where they drank French-pressed coffee together and painted an accent wall. Wore matching Halloween costumes. Put their hands in each other's back pockets while they walked, knowing it was cringey to do so but not caring. Then she remembered where and who and what she was.

"You have a chance to give him a better start than she can," Mickey said, stepping back.

"How?" He threw his arms wide, the exasperation raw in his voice. "No—really—I want know how. What do you suggest I do? Steal him?"

"Talk to her. Help her see that it's an option."

"It's not an option. I'm not his dad."

But he could be. Chris could drive Ian to soccer practices, show him how to tie his shoes, teach him how to cook a steak. There would be hard times—slamming doors and shouting matches—but in the end, they would love each other and keep each other.

"She's blackmailing me," Mickey said.

Chris sneered. Actually. Mickey had never seen someone sneer in real life—before now, she wasn't even sure what such a thing would look like—but there it was. He'd sneered.

"Mickey, come on," he said.

"What? She is. You don't believe me?"

He backed away with his palms turned out, a gesture that said *You're crazy. You're a crazy person.* "I've been really worried about you. You screen my calls, you ignore my messages, and then you show up here out of the blue to yell at me?"

Mickey grew colder as he said this, each word a needle in her spine.

"Who are you to us, anyway? I've known you for two months. Maybe you need to back off a little." Chris must've seen the hurt on her face because he seemed to sway slightly, and his tone softened. "Look—"

"No, you're right," Mickey said. Of course he was right. This wasn't friendship. It wasn't any kind of ship. She and Chris were two disparate humans adrift in the cosmos on the nugget of rock and soil known as earth. They shared nothing but the ground on which they stood. It was a fantasy, and not the future, Mickey had been staring into.

She opened her mouth to say goodbye but then decided it would be silly and probably melodramatic. There was no parting from someone who was never yours.

◎

The last time Mickey saw her mother was the time with the garbage bags. Mama had opened the door a crack and given a clumsy speech about how hard this was for her, and how it broke her heart, and if only there were another way. Mickey had quit listening. Because Mickey was twenty-two and sure of everything.

Now, watching her mother through the window of the hair salon, Mickey wasn't sure of anything at all.

Mama swanned around restocking the shelves, her slim body folding as she scooped up more shampoo bottles from the cardboard box on the floor. She had the same flax-gold hair as always, the same long nose, the same denim overalls. Always so much denim.

One thing had changed: she'd realized her greatest ambition. After all the years of scrimping pennies and scrolling rental listings and doodling logos on restaurant napkins, she'd actually done it.

Mama gathered the empty box in her arms and picked at the tape that held it together. After fumbling with it for a minute or two, she returned the box to the ground and stomped on it until the walls flattened. She picked up this crunch of cardboard and disappeared from view.

Mickey pulled open the door and stepped into her mother's dream.

A slow rendition of "Feliz Navidad" slogged through the air, which smelled faintly of coconut. A jar of pink candy canes sat brightly on the counter beside an animatronic Christmas tree Mickey guessed would sing if she pushed a button. Classic Mama. The business license on the wall bore her name, and hers alone.

Mickey found her sweeping the floor around the hairdresser's chair.

"You got your own salon."

The broom clattered to the tile.

"Jesus Christ." Mama piled her hands over her heart. "You scared the shit out of me."

"Sorry." Mickey searched her mother's face, where a smile hatched, quivered, and fell. Not an expression of unbridled joy, but Mickey would take it. "I came for a cut. That's all."

Mama stared at her so blankly Mickey felt compelled to add, "For my hair. A haircut."

Leaving the broom on the ground, Mama led Mickey to the sink.

Scalp massages had been their ritual since before Mickey could remember. Every evening of her childhood, she would sit on the living room floor while Mama sat behind her on the sofa and kneaded the muscle at the base of her skull. No words were ever exchanged, but Mickey always felt understood. The tradition had petered out in seventh grade around the time she discovered raspberry Smirnoff.

"It's exactly like you wanted," Mickey said, as water from the tap spilled into her ears and down her neck. One of the Christmas garlands strung across the ceiling had come untacked and tossed in the breeze from a nearby vent.

She could hear Mama pumping shampoo, lathering it between her palms.

"The salon? Truth is, sometimes the place stresses me out so much I forget to be thankful. I might hire an extra set of hands in the new year."

"You must be pretty successful then."

A clay-like smell melted in Mickey's nose as Mama worked the shampoo into her hair. The clot in her stomach began to loosen.

"I don't really think in those terms," Mama said.

Mickey remembered the tarot cards, the star charts, the TV psychics with their swirling cosmic backdrops. So great was Mama's distaste for the industrial capitalist complex after Mickey's dad left—crushing debt will do that to a person—that she'd surrounded herself with tokens of the divine and forsaken all pursuit of personal wealth. Except for the Italian leather handbag she bought in the TV auction that one time. And that new dishwasher. And now she was a business owner.

"You haven't changed," Mickey said, containing a laugh.

She waited for Mama to say *Neither have you.*

"They invited me to see your dad's headstone, you know."

Mickey's stomach reknotted.

"They bought him a big fancy one—a tall one, like in a movie. They're getting together next week to unveil it."

"Who's 'they'?"

"The daughter came to see me."

"What, here?"

"Twice."

Mickey imagined her half-sister reclined in this very seat. Surprising how much it bothered her, the idea of Mama washing Charlotte's hair, pressing her care and attention into Charlotte's scalp. And yet she felt a strange pull to know more. "What was she like?"

Mama was quiet for a moment. "Young. And small. Tired, I think."

That would make sense. Just because their father hadn't abandoned *Charlotte* as a child or ruined *her* mother financially, that didn't mean life with him had necessarily been easy. Charlotte would have had to fluff his hospital pillows and stroke his brow while he lay dying. This after twenty-five years of flagrant emotional manipulation. Mickey had dealt with his bullshit for seven years. Charlotte would have dealt with his bullshit her whole life.

"Lonely," Mama added.

The water cut. She began plying the conditioner.

"The thing is next week. Thursday, eleven o'clock, Greenwood Cemetery. If you felt like maybe coming w—"

"Why would you want to go to that?" The mere idea of attending—of celebrating the man who'd so thoroughly derailed their lives—made Mickey's stomach lurch.

"Closure," Mama said, raking conditioner through the ends of Mickey's hair.

Closure. *Closure.* Clo-sure. Nope—no matter how many times Mickey repeated the word to herself, it never got any less absurd.

"We were together a long time," Mama said.

"Stalin ruled Russia for twenty-five years."

"There are people in life who stick with you."

"Chairman Mao, Kim Jong-il, Mussolini."

"Even a long time after they've gone. They color your life in a certain way."

Mickey bristled. What the fuck did that even mean?

Mama stepped in front of the sink, backlit and dripping from her fingertips. Mickey couldn't make out her expression, but her voice was desperate. "I should've left him before he had the chance to dump us. I'm sorry."

Mickey sat up on her forearms. A chill trickled down the back of her neck—dripping water, most likely, or maybe she was having some kind of neurological event. She'd waited a long time to hear those words and now didn't know what to do with them. Forgiving Mama would be a betrayal to her younger self, the tough kernel at her core. But Mickey couldn't deny Mama completely. She needed to offer something in return.

"I stopped drinking?"

The phrase hovered there. Mickey wasn't sure why she'd said it as a question.

"When?" Mama asked.

"Two weeks?"

Again as a question! Why?

When Mama next spoke, she sounded less like herself and more like the user interface for a smart-home system. "Are you getting help?"

Mickey stiffened. Cold is what she was getting. "I have a counselor I see."

"How often?"

"I'm paid up for one more session. I've done six." What did it matter? She was sober. Hadn't Mama heard?

"But you're gonna keep going, right?"

"I don't know. I haven't decided." Mickey laid back down and squeezed her own hair out in the sink. "Why aren't you happy? You wanted me to stop. I stopped."

"Is it enough, an odd counseling session here and there? A lot of addicts"—Mickey flinched; that word, God, that word—"need more support. Especially at the start."

Mama would know this, of course, from all the reading she'd done, the webinars she'd watched, the Al-Anon meetings she'd attended in people's basements during Mickey's university years. She used to come home with armfuls of brochures and buzz-phrases like *Progress not perfection, One day at a time, It's a family disease.*

Then Amsterdam happened, and she quit with all that.

"You think I'm too fucked up," Mickey said.

"No. I don't think—"

"You think I'm beyond repair."

Unbelievable. This was Mickey's mother, the person who'd bathed her and changed her and bandaged her knees after every scrape. Loving Mickey was her one job. If anyone on earth could do it, she could. And yet she chose not to.

Mama drew a slow inhale and let it go as a sigh. Long inhale, sigh.

"Are you taking deep breaths right now?" Mickey asked.

Again: the inhale, the exhale.

"Because that's how much I distress you." Mickey pulled herself upright and flopped out of the seat, the conditioner still thick in her hair. "I'm leaving."

She saw Mama cowed there, shoulders heaving, lashes filmy with tears, and the years peeled back. Mickey was twenty-two again, stepping off that airplane.

This was what she and Mama did, what they'd always done.

ARLO

The journey to her parents' place had never taken this long before. Traffic was weirdly thick for the time of day, and every light was red, and had there always been so many school zones? As Arlo stopped and started and stopped and started, inching her way out of the city and into the suburbs, she quit trying to feel calm and yelled along to "White Christmas" on the radio, only half-aware of the tears on her cheeks and the leering driver in the next lane.

Arlo often consoled grieving clients by saying the dead were never truly gone. *They never leave us*, she'd say, *because we go on carrying their love*. But if this were true, and Daddy's love was still on Arlo's person, bouncing around in her pockets like loose change, then why couldn't she feel it? Arlo couldn't even picture him anymore. Since that last session with Mickey, every image of him had darkened and blurred, as if none of it had ever been real in the first place, like that movie from the eighties where everyone lives on Mars, and they download memories into people's brains from vacations that didn't actually happen.

Everything would be better once Arlo arrived home. She needed to sweep a pile of Daddy's shirts into her arms and squash them against her chest and absorb the smell of his cologne. Nothing cleared the mind like a whiff of Daddy's Dior Bois d'Argent.

The neighborhood lake lay still as she drove past, its waters shining and black. She followed the bridge over the snowy creek bed, passed the outdoor tennis courts, and gunned it up the long slope to her parents' house, a glass ornament at the top of the hill.

Daddy loved these big windows. And the plum tree in the yard—he loved that, too. And the snow-topped hydrangea bushes. In fact, the whole exterior of the house screamed "Daddy." Except the silver Saturn in the driveway, which Arlo couldn't account for. None of her parents' friends would drive a dented piece of shit like this, and mother's cleaning lady drove a minivan.

She parked beside the Saturn and clambered out, pain streaking up her thighs after such a long time seated. Peering through the window of the mystery car, she noted a stray sock in the backseat, a balled-up McDonald's bag on the passenger-side floor, and a paper Slurpee cup in the middle console. A track of footprints in the snow led from the Saturn to the front porch.

Arlo fetched an extra shoe from her backseat—beige pump with respectable heel—and held it at the ready. It was probably just a neighbor or a salesperson or someone collecting money for the United Way, but it might also be a burglar or a murderer, and wouldn't it be prudent to have something pointy on hand? She wasn't thinking about it too hard.

She swung the door. Here was the same old floor mat, the same old foyer table, the same old decorative copper vase, something Mother had probably spent five grand on. Light spiraled down from the chandelier, illuminating familiar chinks and scrapes in the hardwood.

Oddly disappointed, Arlo lowered her shoe and stepped into the living room. Then she gasped.

Gone were Daddy's books and records. The jungle scene painting, which had hung above the fireplace; the turntable that usually shored on the credenza—these things were gone, too. The TV had been set, inexplicably, to a light-rock music channel. Sheryl Crow sang about soaking up the sun.

Men's voices drifted up from the basement.

"*This place is huge.*"

"*You've said that like eight times.*"

"*Well, it is. It's really freakin' huge.*"

Arlo padded through the kitchen and descended the first flight of stairs, pausing on the landing. It did not occur to her that she should leave. This was, after all, her house.

"*You think they like whiskey?*"

"*Don't snoop.*"

"*I'm allowed to open the cabinets. Aren't I?*"

Another person spoke—a woman's muffled voice. Arlo could almost make out the words.

Down she went, treading on the balls of her feet.

At the foot of the stairs, the glass door to the games room stood ajar. The same soft-rock channel wafted from the TV within, the audio playing one or two seconds ahead of its faint echo on the main floor. Two sunken squares of carpet marked the spots where Daddy's Pac-Man and Big Buck Hunter had once stood. It seemed someone had swooped in here with a screwdriver, dismantled the machines, and carted them away on a dolly. Boom, done, as if Daddy's stuff had meant nothing.

The stuff had not meant nothing.

Arlo blamed herself. She should've guarded the stuff better, appreciated it more. She should've spent more time with the stuff while it was still around. People went their whole lives searching for it, this kind of stuff, never knowing what it was like to love a Pac-Man machine, a Pac-Man machine put on earth specifically for them. Arlo knew. She'd always had a Pac-Man machine—the best, bravest Pac-Man machine of all. Now it was stolen, lost, probably resold to a stranger for half its true value, and where did that leave her?

She didn't realize she was running until the hallway blurred, and the living room came into view. She didn't realize she was screaming and waving her shoe until a woman in dress pants crumpled on the ground. Two men—leather jackets, ballcaps—took cover behind the couch.

"Get out!" Arlo shook her shoe some more.

The woman scooted backward on her butt and shielded herself with one raised arm. "Who are you? Get back."

"*You* get back," Arlo said.

"I'll call 911."

"*I'll* call 911. This is my parents' house."

The woman clapped a hand over her eyes and hung her head. "Oh my God."

"What?" Arlo said.

"I'm the realtor."

A realtor. A realtor?

"Who did you think we were?" the woman asked.

Burglars was too ridiculous to say aloud.

"You're clearly showing the wrong house," Arlo said, suddenly very aware of her ears, which she was sure had turned a different color.

The realtor disappeared behind the couch. "I'm so sorry, guys. Are you okay?" She popped her head up and aimed a soldering glare at Arlo. "Maybe you should call your mom."

Arlo made a *pfff* sound. Then she took out her phone.

"Finally," Mother said in place of *hello*. "I left you seven messages."

"I'm at the house," Arlo said, wandering back toward the games room.

"Why? There's a showing."

"I thought they were, like, intruders or something."

"What?"

236

"I stormed into the basement with a . . ." Arlo glanced at the stupid shoe in her stupid hand. "I stormed into the basement."

"Why didn't you call me?" Mother asked. "In the moment."

Once again, Arlo found herself hovering over the patch of carpet where the Pac-Man machine had been. "I didn't think to."

The line fell quiet.

"You thought the house was full of intruders, and it didn't cross your mind to check on your mother." It wasn't a question.

But Mother was missing the point.

"You put the house up for sale?" Arlo asked.

"You didn't notice the sign on the lawn?"

"There's no sign."

"Go look."

Arlo jogged upstairs, went to the window by the front door, and peered into the yard. "It's not a very big sign."

Mother muttered something under her breath.

An ache sprouted somewhere near the back of Arlo's heart. This was her childhood home. She'd practiced cartwheels in the living room and done math homework at the kitchen table and helped Daddy plant perennials in the flowerbeds. This house had made her—these walls, this roof. These floorboards!

"Why is the house for sale?" she asked, gently stroking a nearby sconce. The sconces!

"It's too big for one person," Mother said.

"It was too big for two people."

"Yeah, well, I really notice it now."

"You couldn't have asked me first?"

"You don't live there."

"It's still my home." Arlo went to the living room and swept a hand along the shelf that had once held Daddy's LPs. CCR. Mellencamp. His original 1966 copy of *Pet Sounds*. "And where's all the stuff?"

"I called a junk company to take it all away. The man was very nice. Alex. He got everything loaded up in under two hours. Very, very nice. Great forearms."

Reality rose up around Arlo, engulfing her to the neck, the chin, the nose, the eyes. She was drowning in it. "You're telling me Daddy's things are in a landfill somewhere."

"You told me to throw it all away."

"No, I didn't."

"Yes, you did. On the phone the other day. 'I don't care,' you said. 'Get rid of everything.'"

That conversation in the pawnshop. But had Arlo really said that? If she'd said it, she hadn't meant it. Of course she wanted Daddy's things. If she couldn't keep his money, or his memory, or even his love, then by God, she at least wanted his Bruce Springsteen bobblehead.

"And it was good advice," Mother said. "I felt lighter the second Alex drove away."

Arlo sank onto the couch. "Did you at least save something? Some shoes?"

"For what?"

"I don't know, a keepsake?"

"You need a shoe to remember your father?"

"Of course not. It's just that . . . you know . . . he's dead." Arlo heard her voice splinter into little pieces. "Like, *dead* dead."

Mother was silent.

"Like, actually," Arlo said. "He's actually dead. Gone. Over. The end."

"You're only realizing this now?"

"He won't do anything or say anything ever again."

"That is how death works," Mother said.

Arlo almost hung up then and there. "Don't do that."

"Don't do what? I'm agreeing with you."

Grief was a learned process. As a therapist, Arlo knew this. She was learning to live in a world without Daddy, which would take time and practice. She just hadn't expected to be so bad at it. The more time that passed, the harder it seemed to get.

"I don't know how to be without him." Arlo was in front of the living room fireplace suddenly, gazing up at the pearly white urn on the mantel.

"I get it. Look at me, on my own for the first time in how many—"

"No. You're not listening." She reached out and pressed her fingertips to the stone. Cool, smooth. Almost like touching a face. "I don't know how to *be* without him."

Mother's tone softened. "Do you want to come over Thursday morning? We could drive to the cemetery together."

He was here. He was right here.

"Charlotte? Are you still there?"

Arlo swiped to end the call and swept the urn against her chest.

Six hours before her death, Laura Hedman had given Arlo a locket. "I want you to have this," she'd said, dangling the necklace from three fingers as their final therapy session drew to a close. A small silver heart swished and spun at the end of a long chain. "As a thank you. For everything."

Though Arlo wasn't supposed to accept gifts from clients, the locket was so tiny and tinny—so obviously cheap—that she accepted it without thought and jammed it in her pocket. After arriving home that night, she took the locket and put it somewhere. She hadn't divined a purpose for it. Until today.

She swore she'd tucked it away in the drawer under the microwave in her apartment. The locket had to be there, coiled up behind a deck of playing cards or knotted in some charging cables or buried in a pile of spare change and bobby pins. But even when Arlo dumped all this crap on the counter and combed through it with her fingertips, even when she peered into the back of the empty drawer with a flashlight, the locket did not reveal itself.

Her desk, then. She flung open the drawers and rummaged through stationery, spare pens, crumpled sticky notes, certificates for continuing education workshops she'd attended and promptly forgotten about.

After the desk, she checked her nightstand. After her nightstand, she checked her pockets. Every single pocket in every single item of clothing she owned. Dress pants, jeans, skirts, dresses, sweatshirts, everything. She pawed through each garment before casting it aside on the bed or the floor. Soon she was wading up to her calves in cotton and polyester while her temples throbbed and her heart thudded. The locket wasn't there. It wasn't anywhere.

Arlo tossed one last blazer on the mattress, then tossed herself there, too. Maybe she hadn't brought the locket home at all. It could be in her desk at work or in her car. Maybe it had fallen out of her pocket at some point. The locket could be in the landfill, the gutter, the sewer.

She rolled onto her side and made a tight seed of her body.

And there it was, catching sunlight from the window. The locket dangled from a bedpost, so constant a sight she'd stopped seeing it altogether.

Arlo lunged for the necklace and swiped it off the post. Sweet relief! She'd kept it! She wasn't a bad person!

The heart sank in her palm like a small chunk of ice, heavier and colder than she remembered. It snapped open easily, revealing a hollow that would hold about half a teaspoon of Daddy's ashes—the same amount she'd taken from the urn.

Arlo scanned the wreckage of her bedroom. The ashes. She'd put them down on the dresser in the little plastic baggie she'd taken from her parents' house. Or maybe she hadn't. When she jumped out of bed and crossed the room, the top of the dresser was bare.

Had she left the baggie on her nightstand? On her bed? Arlo shoveled through the clothes that had amassed absolutely fucking everywhere.

"You've got to be kidding me," she said.

She checked the bathroom, the living room, the small table by the front door, the glazed ceramic oyster shell where she kept her keys. She went out to her car and checked the cupholders, the glove box, the pit under the driver's seat full of hair and nickels. She came back inside and checked the bathroom again, lowering onto all fours to peer behind the toilet.

Panic crashed down on her in waves. If misplacing Laura's locket made Arlo a bad person, then losing Daddy's ashes made her a villain. She was Harvey Weinstein. She was Peter Nygard. She was Pol Pot.

She went into the kitchen and combed through the junk drawer again. She rolled the apples around the fruit bowl, peered behind the espresso machine. Maybe she'd put the ashes in the fridge. People put weird things in the fridge when their minds were pre-occupied—wallets, car keys, why not ashes? She yanked it open, blinked at the empty glass shelf, and fumbled through the bottles of soy sauce and expired salad dressing on the inside of the door.

"Where the hell is he!" she cried.

They should never have divided the ashes in the first place. Daddy was Catholic, after all, and how would he rise from the dead at Armageddon if half of him was in the cemetery, half of him was on Mother's mantel, and a speck of him hung around Arlo's neck? Was she overthinking this?

She shuffled into the bathroom again, planted her hands on the counter, and leaned forward until her nose brushed its reflection. "Snap out of it." As she leaned back on her heels, something else in the mirror caught her eye—a bulge in her left pocket.

Oh, right. She'd put him in her pocket.

Arlo pulled out the crumpled sandwich bag.

The ashes weren't what she'd expected—like cinders from a campfire but sandier, with white flecks of what must've been bone or tooth.

She used a tiny funnel to make sure none of the ashes ended up on the kitchen counter instead of inside the locket, then zipped the empty bag nice and tight and set it down on the counter, unsure where it should go. Not the garbage, surely. This baggie, while plastic and disposable, contained microscopic pieces of her departed father.

The two halves of the locket clicked back together. She slipped it over her head and felt it settle in the depression between her collarbones.

After deliberating on the matter of the baggie for some time, Arlo folded it up and placed it in the junk drawer and poured herself a glass of wine.

MICKEY

By the time Thursday rolled around, Mickey had consumed two extra-large cheese pizzas, two bags of Cool Ranch Doritos, twelve cans of Coke, a tub of ice cream, and zero alcohol. Not a lick, not a drop, hell, she hadn't even smelled the stuff. She hadn't consumed any alcohol because to do so would be to concede. She stood on a precipice with the entire world—Mama, Tom, Daria, Chris, the psychologist, everyone, everyone she'd dared to trust over these last few months—shouting at her to jump.

But she would not jump. She would dig in her heels. She would resist. That was why she'd spent the last week eating processed food alone in her apartment. She would simply wait for the cravings to disappear, for the bad thoughts to settle, for the great, big, vacuous hole in her middle to close over.

She stood at the window in her living room with a thrice-microwaved cup of coffee as night shuffled out of the sky. It was seven in the morning, and she hadn't slept much. Not that she ever slept much anymore. Not the way Mama probably slept. Mama probably got eight hours a night. Calm, cool, emotionally stable Mama with her deep breaths and her boundaries.

Mickey found a pizza box under a pile of blankets on the couch, pulled out a hardened slice, and tore into it like a dog.

Mama was going to the headstone unveiling for closure, which was basically the most pathetic thing Mickey had ever heard. How could she still need closure after over twenty-five years? Two and a half decades of reeling from the devastation Mickey's father had unleashed upon their lives, Mickey didn't need closure. Her feelings about her father were one hundred percent resolved—so resolved that, as proof, she found her coat and boots, dragged her ass to the bakery around the corner, picked out a fresh pie, and bought it for her damn self.

Back at the apartment, she took a fork from the sink and sat down on the couch with the whole pie in her lap. The bakery hadn't sold pecan, so she'd gone with pumpkin: an adjacent flavor. The crust made a pleasant crackling sound as she hacked into it. The filling melted on her tongue. Sweet but spicy. A hint of nutmeg.

Silence enveloped Mickey. No one was saying *I'm sorry*, or *I'm proud of you*, or *I love you*. No one was saying anything at all, which was fine because nothing needed to be said.

If Mickey went to the unveiling today, she would watch with only passing interest. If there were speeches, she would only half listen. She would watch her dad's second wife tug back a curtain to reveal an atrociously decadent headstone, something with ionic columns and sculpted lions, and she wouldn't care enough even to scoff. While the crowd whistled and gasped, overcome with emotion, Mickey would feel nothing. Because she was beyond him.

ARLO

Arlo twisted to peer back at the shrouded headstone, rooting one palm on the podium for balance. The black drape fluttered and rumpled in the wind, which still blew even though her father was dead. Snow coated the ground, sparkling under the bright sun even though her father was dead. Birds chattered in a nearby copse of trees, singing their friendly hellos even though her father was, yes, dead. She stood before a great tide of indifference, waiting to be swallowed.

"He would think we're crazy, sitting out here in the cold," Arlo said to the audience. Four dozen mourners shivered on flimsy plastic chairs with their scarves pulled up to their eyeballs. "So I'll try and make this short."

She thanked them all for coming. At least, she meant to thank them. Maybe it was the gravity of the situation, or maybe the low temperature was messing with her sensory-perceptual functions, but for whatever reason, it was hard to tell the difference between the words in her head and the words on her lips.

"He wasn't a perfect man," she found herself saying. "Not even close."

The audience laughed, or maybe that was the birds again. Mother was squinting in the front row, the frost a white rime on her falsies.

"He could be quick to anger. He could be slow to forgive. He ate and drank too much. He kept the volume on everything turned up to like a hundred. If you were in another room of the house, and he wanted to talk to you, he would never walk over and find you. He would just yell and yell and yell until you answered."

More laughter/bird chatter.

"He could get terrible road rage. He hated my boyfriends. He wouldn't eat any of the healthy food I cooked for him. One time in the hospital he took a salad I made and threw it at the wall. The balsamic vinegar left a stain in the tile grout. I bought this special spray—this industrial-strength cleaner—to try and get it out, but nothing worked."

The battle she'd waged against that stain. How she'd pressed her body weight into the floor and scrubbed, scrubbed, scrubbed, because that was her job.

"He was so rude to the hospital staff I was afraid they would kick him out."

Another of her jobs: to worry. To fuss over Daddy's broken legs, his amputated toes, his vomit, God, all the vomit. Red wine vomit, sudsy beer vomit, vomit with chunks of steak mixed in. The dry-heaving, the moaning as he clutched his stomach and spasmed. The number of times she'd thought, *This is it. He's going to die.*

Arlo reached to her throat and rolled the locket between her fingertips. The metal was almost too cold to touch.

"Loss is the other side of love. That's a thing I always tell my clients. Because it makes sense. You can't lose something you never loved, and everything you love, you're going to inevitably lose. Unless you're the person who dies first, I guess. But you get what

I'm saying. Grief, love—it's all the same thing. For years, I have thought this. So, naturally, when my own father died, I assumed I would get to keep the love. His love."

Arlo loosened the top button of her coat. Pressure was building inside her like steam, expanding outward, threatening to split her open. "But do you know something?"

The audience members threw wide-eyed stares, their brows disappearing under woolen hats.

Arlo leaned in close to the mic. "That's all a bunch of horse-shit."

Her seams burst, and what spilled out was laughter. It clouded the air so thickly that the audience disappeared for a whole second or two. She laughed and laughed and couldn't stop. Because it was funny, how wrong she'd been about grief and love and Daddy and everything. It was fucking hilarious!

Yet when the fog cleared, oddly, no one else looked very happy. She would have to explain further, help them understand.

Arlo found the locket again and closed the heart pendant in her fist. "I carry Daddy right here around my neck. A tiny bit of him, that is, a bit of his ashes. Maybe it's his spleen, maybe it's his elbow. I don't know, but it's all I have left. Like, actually all I have left. All my memories of him have been compromised because it turns out he was this huge asshole to everyone, including me, and I just didn't realize it until now."

She didn't have Daddy's love. Maybe she'd never had his love. He was, after all, the worst person ever. And how much lighter it made her feel to speak this truth aloud. She was a feather. She was a snowflake. She was the air itself.

"Not only do I not have his love, but I don't have any of his money either. I don't have any of his money because he cut me out of the will at the last second and gave it all to his other daughter, some girl he hadn't seen in literal decades, whose life, by the way, he totally ruined. I would know this because she's seeing me for therapy—something else my father contrived and further evidence of his being a fundamentally terrible person."

For some reason, a lot fewer people were staring at her now. Most audience members were looking at the ground, or at their own gloved hands, or at each other.

"Like, did the rest of you know how awful he was? I was vaguely aware of some things but not everything. I knew, but I didn't *know*. You know?"

A woman in the third row lowered her scarf, a few twists of hair springing out from under her hat. Deborah. She whispered to the person in the next seat, whom Arlo didn't recognize. But this stranger still caught her eye, and the longer she looked the more this person began to resolve herself into someone Arlo did know. But she belonged to a different part of Arlo's life, this person. She did not belong here in the cemetery with the wind and the sun and the birds that kept singing even though Arlo's terrible father was dead. Arlo's and . . . Mickey's.

Arlo tried to turn and run but couldn't. She was no longer a feather, or a snowflake, or the air. She was herself, and she was frozen. Her muscles wouldn't contract. Her feet wouldn't carry her. And so she closed her eyes and went down into her body and nestled there among her organs, her tissues, her thudding pulse. It was quiet down inside her body.

Until it wasn't.

"Charlotte? Charlotte."

Her name stretched and warped, as if traveling through water.

She opened her eyes. A dog collar, an overcoat, a bad haircut. A priest. Yes, they'd invited Daddy's priest. His hand was on her forearm. He stood very close.

"Charlotte?" he said.

In the audience, Mickey was rising. Yes, Mickey was here, and she'd heard Arlo's speech, and now she knew the truth. Worse, she knew Arlo had kept it from her.

"Charlotte, are you alright?"

Adrenaline coursed through Arlo's bloodstream. Maybe she could fix it. Maybe if she explained? "I didn't know at first," she said into the microphone. Her own voice sprang through the loudspeaker and ricocheted off the walls of her skull. "I swear I didn't."

As Mickey approached, her face showed no signs of sympathy, or anger, or anything. This absence of emotion was more frightening than the most febrile rage would've been. If Mickey were angry—if she were raising her voice in indignation or ripping a tissue into tiny pieces, as she'd done in the therapy room—at least Arlo would've known what was coming.

Instead, Mickey reached the podium and just stood there, long tendrils of breath rising from her nostrils. She wore no scarf or hat, her ears and nose a meaty shade of pink.

The priest regarded Mickey curiously. "Are you a friend, dear?"

Mickey flashed a smile so broad and bracing the sheer force of it set Arlo off balance. "Family," she said.

"We're . . . she's . . ." Arlo didn't know what to say. She wanted to sink her fingers into the past and claw her way back. Why not rewind the last two minutes? It was so short a time, the moment in question so recent. Why couldn't she just undo it?

Mickey nodded at the microphone. "My turn." It wasn't a question.

Arlo stepped aside. Rather than return to her seat beside Mother, she braced her hip against the headstone and gathered some of the velvet drape in her fist.

"None of you know me, but I'm Michelle."

No murmurs, no chatter. No reaction from the audience whatsoever.

"Michelle Kowalski." Her bare hands seemed to vibrate as she flattened them on the podium. "Adam here"—she gestured to the veiled headstone—"walked out on me and my mother when I was seven and left us with hundreds of thousands of dollars of his debt, so I tend to agree with what Arlo said about him being an unconscionable asshole."

Here came the whispers. Arlo crushed herself against the headstone.

"That was after years of him throwing up everywhere, by the way. Years of him stumbling around drunk and passing out in random places, him calling us both stupid bitches. He was an abuser, which makes me wonder why you're all here celebrating him again."

"Mickey—" Tom Samson said. The lawyer was on his feet in the audience, trying to stop whatever this was, this thing Arlo had started.

"How could you love someone like that? What's wrong with you?" Mickey directed the question at Mother, who was weeping silently into her designer gloves, the picture of humiliation, so terrible a sight Arlo had to scrub it out somehow, had to make it end.

"And you," Mickey said, turning to Arlo with a look of anger and hurt, broken trust, shame, and the tiniest bit of fear. "You really are Daddy's little girl, aren't you?"

Arlo promptly shriveled up into nothing. Where had the birds gone? She couldn't hear them anymore. The sun had faded, too. All she could see was Mickey pulling a silver flask from her coat pocket and unscrewing the cap.

"Here's to you, Dad," Mickey said, toasting the headstone. "You taught me how shitty people can be." After a long swill, she wiped her mouth and walked away.

There was nothing for Arlo to do then but pull the drape, which sank into a shimmering pile at her feet.

MICKEY

Mickey raised her flask to the nearest grave and its modest stone marker. "Cheers, Wilfred—beloved husband, father, and grandfather." She squatted on her heels and scraped back the snow at the base of the stone to reveal the dates of birth and death. "Age . . ." (The mental math took longer than it should've.) "Seventy-seven." Not bad. Not good but not bad.

A bouquet of brown carnations lay at the next headstone along with a small wooden cross and a teddy bear holding a satin heart in its paws. Someone had folded a piece of lined paper like a fan and wedged it upright in the snow.

"And you, Luisa. Wife, mother, and Nonna." Again, Mickey raised her flask and did the subtraction. Eighty-four years old. Average or slightly above?

Engines chuffed in the distance, the only sound Mickey could detect besides the creaking of snow under her boots and the clinking of the flask against her enamel. It was a big cemetery, and she'd wandered far, over the crest of a hill and down into the trough of land below, this snowy nook dotted with poplars. Cold air pinned her to the spot.

Her father's headstone unveiling would be finished now, the attendees trudging back to their cars with frostnip on their toes and gossip on their tongues. What a morning they'd had. They would be telling the story for years.

Mickey sat her ass in the snow and eyed the perfect white crust of the hilltop. After the display she'd made, someone would definitely be looking for her. Any second now, a shadowy figure would come skidding down the pathway, eager to pat Mickey's back and dispense their consolations. It would probably be Mama. If not Mama, then Tom. If not Tom, then Arlo, the half-sister Mickey thought she'd never met but who actually she *had* met because *actually* she was Mickey's fucking therapist!

The number of times Arlo had brought up the inheritance during therapy. The number of times she'd raised questions about Mickey's deservingness. Her expression, a collision of sorrow and shame, as Mickey had stepped up to the mic today. It all made perfect sense; Arlo wanted that money for herself. And yeah, her dad—*their* dad—had done a fucked-up thing with the will, but that didn't excuse Arlo's selfishness, her cruelty, her blatant attempts at manipulation. Why wasn't she here right now begging Mickey's forgiveness?

When the flask ran dry, Mickey reached into her purse and pulled out a second one.

"I know what you're thinking," she said to the bank of headstones, "but remember now—I'm a big girl. I'm a grown-up."

She watched the hill for any signs of movement, trying hard not to blink.

If Mama didn't come looking for her, or Tom, and if Arlo didn't come, then surely one of the other attendees would come. One of her dad's friends, maybe, someone sympathetic and nosy. *You don't know me*, they'd say, *but I wanted to make sure you were alright.*

The next headstone had been inlaid with a sepia-hued photograph Mickey found a little narcissistic and more than a little creepy.

The man pictured wore a mustache and a cowboy hat, both too big for his head. He seemed to pinch his eyes at her, smug, as if he were so smart, as if he knew everything.

"Shut up, Phillip," Mickey said with a shudder. The cold had seeped through her jeans, up her spine, and down the backs of her thighs. "What do you know anyway? Just because you lived to be"—more math; this one was a doozy—"ninety-seven years old. Just because you had people in your life who loved you enough to buy you this freaky fucking headstone."

Mickey glared at the other graves, all these beloved so-and-sos with their angel statuettes and little engraved poems. Mickey wasn't anyone's wife or mother or friend. She didn't do people. This was the truth, and it carved her to the bone.

No one was coming. No one would pop out of the trees to offer Mickey kindness. She didn't deserve kindness. She'd stolen and lied. She'd been stealing and lying all her life. She'd humiliated Arlo's mom and everyone else who'd gathered this morning to remember their lost loved one. However cruel Mickey's father had been, there was no denying people had loved him. He'd done a better job than Mickey in that respect.

Ninety-seven years old, she thought, turning to face the cowboy again. She couldn't imagine living that long. Another sixty years of this? Of making one choice after another after another, and somehow always choosing wrong?

As Mickey drew her knees into her chest, shaking, the flask slipped from her grasp and toppled on the ground. "Shit." She moved to right it but froze with her hand outstretched.

The vodka ate through the snow cleanly, tunneling to the pale grass beneath. She watched it flow out in a gush, a stream, a trickle.

A flame lit behind Mickey's heart.

She snatched the flask off the ground and shook out what was left, fine beads of liquid that spun through the air and dappled the snow. When the vodka was gone, she whipped the flask into the bushes. By then she was crying, not from sadness but something else, some strange alchemy of pain and relief. To finally be rid of it—this stuff she carried every day and had carried for most of her life . . . It was like swimming up from the depths with burning lungs, the surface only a few kicks away.

She planted her hands in the snow and rocked onto her knees, rising, leaving the snow and the vodka and the graves far below, feeling if not free, then at least lighter.

The sun peered at her over the crest of the hill, a bright and wild eye.

Mickey found her purse, hooked it over one shoulder, and began to climb.

Half the people looked like moms—women in baggy blouses munching the granola bars and carrot sticks they'd packed in their knockoff handbags. Judging by the hospital scrubs and the tired eyes, one was a nurse. Some people wore paint-stained overalls and steel-toed boots, others three-piece suits. The youngest person was no older than twenty. The eldest person, a crumpled little man with an oxygen canister hooked onto his walking frame, could've been ninety.

"Starting in five," someone said.

People drifted toward the chairs at the center of the room. They were just people. These were just chairs. Mickey knew rationally there was nothing to fear. And yet.

She collected a few squirts of coffee from a big steel urn at the beverage station. Her cup was half-full when the spout ran dry with a sputter. "God damn."

"There's never enough, is there?"

An older man sidled in beside Mickey, filled his thermos with hot water from a kettle, and added a tea bag. She placed him immediately. Who could've forgotten that skintight Playa del Carmen t-shirt?

"You were at the café thing," Mickey said.

"Thought I'd seen you." He introduced himself as Roger and tapped his temple. "Memory's still sharp." He wore one of those oversized, brightly striped knit sweaters from Peru. The patterned alpacas seemed to glare at Mickey accusingly.

"I'm not sober." She'd left the cemetery ninety minutes ago, and the buzz from the vodka still hadn't worn off.

Roger took three packets of sugar from a ceramic holder and ripped them open all at once. "Then you're in the right place."

As it turned out, public AA meetings were held at all hours of the day in every quadrant of the city. This one was being held in the basement of the Danish Cultural Center, where the paintings on the walls depicted stormy battle scenes from Norse mythology, and the ceiling creaked from all the folk dancers practicing in the ballroom upstairs. They'd arrived in their clogs and bright skirts at the same time as Mickey.

"You're shivering," Roger said.

Mickey shrugged. She hadn't changed out of her wet jeans.

"Here." Roger pulled the alpaca sweater over his head and offered it to her. Puffs of white chest hair escaped the ribbed tank top he wore underneath.

"Do you ever start the day thinking you'll end up in one place," Mickey said, accepting the sweater with a rush of gratitude, "and then end up someplace completely different? Or is that the way life works in general? Is every day like that, only sometimes you just don't notice?"

"You *are* drunk," he said.

Mickey eyed the door and the glowing red exit sign above it. How easy it would be to call the whole thing off and slip out.

She pulled the sweater on overtop of her coat. "Can I sit beside you?"

Her phone rang shortly after the meeting adjourned. It was someone from the teachers' union.

"December eighteenth," the caller said. "That's the date."

"For my inquisition?" Mickey fumbled with the phone as she yanked Roger's sweater over her head and offered it back to him.

Busy stacking the chairs, he smiled at her and mouthed, "You keep it."

"*Inquiry.*" There would be a three-person tribunal, the caller explained. "You're allowed to present a character witness in your defense. Written or in-person testimony. In-person is better, between you and me."

"Any other tips?" Mickey asked, crushing Roger's fuzzy sweater against her chest.

"You're allowed to represent yourself, but most people in your position hire a lawyer."

"A lawyer," Mickey said.

Everyone funneled out of the room, and she was alone again.

ARLO

After the ceremony, Arlo found her mother stooping over a cracked bathroom sink inside the cemetery's unheated service building, splashing herself with what must've been ice-cold water. Here was a person who'd been stripped, who'd been shamed, who'd had the last twenty-five years collapse over her head. She would need Arlo's support.

"Mother?"

"I have to get this shit off," she said.

"Mother, are you okay?"

She peeled a string of false lashes off one eyelid and placed it on the edge of the sink. "I look like I was at Chernobyl."

Purple swaths of makeup stained the skin around her sunken eyes. Lipstick smeared her upper lip and chin, her mouth cracked and raw and rimmed red as an infected wound.

"It's not that bad," Arlo said.

Mother went to the dented paper towel dispenser on the wall. Finding it empty, she began drying herself on her coat, smearing blush and foundation all over the sleeves.

Arlo had never felt such pity. "I'm sorry about those terrible things she said."

Mother blinked her raccoon eyes. "What?"

"Mickey. She made you cry."

"No, she didn't."

Arlo buried her gaze in the dingy floor tiles. Their boots had streaked the floor with snow and mud. "I was there, remember? She called you out for still loving Daddy even when he treated you so badly." Arlo had dropped some hard truths during her speech, but at least she hadn't skewered Mother personally. "'He was an abuser.' That's what she said."

Mother snorted. "You think she's the first person to ever say that to me?"

Arlo hesitated, unsure how honest to be. "Yes?"

"You think it somehow slipped past me that my husband of twenty-six years, who used to call me names and decided what I wore every day and never let me have my own money, was an abuser? You may not have realized what he was, but trust me—I did."

"What, so you randomly started weeping for some other reason?" It didn't make sense. Mother hadn't shed a tear all day until Mickey stepped up to the mic.

"I should've taken you and left," Mother said. She was standing close all of a sudden, brushing Arlo's cheek with her frigid fingertips. "I thought about it, you know, back when you were in kindergarten. I should've done it. Before he made you into"—her nuclear disaster of a face twisted up—"whatever you are now."

"Wait," Arlo said, putting the pieces together. It was harder to think in here under the low ceiling and the single sputtering light-bulb. "Are you saying *I* made you cry?"

"Did that woman really come to you for therapy?" Mother asked. Not really? Not exactly.

"It's complicated," Arlo said, trying to forget the way Mickey had looked at her as they stood side by side at the mic. The way anger, hurt, and fear had mingled in Mickey's eyes, as if Arlo, and not their father, was the real monster.

"And you agreed to see her even though you knew who she really was?"

Arlo fought to keep her voice steady. "Again, it's complicated."

"Charlotte, I am not a woman with a particularly strong moral compass. But you have done some fucked-up things here, and I can't tell you how much that depresses me."

Heat rippled up Arlo's arms. "I came in here to comfort you."

"No, you didn't. You came in here so I would comfort *you*."

That was not true. Distinctly, categorically, irrefutably not true.

"I don't know why I'm so surprised," Mother said. "The writing's been on the wall for years. I mean, look at you—you have no friends, no hobbies, no interests of your own. You divorced your own husband because your father didn't like the poor guy."

"Are you talking about me and Hayden?"

"No, I'm talking about you and your other ex-husband."

"I did not break up with Hayden because—because—" Arlo stopped herself. She wouldn't dignify this absurdity with a response. Not when she was the one who'd gotten screwed here. "Daddy gave Mickey all the money he was supposed to give me."

Mother drew a heaving breath. "So what?"

"So, it isn't right."

"Who made you the queen of right and wrong?" Mother started to blubber again, to weep. Parents only cried like this when truly awful things happened to their children—motorcycle accidents, plane crashes, brain tumors. Tragedies.

Arlo felt tears building behind her own eyes. Okay, so she'd spied. She'd abused her power. She'd attempted to con a client—a sister—into giving up a large sum of money. But that wasn't the whole story. There were other factors to consider, factors such as . . . such as . . .

Mother wiped her brow on her sleeve again. "I should've taken you and left."

MICKEY

It was ten o'clock on a Friday—a perfectly reasonable time for visiting a law firm—yet judging by Dean's expression as Mickey approached his desk, her presence both annoyed and frightened him. The door to Tom's office was closed, no movement visible behind the frosted glass.

"If he has a couple minutes," Mickey said, "I'd like to talk to him. Please."

"Who should I say is here?" The secretary's voice betrayed the slightest tilt.

Mickey thought about it. "Tell him it's Michelle."

The secretary picked up his phone and spun his chair to face away. Tom's ringtone—brassy wind chimes, of course it would be brassy wind chimes—tinkled through the walls. After a few moments of muffled conversation, the secretary swiveled back around. "Go ahead."

Mickey made a point to thank him.

Behind the door, a blast of sunlight. As Mickey's eyes adjusted and the office took shape, she almost didn't recognize the place. The blinds were up. The couch was bare of blankets and pillows.

No files or notepads carpeted the floor. No takeout containers cluttered the table. The essential oil diffuser was also absent.

"It doesn't smell weird in here," Mickey said.

Tom sat behind the desk with his gaze bent to the computer screen. "Hello to you, too."

A crystal whiskey decanter shored up on the credenza behind him. Mickey thought instantly of numbness, of being submerged.

"Where's your incense thing?" she asked, forcing her gaze away from the liquor.

"Gave it to a friend."

"And your bed."

"At home."

"You don't sleep in your office anymore?"

"Cutting back on my hours." He looked healthier than normal, and brighter, his spine a little straighter, his eyes a little less bloodshot. "And I'm seeing someone."

"What, romantically?"

"Yes, romantically," he said, a crisp edge in his voice.

Good for him, Mickey thought. He was trying to change, and that was no small task.

She clasped her hands behind her back and rolled her shoulders open, a painful stretch. She wanted to move, to break apart, to wrestle herself to the ground. "I went to an AA meeting."

Tom froze with his hands poised over the keyboard. He closed the lid of his laptop and peered up at Mickey for the first time since she'd walked in. "And?"

"It was weird. But good. Weird but good."

He nodded. "That's how it felt when I started going to therapy. Weird but good."

"Well, you know what they say. The right help is hard to find." Mickey hoped, for Tom's sake, that his therapist was better than hers.

"My gal is annoying," Tom said. "But I guess that's the point."

Mickey gestured to a spare chair. "May I?"

Tom folded his lips under his teeth. A long moment had passed before his mouth rearranged itself into a hesitant smile. "Sure."

Mickey remembered the conversation they'd had that day in his car outside Chris's house. What did he say? *You might get along well with this therapist.*

"You knew," she said. "All along, you knew."

Tom winced. "Confidentiality. It was about confidentiality. But I was so torn. Believe me. I could see the whole setup was unethical. Obviously, your estranged half-sister should not be your mental health therapist. That's an easy one." He spoke quickly and gestured madly. "But I'd already made such a mess of things by sleeping with her—"

"By what?" Mickey imagined Tom and Arlo naked together, and her head exploded.

"I know." He covered his face with his hands and screamed softly. "I know."

"When did you—why would you—I mean, I know why. But *why*?"

"I don't know. She's young and beautiful and I—I'm a creep. I'm a goddamn awful creep."

Mickey said nothing. Some facts, she'd learned, needed room to breathe.

"The will," he said. "Her, you. Therapy. I thought she would figure it out and call the whole thing off. I guess I didn't appreciate how angry she was. Is."

"Did he really cut her out?" Mickey asked. Erasing Arlo from the will without explanation . . . it was a vicious move, even for their father.

"This was back in March. He came into my office and stood right here—no appointment, just barged in—and said, 'I don't want Arlo to get anything when I die.' I was shocked. I remember our first meetings after we started doing the estate planning, oh, two or three years ago. Arlo was all he talked about. How smart and successful she was. How special."

"So then why?" Mickey asked.

"Something about needing to set things right. A 'course correction,' he called it."

Mickey could sort of see the logic? He'd thrown them together—two sisters, messed up in equal but different ways—hoping they might mend each other's wounds and therefore rectify his wrongdoings. As a solution, it was gross, manipulative, and very elegant.

"Well, I get why she hates me now."

"She must've stolen a file from me. I think that's how she figured it out." Tom's expression grew thoughtful. "How many sessions you got left?"

"Just one," Mickey said, as the decanter caught a beam of sunlight.

Tom reached for the whiskey and slyly stowed it in a drawer. "Go see a different therapist for a one-off, and we'll start the process of releasing the funds."

A hollow victory. Mickey could get her money, pay Evelyn what was still owed, and . . . what? Sit around all day watching *Bridgerton*? None of it would matter if she couldn't teach.

"I'm sorry," Tom said. "For not telling you, for everything. And if there's anything I can do to make it better . . ."

Mickey drew a shallow breath. This was her chance.

"Well, that's why I'm here, actually." Did he stiffen slightly, or was that her imagination? "Have you ever gone up against a school board?"

Tom narrowed his eyes at her. "I'm an estate lawyer."

"Would you *consider* going up against a school board?"

"This is about your job," he said.

"They're putting on an inquisition."

Tom pursed his lips. "Inquiry?"

"Yes," Mickey said. "That."

"And legal representation would help," he said flatly. "I see."

Mickey twisted her fingers together and jammed one thumbnail under the other. "Look—forget I—"

"I'll do it."

Whatever Tom saw on Mickey's face, it made him grin.

"I'm a sucker for the underdog," he added. "Being one myself."

The snowman in Chris's yard had seen better days. Its scarf was gone, its hat askew. The three spheres of its head, trunk, and body had smoothed into a single cone. A warm spell had tracked eastward across the mountains, leaving behind slush and sunshine and that grassy smell of spring. Twelve days until Christmas, but it might've been March.

Mickey righted the snowman's dangling nose, pulling it parallel to the ground. The carrot drooped again the second she let go. Poor bastard.

"What are you doing?"

Leaning over the porch railing in gym shorts and a t-shirt, Chris looked every bit the college frat boy. Something about the stubble or the backward baseball hat. Maybe it was the bottle of Corona he held. Odd that someone so silly—a veritable man-child—could make Mickey's stomach flutter.

"I . . . It was sad." Mickey tried not to stare at the beer. Tried not to imagine how each sip would froth between her teeth and glide down her throat. "Is. Sad."

Chris nodded, gestured meekly to the sky, nodded some more. "It's so nice out. Isn't it nice out? Except for—yeah, our guy kind of sucks now. I've been meaning to come get the carrot before it rots, but I just keep, um . . . I keep forgetting."

They stood there for a moment, not quite looking at each other, while snowmelt dripped steadily from the eaves.

Chris dangled his beer by the neck and drew circles with it. "About last time—"

"I'm sorry," Mickey said, surprised how easily the words arrived. She'd overstepped, budging her way into a family that wasn't, despite what she might wish, her own. "I shouldn't have—I mean, it wasn't my place to, you know—so, yeah. I'm sorry."

She steeled herself. *It's a little late for that*, he would say. *I think you should leave.*

"Thanks," he said, smiling with genuine warmth, with kindness and maturity, because he wasn't really a man-child. He wasn't silly at all. And while Mickey had disillusioned herself of the accent wall and the French press and the matching Halloween costumes, she hadn't stopped wanting these things. She wanted them badly.

Mickey checked the time on her phone. Twenty-six hours sober. In eleven minutes, it would be twenty-seven. "Is Evelyn around?"

"Out buying a purse from someone. She finds this stuff on Facebook Marketplace and flips it for a profit. It's really smart, actually."

"She is a smart one."

He set his Corona on the porch railing, then picked it up again. "So, you came here to talk to . . . Who did you come here to talk to?"

"Ian," Mickey said. "If that's okay."

She couldn't let him go without saying goodbye. He had been her favorite student—her most beloved little weirdo.

And if there was time to talk to Chris about the other thing, well, great.

"I took the day off to help them pack," he said.

Mickey wasn't sure if this meant yes or no. But then he turned and retreated inside the house, leaving the door open behind him, and she took this as her cue to follow.

They found Ian at the kitchen table hunching over a bowl of cereal. He scooped some milk on a spoon, poured it back. Scooped some, poured it back. The corners of his mouth sagged a little deeper than usual, lending him the disillusioned air of a middle-aged office worker.

Mickey sat beside him, a mere five feet from the fridge that probably contained more beer. "I'm sorry I hurt your eye, Ian."

The spoon fell into the bowl with a splash and a clatter. Ian readjusted the strap of his eyepatch. "You said that already."

"I'm still sorry."

"I still forgive you." He pushed the bowl away.

"I heard you're going on an adventure with your mom." Yes, Mickey was stalling. She couldn't help it. Once this conversation was over, she'd never see him again.

"We're going to Trail."

"That counts as an adventure."

He looked skeptical.

"Seriously," Mickey said. "And then you'll start grade one." He grew to a middle grader in her mind, then a high schooler, then a university student.

"Stop," Ian said, somewhat pityingly, as if he could see inside her brain.

Really, she shouldn't be so sentimental. He was always meant to grow up and forget her. She, meanwhile, would keep him in her mind forever. That was her privilege, and her sorrow.

"I hope you get a good teacher," Mickey said.

"You, too." Then he was reaching out and falling into her arms.

Mickey's heart rate slowed. Her blood pressure dropped. He was a flimsy thing, so light and breakable, yet at the same time so

266

significant. He was the most important person in the world, and his hair smelled of apples.

He pulled back, and the hug was over as swiftly as it had begun. He leapt off the chair and tottered away without another word.

"I've never seen him hug anybody." Chris stood at the counter smearing peanut butter over slices of thick white bread. "Not even Evie."

So long had it been since Mickey felt any pride that she almost didn't recognize the feeling. "I went to my first AA meeting."

It was getting easier to say, starting to feel more like the truth.

Chris clapped two pieces of bread together. "I have a buddy who goes to that. He says they have good doughnuts. Not that—obviously, you don't go there for the food. I was just trying to think of something to say, and . . . yeah. But that's great."

As he stuffed his mouth, Mickey filled with an impulse to relieve him of all life's burdens. He was so awkward and wonderful. "It's okay," she said.

"Hafforoo," Chris said through his still-full mouth.

"What?"

It took him three or four swallows to get it all down. "I'm happy for you."

Despite everything, Mickey's heart lifted. "Thanks."

The television clicked on in the other room, and the posh tones of British pigs filled the air. Chris shut his eyes for a moment.

"When are they leaving?" Mickey asked.

"Couple days after Christmas. I'm gonna miss the little guy." He said it too lightly, the cheer in his voice overwrought.

Mickey tried to think meanly of Evelyn but couldn't manage it today—not while she remembered the decanter, the cat, the cemetery, the million other shitty things she herself had done to people. Mickey's misdeeds had piled so high she sometimes thought there would be no digging out from under them. But she would try.

Chris's shoulders, and his smile, began to sag. "This whole time, I wanted him gone, but now that he's going . . ."

"You're sad," Mickey said.

Chris placed his mangled, half-eaten sandwich on the counter. "I'm so fucking sad."

"He's a special kid."

"He *is* special!"

"He was my favorite out of the whole class."

"Are you supposed to have favorites?"

Mickey rose from her chair and joined Chris at the counter. She reached up to touch him but froze halfway. Her hand dangled there for a while, doing nothing, before she lowered it again.

"Any news on your job?" he asked with the smallest step backward.

"I actually wanted to ask you something about that." Mickey's mouth went dry. She sucked on her tongue to try to produce more saliva, which kind of worked? "There's this inquiry thing happening to see if I can get my position back. I get to present a character witness in my, you know, defense or whatever."

He inched further away. Not a good sign. Or maybe she was reading too much into it?

"I was wondering if you would do it. The character reference."

He tented his fingertips, a gesture she'd never seen him make. Definitely not a good sign.

"I feel like I—uh, this is hard to say," he began.

It was a no. Of course it was a no. This was so dumb, coming here. Mickey was so dumb.

"I feel like I might not actually know you that well? It's been, what, two months since you showed up here with Ian? Don't get me wrong—I think you're great. I'm glad things are coming together for you. But I feel like, with this, I maybe don't know what I'm getting myself into."

Mickey wrapped her cardigan tighter around her ribs, wishing she could furl her whole body inside like some pathetic little bat. "Forget I mentioned it."

"And because my family was involved in the whole thing, I don't know, it feels messy."

"No, totally." He was right. Obviously, he was right. "Seriously—forget it."

The fridge hummed and clanked and made a mechanical retching sound.

"Ice machine," Chris muttered. He ripped what remained of his sandwich in two, examined the halves, and set them down again. "So, the plan is to go back to work?"

Mickey tensed. It was back—the false cheer.

"Yes," she said. "Why?"

"I don't know. Let's say you go to a couple AA meetings a week."

Mickey studied the tiny beads of sweat that had emerged along Chris's hairline. No way was he really about to go there. No way was he really about to do this.

"Will it be enough?" he asked, and yep—there it was. A question of willpower against biology, of whether Mickey's beleaguered heart could outmatch her haywire brain.

Her eyes watered. Her cheeks burned. Her ears began to flutter uncontrollably. She couldn't make them stop. "Enough to what, fix me?"

"Yes. No." He shook his head. "I—"

"That's a bold question for someone who was just saying they don't actually know me."

"Going it alone doesn't work. You need more help, more—"

"Have you ever quit drinking before, Chris?"

Regret exploded across his face. "I'm sorry. I'm stupid."

Mickey opened her mouth but wasn't sure what else to say. There were too many thoughts niggling at the back of her mind, not least of which was this: Chris wasn't stupid. Careless, maybe, and clumsy with his words—but not stupid. He kept a level head. He asked good questions. He saw things for what they were. Usually.

After a moment, he offered her a scrap of his sandwich. "Want some?"

"It'll be enough," she said, and left him there with his hand outstretched.

ARLO

Arlo pressed 1.

Heya Arlo girl. It's, uh . . . it's . . . Dad. You left a minute ago, or maybe it was ten minutes now. I don't know. I . . . I wanted to tell you something, see, and the whole time you were here, I kept trying to do it, but there wasn't a good moment. Life's like that. There's never a right time for anything. You have to make do with the wrong time and hope for the best. Which is sort of what I wanted to tell you. Things happen in a life. Mistakes happen. You can't be at your best every day. Me, I did wrong by just about everybody. But I'll make it up to you. I'll fix it. I know it'll be hard for you at first. I can see that already. But life's like that. Never easy. And, uh . . . there was more I wanted to say, but I can't seem to . . . I can't . . . The nurse gave me my meds just now. You left only a minute ago, or maybe it was longer. I don't know. I love you, Arlo girl.

Arlo listened to the voice message over and over until she'd memorized not only the words but the pauses between them. The erratic metronome of a monitor beeping in the background. The ocean between *it's* and *Dad*. The certainty in his voice when he said, *I'll fix it.*

She sat alone in her car, engine off, breath shimmering. Though the windshield was starting to fog up, she could still make out the headstone in the distance.

Three days had passed since the ceremony. Each of those days, she'd driven here and hung out for a while in the parking lot to watch the sun rise over that pearly face. They'd done well choosing the marble. Only the best for Daddy.

While his message played for the thirtieth time, Arlo unclasped her necklace, letting it unspool down her front and into her lap, and only then did it occur to her how super fucking weird this all was. Not keeping Daddy's ashes inside a locket—plenty of people did that. The fucked-up-ness lay elsewhere.

She took her phone from the cupholder and dialed a number she'd never forget. The line connected after one ring.

"Char?"

Still the most normal thing in the world, hearing Hayden call her that.

"Charlotte? Hello?"

She tried to remember the last time they'd spoken. It would've been a brief conversation, very civil, something about who was going to keep the TV stand or the kitchen chairs. Their divorce had been so swift and painless she sometimes wondered if it had really happened.

"Char. Did you mean to call me?"

"Why did we split up?" Arlo asked.

She knew the answer. Rather, she knew one answer and was hoping it wasn't true.

Hayden coughed. It sounded fake. "I heard about your dad. I'm really sorry, but this isn't a great—it's not a great time."

Of course, it wasn't a great time. He would be hovering over the stove right now, cooking up breakfast—eggs Benedict, it would be eggs Benedict—for a tall, pretty, successful girlfriend, someone who hadn't smashed her life to pieces with a sledgehammer.

Arlo's relationship with Daddy had gotten in the way of a few things over the years, but never like this. Lately, it was as if a stranger had animated her body, and all she, the true Arlo, could do was watch helplessly from inside her own head while the wreckage piled up. Manipulating a client was selfish. It was cruel. It was predatory. And worse yet, she'd failed to recognize it as such. Mother—Mother, of all people—had made her see.

Which made Arlo wonder what else her mother was right about.

"Please," she said. "Humor me."

"You want me to tell you why we broke up."

"From your perspective. Tell me why it didn't work."

"We haven't talked in like a year." Hayden sounded more tired than angry.

"I'll never bother you again after this. I promise."

Tendrils of ice had grown across the windshield, obscuring her view of Daddy's headstone in the distance. She turned on the engine and hit the defrost button.

"Well, for starters, we were too young," Hayden said.

"But that wasn't the only thing."

"No, that wasn't the only thing."

The ice began to melt, and a patch cleared at the center of the pane.

"I never came first for you," he said. "There were always more important things."

Arlo recalled the long hours she'd spent poring over case files during her student internships, how Hayden used to bring her plates of food while she studied. She had wanted to be a psychologist since age ten, back when she used to counsel her Barbie dolls and Beanie Babies. She would line them up in a row and tell them about their ids and egos and superegos. Charged them imaginary money, too.

"Things like my job?" Arlo asked.

"And your dad," Hayden said.

There it was. There *he* was. Daddy.

"You had to be the one to help him all the time. You couldn't let anybody else drive him to those appointments."

Yes, that was true. Everything she'd done for Daddy—every mess she'd cleaned and toenail she'd clipped—was to hold her keep as his number-one person, as if his heart were a plot of land she had to constantly inhabit, lest someone else come along and snap it up.

"Whenever you got good news about something, he was the one you called, not me. It was like you didn't have space in your brain for anyone else."

Arlo thought of her nonexistent friends. The big apartment she shared with no one. Mother, who wasn't speaking to her. Mother, whose incessant calls and punctuation-less text messages Arlo missed pretty badly, it turned out.

"You needed his advice to do anything. You couldn't make a single decision without talking to him first."

What car to buy, what clothes to wear. Which investments to make, which boys to date. Where to shop, where to live, and should she buy renter's insurance? Yes, she'd asked him everything. He'd always had answers. Even in death, he was still trying to solve her problems. He'd thrown his daughters together, damn the consequences, in the hopes they might, what, fix each other? And in so doing, wipe his own slate clean?

It was the stupidest thing she'd ever heard.

Arlo was still here, still breathing, still living this busted life of hers. *She* had to fix it. And she couldn't do that with Daddy's weight around her neck.

"I don't know how you can even do your job with—"

Arlo thanked him, hung up, and threw open the car door. She'd heard enough.

The rising sun singed her retinas. She'd forgotten her Ray-Bans in the console but couldn't go back for them now, not while she had momentum. A difficult past lay behind; a brave future lay ahead. She needed only seize it.

Standing between two rows of cars, Arlo cupped the locket in her palm and pried it open with a thumbnail. The ashes spilled against her skin.

"I love you, Daddy." She shook the rest of the ashes into her hand and began rotating her palm toward the ground.

A dart of panic shot through her diaphragm. She stopped, righting her hand before any ashes had spilled.

Arlo couldn't spread her father's remains in a parking lot. There were cigarette butts and wisps of receipt paper as far as the eye could see. No—the sensible thing would be to scatter his ashes over the actual grave. It would happen in slow motion, she imagined, the ashes melting into a soft gust of wind and birdsong. And then they would both be free.

She cupped her free hand over the ash-holding hand and made a mental note to complain about the trash at some point.

But as she gazed at the snow that had fallen around Daddy's headstone, Arlo realized this wouldn't work either. The breeze had died down, and the ashes would sit there like a stain.

Thus began an hour of racing through the cemetery in search of an appropriate tree. Pines were too common, shrubs too inelegant. Arlo found a promising elm only to spot a plaque at the tree's base and realize it was already taken.

Eventually, she returned to the grave and overturned her palm with a defeated sigh, watching the ashes fall at her feet, glad to her bones that it was done and so, so certain things would be different now.

A text was out of the question. There was too much to type. An email, on the other hand . . . that wasn't a bad idea. An email would let Arlo explain properly. But how to keep Mickey from deleting the message the second it reached her inbox? Any letters Arlo sent would probably be returned unopened, if not burned. Arlo could knock on Mickey's door and plead with her in person—after all, she knew where Mickey lived—but this would probably constitute an abuse of power, and Arlo had renounced all unethical behaviors. From now on, she would be her best, most moral self.

"Oh, fuck it." Arlo rolled over and reached for her phone on the bedside table. It was only ten. Not like it was too late or anything.

Hey, can we talk?

The message looked punier once she'd hit send. Four words? All she'd come up with were four measly words? She had to do better than this tiny blue speech bubble. She didn't believe in the soul, consciousness being a function of the brain, but if there *was* such a thing, then surely hers was hanging in the balance right now, a blackened tatter caught on a metaphysical fence nail. Only Mickey could take it down and wash it clean.

There are some things I'd like to explain.

Arlo waited for an ellipsis to appear at the bottom of the screen—that merciful signal that the recipient had read the message and was typing a reply. But the ellipsis did not appear. Arlo stared at her phone until it went dark, then tapped the screen to illuminate it again. When the screen darkened a second time, she forced herself to put the phone aside. She clicked off her lamp, pulled the covers up to her ears, and tried to sleep.

Maybe Mickey wasn't looking at her phone right now. Maybe *she* was asleep. Yes, that was probably it. Mickey hadn't even seen the message yet. Morning would come, and Mickey would check her phone, and they would set up a time to meet.

Unless.

Unless Mickey *had* seen the message and chosen to ignore it. And why wouldn't she ignore it? Arlo had betrayed her client's trust, the very foundation of their therapeutic relationship. If only Mickey understood how deeply Arlo regretted that.

Arlo reached for the phone again.

But only if you want to. What you want is the most important thing. You're the victim in this situation.

Oh, God. Why had she said that?

Not that I see you as a victim. You're a survivor. You're a really strong person, Mickey. I admire you a lot.

Arlo couldn't stop her thumbs from typing. The words streamed out and piled up.

I'm sorry. Genuinely really sorry. None of this should've happened. I should've told you the second I found out. What I did was wrong and bad and I wish I could take it bark.

*back

Something else occurred to her then.

This is Arlo.

For clarity, she added:

Fink.

Arlo Fink.

It's my married name.

I'm divorced.

She reread the messages. The phone found its way onto the floor. Maybe it had fallen, maybe she'd thrown it. Whatever.

Arlo needed sleep. She deserved sleep. Okay, so she'd done a bad thing. But she was still a human being, and as a human being, she deserved to sleep. Sleep was essential for repairing her body's damaged cells, clearing the waste from her brain ventricles, and

consolidating recent events into memories that could be catego-
rized and tucked away. The world would be a different place in the
morning, and she a different person. In the morning, she would
be calm. She would breathe deeply. She would face the new day
with courage and poise.

The phone pinged, fanning an arc of white light across the room.
Arlo dove out of bed, her ribs slamming the floor.

It was Mickey.

I would be good to meet.

Arlo cried out with joy. She was saved!

Another message from Mickey arrived:

When and where?

They would have to meet on neutral territory—in public, pref-
erably. Mickey wouldn't hit her if they met in public.

Mickey's face drifted in and out of focus in Arlo's mind for the
next several hours as she rode the edge between asleep and awake.
She scraped herself out of bed around three, resigned to keeping
her eyes open if only to see something besides that shiny, bouncy
hair and that broad forehead and their father's clear blue eyes.

The coffee Arlo bought at the McDonald's that morning was
already her fourth of the day. She arrived early and found a seat by a
window and blinked out at the sunny street, thinking about climate
change while "Carol of the Bells" crashed down from the ceiling
speakers. Her drink was gone in two slurps. She went back to the till
and bought an extra-large container of fries but found she couldn't
eat them. They sat there in the grease-blotched cardboard, growing
hard and cold and glistening under the lights.

Chair legs ground against the floor.

Arlo jolted, flailed, knocked the empty coffee cup on its side.

Of the three empty seats at the table, Mickey took the one
diagonal to Arlo. She didn't look angry. She didn't look much of

anything besides tired. She wore a fuzzy sweater with pink and green stripes and little patterned alpacas, which seemed kind of random.

"I wasn't sure you'd show," Arlo said. "Not that you're the sort of person to stand someone up. I wouldn't blame you, is what I mean."

Mickey seemed to register the empty coffee cup and untouched fries with a certain wariness, chin tucking into her neck.

"I've been thinking about this, and I'll say you did all seven sessions. I'll sign something for the law firm—whatever you need. You'll get your money."

Mickey pulled the elastic from her hair and said nothing at all. Had Arlo offended her? Already, five seconds in?

"It's about more than just the money, obviously. I should've told you the second I found out we were—" Arlo still couldn't say it. "When I found out about our connection. I'm sorry."

Mickey looked away, her gaze roaming the generic wall art and the big glowing screens of the self-service kiosks. She regretted coming here. It was obvious. Any moment now, she would rise from the hard plastic McDonald's chair and stride stoically toward the exit.

But then she turned to Arlo with an oddly hopeful look in her eyes and asked, "What did you want to explain?"

"Hmmm?"

"In your text you said there were things you wanted to explain."

Yes, Arlo had said that. She'd committed to telling the whole, miserable truth.

MICKEY

"I wanted him all to myself. His time, his attention, his approval. And this stuff with the will—with you . . . it was like a threat. Like, the more I thought he cared about you, the less it was possible he cared about me. That's what I thought. Which is funny because now I'm starting to doubt whether he actually cared about anyone besides himself, ever. And I don't know why *I* care so much about whether *he* cared, but the fact is that I do. I can't get over it. I can't."

Arlo was spiraling. It was obvious from the pouches under her eyes, the way her hands trembled as she spoke, the empty coffee cup—probably her third or fourth of the morning—she'd knocked over with her elbow. Her glasses were askew. Her shirt was on inside out. All this made such a painful sight Mickey had to avert her gaze at first. But then the empathy kicked in; spiraling was, after all, an experience Mickey knew well.

Ever since her conversation with Chris, she'd been feeling small, unworthy, doomed to failure, and terribly alone. Most of her waking hours had been spent wandering from room to room eating Fritos or trying to read the Hillary Clinton book but getting too distracted by her own bone-crushing loneliness. Then Arlo's messages had arrived.

280

"He had a way of messing with people's heads," Mickey said.

Arlo looked surprised. "Even yours?"

Mickey tugged her sleeves down over her wrists. She'd worn the fuzzy sweater today in hopes the alpacas would bring her comfort and strength. "Part of me still thinks he'll show up at my door one day and go, 'You know what, kid? You were right. I was an asshole. But look at you now. Look what a good job you've done of your life.' Which I haven't, of course. I've done a terrible job. I have nothing. I've burned literally every bridge."

Arlo picked up a fry and frowned at it. "Surprisingly easy to do, isn't it?"

The headstone unveiling, she meant. Her very public breakdown at the mic.

"Listen—" Mickey began. The more times she'd gone over Arlo's speech in her mind, the more it had niggled at her. "About what you said at the thing."

Arlo chewed the fry slowly, grimacing.

"I actually don't think he was one hundred percent terrible," Mickey said.

A strange noise, half cough and half whimper, escaped Arlo's throat. She covered her mouth and looked away.

"If he were one hundred percent terrible, that would be easier," Mickey said. "But he was—well, you know. He was sweet and silly. Loving."

Mickey had been running from her father all her life. But no matter how far she traveled—no matter where the buses and airplanes took her—she always found her way back. And he was always right where she'd left him: down at the pond with his shirtsleeves rolled up and the sun on his face, sprinkling bread for the damn ducks.

"I was angry at him for leaving because he blew up our lives. But also I was angry because I genuinely missed him. Do you remember that Tigger impression? It was flawless. I mean, don't get me wrong. Obviously, he was still terrible."

Arlo lowered her fist to reveal a fledgling smile. "But only, like, ninety percent?"

"Yeah. Exactly. Ninety percent terrible."

The distance between them seemed to shrink somehow, and suddenly, everything felt the tiniest bit more possible. Mickey would stay sober. She would get her job back. She would establish meaningful relationships and a consistent bedtime routine. And Arlo could be counted on to cheer for her every step of the way even if no one else would. Especially if no one else would. That was why Arlo had invited Mickey here today—to apologize, yes, but also to help. To express support. To bond!

Mickey lay her hands flat on the table. She'd picked a weird place to sit, their bodies not quite facing each other. "It was shitty of him to cut you out. You took care of him all these years— basically kept him alive—and in return he—" Stuck her with Mickey, his biggest mess of all, the case no therapist could crack. "Honestly! Fuck!"

A trio of old people in the corner turned and scowled.

"It's not my place to ask," Arlo said, "but—"

"Ninety-one hours," Mickey said.

"That's great," Arlo said, though her face had filled with pity.

She was probably thinking of all the alcoholics she'd ever met. Which ones had relapsed. Which ones had ended up with spinal cord injuries or skull fractures or hepatitis. Which ones had ended up dead. And the few who had made it, who were still sober two and five and twenty years later, because surely there had to be some. Statistically, not everyone could fail.

"I'm going to AA right after this," Mickey added.

"That's great," Arlo said again.

Mickey waited for more. Any second now, Arlo would chime

in with a corny line about hardship and the resilient nature of the human spirit. *You can do it,* she would say. *The odds are soul-destroyingly slim, but you can beat them.*

"So, does that mean you . . . I mean, what do you think?" Arlo folded her arms across her stomach and gripped some of her shirt in each hand. The gesture wasn't quite right.

"About what?" Mickey asked.

"Are we . . . okay?"

Mickey felt the prick of a balloon bursting, all her desperate hopes siphoning out. "You're asking forgiveness."

Arlo's eyes widened with guilt.

"You are. You're asking if I forgive you."

There would be no encouragement, Mickey realized. No reassurance or corny psychobabble. Arlo hadn't come here to help or express support or bond. For her, this meeting was just another transaction—another fifty minutes of false intimacy, which she offered for no reason beyond clearing her own conscience.

"I only meant that—" Arlo's gaze darted back and forth between the fries and the coffee cup. Her brow had developed a sheen. "I thought maybe some good could come out of the situation. Maybe you and I could be, I don't know, friends."

A laugh erupted from deep in Mickey's chest. "You don't want that. All you want is not to feel so guilty anymore. You want me to tell you not to worry about it, because then you can go on your way and forget this ever happened."

Even now, Arlo was thinking only of herself. She was that callous, that selfish. Ninety percent terrible at the very least. Maybe ninety-five.

"You're right," she said. "I'm so—"

"You're sorry," Mickey said, lurching to her feet. "I get it." After all, she'd said those words a few times herself. She knew how little they really meant.

The man in the Santa hat glanced at his pile of papers. "You must be Mickey Morris."

"Yes," she said. "Sir."

Beardless and moonfaced, he struck Mickey as too young and too ridiculous to be a sir, but better to err on the side of caution.

He introduced himself as Mr. Cook and said he'd be leading the inquiry. "Happy holidays."

"Happy holidays," Mickey and Tom droned in unison.

A receptionist had led them down a series of windowless corridors lined with photographs of old white men in suits, a parade of intendents and superintendents and super-super-intendents. The years ticked further back the deeper they went into the labyrinth, the pictures fading from color to sepia to black and white. Around 1950, they reached a cramped conference room full of orphaned keyboards and old overhead projectors where pipes burbled behind the walls and the air smelled faintly of diesel fuel.

Beside Mr. Cook sat his two colleagues, a washed-out blonde woman and a middle-aged man who appeared to be asleep. The woman wore too much mascara, her lashes clumping into four or five spikes per eyelid, and she wouldn't look up from her phone.

Mr. Cook ducked under the table and emerged with a bundle of red cloth: two more Santa hats, each trimmed with white fur. "I thought this might make the occasion a little more festive," he said, sliding one across the table to Mickey and the other to Tom.

Mickey, having no pride left, donned hers without a second thought. Tom appeared more hesitant. He poked the fur trim with the tip of a pen.

Mr. Cook flashed his teeth. "Why so glum, chum?"

"This is a legal proceeding," Tom said.

"I have cookies for when we adjourn. Shortbread. My great-grandmother's recipe."

"Oh, good." Tom pulled the hat down over his ears and crossed one ankle over the opposite knee, his pant leg hiking up to reveal a sock patterned with cartoon avocados. Mickey might've smiled had she not been dying inside. She hadn't found anyone—not one person on a planet of several billion—to provide a character reference. She was doomed.

She slid the purse off her shoulder, let it fall to the floor, and tried not to think about what she'd stowed there. She didn't need it. She certainly didn't want it. She'd only brought it as a precaution— an insurance policy. The stuff she'd brought had many uses. It could remove nail polish . . . disinfect wounds . . . fuel certain engines, maybe . . .

Mr. Cook removed a pair of Buddy Holly–style spectacles from the breast pocket of his three-piece suit, pushed them up his nose, and described the order of the day's events: opening questions followed by any additional testimony.

"Everything will be recorded on tape." Mr. Cook nodded to the brown brick on the table, the first cassette deck Mickey had seen since childhood. "Then the panel will adjourn to make its decision. All that sound hunky-dory?"

"Hunky-dory," Mickey said.

Mr. Cook set his wide eyes on Tom, who kept glancing between his watch and the door. Envisioning his escape, probably. He must've known today was a lost cause.

"Hunky-dory," Tom said.

Mr. Cook nudged the sleeping panelist, who jolted awake with a sputter and a snort. "Larry. We're starting."

The blonde woman set her phone on the table. It appeared she had two guesses left for today's Wordle.

Mickey scanned the room for the most appropriate place to vomit, should that be necessary.

"Ms. Morris," Mr. Cook began, reading from scribbles on a yellow legal pad, "is it true that you took the child in question off the school premises without the permission of his guardian?"

"His mom didn't come to pick him up, so I—"

"Yes or no, if you please." His mouth set into a firm line that made Mickey's own lips quiver.

"You can't make a witness answer only yes or no," Tom interjected.

"I'm not making her. I'm asking her." Mr. Cook gazed at Mickey expectantly.

"Yes?" Mickey said. "I guess."

"Was the child in any danger at this time?"

"No," Mickey said. "Except yes, sort of. Well—"

"I'll ask again." Mr. Cook leaned forward, the pom-pom of his Santa hat flopping down over his temple in a strangely menacing way. "Was the child in any kind of *direct danger* that warranted his *immediate removal* from the school premises *at that time*?"

Mickey found her purse and held it tight. "No."

"Again—you have to let her elaborate," Tom said.

"And is it true that your supervisor that day, a Principal Jean Donoghue, gave you explicit directions to call the authorities should the child's guardian not present herself?"

Mickey opened her purse by a crack and peered down at the bottle of Smirnoff. The red cap beamed as brightly as Rudolph's nose. "Yes."

"And were you aware that by disobeying these directions, you were violating not only the school policy but also the code of ethical conduct outlined by the teachers' association?"

"If I may," Tom cut in, sweet, earnest Tom, "I'd like to point out Provision 42B of the Teachers' Code of Conduct, which states that a teacher may violate certain articles in order to act in the best interests of the child's 'physical and emotional well-being.'" He slid one of his papers across the table.

Mr. Cook didn't pick it up, didn't even look at it. "But your client has already agreed that the child was in no direct danger."

"Yes, but—"

"Do we need to review the tape? We can."

Mickey lay a hand on Tom's elbow and whispered in his ear, "It's okay. There's still time to sway the other two."

In truth, she wasn't so sure. Wordle Woman was down to her last guess for today's puzzle. Sleepy Guy, while conscious, looked disinterested, scraping out the undersides of his fingernails with his incisors.

"So, Ms. Morris?" asked Mr. Cook. "Were you aware that you were violating the code of ethical conduct?"

Mickey swallowed hard. Two minutes in, she was already dead in the water. "Yes."

Mr. Cook flipped the page of his legal pad with distinct relish. "There's also the matter of the following Monday."

Mickey was taken aback. "Monday?"

"I have it noted here that when Principal Donoghue informed you of the suspension and asked you to leave, you refused."

Ah, yes. The following Monday.

"I—I didn't understand what was happening," Mickey said. "That's all."

"Is that why you aggressed against a substitute teacher? You didn't understand?"

"I did not *aggress*"—Mickey almost laughed—"against anyone. I think I grabbed some toys from her, that's all, and to be fair, she obviously did *not* know what she was doing. You can't put out the toy trucks first thing in the morning and not expect a bloodbath."

"You must think highly of your own abilities."

"Well, yeah." Was that bad to admit? "I've been doing this over a decade. I know kids. I love kids. Kids are the only thing that make sense in my entire life."

"What do you mean by that?" Mr. Cook asked as he jotted feverish notes.

Tom spoke up then. "I'm not sure that—"

Mr. Cook hushed him. "Ms. Morris?"

For the first time in over a decade, Mickey couldn't think of a good lie. Instead, she panicked and told the truth. "What I mean is that my life outside of work is kind of sad and empty and devoid of meaning?"

Tom sighed. Mr. Cook simpered.

"I don't have any friends," Mickey went on, thinking maybe it would sound better if she explained in more detail. "I used to believe all adults were inherently selfish and corrupt, which is also why I've always had this weird inclination toward kids. I mean—not *weird* weird. Not like—" Oh, God. "I have abandonment issues because of all this stuff with my dad. Not that—I mean—I'm working on it." Oh, *God*. "Since my own upbringing was so traumatic, that's why I work hard to be a good teacher. I want to provide safety and stability for the kids so they don't turn out quite as messed up as . . . as I did."

They sat in silence while Mr. Cook scribbled more notes. It took quite a while.

When he'd finally finished, he looked up and said, "Well, that's that bit. Now, are we ready for—"

The door swung wide, and in burst a petite freckly redhead dressed in cashmere everything. She carried a leather briefcase over one shoulder and a Canada Goose jacket under the other arm.

"I'm so sorry. I couldn't find parking. And then I got lost down here. Again, I'm so—" Arlo broke off; she had perhaps registered the Santa hats.

Yes, Arlo was here. At Mickey's inquisition. But why? Unless—

"Ah," said Mr. Cook, glancing again at his legal pad. "You must be Ms. Fink? Here to give a character reference?"

"No," said Mickey.

"Yes," said Arlo.

Mickey had no clue what Arlo would say on her behalf but couldn't imagine it making the situation any better. What kind of self-interest was she serving here? "I really don't think—"

"Yes, I'm here for the character reference." Arlo plopped into an empty seat beside Tom, who was grinning. She leaned across his lap and whispered to Mickey, "Let me help you."

Mickey could smell the fruity notes of Arlo's perfume, could hear the faint gurgle of her stomach, could see the tiny blood vessels that had broken in her cheeks. To think that in another life she might've run through lawn sprinklers with this person on hot summer days. Built snowmen. Roasted marshmallows on sticks.

"Ms. Morris?" Mr. Cook looked impatient. "Shall we proceed?"

Mickey managed an affirmative squeak, not at all ready to proceed.

Everyone turned to Arlo, who seemed to be sweating, her glasses fogging each time she exhaled. Red blotches appeared up and down her neck.

After introducing herself as Mickey's therapist, she cleared her throat and began reading from a note in her phone. "It wasn't long after I'd started working with Mickey that it became obvious how much she loves her job. When I asked whether her students were important to her, she replied, without hesitation, 'The *most* important.'"

Yes, Mickey had said that.

"She's always thinking about lesson plans for printing practice, which songs to sing at circle time, and which children need extra help to put on their mittens."

More things Mickey had said during therapy and which Arlo had remembered. Apparently, she'd been listening as well as scheming.

"It comes as no surprise, then, that Mickey would take the time and initiative to drive a child home herself rather than call the authorities on a parent—a good parent—she knew to be marginalized and struggling financially. Mickey sees the forest for the trees."

Mickey's chest tightened up. Did Arlo . . . *know* her?

"But beyond her caring nature and skills as an educator, Mickey has another rare quality that bears mentioning. Allow me to digress here for a moment."

Mickey tried to breathe, but her lungs could barely inflate at this point. *Digress* was not a word that usually boded well.

"Within the field of psychology, we often refer to what's called the Transtheoretical Model—"

Every eye in the room glazed over instantly.

"—which posits that people move through certain stages of change. Our vices are hardwired into our brains, and before we can start to do things differently, we must journey through a stage of contemplation—of *thinking* about making the change. People float around in this period for years."

Mickey hung her head. This wasn't a character reference; it was a psych lecture. And they'd been off to such a promising start.

"I try to help my clients along, but really, the shift from contemplation to action has to come from them. A lot of people never get there. If I'm honest, seeing this—seeing people flounder—makes me wonder why I do my job."

Mickey reached inside her bag and gripped the liquor bottle by its neck. This meeting would take, what, fifteen minutes? Twenty, tops. She would make it to the end, slip out, find the closest bathroom, get cozy in the stall, and . . . yeah. If she wanted to. Did she want to? Obviously, she wanted to. But on a deeper level?

"Every so often, though, someone will come along who surprises you. Mickey has struggles, like everyone. I won't say what they are because that's her business. But suffice it to say that when she plans for a change, she sticks with that plan. I can't tell you how rare that is. She acts. She commits."

Shame rolled in, a sinister fog. Mickey hadn't committed to anything. She'd shaken out her vodka in that graveyard feeling so enlightened, so self-actualized. As if that could really be the end of it. One toss of that flask into the bushes, and whammy, addiction over. Ha!

Mickey remembered all the other times she'd tried to quit drinking, because there *had* been other times, of course there had. She always did this—shed some tears and poured her liquor down the drain and convinced herself that this time, *this time*, it was really done.

"There are setbacks, of course. We fall off the wagon, then we get back on again. At least, some people do. Mickey does. No matter how many times she stumbles and falls, she picks herself up. That—*that*—is the difference between stagnancy and meaningful change."

She'd stayed sober a whole month after the Amsterdam thing. She'd stayed sober eleven days when she was twenty-four. Eighty-nine days when she was twenty-eight. Forty-two days when she was thirty. She'd seen half a dozen therapists, been to plenty of meetings. She'd read the Big Book, or at least some of it. She still had it somewhere—in a closet, maybe, squashed away with the yoga mat and the dumbbells and all the other things she didn't use because she wasn't that good a person. Because she didn't deserve a care from anyone, least of all herself.

Her father had thrown her away like one of his empties because that's what she was worth to him. And so she'd gone through life believing him, it, this story that she was worthless, unlovable, unhaveable. She'd slept with randoms and woken up in strange places.

When that got boring, she shut herself away from the world completely. She drank vodka on buses and devoted herself to the only thing that mattered, the only thing she'd ever been any good at.

Arlo set her phone and her speech aside, looking directly at the panel for the first time. "Something you have to understand is that everybody's got problems. Even the people who seem like they have it all together. Look at me. I have a master's degree. I'm a respected professional. It's my job—my literal job—to help people make better decisions. Do you know what I did the other day? I lied to a client for my own personal gain. For *money*."

The panel exchanged dark glances. Mickey's eyes went to the tape recorder, which crackled and hummed, recording Arlo's every word.

"I lied, and then I lied about lying. I had plenty of chances to come clean—to make a bold change—but didn't. I was too afraid." Arlo spoke evenly, as if she hadn't just hit the self-destruct button on her whole life. "Not Mickey. Mickey has the courage to face herself head-on. *That's* how she sets such a good example for her students. *That's* why you'd be remiss to fire her."

The problem was one of square footage, of whether Mickey's life held enough space for a teaching career and a problematic affinity for alcohol. Could she be a person who minded children and also a person who brought vodka everywhere? A person who eyed the clock all day, counting down to the first drink at five? She'd been doing it for ages, of course. It hadn't seemed like an issue until recently.

Arlo picked up her phone again and scrolled to the bottom of her note. "Life is hard for everyone, and especially hard for some. It's no wonder we question whether people can get better. Do they really change? Mostly, unfortunately, the answer is no."

Their father was in the room, it seemed, casting his long shadow over them both. Then Mickey decided she'd had enough of his stupid bullshit and swept him from her mind forever—or at least for now. *The Goodbye Train is coming, bye to you! Choo-choo!*

Arlo was smiling. "Now I can say with confidence that sometimes—rarely—people do."

While the panel weighed their decision, Mickey, Arlo, and Tom sat in a row of sad chairs in the hallway and ate Mr. Cook's great-grandmother's shortbread.

"I hate to admit it," Tom said, lifting another cookie from the mistletoe-patterned paper napkin he cradled in his lap, "but these are actually pretty tasty."

"Super tasty," Arlo said. Crumbs had caught in the ends of her hair.

Mickey glanced back and forth between her lawyer and her sister. They seemed an unlikely combination. "I still can't believe you two really—"

"Let's not speak of it," Arlo said.

Tom grunted in agreement.

"This was all you, I'm guessing?" Mickey asked him. Not that she was angry.

"I thought she'd stood us up," Tom said.

"Sorry. I got really lost down here." Arlo grimaced at their surroundings. "Why are the floors so squeaky?"

"School boards are weird about polishing floors." Mickey rubbed her eyes. The fluorescent tubes in the ceiling flickered and hummed and sent their light crashing into the pukey-green, aggressively shiny linoleum. "It's an industrial-capitalist thing."

"It's a fucking nightmare, is what it is," Tom said.

After polishing off one last cookie, Arlo wrung her empty napkin between her fists. "I meant it, you know. Everything I said."

"Thanks," Mickey managed to say. Arlo had basically incriminated herself to make Mickey sound better by comparison. As a gesture, it was totally unhinged. And deeply touching.

She almost told Arlo and Tom about the vodka right then and there—almost divulged the shame of having brought a copious amount of liquor to a disciplinary meeting. But talking about it would mean acknowledging what it meant.

When she'd told Chris about AA, he'd asked her if it would be enough. Now that question was everywhere. She saw it in the stern, bespectacled faces of the superintendents whose portraits lined the opposite wall. She felt it in cold air. She heard it in the rhythm of her own heart: *Is it enough, is it enough, is it enough.*

The door to the conference room creaked open.

Mr. Cook stuck his head out and peered at them with unbridled anticipation, his eyebrows disappearing under his Santa hat. "Well? How were they?"

"Fabulous," said Tom.

"Truly," said Arlo.

Mr. Cook clapped with delight. "I told you." He addressed Mickey as if in afterthought: "You can come back in now."

Inside, Sleepy Guy appeared to have packed his briefcase, which lay on the table in front of him, and Wordle Woman was scrolling pictures of corgis on Instagram. Had she solved the day's puzzle? Mickey would never know.

"Let me get this thing working again." Mr. Cook poked a button on the cassette deck. Nothing happened. "Hmmm."

Mickey bit the inside of her cheek hard enough to draw blood.

Mr. Cook poked another button. The machine began to whirr. "Aha! There." He clasped his hands. "Now, I know we're all eager to start our holidays, so I'll get right to it."

Is it enough, is it enough, is it enough.

"This panel has voted by a count of two to one—"

Is it enough, is it enough, is it enough.

"—and decided, with some reservation—"

Is it enough, is it enough, is it enough.

"—to reinstate Ms. Morris in her position as teacher."

"I need to take some time off," Mickey said.

The cheers that had erupted to her left and right swiftly fell silent.

Mr. Cook blinked. "What?"

"Sick leave. I need to take sick leave."

Wordle Woman, who had emerged from the depths of Instagram to hear the verdict, returned to her phone. Sleepy Guy sighed and checked his watch.

Mr. Cook removed his Santa hat. He looked so forlorn without it. "But . . . we just granted you your job back."

"I'm entitled to sick leave. It's in the union contract." Mickey turned to Tom. "Isn't it?"

Tom's smile widened yet further, if such a thing were possible. "Definitely."

"See?" Mickey said.

"Yes," Mr. Cook said, "but—"

"I'm not well. That's the truth of it. It's not my fault that I'm like this, but it is my job to get better." Mickey found Arlo, whose eyes shone as vacant and glassy as a doll's. "That's the only job I want right now."

ARLO

Arlo clicked through her Google calendar at random, hopscotching across days, weeks, and months while morning light squeezed through the window blinds. She'd arrived at work two hours ago, and at last, the sun was rising.

December twenty-third. No appointments today—only some reports to finish, some referrals to send. Then she would sign off for the Christmas break and arrive back at work on the twenty-seventh, a full day of soothing clients' post-yuletide woes. Arlo thought of the anorexic medic sitting alone on his sofa with a box of cereal in his lap and a nineties sitcom on the TV. How the laugh tracks must fill his apartment.

She spun to face the wall opposite her desk. There hung her master's degree, a big piece of beige paper with a gold seal and some strangers' signatures. The sum of her six years in university: MASTER OF SCIENCE IN CLINICAL PSYCHOLOGY. Daddy had paid for the entire degree. He'd even paid to frame it. *Do you know how big an achievement this is?* he'd said. *If you don't put it up in your office, I'm putting it up in mine.*

Arlo let herself smile at the memory.

On impulse, she went to lift the frame off the wall, but it wouldn't budge. After a few tugs, it finally came free, and the sudden weight sent her staggering backward. She flopped into her chair as the corner of the frame stabbed her armpit.

She sat like that for a long time, holding the past close.

Option B hadn't fully materialized in her mind. It wasn't an idea so much as the absence of one. Instead of going back to work after Christmas, she could simply . . . do nothing. She could go nowhere, talk to no one, just sit alone in a quiet room. A painful thought, that she might be better off doing nothing than doing this, but the evidence had piled too high to ignore.

It isn't my fault that I'm like this, Mickey had said, putting her life's work aside in pursuit of meaningful change, *but it is my job to get better.*

If someone had asked Arlo a year ago where she'd expected to be in twenty, she would've had a quick answer: heading a renowned psychology practice, publishing papers, writing bestsellers, giving sold-out talks at international conferences. She would be loved, feared, distinguished. She would be someone like her boss.

Punam was at the computer in her office when Arlo knocked on the half-open door.

"Do you have a minute?" Arlo asked.

"Hey! Come on in. I was just looking at places for spring break."

Arlo eyed the window at the back of the room. She could probably fit through, and the drop to the ground would only be, what, five feet?

"First vacation in about a million years." Punam gestured to a chair opposite her desk. "So nice having someone to cover my caseload."

Arlo took a discreet sniff of one armpit as she lowered. Tangy. Sharp. "Look, Punam—"

"Check this one out." Punam angled the monitor toward Arlo and scrolled: a bungalow with a terracotta roof, an enormous bed of white linen, a beachfront of blonde sand. "Do you see that? That hammock? I could be lying in that hammock ninety-one days from now." She laughed. "Not that I'm counting."

"There's something I—"

Punam reached under the desk for the sort of straw boater hat Gatsby or Coco Chanel would have worn. "I know it's slightly ridiculous," she said, placing it on her head at an elegant angle. "But you have to imagine it by the beach."

"You could never be ridiculous." Arlo respected Punam. She admired Punam. That was the worst part. "I know there have been some bumps in the road, but I really appreciate everything you've done for me. Taking me on, teaching me."

"Of course." Punam removed the hat and set it aside. She'd clued into something. But did she know what was coming next? God, Arlo hoped so.

"You didn't have to take me back after what happened with Laura, but you did. Thank you for that."

"Shit happens over a career. You'll see. Trust me." Punam's smile expanded, then faltered. "What is it?"

The words were right there at the back of Arlo's throat. She needed only expel them. "I don't think I should do this anymore."

"Do what anymore?"

"I don't think I should practice psychology."

Punam shook her head, and kept shaking it. "The first few years are tough. You're learning. And Laura Hedman? You'll process it. It'll take time, but you will."

"There are some things I never told anyone," Arlo said. "About Laura."

Punam planted her hands on the surface of the desk and splayed her fingers wide. "What kind of things?"

The first forty-six minutes of the therapy session had passed without incident. Fortunate, seeing as Arlo needed to leave right at five today. She'd read a lit review about anti-inflammatory diets and liver disease—promising stuff—and had a long list of questions to ask Daddy's dietitian.

Arlo flipped through the tattered day planner she carried everywhere. "So, in terms of our next session, I was thinking maybe two weeks from Friday?" Thursday wouldn't work; that was the meeting with the palliative care nurse. Wednesday was no good either; she had to buy a two-wheeled walker and a raised toilet seat from the medical supply store.

Laura stared at the patch of wall below the lighthouse picture. "I think I'm done."

"With therapy?" Arlo asked. That wouldn't be the worst thing. Laura could only meet in late afternoons, which were prime time for Daddy's appointments. "That is completely your choice. I think sometimes a break can be really positive."

Laura blinked her big, dewy eyes. "Done, like, with everything."

"Everything, like . . ." Arlo pulled back her sleeve and glanced at her watch. Thirteen minutes to five.

"I don't know. I don't know what the point is anymore."

A dark, swirling, galaxy-crushing vortex opened in the pit of Arlo's stomach. Not this. Not now. "The point of what, exactly?"

"It shouldn't be this hard, right? It takes so much effort for me do anything. I'm talking about simple things. Getting up, brushing my teeth. That's not normal, is it? Living isn't supposed to be this much work?"

Arlo felt a spike of bad adrenaline. This wasn't happening. It couldn't be. She needed to leave. She needed to ask a dietitian about monounsaturated fats and vitamin K and whether eating more collard greens would keep Daddy from dying. She couldn't sit here with Laura for another hour talking about—about—

She pushed away the thought. It wasn't happening.

"We all have bad days. Cut yourself some slack."

"I'm not talking about a bad day," Laura said. "I'm talking about a bad year, a bad decade. I have never not felt like this, and it is exhausting."

"You mentioned before"—twenty minutes ago, Arlo thought, it had only been twenty minutes—"you were having success with that meditation app?"

The entire session, they'd talked of nothing else besides how well Laura was doing. The tools were working, she'd said.

"Yeah. I lied about that. I haven't used it. I haven't even downloaded it."

"And the thought record?"

Laura laughed bitterly. "See? This is what I mean. I can't even do simple things. I can't open an app on my phone. I can't even open the app to *buy* the app. I can't be bothered to pick up a pen to write down what I'm thinking. Do you know how much time it takes me to get ready and come here every two weeks? To put all this on?" She gestured to herself: touch of mascara, messy-perfect Dutch braid, ruffled blouse under a pinafore-style dress. She looked, as ever, like she was about to go foraging for mushrooms in a nineteenth-century novel. "Three hours. It takes so much effort that when I go home, I go straight to bed and sleep for almost a day."

Arlo's watch ticked in her ears. This was too much information to receive with only three minutes left in a fifty-minute therapy session. It wasn't fair.

"That's why I think I'm done." Laura reached beneath the collar of her shirt for a small necklace and fiddled with the pendant absent-mindedly.

300

Maybe if Arlo redirected the conversation . . . if she nudged them toward something bright, something happy? There wasn't time for a proper crisis intervention. Unless Laura wasn't really in crisis? Everyone's moods oscillated over the course of the day. Laura might step outside and feel the sun on her face and decide everything was going to be just fine.

"What's that?" Arlo asked, gesturing to the necklace.

Laura undid the clasp. The chain spooled into a small pile of silver in her palm. "This thing? I've had it forever." A smile. There— better already. "My grandma gave it to me." Her gaze flashed up, wide and clear as daybreak. "Do you want it?"

"You don't?" Arlo asked.

As Laura slid the necklace across the table, the heart-shaped pendant glimmered and spun and made a scraping sound against the laminate. "Take it as a thank you for helping me. You have a hard job."

Arlo stole another peek at her watch. Eleven minutes to five. One minute left of session. One minute to make extra sure. "What are you doing tonight?"

Laura supplied an answer without hesitation: "Probably watch a movie with Mom."

"And tomorrow?"

"Homework."

"By yourself?"

"My friend Lydia is coming over."

"What time?"

"Ten."

"What homework?"

"Econ."

Good. This was good.

"What about the day after?" Arlo asked.

"Helping Dad in the garage," Laura said.

"And what time are you doing that?"

"Sometime in the afternoon, I think. I forget what he said exactly."

Arlo nodded. Laura had plans for the immediate future. This was positive. This was enough. If—*if*—Laura was having . . . *those* . . . thoughts, there would be time to deal with them. They would talk about it more next session. "And then you're coming back to see me. Two weeks from Friday, same time."

Laura smiled again. "Two weeks from Friday, same time."

It was still 4:49 when she shrugged on her coat and moved for the door. What a relief to finally see the back of her.

○

"Okay." Punam rose from her chair and began to pace. "Okay. Okay."

"I forced her out the door," Arlo said.

"Becoming a therapist doesn't automatically make you a perfect person. We can—and do—screw up sometimes."

"It was a dietitian appointment. It wasn't even that important."

"Everything is important when it's your loved one," Punam said. "Look what you were going through. Your father was dying."

How to make Punam understand? Arlo barely understood. "I loved my dad so much it hurt. Actually. It hurt me. I gave and gave. He took and took."

And it hadn't stopped, the giving, the taking. Arlo was still pouring all her time and energy into Daddy, or what remained of him. There was nowhere else to put it.

Punam began to pace faster, from one wall to the other and back again. "Your dad was an alcoholic, right? Codependency. It happens."

"I don't have friends, Punam. Not one. I don't have hobbies. I don't have interests. My relationship with Daddy has consumed

302

my entire life since before I can remember. I divorced my husband because Daddy thought he wasn't good enough for me."

"And that lived experience—that compassion—is what makes you a good therapist, and what will continue to make you a good therapist. You can get help *and* do your job, Arlo. It's not one or the other. I mean, shit—you think I don't need counseling? Twice divorced over here, with a son who won't speak to me. Don't quit because you made one mistake."

"There's other stuff," Arlo said, as her misdeeds piled high inside her head.

Punam's voice dropped half an octave. "Seriously?"

Arlo was so tired of keeping it all inside. She wanted someone to sit across the table from *her* and nod along while *she* talked. And not a therapist (though she clearly needed one of those, too). She wanted someone who'd listen not because it was their job but because they simply . . . valued her. Someone she could send funny GIFs to. Someone she could meet for coffee at McDonald's *without* an ulterior motive. But Arlo knew it would take time to earn such a friend.

"This place"—Arlo gestured to the office, the two armchairs in the corner, the box of Kleenex on the little table—"is not where I should be. I mean, I should be here. But I should be getting the therapy, not giving it."

"I'm telling you," Punam said, "you'll look back five years from now and regret this."

"I don't think I will." Arlo's pulse thumped in her ears. "I don't like this job. Having to forget yourself at the door and devote every ounce of brainpower to someone else and their problems? It wears me out." All this was true. It had been true since the start. "People are too much for me."

"You love people," Punam said, the calm waters of her face at last starting to ripple. "You love their spirit."

"In an abstract sense, yes."

"See? There you go."

Counseling a human being was like combing apart a bundle of hay. Arlo used to find the work slow and meticulous but deeply rewarding. Now she found it frustrating and tedious. "People are so complicated."

"And you've just discovered this?" Punam snapped.

They floated around in the silence, eyes bobbing toward each other but never quite meeting.

"I do love people," Arlo said. "But having to actually sit down with them for hours and hours . . ."

". . . is a privilege," Punam said.

". . . is a burden."

Punam threw the boater hat back under her desk. "What else would you even do?"

Arlo licked her lips. The thrill of what she was about to say boiled up and spilled over. "I have absolutely no idea."

MICKEY

Rybka squirmed in Mickey's arms as the elevator doors rattled open. The cat hadn't met her gaze once—not at the pawnshop, not on the bus, and certainly not here, mere feet from Daria's apartment and Rybka's rightful home. Mickey didn't blame her in the slightest.

"Okay, okay. Here you go." Mickey crouched, and the cat sprang free. Rybka crossed the hall in three strides and scratched at Daria's door until it opened.

Behind it stood not Daria but a man in a dress coat.

"Tom," Mickey said.

His face lit at the sight of the cat, who had reared up on her hind legs and begun batting Tom's shins with her paws. "Didi! Come see."

Mickey tried and failed to process this. "*Didi?*"

Daria bustled into the doorway and scooped Rybka off the floor, crying from her hard-ass, unflappable Slavic eyeballs as coos of sweet-sounding Polish left her lips. Tom kissed both cat and woman on the tops of their heads, the very picture of . . . sweetness and affection? Honestly, Mickey wasn't sure what she was looking at. The whole thing felt too wacky, like something her unconscious might've cooked up in a particularly head-scratching dream.

"Are you two seeing each other?" she asked.

Daria continued to coo. Blushing, Tom stood up a little straighter.

"I was just on my way out," he said, sidling past.

Mickey felt a strange pang in her chest. As shocked as she'd been to find him here, she was just as sad to watch him stride away. He'd helped her more than anyone these last few months. He'd been a friend. "Hey—Tom?"

He turned and looked back.

"You're a good person," she said. "In addition to being a goddamn awful creep."

Tom laughed. "Thanks." He gave Mickey a tiny but encouraging smile—a gift—and carried on down the hall.

Then it was just Mickey and Daria, who lifted her shining chin in a way that said *Go ahead. Try to justify it. Just try. I dare you.*

But Mickey could not justify it. Although she'd tossed in bed the whole previous night brainstorming, there simply was no excuse for stealing and pawning a friend's beloved cat.

She buried her hands in the front pockets of her jeans and said the only thing she could think to say: "Merry Christmas Eve Eve."

Daria's stare radiated a nuclear heat. Land-razing. Flesh-melting.

"I . . . I found . . ." No. Mickey wouldn't lie about this. "I got her back."

"You got your money, I am assuming," Daria said.

The bank transfer had arrived that morning, December twenty-third. Besides buying back the cat and paying off Evelyn, Mickey would use the money to stitch the torn scraps of her life back together again. Somehow. She was still blurry on specifics.

"I did something very cruel to you," Mickey said. She'd discussed it with the new therapist she'd found on Google, an older lady named Sabine who wore elegant neck scarves and used words like *transference*.

Rybka nestled into Daria's throat.

"It is cruel world." Daria's glare dimmed by a few watts. "You will come in?"

They settled at the kitchen table, the same place they'd once swilled vodka together. Without asking, Daria plunked a cold can of Fanta in front of Mickey and shook some chocolate-covered biscuits out of a box and onto a plate. Rybka ate from a bowl of canned tuna on the floor, nibbling softly. It was late morning, and a bright winter sun blasted through the east-facing windows. Mickey undid the top button of her blouse and tried to think cool thoughts.

She sipped the Fanta: sudsy and chemical-tasting and totally not what she wanted.

"How was all the therapy?" Daria asked.

"Parts of it were good." Mickey set the can down and watched a bead of condensation glide down the side. Were the biscuits and the orange drink meant to amplify her guilt? Or maybe Daria was really that hospitable, her instinct to feed a guest even stronger than her desire to obliterate said guest for said guest's unforgivable betrayals.

"Which parts?" Daria asked.

Mickey's sessions with Arlo had already receded into distant memory. She could no longer recall who had said what, which things had happened when. All she knew for sure was that she'd left her old self behind. And thank God. "Oh, I don't know."

Daria gave a grunt of obvious disappointment. She had a talent for vulnerability, always baring herself to others so easily. Well. Maybe it wasn't easy. But she managed it.

Mickey tried again. "It can be good to say things aloud that you've only ever thought before. And then you find out some of those things aren't even true. Which is actually nice. It's nice to be wrong about yourself sometimes."

"I used to think I was a loner." Daria laced her fingers behind her head, elbows pointing outward. She looked like a painting, sitting there with the sunlight grazing her shoulder. "My whole life, I am always alone. Always one-bedroom apartment, no friends, no family, not even roommates. Lovers, sure. But nothing long-term." She laughed. "Who am I kidding? Me? I am people person. I crave them. I need them. If I am fish, people are my water."

Mickey dredged up what vague memories remained of her birthday dinner. Daria and Tom locked away in a corner together. Tom talking about Bill Murray. Daria smiling—smiling!—of all things. They made an odd couple, he a straitlaced lawyer and she an avant-garde sculptor who read horoscopes unironically and considered nipples a fashion accessory. But maybe odd was good.

"You and the pretty man," Daria said. "Tall, big eyebrows. What is his name?"

"Chris." Mickey shoved a cookie in her mouth.

Daria swept her legs up beneath her. "You and him?"

Mickey and Chris? Pipe dream. Except not, because for something to be a pipe dream, she would have to want it, and she definitely didn't want that. Not anymore. She *definitely* didn't want to wake up beside Chris on, say, a sunny Saturday with her ear pressed against his chest and his arms looped around her waist. That sounded terrible.

Daria grew a sly smile. "You will call him?"

Mickey tried to speak, but cookie had gummed to the roof of her mouth. By the time she got it all down, she found she was no longer sure what to say. "Maybe."

"I love this word. *Maybe.* This is life, this word. Life is cruel things, I said before. But also, you know, life sometimes gets better. It's like, you have to wait and see. Life is maybe."

This sentiment sounded very wise, very true, and like the soda Mickey was drinking, completely unsatisfying. There was a reason small children hated waiting for things. They hated waiting because waiting, as an activity, was legitimately the worst thing ever. Waiting for recess, waiting for snack time, waiting for the end of the day. Waiting for one's brain to heal. In a kinder world, there would be a fast-forward button.

"What will you do with the rest of it?" Daria asked.

The money, she meant.

"Maybe go away for a while," Mickey said.

She'd clicked through every page on the SkyView website, read dozens of reviews, even memorized the intake phone number. The facilities had everything: a bright gym, a yoga studio, expansive grounds with manicured shrubs and a flagstone walking path and a gazebo. And yet. As much as she knew it was the only way forward, she hadn't committed.

"You are scared," Daria said quietly.

Rybka sprang off the cat tree in the corner, crossed the kitchen floor in two strides, and leapt onto Daria's knee. To be the cat in that moment, the world a small and simple place.

"I'm so scared," Mickey said.

"It's normal, I think."

Rybka purred: a soft, ceaseless vibrato.

"How many days now?" Daria asked.

"Eleven." Eleven days, three hours.

"And tomorrow will be twelve."

"I don't know if I can do it," Mickey said.

A lot of people walked out after sixty days in rehab and went straight to the nearest liquor store. It happened all the time. People relapsed. People failed.

"Ah, yes, that is good question." Daria stroked Rybka between the eyes with slow upward motions of her finger. "Maybe you can't. And maybe you can."

Mickey's nose began to sting. And her throat. And the corners of her eyes. "Maybe?"

"You can make call right now." Daria stole away the Fanta and the plate of biscuits. Mickey had nothing left to hold. "Go on."

Mickey's hands were shaking as she found her phone, set it on the table, and stared into the black void of the screen. It still felt like her sinuses were getting fumigated.

Daria sighed. "So dramatic, oh my God."

"No—I just—"

"Is fine," Daria said. "I wait. After, we have cake."

Mickey keyed in the number and tapped the green button to dial. "I have another call to make after this," she said, raising the phone to her ear.

Evelyn peered down into the plastic bag, expressionless.

Too lazy to find an envelope, Mickey had tossed the cash—four bricks of ten grand each—in a ragged old Safeway bag from her kitchen pantry and called it a day. "We good?"

Evelyn hooked the bag over one wrist, her gaze skating back and forth across the frosted cement at their feet. "Ian is here if you want to say hi."

Through the front door, Mickey glimpsed a shimmering, if scraggly, Christmas tree, the bottom third cluttered with tinsel and ornaments while the upper branches remained mostly bare.

"We already said our goodbyes." She wanted far away from here. Well—not actually. Actually, she wanted to come inside and stay forever.

"He made you a card. Let him give it to you."

"I don't think . . . I don't know."

"Please," Evelyn said. She looked shorter today, leaning against the doorframe in a pair of dingy sweatpants and a huge, half-faded Donald Duck t-shirt she'd probably worn to bed every night since she was twelve, which wasn't all that long ago, come to think of it.

Mickey checked her phone for the time. "Just a quick ten minutes? I'm supposed to be meeting someone."

Ian and Chris were on the floor in front of the TV. Ian greeted Mickey with a wave, even glancing away from *Rudolph* briefly—as fine a compliment as a five-year-old could pay—while Chris offered her a weak smile, his eyes big and uncertain.

Mickey felt her cheeks simmer. Chris must've seen her blushing, because then *he* blushed, making her own face burn even hotter and, in turn, his even brighter. Mickey couldn't handle it.

She sank beside Ian and fixed her gaze straight ahead on the screen. "What a classic."

"It would be better with spaceships," Ian said.

"True," Chris said.

They'd reached the part where Rudolph leaves his friends in the night, convinced they'll never be safe as long as he and his pesky nose are around. As the reindeer was drifting out to sea on his ice floe, darkness setting in around him, the screen froze.

Mickey glanced up to find Evelyn standing over them with the remote.

"Go get her card," she told Ian. "We'll watch the rest after."

Ian whined a little before running off. Evelyn, too, wandered away, leaving Mickey and Chris together on the floor with nothing and no one to distract them.

Chris rearranged his legs to try and sit cross-legged but obviously wasn't flexible enough, tipping backward with a huff. He flopped onto his side, then his stomach, then found his way onto all fours and came to sit with his knees drawn into his chest. Mickey might've laughed if it wasn't so completely, utterly, disgustingly adorable.

"How are you?" he asked.

But Ian returned at that moment with a piece of folded red construction paper and a two-inch-thick hardback book. He handed over the card first.

He'd written *Mery Chrismas* on the front in big wobbly letters and drawn a lopsided tree on the inside, a series of green triangles stacked one on top of the other. It was the most perfect card Mickey had ever received.

"I love it," she said.

Ian pushed the book across the carpet. "I want you to have this, too."

Five-Minute Stories read the gold-embossed title.

It wasn't a lump so much as a ten-ton hunk of granite that formed in Mickey's throat.

A blast of sentimental string music. Rudolph was back, and so was someone else.

"Can I talk to you for a sec?"

Evelyn was standing over them again. She was still pointing the remote at the TV but seemed to be staring at the wall behind it, at nothing.

"Me?" Mickey asked, but Evelyn was already striding away.

Chris followed them. Mickey did her best not to turn and look but could hear his footsteps at her back. What was this about? Was she about to be murdered? She honestly had no idea.

In the kitchen, Evelyn slid the bag of cash across the counter. "Here."

On her face was the familiar desperation of a person trying to scrabble up from the deep, shameful hole she'd dug herself. A person who couldn't quite find purchase.

Oh, Mickey thought. She thrust the money back. "Just keep it."

"I don't want it," Evelyn said.

"Yes, you do."

"I found some Louboutin shoes at Goodwill I can resell for like a grand. I'm good."

"Is that a grocery bag full of money?" Chris interjected.

"I was kind of, like, half blackmailing her," Evelyn said.

Chris looked suitably horrified. "As in, for cash?"

"But I'm not anymore," Evelyn added, "so it's cool."

Mickey planted her elbows on the counter and bowed her head for a moment, remembering something her new therapist had said about inserting oneself into others' domestic dramas and why this strategy was generally unadvisable. The advice was starting to make sense.

Chris was still staring at the bag. "She said—but I didn't think it could be true. I didn't think—"

Evelyn gestured vaguely at her brother and said to Mickey, "Forget him. He's a dumb-ass."

Chris did not refute this. He didn't say much of anything, only sputtered softly to himself. Again: completely, utterly, disgustingly adorable.

"My kid clearly loves you," Evelyn went on.

The hunk of granite wedged itself yet deeper in Mickey's throat.

"I'm going to do better from now on. I have to do better." Evelyn shoved the bag across the counter again. "Which is why I don't want this anymore."

Mickey blinked at the pile of cash, dumbfounded at what she was about to say.

"*That*"—she nodded at the money—"is a drop in the bucket for me. I have a lot of money, Evelyn. Like, a lot of money."

Maybe it was stupid for Mickey to show her cards. Oh, well. Mickey had more money than she could properly conceptualize. She could buy a house. She could buy a boat. She could buy a house *and* a boat. Ten boats, probably. Twenty!

"I don't care how rich you are," Evelyn said.

"Put it in a college fund or something if you don't need it."

Evelyn pouted for a long moment. "I guess I could do that."

Chris, it seemed, could take no more of this conversation. "Can we have a minute, Evie? Thanks." He spun Evelyn by the shoulders and shooed her into the hall.

Once she was gone, he turned back to Mickey, spread his arms wide, and glanced at the ceiling in pure surrender, as if offering himself for sacrifice to some bloodthirsty god. *Go ahead,* said the miserable expression on his face. *Drown me in your flood. Bury me in your landslide. Impale me with your thunderbolts. I deserve it.*

But Mickey was feeling generous. "I wouldn't have believed me either."

He dropped his arms and stared at her through his eyebrows, clearly not buying it.

Mickey checked the time again, remembered the task ahead of her. "I really have to go."

"Then come back so we can talk properly," he said. "If—if you want. Whether it's tonight or tomorrow or next month. Whenever. Just . . . come back."

Suddenly they were standing close, and Mickey wasn't sure whether he or she—or maybe both of them—had narrowed the gap.

She couldn't bring herself to take his hand, but she did hook her pinkie finger around his in a way she knew was awkward but hoped was maybe, just maybe, a tiny bit sweet as well.

"I'll come back," she said.

And she would, eventually.

◎

"Thank you for reaching out in advance instead of showing up out of the blue," Mama said.

Shame seized Mickey's body like a sudden flu. Nausea, fatigue, lightheadedness, and a fierce will to make it end—to throw back a

314

handful of pills and lie in bed until she felt normal again. Which was, of course, not an option.

"You shouldn't have to thank me for that," Mickey said quietly. "It's common courtesy. Or it should be."

"Still."

They sat together on a park bench overlooking the half-frozen river. A thin stream chuffed along between two wide banks of ice. The sun was close to setting.

"This was a good suggestion," Mickey said, chipping into the packed snow with her heel.

"I come here all the time to eat lunch," Mama said.

Mickey held out the box of doughnuts she'd picked up on the way from Chris's place as a kind of high-calorie armor. "You want one?"

"Glazed chocolate?"

"Obviously."

Mama took a doughnut. "So?"

"So." Mickey set the box between them on the bench. Her body didn't want to be here, but she was getting used to the idea that her body didn't always want the best for her. Her mind didn't always tell the truth. "I'm just going to say it—I'm sorry. Very, very sorry."

"For what part?"

"Everything. All of it. All the times I made it about me. All the times I made you worry."

A shadow of hurt flickered across Mama's features. "What did that girl say at the thing? 'Loss is the price of love'? Something like that?"

Arlo and her bullshit, Mickey thought, not without fondness. "She doesn't know what she's talking about. She's confused."

"She does have good hair, though."

"She does," Mickey said. "She does."

Mama glanced at the doughnut in her hand. "So, this is what I get after all these years. Baked goods and a blanket apology."

Mickey's body told her to get up, to run, to fucking flee.

"I have a lot of feelings about this, Michelle. Do you know how many times I've heard you apologize for shit?"

"I know," Mickey said miserably.

"Do you? Do you actually?"

The ache in Mickey's chest doubled. But how to explain it? How did people do this all the time? How did they take everything they felt and squeeze it into words that could be spoken, heard, understood? It was impossible.

"Maybe this was wrong," Mickey said, willing herself to at least try. "Me coming here, saying these things. I don't know, Mama. I don't know yet. I'm trying. For real this time. And I know I can't fix it overnight. If you want to keep your boundary, I get it. You should keep your boundary, actually. That would be smart." Mama had found a way to reinvent herself. Mickey wouldn't mess with that. "I'm happy you're happy."

Mama's face did that thing where it squished up like a frog's. "You're happy I'm happy."

"You have your work, your friends. Things turned out well in the end."

"No," Mama said, with a thin laugh. "No, they did not *turn out well*." She threw the half-eaten doughnut back in the box and brought her palm, still grainy with sugar, to Mickey's cheek.

Mickey let out a tiny yelp, a sound she'd never heard herself make.

"I'm estranged from my only child. That's not okay."

"The garbage bags," Mickey said. "I get why you did it. Your life already revolved around an alcoholic once. You couldn't do it all over again."

Mama's hand fell. She turned away.

"This whole time," Mickey went on, talking to the back of her mother's head, "I thought you kicked me out because you didn't care about me, which is obviously not true. I get now that it wasn't about that. I mean—you kicked me out *because* you cared about me, and you knew things couldn't go on as they were, which, you were right, they couldn't. But also, I think, you were taking care of yourself. It was an act of self-respect. And I admire you so much for that."

A moment passed. The sky darkened by a shade.

"You sure made a hell of a scene at the thing, you know," Mama said, still facing away.

How painful it must've been to watch Mickey ramble in front of a crowd. To watch her swill from a flask at eleven a.m. on a Thursday. Not painful—traumatic. It would've been traumatic, and worse yet, the thought hadn't crossed Mickey's mind until this very second.

Mickey rubbed the tops of her thighs, gave them a pat, rubbed them some more. She just had to say it, do it, get it out, get it over with. "I'm going to treatment."

When Mama turned, her eyes were as pink as the sky. "What—like . . ."

"Live-in rehab. Group therapy, bed checks, the whole shebang."

"Seriously?"

"I start first week of January."

"For how long?"

"Two months." God, that felt like a long time.

"Where is it?" Mama asked.

"Some town on the West Coast?"

The school board had approved Mickey's medical leave. Daria had agreed to water her ferns. Everything was taken care of—everything except the gnawing sensation in her gut, but she suspected that wasn't going away any time soon.

"Are you allowed visitors?" Mama asked.

Mickey tried not to smile. "I don't know. Probably."

"I might not come," Mama said quickly. "But I will think about it. If that's what you wanted."

"Okay."

"Okay what?"

"You think about it, and I'll also think about it."

"Great," Mama said.

"Great," Mickey said.

They sat there a while longer and watched the river flow.

ARLO

"Mother?" Arlo called, slipping through the front door.

A Christmas tree towered in the foyer: ten feet of winking bulbs and glittery baubles. The sun had set, and the house was dark, the tree shimmering white and gold among the shadows.

"Hello?" Arlo held still, training her ear for any signs of life. "Mother?"

Air droned through a nearby floor vent. At least three clocks were ticking, their second hands all slightly out of sync, while the gurgle of the dishwasher carried from three rooms over. If Arlo hadn't texted ahead of time, she would've guessed the house was empty.

The house was not empty. Mother was here somewhere, probably holed up with a gin martini and a show about the Kardashians. Arlo would find her, stare her straight in the face, and say what she'd come here to say. She'd already quit her job today, so this—uttering two short words—should be easy.

She slipped off her boots and padded along in search, her damp socks squishing underfoot. A triangle of light fell onto the hardwood at the end of the hall, where the door to her parents' bedroom

319

stood ajar. Music drifted from within—something synth-infused and atmospheric. And was that a woman's voice?

Arlo entered. Her breath caught.

Mother prostrated in Child's Pose on the floor in front of a laptop, her shins, palms, and forehead flat against the yoga mat. Yes, it appeared Mother owned a yoga mat.

"*Balasana*," intoned the teacher on the screen, a white woman in leopard-print tights and a matching sports bra.

"*Balasana*," Mother repeated piously.

The teacher pressed off the floor and into a push-up position. "*Phalakasana*."

Mother rocked forward onto her hands and straightened her legs, rising into a shockingly firm plank. "*Phalakasana*." Her gaze flickered briefly toward Arlo, but she said nothing.

Arlo cleared her throat. "Hello?"

"This'll be over in three minutes," Mother said.

"Oh. Okay." Arlo perched on the edge of Mother's unmade bed, where a duvet comforter and an excessive number of pillows were balled on the bare mattress. None of this made any sense. Since when had Mother worn Spandex? And how were her arms so toned?

"*Chaturanga*," said the teacher.

Mother lowered to the mat. "*Chaturanga*."

Arlo watched Mother kneel, squat, bend, twist. Eventually, Mother followed the yoga teacher into a cross-legged seated position and closed the practice with three deep breaths: in through the nose, out through the mouth.

"*Namaste*," said the teacher, before the screen faded to black.

"*Namaste*." Mother bowed her head reverently, then got up and began rolling her mat. She couldn't keep the edges aligned, twice flopping it flat again and starting over.

"What . . ." Arlo gestured vaguely at the spot on the carpet where all this madness had transpired. "What was that?"

"The word *yoga* comes from the Sanskrit 'to unite.' It's about bringing the body, breath, and mind together. Amber G. taught me that."

"Wow," Arlo said.

Mother snapped the laptop shut. "Don't do that."

A prickly sensation spread across Arlo's chest. "Do what?"

"This practice is helping me. You should try it."

Arlo softened. Here was an opening, a chance to say those two little words. "I—"

"I only have a few minutes," Mother said, stashing the disheveled yoga mat in one corner of the room. "I need to shower, the home inspector is coming later, I'm supposed to meet Soleil for tea. It's a big day."

"The house sold?" Arlo asked. This news didn't rattle her as badly as she might've expected. Mostly, she was surprised. And confused. "Also, who is Soleil?"

Mother strode into the ensuite bathroom and patted her shining brow with a facecloth from the vanity. "I met her at a meditation class."

Ah. Of course.

"I wasn't sure how to tell you," Mother added.

"About Soleil?"

"Be serious, Charlotte."

Arlo would've felt shame if that emotion hadn't already permeated every aspect of her being. "Okay, okay. You're right."

Mother disappeared into the walk-in closet. "What did you want to talk about?"

Well, what Arlo wanted to say was something along the lines of *I quit my job because I think I need serious help but don't know how to start and also I'm terrified and please, pretty please, will you help me? Please?*

But today was not about that.

"I think it's really great how you're moving forward," Arlo said. "Reinventing yourself."

Mother emerged from the closet a moment later dressed in slacks and a V-neck tee Arlo had never seen before. Age spots spattered the pale skin below her clavicle. "It feels a little silly at my age," she said.

"That only makes it more impressive."

Mother arched a brow. "Impressive?"

"I . . . admire you."

Mother's expression shifted from disbelief to something more like suspicion. Arlo could hear the dishwasher again.

Two words. They were just two words. She would say them, and she would be free.

"Thank you," Arlo said, at last.

Mother blinked. "For what?"

"Yelling at me. I needed it."

Mother slumped beside Arlo on the edge of the bed. "I should've yelled at you a lot sooner."

"No, none of this is on you. I'm a grown-up. I'm responsible for my own choices. Lately, they've been bad ones."

Mother shrugged. "You're twenty-five."

"Does that really absolve me?" Arlo had her doubts.

"All I know is it takes a long time to figure out your shit," Mother said. "Changing it takes even longer. Be patient with yourself."

The prickly feeling took root in Arlo's chest again. Not to say that Mother was wrong; she wasn't. Personal growth did take time. Arlo used to say as much in an oft-recited speech about neural pathways and behavior change. Now, suddenly, she hated that speech. Now, all she wanted was a fast-forward button.

Mother glanced at her Apple Watch. "Do you want to come? To tea? Soleil wouldn't mind. She's always—"

Arlo declined. She wasn't in the mood to meet anyone called Soleil. "I'll come back tomorrow for Christmas Eve, though? There are some other things I'd like to talk about. Run by you. If that's okay."

"You want my advice?" Mother asked, peering at Arlo doubtfully out the corner of her eye.

"Yes, Mother. I want your advice."

Mother's mouth dropped open. But she soon recovered, setting her face into a neutral expression as she put an arm around Arlo's shoulders and squeezed.

EPILOGUE

MICKEY

Five weeks later

One of the first things Mickey learned in treatment—one of the best things, she would later reflect—was to make her bed every morning. "How will you kidlets ever stay sober," Lionel had said to the group on Mickey's first day, when everyone sat around in a circle and stared at their hands, "if you can't even straighten up a few pillows?"

The bed itself was a twin with a scratchy quilt—surprising given the price tag for an eight-week stay. Mickey hadn't expected to share the room either. Her first roommate, Danielle, suffered from sleep apnea and emitted snores so howling Mickey had thought it was a joke. Danielle checked herself out of SkyView after eleven days and was swiftly replaced by Taissa, who had a heart attack that same morning and later died in hospital.

"Anyone coming to see you today?" asked Angelique, Mickey's third roommate, as she tucked one corner of her top sheet under the mattress. Angelique was ex-military, and the bed-making seemed to come naturally.

"Maybe." Mickey had already tidied her bed and now sat on the quilt flicking through a local newspaper. A stolen pickup truck had been returned to its owner; the high school basketball team was going to the finals; oysters harvested in a nearby bay were making people sick and had to be recalled. She ran her eyes over the headlines without really reading them, turned the pages without really feeling them. "Will you hurry up? I'm hungry."

"You afraid they won't show?" Angelique asked.

"I'm more afraid they will," Mickey said.

Today was the last Saturday of the month: Visiting Day. The counselors had spoken of it in low, foreboding tones all week. There was a reason why patients' devices were locked away upon admission, their contact with loved ones limited to once-weekly calls on the first pay phone Mickey had seen in about a decade and a half.

"You must be excited," Mickey said.

Angelique fluffed and refluffed a pillow, walloping it with the heel of her hand as if to enact vengeance. "It's a long time to be away from my girls."

Mickey flipped to the obituaries and scanned for anyone she knew. There was, of course, no one. "I bet." She folded the newspaper and set it aside. "You ready?"

"You're not changing?" Angelique asked with a scrutinizing glance. She'd donned a maxi skirt and tucked a flowery top into the waistband like she was going to a backyard barbecue or a cousin's bridal shower or something.

Mickey looked down at the jeans and t-shirt she'd thrown on. She hadn't done her hair—curling irons, like phones, were forbidden—but at least it was clean. "No?"

"Don't you want to impress your people?"

Mickey laughed. "Loaded question."

"Put on that nice sundress."

"It's cloudy out," Mickey protested.

"Those jeans make you look pregnant."

"Uh, rude."

"And that t-shirt stinks."

"It does not."

Angelique sat at the foot of her immaculate bed. "Go on. I'll wait."

Grumbling, Mickey went to her dresser.

In the dining room, she hardly recognized a soul. Lawrence, a long-standing member of the Hells Angels, had oiled his beard and gelled his hair. Minjung, an artist type who tended to prefer denim and corduroy, was wearing suspenders and a bowtie. Even Tony, the drummer for a semi-famous punk band who usually went around shirtless to the constant dismay of the staff, had put on a collared button-up and leather brogues.

Mickey went to the beverage station and sloshed some coffee into her mug from the carafe. This was ridiculous. Today was no big deal. She would sit across from her visitor and smile benevolently, calm and in control of her own actions. She would stay in the present moment. She would not lose herself in the thorny overgrowth of her own mind. The question she planned to ask her visitor. The offer she planned to make.

Pain raked her knuckles. "Shit." Coffee had brimmed over the sides of the mug and down her arm and was now pooling absolutely everywhere.

When Mickey finally took a seat, plate of runny eggs in hand, Angelique was describing her daughter's hair color to Lionel, who stood over the table slurping a shimmery pink iced beverage from Starbucks. The staff never joined clients for meals, only paused for a few moments of chat en route to the breakroom. Which made sense.

"I wouldn't say it's red, but it definitely has red undertones."

Lionel rattled his ice cubes. "Uh-huh."

"Strawberry-blonde. That's the term for it."

Mickey cut a piece of egg with the side of her fork but found she couldn't lift it to her mouth. Her limbs weren't cooperating this morning.

"Not in summer, though. In summer, her hair goes—"

"You're freaking out a little bit, hey?" Lionel said. "Why?"

Why, indeed. Why, why was Mickey so nervous?

"It's a big day." Angelique sipped her orange juice, the only thing she'd taken from the breakfast buffet.

"Only if you want it to be." Lionel picked some lint off his uniform, a polo shirt with the SkyView logo stitched on one shoulder. They put that little rising sun on everything from the pillowcases to the glassware. *Hope!* it seemed to shout. *You will have hope!*

"I keep wondering if the girls'll recognize me."

"You've only been here ten days," Mickey pointed out.

Angelique eyed Mickey's dress. "Did you spill on yourself? Already?"

"You got anyone coming today?" Lionel, too, was examining Mickey with interest.

Mickey did not like it. "A friend," she said, unsure if the word fit. If one person was an infinitely complex creature, then the relationship between two people was twice as unknowable.

"So secretive all the time," Angelique said.

"Remember your own shoes," Lionel said, dispensing this warning in a wary drawl, as they all did. All of them—the counselors, the support staff, the receptionists. Mickey had even heard the cleaning staff say it a couple times. *Stay in your own shoes. Focus on your own actions. You've made it this far, so don't fuck it up now.*

And what had Mickey, in her infinite wisdom, gone and done anyway? Filled her head with someone else. Now that someone was on her way here. She might be pulling up in a cab this very second. Stepping out on the curb. Steeling herself for the visit, which was sure to be awkward and terrible. They would wind up sitting at a picnic table for sixty excruciating minutes, not quite looking at each other, breaking the silence with occasional comments about the blueness of the sky or the greenness of the grass. By the end, they would reach an implicit agreement to never see each other again.

Mickey pushed out her chair. "Excuse me."

She ran for the bathroom, where she threw herself into a stall and folded over her knees on the toilet, inspecting the rust-brown stone tiles at her feet.

"Idiot," she said. "Stupid, stupid idiot."

A familiar voice rang out from the next stall. "Mickey?"

Or maybe it hadn't. Maybe no one had spoken her name. A whooshing sound had flooded Mickey's ears, and she no longer trusted them.

The voice came again. "*Mickey.*"

She didn't have to reply. She didn't have to say anything. She could stay right here in this bathroom forever and ever, or at least until visiting hours ended and the staff came searching. That was a legitimate option.

The next toilet flushed. Mickey bent far enough forward to peer under the stall door and watch a familiar pair of loafers stride toward the sink.

Mickey forced herself upright and reached for the latch.

There she was, lathering soap between pinkish hands. Her eyes met Mickey's in the mirror. "I was early, so I . . . Hi. Hi, Mickey."

"Hey, Arlo."

◎

Mickey was about to give Arlo some money. A lot of money, actually—half the inheritance. But was it enough? Arlo had spent more years than Mickey shackled to their father; maybe she deserved greater compensation. Not that Mickey could probe her feelings on the topic. *How damaged would you say you are, exactly? Would a million bucks about cover it? Two million?* No—safer to split it down the middle and be done.

At the end of the day, he'd fucked them both up pretty bad.

"Beautiful day," Arlo said.

"Isn't it?" Mickey said.

The cherry trees had bloomed early this year, or so everyone was saying, and as they wandered the pathways, Mickey trained her gaze on their narrow limbs and cotton-candy petals, which like her were shivering. The breeze was just cold enough to sting.

"It's so green here," Arlo said.

"So green," Mickey said.

"And the sky. It's so blue."

"So blue."

A wall of brush rose up on one side of the gravel path, the shrubs thick enough that Mickey could feasibly crawl inside and not be seen by anyone except maybe the squirrels and the puffy little birds that flitted from branch to branch. It would be warmer in there. Easier.

Arlo halted in a strip of shade and peered at Mickey over the tops of her glasses, which had slid halfway down her nose. "Why are you weird today?"

A stabbing sensation flared up in Mickey's stomach. "I'm not weird. You're weird."

"You've barely looked at me."

"That's not true," Mickey said, definitely looking at the ground again.

What followed was the kind of stiff silence real sisters would never share. When *real* sisters shared a silence, it was comfortable, even cozy. *Real* sisters didn't need words in the first place. They could intuit each other's thoughts and feelings based on the way they carried themselves, the micro-movements of their eyebrows, the energy in the air.

Mickey felt gloriously stupid for bringing Arlo here. What had she honestly expected would come of it? Monthly lunch dates at overpriced fusion restaurants? Two-hour phone chats? Mani-pedis? How would it even work? How did she think they could ever—

"I thought you should have this."

Arlo was holding something out to her—a photograph, Mickey realized, stepping closer and taking the glossy paper in her hands.

"He used to keep it in his wallet," Arlo added.

The photo had been folded many times and smoothed flat again. An especially thick crease ran vertically between the two subjects, a man with a sandy-colored mustache and a little girl on his knee. The man was looking down at her with a bemused expression as she smiled wide, her mouth slightly open and her tongue slightly blueish. She'd just eaten a popsicle, Mickey remembered. Yes— there was the wrapper, right there on the picnic table! Immediately after this photo was taken, Mickey's father had scooped her up in his big arms and tipped her upside down. How hard she'd giggled as the blood rushed to her head.

Mickey tried to say "Thank you," but what came out was "You quit your practice."

Arlo adjusted the plaid shacket she wore over her shoulders like a cape, her expression stony. Shit. Mickey had offended her, or embarrassed her, or maybe both.

"I heard it from Tom who heard it from your mom," Mickey added quickly, for some reason thinking this would make it better.

"I've been crashing with her in the new condo. She decorated the whole place floor to ceiling with macrame and"—Arlo wrinkled her nose—"little cacti."

A blossom drifted across the sky and settled in her hair. She seemed every bit the child, small and pretty and totally lost. How natural it would feel to embrace her, to save her, to write her a check and send her off toward a (slightly, at least) brighter future.

"How long will you stay?" Mickey asked.

"I don't know."

"What will you do for money?"

"Don't know that either." Something gave way in Arlo's expression. "Stop that."

"Stop what?" Mickey asked, as the stabbing sensation reared up again.

"That look."

"What look? Two seconds ago, you were mad at me for not looking at you."

"Yeah, but now you're looking at me like . . ." Arlo turned away. "Like I'm some precious little thing."

And why not? Why shouldn't Mickey regard her half-sister/ex-therapist with tenderness? Even if they weren't *real* sisters, they shared a history. No one else in the world could possibly understand what had happened to them. Who had happened to them.

Mickey glanced at the photograph again, her mind made up. "Let's split it."

Arlo spun. Her eyes were very wide. "You don't mean—"

"It's not because I feel bad for you or anything," Mickey said.

"I'm not taking it." Arlo shook her head. "I won't."

"It's not a pity thing. It's about what you deserve."

"Just invest it or something. Put it in a savings account and forget about it."

Mickey raised her chin. "If you don't want your half, I'm giving it away."

"Well, hang on now," Arlo said quickly. "Don't do that."

They shared a laugh.

The wind shifted, and for the first time all morning, Mickey smelled ocean on the air. Though the Pacific lay a short car ride to the west, she hadn't seen it yet except from the plane and wouldn't see it again until her eight weeks at SkyView were up. But she knew it was there waiting. The ocean, and a lot of other things.

"I'm seeing a therapist," Arlo said as they started walking again.

"She any good?"

"She is, yeah. Kind of annoying, though."

"That checks out."

A grove of spruce trees pushed in around them. Eventually they reached a place where the path turned boggy, a mire of roots and muck, and they clung to each other to get through.

ACKNOWLEDGMENTS

This book was inspired in part by my own struggles with mental health and the question of whether people can really get better. (If you've made it this far, then you know my answer!) To anyone out there who's struggling—please know you're not alone. And please seek help. Life can change in ways you never thought possible.

To my parents, Jon and Silvana—thank you for the endless love and encouragement. And for feeding and sheltering me while I learned to write! This book exists because of you.

My older siblings, Candice and Kyle, were like a second set of (super cool) parents to me while growing up. Now I'm grateful to call them friends. Candice—thank you for being my role model and confidante. Kyle—thank you for always speaking so frankly about your experience and sharing it with others. You're my hero!

To my editors, Bhavna Chauhan, Rosa Schierenberg, and Laura Tisdel—you've taught me so much. Shaping this story together has been my favo(u)rite part of the whole process. Thank you for making this book better.

To my agent, Jemima Forrester, who is so good at all aspects of her job it's actually bananas—thank you for believing in me and my book. And thank you for responding kindly and patiently every time I sent you an email with phrases like "tax problem" and "anxious spiral" in the subject line.

Thank you to Maria Golikova, Megan Kwan, Kate Sinclair, Kate Panek, Kaitlin Smith, Val Gow, Amy Black, and everyone at Doubleday Canada. Publishing in our country is so much better and brighter for the powerful work you do.

To Harriet Bourton, Charlotte Daniels, and the whole team at Viking UK—thank you for championing this book in Britain and beyond.

Thank you to the team at Viking in the US, including Paloma Ruiz, Jenn Houghton, and Lynn Buckley, for bringing Mickey and Arlo to readers south of the 49th parallel.

I wrote the first draft of this novel while an apprentice in the Writers' Guild of Alberta Mentorship Program. Thank you to my mentor, Vern Thiessen, whose valuable insight gave me the tools and courage to work through a second draft (and a third, and a fourth…). To Jason Norman and everyone at the WGA—thank you for supporting writers in our province so fearlessly and tirelessly. Thanks also to Susie Moloney and all the other participants of the 2022 program.

It's a fact that writers need other writers. To Tim Ryan, Sarah Butson, Ron Ostrander, Elena Schacherl, and Karen Craig—thank you for the feedback and companionship. I miss our Monday nights together!

Thank you to Melanie Little for the wise and insightful copyedit. (And for teaching me what the word "shirk" actually means, because despite using it eighteen thousand times in this manuscript, I definitely did not know!)

Thank you to everyone at David Higham Associates, especially Clare Israel, Sam Norman, Giulia Bernabe, Sophia Hadjipateras, Ilaria Albani, Sanskriti Nair, and Sarah Vanden-Abeele. Special thanks to Hitesh Shah for your help with the aforementioned tax problem. (Sorry, again!) Thanks also to Carolina Beltran.

To Sakshi Sharma for your lawyer superpowers and for always believing. Andrea Johancsik, Katrina Waldhauser, Megan Schmidt, and Anastassia Martynova—thank you all for your friendship and many pep talks.

I also want to give a shout-out to my therapist, who I won't mention by name because that would be kind of weird? But trust me when I say she is amazing. (And much better at her job than Arlo…)

Lastly, to Eric—oh boy, I don't know where to start. I know you hate cheesy stuff, so I'll try to contain myself here. Thank you for making every day better and for coming with me on all the ups and downs of this journey. "Milo and Orloff" wouldn't be here without you.

QUESTIONS AND TOPICS FOR DISCUSSION

1. Oftentimes after facing a loss, people struggle with the idea of grieving in the "right way." How do Mickey and Arlo differ in their approach to grief?

2. Tom Samson becomes a rather key figure within the story. Were you surprised by the evolution of his character? Why do you think the author chose to give him such a substantive role? How do you think his relationship with both sisters influenced the direction of the novel?

3. For much of the novel, Mickey is in denial about her alcoholism—and it is only addressed by the other characters after her birthday. How does this addiction, and Mickey's masking of her mental health, impact her relationships with other people?

4. Although Arlo initially feels entitled to receive the inheritance, she changes her mind over the course of the novel. What would you say is the turning point for her?

5. Boundaries are a key theme throughout this novel. What are the various boundaries that are crossed? What are some that are upheld?

6. If this book were to be adapted for the screen, who would you cast in the roles of Mickey and Arlo? Who would you want to play Chris, Tom, Deborah, and Daria?

7. The novel is told from both Mickey and Arlo's perspectives. How do their alternative points of view enrich the narrative?

8. Compare Mickey's relationship with her mom to Arlo's relationship with her own mother. How did their father's actions influence both mother-daughter relationships?

9. What were Arlo and Mickey's first impressions of each other? What assumptions do they make about each other in their first therapy session? How accurate were these assumptions?

10. What roles do favoritism, envy, and comparison play in shaping Mickey and Arlo's relationship as half-sisters? How do they overcome these limiting beliefs about themselves and each other?

11. How is Arlo and Mickey's relationship shaped by their initial therapist/patient dynamic? How does that continue to shape their relationship as half-sisters?

12. Grief is a nuanced thing, something that different people experience differently. How do Mickey and Arlo experience grief? What are the various types of grief on display throughout the story?